RIPENESS IS ALL

Also in this series:

ERIC LINKLATER

RIPENESS IS ALL

A novel

> 'What, in ill thoughts again? Men
>   must endure
> Their going hence, even as their
>   coming hither:
> Ripeness is all.'
>
> KING LEAR

MACDONALD PUBLISHERS
EDINBURGH

Published by Macdonald Publishers, Edinburgh
Edgefield Road, Loanhead, Midlothian EH20 9SY

ISBN 0 86334 038 5

The Publishers acknowledge the financial assistance of the Scottish Arts Council in the publication of this volume.

Printed in Scotland by Macdonald Printers (Edinburgh) Limited

To Compton Mackenzie, Esquire
  Isle of Barra

My dear Monty,
  I can think of three sufficient reasons for offering you
the dedication of this small comedy. In the first place,
your name on this page will advertise my good judgment
in being, and having been for many years, a most warm
admirer of your work; though indeed the great host, not
only of readers but of writers, who have travelled by way
of Sinister Street – if seldom to country so diversified as
yours -- makes such judgment seem, to the honour of your
contemporaries, the merest commonplace. Secondly, we
are about to become neighbours in some sort, and though
the walls of our houses are as yet but little advanced, I look
forward to the time when the way between us, doorstep to
doorstep, shall be the Minch and the Pictland Firth; and
in your non-existing tray, on your table as yet unbought,
in your hall unbuilt, in your house not roofed, I drop this,
your first visiting-card. Thirdly, I want to affirm my
friendship for you. It is a large and delighted friendship;
but if I do not protest it now, in public, and at a distance,
it may go unspoken for long enough. For as soon as we
meet again there will be talk on noisier subjects, more
inflammatory subjects, on a multitude of very arguable
subjects, and a host of inordinately comical subjects; we
shall certainly not bother about a topic as quiet as friendship. Indeed, had a stranger listened to our last debating
with Norman Sturrock, and Willy Mackay Mackenzie,
and Moray Maclaren, he might well have thought we
were each and all devoted enemies: for you have the gift
of contagious passion in argument on subjects so remote

5

and disparate as, if I remember rightly, Turkish mathematics and Jack the Ripper; and you and Willy and Norman are experts in the old Scots game of flyting. Let me protest my friendship, then, while the breadth of Scotland is between us, and let us soon dispel any memory of this sentimental admission in new controversy, in Edinburgh, Orkney, Barra, or where you will.

Yours ever,

ERIC LINKLATER

ABERDEEN
January, 1935

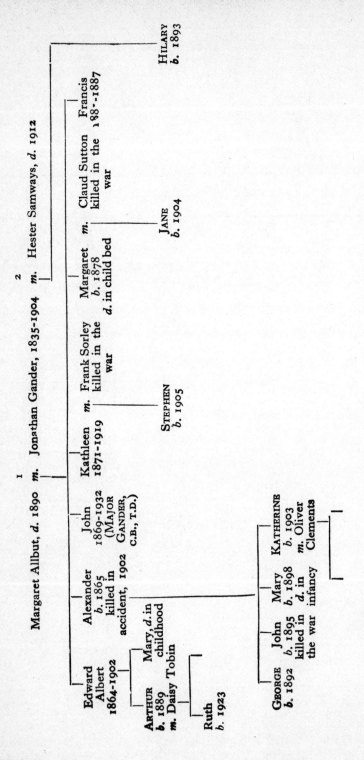

Margaret Allbut, d. 1890   *m.*   ¹   Jonathan Gander, 1835–1904   *m.*   ²   Hester Samways, d. 1912

Edward
Albert
1864–1902

Alexander
b. 1865
killed in
accident, 1902

John
1869–1932
(MAJOR
GANDER,
C.B., T.D.)

Kathleen
1871–1919   *m.*   Frank Sorley
killed in the
war

Margaret
b. 1878
d. in child bed   *m.*   Claud Sutton
killed in the
war

Francis
1881–1887

HILARY
b. 1893

ARTHUR
b. 1889
m. Daisy Tobin

Mary, d. in
childhood

STEPHEN
b. 1905

JANE
b. 1904

Ruth
b. 1923

GEORGE
b. 1892

John
b. 1895
killed in
the war

Mary
b. 1898
d. in
infancy

KATHERINE
b. 1903
m. Oliver
Clements

Table of Jonathan Gander's descendants by his two marriages

Lammiter, 1933

SERGEANT PILCHER was not one of those bull-mouthed swarthy red soldiers, common enough twenty years ago, who larded instruction with oaths and kept conversation buoyant on their flotsam of Hindustani and a flood of beer. He belonged to the new post-war army, whose virtues are those of the mechanic and the clerk, and whose vices are negligible. He wore his uniform with neatness so pronounced as almost to be nattiness, and his voice, explaining the detail of reversing arms to the thirteen men before him, had the precise inflections of a demonstrator in a chemical laboratory; but a demonstrator not too sure that the experiment was going to be a success, for the 4th Brackens — a Territorial battalion — were infrequently required to supply a firing party, and Sergeant Pilcher had had but little time to teach his men the necessary drill. This was their last rehearsal, a lesson thrust into ten vacant minutes while they waited for the funeral company to be paraded.

The firing party stood with their rifles held out before them, perpendicular at the full stretch of their arms, and waited for the next command.

'Now on the word *Two*,' said Sergeant Pilcher, 'I want to see you bring the butt of the rifle towards the body, passing it inside the left arm, and turning the muzzle over to the front. At the same time change the position of the hands, bringing the left hand to the small, and right hand to the point of balance, the rifle still remaining at the full extent of both arms.'

Unless one is expert in handling the heavy service rifle this movement, that turns it upside down, is difficult to perform smartly, and Private Ling, a romantic young man who cultivated military drill in order to equip himself for a Fascist revolution, painfully struck his nose with the brass-bound toe of his butt.

'Now,' said the Sergeant, 'on the word *Three*, give the rifle a cant under the left armpit, bringing the muzzle to the rear, sling uppermost, keeping the left elbow — 'Ere, what's the matter with you, Ling?'

Private Ling sniffed and answered, 'My nose is bleeding.'

'Fall out and wipe it,' said the Sergeant. 'You can take my hanky if you haven't got one of your own,' he added kindly.

The firing party, their extended forearms sagging with the weight of their rifles, waited anxiously while he rubbed a spot of blood from Private Ling's tunic. He returned with military precision to his post in front of them. '*Three!*' he commanded. They tucked their rifles under their left arms, and would have felt a little happier had not a shower of rain, needle-like, assaulted them at this very moment. A variety of expressions upset the impersonal rigidity of their features that discipline dictated: ire and vexation humanized them, a shiver disturbed them, and the prospect of a cold, wet afternoon elicited, as natural as an eructation, a little muttering of blasphemy from the rear rank. Sergeant Pilcher, cherishing as far as possible the comfort of his men, promptly marched them into the drill hall, and in its hollow gloom earnestly explained, during the five minutes that remained to him, the complicated procedure of firing a salute.

The cause of this activity — the body of Major Gander, c.b., t.d. — lay meanwhile, richly encoffined, flag-draped, crowned with roses and a sword, in the hall at Rumneys, lately his house and now, if rumour were correct, his legacy to his sister Hilary.

Hilary Gander was one of those women whose unmarried state impugns the sagacity of men and condones, or rather justifies, the occasional extension of maidenhood into middle life. She was at once the most pleasant and most sensible of the Ganders. Her brown hair was strawed with grey, and her eyes were an agreeable blue. Her other features were good without being strikingly good, and her figure was sufficiently generous to show that maternity had been her natural function. That she had failed to achieve maternity was due to her unfailing common sense: she had never yielded, that is, to the romantic illusions which are the general preamble to marriage, and common sense, useful though it is in many ways, is starvation to a young man in love. She was a sound churchwoman, unaffectedly devout, more immediately concerned with works than faith, and happy in her ability to accept a mystical thesis without being really aware that it was mystical. She was intelligent though by no means intellectual, and her principal contribution to humour was good humour.

She listened, while they waited for the arrival of the gun-carriage, to the Vicar's animadversions on the weather.

'I like weather to be appropriate,' he said. 'I like a grey November, a white Christmas, a rainbow April, and a fine sunny June. I have faith in the validity of the seasons, and I like my faith to be justified. This wind and rain, these bitter skies, are a kind of anarchy at midsummer. They annoy me intensely. They're out of harmony with June, and I value harmony above most things.'

'I think the weather's quite suitable for the occasion,' said Hilary. 'I like a fine day for a wedding, but I much prefer a really miserable afternoon, like this, for a funeral.'

'But the prospect for to-morrow is no better,' said the Vicar. 'My barograph is steadily going down, and Caroline's garden party will be ruined. She's made most elaborate preparations for it, and she'll be bitterly disappointed if it isn't a success.'

The Reverend Lionel Purefoy, Vicar of Christchurch in Lammiter West, was a handsome tall man, red-faced, a fox-hunter. The natural dignity of his appearance was impressive, but it was sometimes impaired by an overlaid pomposity, sometimes by unaccountable irritation, and his devotion to his wife, which was quite sincere and for which he was much admired, was largely due to her being the fifth daughter of the fourth Duke of Starveling. He

12

was at his best when she was beside him, and when he was separated from her, though by nothing more than an intervening room, he would bring her name into the conversation, perhaps with unnecessary frequency, to comfort himself by reiterated assertion of his alliance to the daughter of four dukes, of his relation through her to a score of diminished titles, to a cousinhood of Rear-admirals and Major-generals and deputy Lords Lieutenant. In Rumneys more than in most places he felt the need for this circumvallation of kinsmen and pedigrees, and in Rumneys he was especially liable to irritation and compensatory pomposity.

Now, with sudden spleen, with a quick freshet of anger in his blood, he turned away from Hilary Gander and surveyed the other mourners, the murmurous sombre coveys in the corners of the room, with upflung head and hostile eyes. A happy relief among so many black shapes were the scarlet and gold Staff badges of Colonel Swan, whom the War Office had grudgingly detailed to attend the funeral. The Vicar caught the Colonel's eye. They turned their backs upon the coffin and began to discuss the weather.

'Filthy day,' said the Colonel. 'I'd hoped to get a round of golf before going back to town.'

'An abominable day. We've a right to expect better things in June. My wife's garden-party to-morrow is going to be ruined. It's in aid of the Brackenshire Association for Improved Slaughter-houses, and we've made really quite elaborate preparations for it. My wife has set her heart on its being a success, and I'm afraid she's going to be sorely disappointed.'

'Too bad,' said the Colonel, 'too bad indeed.' And he looked at his watch.

Stephen Sorley, nephew of the dead man, stood with his friend Wilfrid Follison before the fireplace and disputed with his cousins, Katherine Clements and Jane Sutton, the charge of selfishness they had preferred against him for the extravagance with which he absorbed the heat. He was a pallid plump young man, with smooth black hair and very red lips, and he might have been handsome were it not for a thickly-rooted snub nose. He was tall and broad and too fat for his twenty-seven years. He was richly and carefully dressed — he wore a black satin stock, a watch-chain with a pendant jewel, a couple of rings — and he stood astraddle before the fire, and contemplated his fine white hands, and ignored his cousins' expostulation. But Wilfrid, a slim pretty fair-haired youth with long eyelashes and a sweet bubbling voice, defended him and cried indignantly, 'Stephen's *quite* right to keep warm as long as he can. He had a terrible cold last month, and he isn't properly better yet, and he oughtn't to be out at all in weather like this. But he's terribly conscientious, and he said it was his duty to come to the funeral, and nothing I could say would stop him. It's perfectly hateful of you to grudge him a place by the fire, and want him to stand in some draughty corner where he'll just catch another cold, and then Mrs. Barrow and I will have to nurse him for weeks and weeks.'

Jane shrugged her shoulders. 'Oh, all right,' she said. 'Stay there if you want to, Stephen, but it's damned silly to toast yourself like that just before going out.'

'Whatever I do now I shall be miserable in half an hour,' said Stephen, 'so I might as well be comfortable while I can.'

Jane was a bulky girl with a broad chest, a weather-beaten face, and thick muscular arms and legs. She was captain of the Brackenshire Ladies' Golf Club. She walked like a heavy-weight boxer, and except for her skill in approach-shots, putting, and the like, she possessed few of the arts of life. Because she had no taste in dress she valued her friendship with Stephen and Wilfrid, who helped her to choose clothes that would minimize the rugged opulence of her figure. Wilfrid had once knitted for her a silk jumper of alternating leaf-green and jade-green diagonal stripes, in the hope that this clever lineation would, like the zebra's among trees, or the dazzle-painting of a tanker in war-time, make her line, size, and shape less obvious. The jumper had been only moderately successful in its purpose, but Jane had never ceased to be grateful to Wilfrid for his good intention. Now, for his sake, she abandoned her attempt to shift Stephen from his place in front of the fire: even if she did succeed she would only make room for Katherine, and Katherine, babbling like a brook and shallow as a brook, was one of those women with whom men flirt at sight and whom women hate at sight: a despicable creature, thought Jane, glancing enviously at Katherine's pale

15

mourning *maquillage* and exquisite funeral attire. She crossed the hall to speak to her cousin Arthur.

Arthur Gander was standing at ease — in the military sense of the word, that denotes not ease but rigid composure — before the flag-draped coffin. He cultivated a soldierly bearing that his appearance did little to assist, for he was short in stature, bald in front and behind — a median waft of hair separated the occipital bareness, which was quite round, from the arid horseshoe in front, on which a few isolated hairs still weakly grew — and his slightly protuberant eyes were velvety and brown. A closely growing cropped moustache did something to counteract their mildness, and a Socratic nose, indicating the robustness of his constitution, excused his little basin-shaped paunch. So much for the exterior: of the inner man, of his mind, of his spirit, of the flux of his emotions, it is less easy to speak, for he was very subtly compact of honesty and dishonesty, of noble perception and trivial performance. He stared at the coffin, and in his imagination this corruptible, this clay that would soon be dust and once had been a soldier, had put on its incorruption and was already a unit in that eternity-serving army whose muster-roll is the battle-honours of England: he saw the Major as fellow-ghost with veterans of the Peninsula and older shades from Malplaquet: he beheld, as on a parade ground, company behind company into the darkness, the armies of England in khaki and in scarlet, splendid in the Hussars' pelisse and seven feet high in Grenadier caps, in steel harness, in leather jerkins, pike-bearing, carrying long-bows, carrying Saxon swords: he descried continuity from Battle Abbey to the last battle of Ypres, and he perceived, as engagements in one mystical campaign, Agincourt, Oudenarde, and Seringapatam; Alma, Dargai, and Arras, and the Somme. — Yet seeing all this he still had vision left to see himself standing soldierly beside a soldier's coffin, and his velvety brown eyes were alert to watch the effect of his disciplined immobility on any who should notice it. His attitude invited attention. It proclaimed that he also had been a soldier, that he, mourning the dead Major, knew grief more poignant than the other mourners. He frowned a little, contracting his features to harsh significance. Nothing, at this moment, would have given him more pleasure than to hear someone whisper, 'Look at Arthur! How well he carries himself, as though he were on parade!' — And the proper answer would have been, 'He is mourning a lost comrade. It is a soldier's grief that his attitude bewrays.' But no one, at least in his hearing, made so understanding a comment. His reverie, indeed, was untimely interrupted by Jane who asked, as loudly as the circumstances permitted, 'Hullo, Arthur. What's the matter? Trying to see how long you can hold your breath?'

Arthur was saved the task of replying to this foolish question by a warning sibilation. Hilary was the first to say 'Hush!' Others repeated it, and a slight hissing ran through the room as though from a flock of resentful geese. Silence succeeded.

So that he and the 4th Brackens need not, in this inclement weather, stand by the grave too long a while, the Vicar had decided to read part of the Burial Service before they left Rumneys. His vestments gently rustled. 'I am the Resurrection and the Life,' he said. His voice carried a churchly echo, and like homing doves the words came through the quietness of the hall. He read the ninetieth Psalm: for the alternative contains the words 'Every man living is altogether vanity', and Mr. Purefoy thought such extravagant humility, suitable though it might be for Jews, inappropriate for Englishmen. But he enjoyed reading *Domine refugium*, and the doves became eagles at 'the glorious Majesty of the Lord our God be upon us: prosper Thou the work of our hands upon us, O prosper Thou our handy-work.'

He turned the pages and read the Corinthian mystery. He asked the statutory riddles. Bearers raised the coffin and carried it out to the gun-carriage that had just arrived, where the wind raised the skirts of the flag, and the rain darkened the red cross upon it, and Sergeant Pilcher's men gravely presented arms. The civilian mourners hurried into their motor-cars, and the whirring of electric starters, the purring of engines, competed with the wind in the trees and nearly defeated the subdued staccato of military commands. In the road, beyond the debouchment of the drive, stood the escort clumsy in their greatcoats: there were a nominal company of the 4th Brackens, Gunners, Engineers, a Field Ambulance section, and a detachment of what had once been the Bracken-shire Yeomanry, and now, its glamour gone but its efficiency increased, was an Armoured Car Company. They were all Territorials, and few of them did not feel the injustice of being rained upon, and coldly blown upon, when they had already sacrificed part of their Wednesday half-holiday to give the funeral its proper honour: Major Gander had been President of the local Territorial Army Association.

The procession was formed, and the muffled drums, mournful beyond words in such weather, beat their march between wildly fluttering hedges. The firing party, their brows constricted with thought, endeavoured to visualize the part they were about to play. In the motor-cars the weather continued to be the principal topic of conversation, and the Major's will, whose provisions were as yet known only to Mr. Peabody, his solicitor, was so absorbing a subject for private speculation that none complained of the monotony of meteorological discussion. At the Churchyard the lesser mourners, those more remotely sorrowful, waited under their umbrellas: they stood like a spawning of giant black mushrooms, a tropical growth of dingy cryptogams, and felt dampness invade their shoes, but stayed resolute to show themselves at the obsequies of a wealthy neighbour. The drums came nearer. The soldiers trod heavily along the broad path between the tombstones. Sergeant Pilcher shepherded his firing party into their proper position by the grave, and told them in discreet tones not to be flurried when the moment came for them to load, for he would give them plenty of time to execute his orders. They listened gloomily, resting on reversed arms, and felt the rain trickle down their necks.

'Man that is born of woman hath but a short time to live, and is full of misery,' said Mr. Purefoy. He read the service quickly now, and when the wet soil fell upon the coffin, when earth, ashes, and dust were committed to their like, Arthur Gander was seized by a curious notion that mud also should be mentioned, and for the next few minutes heard nothing of prayer or collect, being intent on a debate between the rival qualities of dust, that sterile pricking in the eyes, and mud, the gravid floor of crops, and was very perplexed that the former should be preferred for ritual remark. He was roused from this unprofitable logomachy by the loud command, 'Firing party, present arms!'

The firing party hoisted their rifles into the required position. 'Salope arms!' said the sergeant. They transferred their rifles to their left shoulders. The preparatory order 'Volleys!' was succeeded by the injunction to load. They stuffed blank cartridges into the breech, thrust in the bolt, and, pointing their rifles to the sky, waited for the word to fire. Sergeant Pilcher hesitated: he looked anxiously to see if all were ready: and in that surplus second Stephen Sorley, harshly and abruptly, coughed. To Private Ling, eager as ever to be smart, the crackling noise seemed very like a military command, and he pressed his trigger. Privates Butt, Jenkins, Gotobed, Blair, and Hopkins followed suit, and the result, most inappropriate for a funeral, was a *feu de joie*.

'Wait for it, you bloody fools!' cried Sergeant Pilcher, and wished for one agonizing moment that he had at his command language equal to the daedal invective of a pre-War N.C.O. But the next two volleys were fired in gratifying unison, his anger evaporated, and he listened with composure to Bugler Bliss's attempt to sound the Last Post. Bugler Bliss's tongue was imperfectly taught, and that poignant call, that may summon the heart to a loneliness like the outer stars', brayed with his breath like a tinker's moke.

Major Gander's life had not been happy, and the ceremonies attendant on his death were correspondingly mismanaged.

SERGEANT PILCHER, walking with a young woman past Rumneys in the late afternoon, when the weather had moderated, stopped to admire its handsome front, and remarked with envy and awe in his voice: 'To think it's all made of toffee!'

His observation, well contrived to arouse interest, was however inaccurate: Rumneys had not been built of toffee, but bought with toffee. Jonathan Gander, who had died in 1904 worth £84,000, had been a man of great business ability and the fortunate owner of a sweet tooth: but a sweet tooth of discrimination, of delicate appraisal, a tooth as sensitive to the various flavours of butterscotch and fondants as the palate of a wine-taster is to the exquisite difference between the growth of contiguous vineyards on the Slope of Gold. This refinement of taste he had inherited from his mother, who, being left a widow in the days when Lammiter was little more than a village, had turned to good account a nice hand for butter toffee and what were known as Grandmama's Bonbons. Filling the kitchen of her cottage with sweet odours, she had made enough money to pay for the schooling of her family, and before she died she had been repaid by seeing most of them settle down as respectable tradesmen. But Jonathan, the tallest, the strongest, and by far the most independent of her brood, had excited the derision of the neighbours and astonished his mother by refusing to work anywhere except in the kitchen. There, among a host of lesser confections, he had invented that most satisfying of all sweetmeats, Gander's Nutcream Toffee. But in him the artist was allied to the business man: quite early in his career, for instance, he found that barley-sugar acquired a quicker consistency and a greater bulk by the addition of a little flour, and this discovery revolutionized his production of Grandmama's Bonbons. Art and acumen continued hand in hand throughout his career, and in forty years the copper pot in the kitchen had grown into a factory whose products were known throughout the kingdom. Gander's Nutcream Toffee became as integral a part of English childhood as Mother Goose and Robinson Crusoe, and Jonathan himself continued to eat it till the day of his death. He neither drank nor smoked, seeing tobacco and wine as mortal enemies to toffee, and he firmly believed that the surest way to good health was an inordinate consumption of sugar.

He had married twice. His first wife had borne him six children, of whom two had predeceased him. Hilary Gander was the sole issue of his second marriage.

The Major, his third son, had died a bachelor. A romantic attachment to a young lady called Evelyn Sotheby had ended, disastrously for him, during the siege of Ladysmith. While the Major — he was a Captain then — was shut up in that unfortunate town, Miss Sotheby married a man called Hubble, whose father, known in Lammiter as Hubble-Bubble, was a wealthy manufacturer of aerated waters. Now the Major had loved Evelyn Sotheby for ten years and never told his love. He was a shy man, to whom words came reluctantly, and Evelyn was a child of sixteen when he first saw her and knew, at that moment, that no other woman in the world had any meaning for him. His regiment was ordered to India and he went with it, hoping to find in the years of their separation words to woo her when he returned. He carried her photograph with him through the Tirah campaign of 1897, and he had another in his pocket — for the first had faded — when the Boers invested Ladysmith. The South African War interrupted his courtship for the second time. He had come home from India, a soldier proved in battle and toughened by service in the northern passes, and for three months he danced attendance on Miss Sotheby, and his love for her grew day by day, and he never said a word to hint of its existence. He waited for a miracle to make his heart speak for him, for a tongue of Pentecostal flame; but the Boers spoke first, and the Major went to war again. In the troopship he swore to himself that the first words he would utter on returning to Lammiter — if he lived to return — would be: 'Evelyn, I love you. Will you marry me?' But young Mr. Hubble stayed at home, and when Ladysmith was relieved the first news that the Major read was an intimation of Evelyn's marriage.

This seemed to him the blackest treachery, and for a couple of years his prevailing mood was bitter pessimism. As soon as the war was over he resigned his commission and went to shoot lions in Uganda. This salutary exercise restored his morale, and when he heard that his two elder brothers had both died within six months — Edward of pleurisy, Alexander in a motor-car accident, for motor-cars were just beginning to go fast enough to be dangerous — he returned to Lammiter and entered the family business. He soon revealed so sound an understanding of its problems, so remarkable an ability for negotiation, that when old Jonathan died of diabetes, eighteen months later, Gander's Nutcream Toffee had increased its sales by ten per cent, and several new chocolate varieties of Grandmama's Bonbons were already on the market.

The Major's energetic application to business was undoubtedly influenced by the desire, sometimes hardly conscious, to make a larger fortune than the Hubble-Bubbles'. Young Hubble and his wife had gone to live in London: he had bought a new factory site in Woolwich: 'He can fill his lemonade bottles from the Thames, he won't need to flavour them now,' said the Major bitterly, and resolved to show Hubble-Bubble, and Mrs. Hubble-Bubble too, that Lammiter toffee was a better proposition than London lemonade. The business of selling sweets became a romantic quest, and he pursued profits as though they were the path to virtue, leading an ascetic life and reading Malory for recreation.

From this monopoly of his interest he was rescued by the Great War. Leaving his manager to look after the business, he immediately offered his services in the national cause and was rewarded for zeal by a succession of the dullest duties imaginable. He guarded waterworks, he did garrison duty in Ireland, he conducted drafts across the Channel, he suffered heat, boredom, and flies in Salonika, and the conclusion of hostilities found him as Officer in Charge of Embarkations in Bombay. But his return to uniform filled him with enthusiasm for military service that even these elaborate variations in monotony could not kill, and when the war was over he devoted himself with such zeal to the affairs of the Brackenshire Territorial Army Association that he soon became its President.

The toffee business had suffered losses during the war, and the Major was no longer interested in it. He effected some perfunctory reforms, however, and in the boom that energized the first years of peace it again showed handsome profits. But in 1921, with the consent of old Jonathan Gander's remaining descendants, he sold it outright to the mammoth corporation of American Candy, Inc., for £120,000. For many years he had held a controlling interest in the business — it had been a private company — and he was now able to retire with a handsome fortune. Having abundant leisure he added Boy Scouts, Girl Guides, the Lammiter Children's Hospital, and a couple of orphanages to his Territorial hobby, and among such a crowd succeeded in losing the greater part of his bachelor loneliness. For in his latter years he became a prey to the fear of loneliness, and his once romantic temperament was progressively infused with sentimentality. He was delighted when the Girl Guides and the Orphans nicknamed him Uncle John.

He was sixty-three when he died, and his death was due to heart-failure after shooting for the Officers' Cup at the Brackens' Rifle Meeting.

He had spent a lot of money on these organizations, but his wealth was so ample that everyone realized a fortune must still remain to be divided among his nephews and nieces. To estimate its extent had for years been a favourite amusement of the people of Lammiter, and extravagant opinions had frequently been hazarded. Poor and simple people, as well as charitable associations all over the country, regarded him as a millionaire; and even the sophisticated, who scornfully pooh-poohed such rumours, would often say, 'Take my word for it, he won't cut up for a penny less than £150,000'. But speculation now had changed its front: the aggregate of his fortune was no longer of much interest compared with the manner of its distribution. The Major was survived by his half-sister Hilary, by two nieces, and by two nephews, or three if one counted George, who drank, and who was now living obscurely in India or the United States: opinion, though unanimous about his evil nature, differed as to his whereabouts.

It was generally agreed that Rumneys would be left to Hilary, who for many years had kept house for the Major; and well-informed opinion expected that she would also inherit the greater part of his whole estate. There were others who tipped Arthur Gander as the heir: he had lost most of the money left him by his father, he had a wife and child, he needed help: and many well-disposed people hoped he would get it. The Brackenshire Ladies' Golf Club, on the other hand, nursed an uneasy fear that Jane Sutton would be the lucky one; it must not be thought, however, that she was unpopular in the Club: many of the members were sincerely fond of her: but altruism has its limitations, and to see a woman, who can already give you half a stroke and beat you, inherit £150,000, is not the sort of thing to make a female golfer happy. Another school of thought expected that Katherine Clements would be the winner: these, for the most part, were spinsters and neglected wives: they darkly said, 'A woman like that can twist any man round her little finger', economically declaring, by this judgment, their contempt for men and their dislike of Katherine in one breath. The last of the known claimants for the Major's fortune, Stephen Sorley, was favoured only by Wilfrid Follison, his devoted friend, and by Mrs. Barrow, their faithful housekeeper.

Happy were those whose curiosity was academic only, who could speculate upon the incidence of wealth without hope of their own gain or fear of their own disappointment. The state of mind of the possible heirs was far from pleasant. Hilary alone was comparatively calm, and even she was aware of a feeling like indigestion, of a certain discomfort in the chest, of a tendency to yawn, as though she were crossing the Channel in rough weather. Arthur, who for several days had been inventing variations on the theme of a beneficent squiredom — he being the squire — had just been made miserable by a whisper from Jane: 'Have you bought Lammiter Priory yet?' Arthur fully intended to do this if his share of the booty were sufficient, and to be surprised in his secret ambition was painfully embarrassing. He was offended, too, by open discussion of the pecuniary significance of his uncle's will: he himself was prepared to regard it as a covenant rather than a testament, as an ark to be conveyed into his care — he the chosen Levite.

'I have more respect for Uncle John than to try and anticipate his last wishes,' he answered stiffly.

Jane whistled and felt unhappy. Arthur's self-righteousness suggested that he knew more than he cared to admit, and an awful fear assailed her that she might be left out in the cold. Her vision of girdling the globe with birdies and her unerring mashie faded like a fire in the sun: she had already planned her tour of the world's golf-courses, from St. Andrews to Del Monte in California, and now that god-like progress dwindled to hacking her way for evermore down the familiar fairways of Lammiter Heath. Arthur would get the money and she would be left as poor as ever. Her enormous muscles felt limp and tired, and a bitter taste came into her mouth.

Katherine Clements, meanwhile, was foolishly confessing her hopes to Stephen Sorley. 'Uncle John was terribly fond of me, I'm sure of that,' she said earnestly. 'And he knew how poor we are: it was only the other day that he said he simply couldn't think how I always managed to dress so well, for Oliver of course, has practically nothing but his pay, and it costs a lot to live in a cavalry regiment, even an Indian one. I do think Uncle John *must* have left me something pretty decent: well, £20,000, perhaps: don't you?'

'No,' said Stephen. 'I shall be amazed if he has left you anything at all.'

He was already busy with plans to purchase a charming little Queen Anne house, five or six miles away, where he and Wilfrid could live, not in luxury, but in exquisite refinement. They could give up their sordid occupation of teaching illiterates, at ten guineas a time, to write articles for the popular magazines and newspapers: twenty lessons, by correspondence, and the illiterates were supposed to learn an easy and congenial method of supplementing their income by journalism and the minor pangs of literature! How inexpressibly debasing! But what else could a man do to keep body and soul together? How different would life be if he were only moderately wealthy! He would have a secretary, a chauffeur, and a buttoned page in the little Queen Anne house: he knew a delightful boy, two years his junior at Oxford, who would make an admirable secretary, and young Herbert Ling — he had looked really handsome at the funeral, except that his nose was rather red — was very knowledgeable about motor-cars. They would live a trim monastic life, safe from the noise and importunacy and assertiveness of women — though he would keep Mrs. Barrow, of course — and Wilfrid would have the opportunity he wanted to paint water-colour pictures, and design Gothic ornaments for goldfish bowls, and play the piano, and talk. How endlessly, with what infinite pleasure and ceaseless wit, they would talk together! There were days when he wanted to do nothing but talk, to spin like a silkworm his whole being into shining threads of conversation. And as things were he had to listen to this dreary woman Katherine, who smelt of a perfume called Deep Night and talked interminably of her shrill need for money and of her oafish husband who was a soldier in India: a Lancer or some such prehistoric monster.

'It might have made a world of difference if Oliver could have got home in time,' she was saying. 'He's on his way now, you see: if he leaves the boat at Marseilles, as he said he would, he'll be home in a day or two. And he used to get on so well with Uncle John, they were both soldiers, you see, and he could easily have said something about the future, nothing about money, naturally, but just a reminder that if I had an independent income things would be much easier for him. Uncle John would have understood him perfectly, and I might have been saved all this worry. Not that I'm actually worrying, of course, for I know that Uncle John must have left me something: but if I only knew how much . . .'

It was at this moment that Sergeant Pilcher, pausing outside, his right arm snugly round a young woman's waist, looked with envy and awe at Rumneys and remarked, 'To think it's all made of toffee!'

No sooner had the sergeant resumed his walk than a car entered the drive, and Mr. Peabody, the late Major's solicitor, got out and rang the bell. He apologized for his lateness: Lady Caroline Purefoy had called to discuss with him certain arrangements for the garden party, for which he was acting as honorary treasurer, and he had found it difficult, well, not to get rid of her, but to persuade her to expedite her business. Mr. Peabody smiled: a few ingratiating wrinkles appeared on the smooth tight skin of his face, and vanished like errant ripples on a mill-dam: 'But I expect you are anxious to hear the contents of the will,' he said.

He was answered by a little symphony of deprecatory ejaculation, hoarse agreement, and Katherine Clements' frank admission, 'Oh, yes, Mr. Peabody!'

'It was the Major's wish,' he continued, 'that you should all be apprised of the disposition of his property at one and the same time, in order, as he himself said, that you might start at scratch. I regret that I have not yet been able to get into touch with Mr. George Gander, but with his exception everyone is present who may expect to benefit by the terms of the will. I refer, of course, to the residuum of the estate, for there are certain legacies which are independent of the condition that governs its disposal. These minor legacies are as follows.'

Mr. Peabody thereupon catalogued the lesser beneficiaries, who included servants, a few friends, the Officers' Mess of the Major's old regiment, the Boy Scouts, the Girl Guides, the Brackenshire Territorials, the Children's Hospital, and the two

Orphanages. Obvious anxiety accompanied his relation of these preliminary bequests, for though none of them was large, the list of them was long, and relief was audible when he declared, 'That is the sum total of what I may describe as external legacies. The majority of them, as you have observed, are token gifts only, for the Major had already given large sums to these organizations during his lifetime. The last of the unconditional bequests is Rumneys itself. This, with its land, the furniture, and other appurtenances, becomes the property of Miss Hilary Gander.'

There was a murmur of congratulation. 'Oh, how nice for you, Hilary,' cried Katherine impatiently, and Jane said 'That's decent,' in a gruff hearty way as though she had seen a ten-foot putt slide into its hole.

Mr. Peabody spoke again: 'And now we approach the more interesting and, I must admit, the more unexpected part of the will. I should like to say, in the first place, that I myself was entirely ignorant of its contents until four days ago. The Major did not ask my advice in this matter: he devised the will himself, wrote it in his own hand, and kept it in his own possession until his death. It is, however, a valid testament, and with one possible exception, which I will mention later, its meaning is clear beyond doubt or cavil.'

The potential legatees grew apprehensive. This was no way in which to introduce an equitable division of the Major's property. This talk of clarity and conditions might be the prelude to some hideous freak of fancy, some deathbed mockery. Stephen Sorley swallowed another bismuth tablet — anxiety had reinforced the heartburn to which he was subject — and Arthur nervously wondered if a romantic trial of virtue were to be announced: his spirit flickered with excitement, and his heart quailed at the thought of hardships which might have to be encountered in the quest for fortune.

'The preamble to the second part of the will is rather long,' said Mr. Peabody, 'but I do not think you will find it uninteresting, and it is necessary that you should be aware of the preliminary reasoning in order to appreciate the logic of what I may call the executive clause. I shall therefore read it to you in full.'

Mr. Peabody cleared his throat and turned a page. 'These are the Major's own words,' he explained.

' "The name of Gander is a name to be proud of. It cannot claim the historical prestige of such names as Howard, Sackville, Cavendish, and so forth, but for hundreds of years the Brackenshire Ganders were loyal, honest, and God-fearing people of the type that can justly be called the backbone of the nation. Early in the Nineteenth Century, however, they fell upon evil days, and when my grandfather died his widow was left in comparative poverty. The re-establishment of the family in circumstances of dignity and affluence is wholly due to the genius and energy of my father, the late Jonathan Gander. Not only did he restore our fortunes — which were, I believe, of considerable extent in the early part of the Sixteenth Century — but having achieved a social eminence unknown to any Gander since the time of the Commonwealth — and I say this without a trace of snobbery — he did his best to ensure the perpetuation of the name by becoming the father of four sons and three daughters. Such a family, though not large by former standards, might well be thought large enough to guarantee the survival of their name. But facts have proved otherwise.

' "My father had seven children. None of those children has shown a like capacity or inclination for parenthood, and of Jonathan Gander's eight grand-children only five are now living: I wish to record here the name of my nephew John who died on active service while serving with the Brackenshire Yeomanry in 1917.

' "It is with a grave sense of my own deficiencies in this direction that I note here a regrettable tendency of the times, viz. to avoid the responsi-bilities of parenthood, and I am filled with dismay to think that this evil practice . . ." '

'Or lack of practice,' observed Jane.

' ". . . this evil practice," ' Mr. Peabody re-peated, ' "which indeed is tantamount to race-suicide, may be prevalent among my own nephews and nieces. Their matrimonial record has so far done very little to dispel my fears, and even those who have had the opportunity to become parents do not yet seem to be aware that the chief ornament of marriage is a full quiver. I, in my advancing years, daily grow more convinced of the truth of Sir Francis Bacon's observation: that children sweeten labours and mitigate the remembrance of death. They are the crown of married happiness. They are the ripeness of the fruit of the Tree of Life. And, as Shakespeare says, Ripeness is All.

' "These few remarks will, I hope, adequately explain and justify my choice of a residuary legatee, for it will now be apparent that my intention, or at least my hope, is to promote the happiness of all concerned and to perpetuate the name of Gander. I therefore will and bequeath that part of my estate which shall remain after payment in full of the aforementioned legacies to whichever of the late Jonathan Gander's progeny shall, five years from now, have become the parent, whether father or mother, of the greatest number of children born in holy wedlock, the said residuum to remain in the interim in trust under the trusteeship of William Peabody, Esquire, and Miss Hilary Gander." '

Having read this disconcerting document, Mr. Peabody rose from his chair, and walking to a wall where hung a series of fine engravings, ostentatiously devoted his attention to the problems of Marriage à la Mode as depicted by Hogarth. Meanwhile a silence of stupefaction lay on the potential legatees. But in a moment or two the silence was broken, splintered rather, by incoherent protests, by indignation that could not, for a little while, find its feet in words, and by dismay that impotently gaggled and beat the air.

Hilary, who had gone very red, was the first to regain composure. 'That finishes my interest in the will,' she announced, and looked benevolently at Arthur. 'You're well placed, Arthur,' she said. 'You've got a daughter, which is more than any of us can say.'

'Yes, but she's got mumps,' said Arthur unhappily, 'and — well, the fact is that one's not very many.'

Stephen cried shrilly, 'It's outrageous! Uncle John must have been in a disgusting state of mind before he could make a will like that. It's barbaric, it's insane!'

'And it's so *unfair*,' said Katherine. 'Mr. Peabody! Do you think Uncle John was mad, just a little mad perhaps?'

'Major Gander's sanity cannot be questioned,' answered Mr. Peabody without turning round. His words echoed coldly off the glass of Marriage à la Mode.

'You've got nothing to grumble at,' said Jane to Katherine. 'Your husband's on his way home: you can start at once.'

'But I don't want to!' cried Katherine. 'I hate children, and they might all be wasted, anyhow. You might have lots more than me, a great big creature like you.'

'I'm certainly not going to spoil my golf by having babies,' said Jane decidedly, and Arthur looked at her with gratitude.

'Before you make your plans for the future,' said Hilary, 'it might be as well to hear how much money John has left. Mr. Peabody hasn't told us yet.'

Mr. Peabody returned to his chair and consulted the calculations he had made. 'I cannot as yet tell you the exact amount,' he answered, 'but I have made an approximate valuation of the estate, and after deducting the minor legacies and an approximate sum for death duties, the reversion will, I think, be in the neighbourhood of £70,000.'

'Seventy thousand!' Katherine whimpered. 'Oh, I shan't know *what* to say to Oliver! It's such a lot of money.'

'But we're not going to submit to this,' cried Stephen. 'I refuse to be bullied into marriage by anybody, and if we all stand together, and come to a decent arrangement, we can upset this wretched will, or ignore it, and simply divide the seventy thousand between us.'

Katherine looked at him with calculation in her eyes. If Stephen declined to marry, and Jane refused to let babies interfere with her golf, and Hilary — well, Hilary was thirty-nine — then the contest lay between her and Arthur: and Arthur's wife was a lean spectacled vegetarian who had produced a daughter nine years ago, and nothing since. Katherine began to think more favourably of the will. She was certainly not prepared to sacrifice her chance of seventy thousand pounds for Stephen's sake.

'Oh really!' she said. 'And why should we ignore Uncle John's wishes just for your benefit? It was Uncle John's money, and he had the right to do what he pleased with it. If you don't want to get married, that's your business. But some of us are married, and if we have children, which is the natural thing to do, then I don't see why we shouldn't benefit by them. As a matter of fact, Oliver is very, very keen on having a family, and I expect we'll have quite a large one in time.'

Mr. Peabody, who had paid no attention to this change and exchange of views, now said: 'There is, as I warned you, one small uncertainty in the will. The executive sentence reads, as doubtless you remember, "whichever of the late Jonathan Gander's progeny shall within the space of five years *from now* become the parent of the greatest number of children" — and so forth. But the will was made three years ago: it is dated 1930. The Major's intention was probably to allow you five full years in which to decide the issue, or perhaps even more, for there is, as you can see, a faintly pencilled question-mark above the word 'five'. But as the will stands the meaning is five years from 1930, and I do not think we can let supposition, however plausible, interfere with that reading. The result of this unfortunate error — if it is an error — is that instead of five you have only two years and three months in which to — ah! — compete for this very substantial legacy.'

'That puts a premium on twins,' said Jane.

'Oliver's mother was a twin,' exclaimed Katherine.

'I'm going home,' said Stephen angrily. He was looking white and ill, and he had finished his bismuth tablets. 'I'll come back to-morrow, and if you've recovered from this lunacy by then, perhaps we can think of some sensible arrangement.'

'I think I had better go home too,' said Arthur.

'Daisy will be anxious to hear all about this, though I don't think she'll be pleased when I tell her.'

'I'm coming to see Ruth to-morrow,' said Hilary. 'I do hope she's feeling better, poor little soul.'

'Mumps are so infectious,' said Arthur unhappily. 'I hope Daisy doesn't take them. I've had them myself, of course, so I'm all right.'

Stephen moved impatiently to the door, but before he reached it it was opened by a parlour-maid, who came in with a telegram. 'For Mrs. Clements,' she said.

Katherine tore the envelope. 'From Oliver,' she exclaimed, and read aloud: ' "Arrived Marseilles to-day coming overland may stop two days in Paris love Oliver". — Two days in Paris,' she repeated. 'Oh, my God, not Paris! Give me a piece of paper: tell the boy to wait: I'm going to wire at once. Two days in Paris indeed!'

THE Vicar's barograph rose a little towards night,
drew a straight line during the darkness, and in the
morning oegan to engrave a melancholy declina-
tion. No rain fell before lunch, however, and Lady
Caroline, after lifting an eye at the weather, grew
more and more cheerful. She was a little plump
woman, brown faced, and the eye she cocked at
heaven was bright and lively as a robin's: few
creatures save robins and Lady Caroline, indeed,
could have looked at such a sky so livelily, for it
hung like an old tarpaulin over the earth, heavy
with unshed rain. But Lady Caroline's optimism
was a product of her enthusiasm, a kind of bow-wave,
and as her enthusiasms were always intense, so was
her optimism large and high and independent of
everything save the progress of her current enterprise. She was a woman of many hobbies, all
benevolent. She did good deeds with ruthless
excitement, and in successive years she had stirred
Lammiter to work for the League of Nations Union,
the protection of wild birds, the provision of window-
boxes for the poor, a new reredos for her husband's
church, the revival of maypole dancing, and now for
the introduction of more kindly methods to local
slaughter-houses. She had been active in this last
campaign for several months, and the prospective
garden-party was but one of many engagements:
but as more than seven hundred tickets, at half a

crown a piece, had already been sold for it, it was not without importance.

The Vicarage garden, uncommonly large and very prettily laid out, was well worth seeing. It contained a parterre of formal beds, a rose garden, a pergola most gaily flowering with yellow Banksias and crimson Ramblers, a lily-flanked pond, and a rhododendron dell: the rhododendrons had unfortunately flowered too early to abet the roses, but, as Lady Caroline said, 'You can't expect nature to make special arrangements for half a crown.' The previous day's inclement weather had also diminished the glory of the pergola and the multi-coloured gaiety of tne parterre. The Vicar shook his head to see turf and soil pied with a myriad fallen petals, but Lady Caroline cheerfully remarked, 'I think they look very pretty lying there, like confetti'. And she so vigorously agitated the adjacent Duchess of Athol that a shower of lingering rain-drops leapt from its leaves like the quicksilver scuts of invisible rabbits.

The earliest visitors came at half-past three, and by half-past four there were nearly two hundred people in the garden. They went walking under the pergola with quick uneasy steps, their shoulders humped as a protection against the dismal leaf-drip, the cold stillicide that contrasted so unhappily with the would-be gaiety of the crimson and the yellow roses; they trod mincingly between the puddles on the paths and told each other, with an effort to enjoy themselves, how sweet the stocks smelt after rain; they looked with perfunctory interest at the muddied waters of the pond and the adjacent bank of wet white lilies; and with a shiver they peeped into the sodden jungle of the dell, where a few syringas and late azaleas did a little to break the drenched and flowerless monotony of the rhododendron bushes.

Moving briskly among the guests, Lady Caroline fortified their failing pleasure with mysterious references to the entertainment, unusual in kind and specially planned, which they might expect in a little while; and refuted the impending sky. 'No, no, no,' she said, 'there'll be no rain this afternoon. And even if there are a few drops you won't notice them, you'll be so engrossed by the demonstration. Oh, I'm not going to tell you what it is: you'll see for yourselves in half an hour. Look at these geums, poor things: they were in perfect bloom two days ago. But we couldn't have enjoyed them till poor Major Gander was comfortably buried, so perhaps everything was for the best after all. And the rain quite spoiled his funeral, of course. The Vicar said that everybody was looking miserable, and I'd have felt just a little bit unfair if my geums hadn't suffered too. Is that Mrs. Ramboise? I must go and speak to her. What a great big girl her daughter is!'

The Vicar, whose spirit was hardly so dynamic as Lady Caroline's, preferred a more stationary form of hospitality. He stood by the buffet that had been erected in the dining-room, and his conversation was like a melancholy countermure for the defensive optimism of his wife. 'We've been very unfortunate,' he said, 'and my only hope is that we

43

shall be spared further mischances. The rain *may* hold off for another hour or two: I hope so, I certainly hope so. This performance that my wife has arranged is going to be a demonstration of the case for reform in our slaughter-houses, and under the circumstances I think we might have expected better weather. No, I don't know what the demonstration's going to be, but my wife assures me that it's quite remarkable and very dramatic. Have you had any tea yet, Mrs. Bulmer? There's Mr. Follison, he'll look after you.'

Wilfrid Follison had already procured a cup of tea for Mrs. Bulmer, and now, with patience for a hook and charm for a bait, he was fishing for a plate of cucumber sandwiches in a chattering eddy by the urn: Mrs. Fowler, Mrs. Sabby, Miss Foster, Mrs. Corcoran, and Miss Montgomery had lived in the aggregate three hundred years, and their fund of small talk was proportional to such experience of life, their tea-time appetite commensurate with so long practice. But presently, without offending any of them, Wilfrid secured the remainder sandwich for Mrs. Bulmer, and turning to the Vicar said impulsively, 'It *is* a nice party! I wish Stephen could have come.'

'None of them suffered from the wetting they got?' asked the Vicar.

'Stephen was shivering when he came home, and I made him stay in bed to-day,' said Wilfrid, 'but it wasn't the weather that upset him, it was the will.'

'He was disappointed, was he? Who were the lucky ones?'

'Everybody was disappointed,' said Wilfrid earnestly, 'and more than disappointed. They were *shocked*. Major Gander must have been mad. There was nothing but a lot of immoral suggestions in the will, and even if we hadn't all decided to keep it a secret, as long as we can, I couldn't possibly tell you about it, because it's *too* disgusting.'

'Good heavens!' said the Vicar. 'You don't mean to say that Gander was insane?'

'He must have been,' Wilfrid assured him.

'Then the will's invalid?'

'No, it isn't, and that's why we're all so upset. Mr. Peabody says there's nothing wrong with it in the legal sense, and Stephen's making himself perfectly ill with worry.'

Controlling his curiosity with praiseworthy strength of mind, the Vicar said stiffly, 'As I don't know the contents of the will I can't make any useful comment upon it. But I always had a great respect for Gander, and I think you're probably exaggerating some small eccentricity he has been guilty of. You mean, I suppose, that he didn't make provision for the family?'

'That's just the trouble,' said Wilfrid. 'He did.'

Before he could be tempted to further indiscretion Mrs. Corcoran pulled his sleeve and asked him to get her another cup of tea. The Vicar, whose curiosity now easily exceeded his self-control, caught sight of Mr. Peabody in a far corner of the room, and made towards him through the crowd. Wilfrid continued to serve the needs of elderly and middle-aged ladies with deft and charming alacrity. He was a great favourite with the old ladies of Lammiter, and always remembered who among them took sugar in their tea, and who objected to having the cream put in first.

Meanwhile, unaware of the important part they were shortly to play and as yet unseen by the two or three hundred guests, two well-grown young pigs, of the kind called Large Black, lay upon straw in one of several outhouses that projected from the east wing of the house. With them sat a little man called Bowles, lately a butcher and now a market gardener, and four of the Purefoy children: Cecily was twelve, Patrick ten, Rosemary seven, and Peter was approaching his fifth birthday. The two older boys, Denis and Rupert, were at school, luckily for Mr. Bowles: they were daring and imaginative boys, and Mr. Bowles's stories would soon have tempted them to mockery and rude parody. But the younger Purefoys sat enthralled by his tedious and prolix descriptions of the pole-axing of bullocks and the slitting of sheep's throats. Though comparatively quiet and well behaved, they were not squeamish, and Rosemary and Peter were still young enough to confuse blood-letting with heroism: they listened to Mr. Bowles's stories of the abattoir and saw him, in imagination, as kinsman to Blackbeard the Pirate, du Guesclin, and the Light Brigade; for Rosemary was a constant reader, and Peter was always her willing audience. Cecily and Patrick, however, had no need of literary illusions with which to sustain their attention: they were interested in killing for its own sake, and as they took great delight in shooting

46

rabbits with a small rifle and hunting rats with a fox terrier, so they suspected major pleasure in the pole-axing of beeves. But what none of them could understand was why Mr. Bowles had given up this absorbing occupation and taken to market-gardening.

'There can't be much excitement in growing lettuces,' Cecily protested.

'There's the satisfaction of knowing that you're producing good 'ealthy food,' said Mr. Bowles. 'A lettuce is very cleansing to the blood, and the more you eat the cleaner your insides'll get. There was a time, mark you, when I thought there was nothing tastier than a nice cow's 'eel. But I know better now. I'm a vegetarian, and 'ave been these last two years.'

'I like meat,' said Peter.

'Vegetarians are generally atheists,' observed Patrick.

'You've no call to say that,' Mr. Bowles replied. 'I'm a Wesleyan and always 'ave been, and you can be a Wesleyan on lettuces just as well as you can on cow's 'eels.'

'Tell us more about killing things,' said Cecily.

'Not if you're going to misunderstand me,' said Mr. Bowles. 'I've only been telling you about slaughter-'ouses and so on to show you what 'orrible places they are. It's because I came to realize what a 'orrid life I was leading that I gave up being a butcher and took to market-gardening. I 'ad a dream one night, a nightmare I suppose you would call it, though perhaps it was a vision. I was standing in the slaughter-'ouse, at least that's

47

what I dreamt I was doing, and there in the corner was an old sheep looking at me in a most peculiar way Well, I went up to 'er, with my knife ready, and I'm blessed if she didn't get up on her 'ind legs and begin to dance. So I stopped short and said "'Ere, that's no way to behave!" But she just went on dancing, looking at me in a very curious manner, and presently she stepped right out of her skin and was dancing bare naked. And then I saw it wasn't a sheep at all, but a girl called Gladys Hoops, that used to be well known in Lammiter and went to London to go on the stage. Well, it shook me, that dream did, and the next day I 'adn't any 'eart for my work through thinking that all the sheep I was killing might be Gladys Hoops under their skin. So I went to a doctor, and 'e told me I'd got blood pressure and ought to stop eating meat and look for an easier job. So what with that, and the 'orror I began to feel about butchering, I gave it up, and I wouldn't go back to it now not if you paid me a thousand a year.'

'When are you going to show us that pistol you were talking about?' asked Patrick.

One of Mr. Bowles's several talents was a certain mechanical faculty, and he had lately given practical expression to his revulsion against the horrors of the slaughter-house by inventing a new kind of humane-killer. Neither its killing-power nor its humanity had as yet been sufficiently tested to substantiate his high opinion of the weapon, but he could be very eloquent about it, and his commendation of it had persuaded Lady Caroline that the Bowles Humane

Pistol, as it was already christened, was the most efficient thing of its kind, and the bullocks and the wethers of England would be happier beasts on the day when it was generally adopted by the abattoirs. She hoped to demonstrate its advantages to Lammiter this afternoon.

Mr. Bowles took the weapon out of a battered cardboard-leather attaché case, and proudly showed it to the children. It had been originally a wheel-lock pistol of the largest kind. It was about two feet long. Rosemary and Peter immediately conceived a new image of Mr. Bowles: they saw him, black-visored, voluminously caped, riding along the Great North Road by Dick Turpin's side, and heard his somewhat meagre voice command affrighted travellers to stand and deliver. But Mr. Bowles was explaining the action of the pistol in technical terms that would have puzzled the highwayman. He had designed a new breech, and the barrel had been rifled. The projectile was a steel bullet, sharply pointed and nearly three inches in length. This made the cartridge so long that he had been compelled to use a bolt like the bolt of a service-rifle, and the pistol had a curiously hybrid appearance. Mr. Bowles said the muzzle velocity was uncommonly high, and the rifling of the barrel gave to the sharp-pointed bullet such power of penetration as would kill an elephant, and, moreover, kill it before suspicion rose in its mind that death was on the way.

'What if the bullet comes out on the other side?' asked Patrick.

'That won't matter, so long as there's nobody standing there,' said Mr. Bowles.

Further discussion was stopped by the arrival of Lady Caroline. She had acquired a certain air of untidiness, as though her excited mind had produced a homologue in the disorder of her dress. Her voice was pitched a little higher than usual, and its inflection had a taut and nervous quality. She was intensely anxious for the success of her demonstration, and she had found the strain of waiting for it almost intolerable. She was tired, moreover, by ceaseless conversation with her guests, and her recent efforts to parade them in seemly order for the performance had been exhausting.

'They're all waiting for you, Mr. Bowles,' she said. 'Have you got everything ready?'

'Yes, your ladyship. I'm ready.'

'And Cecily and Patrick will be able to help you? You won't require more assistance?'

'I think they'll be able to do what's wanted, your ladyship.'

'Of course we shall,' said Cecily and Patrick.

'Us too,' demanded Rosemary and Peter.

'No, no,' said Lady Caroline, 'you'll come with me. I don't believe in pampering children, Mr. Bowles, or encouraging them to be frightened of things, but Rosemary and Peter are too young to be really helpful. They have excellent nerves and they wouldn't be alarmed by the demonstration, but they *might* get in the way. Now be sure you do exactly what Mr. Bowles tells you, Patrick, and don't jerk the pig's leg like that. Persuade it to go with you, don't bully it.'

With some difficulty the pigs were coaxed out of the shed and driven towards the garden. Each was held by a rope tied to its near-side foreleg, and this arrangement, though fairly effective in preventing them from running away, was of little help in guiding them. With Lady Caroline's assistance, however, they at last reached their destination, and when Rosemary and Peter had been given into the hands of Miss Foster, who volunteered to look after them, the little group of Lady Caroline and Mr. Bowles, Cecily, Patrick and the two pigs, advanced to a central position before the middle bed of multi-coloured antirrhinums.

The majority of the guests stood facing them, and at some height above them, on the broad terrace that fronted the house. A curtain of wistaria climbed the stone walls, its pendant clusters still grey-green at the point but opening above their soft mauve plumage; and separating the onlookers from the imminent demonstration were a green bank and a generous border, hedged by dwarf box, of poppies and pyrethrums, lupins, geums, and petunias. To Lady Caroline's right stood other rows of spectators with the pergola for their background; and on her left were as many more, in a double or treble rank, on the high path that separated the parterre from the rhododendron dell. Behind her, between her and the rose garden, a mere score or so of people, of the kind that always stands separate from the crowd, completed the attentive square. Without any formal introduction, Lady Caroline began to speak.

'You all know the purpose of this garden-party,' she said. 'The principal object, the ostensible object, was to raise funds for the B.A.I.S. — the Brackenshire Association for Improved Slaughterhouses — and though there aren't quite as many people here as I'd hoped to see, the inclement weather may be responsible for that deficiency, and after all it doesn't matter much, because we sold a great number of tickets, and from the financial point of view we've done very well indeed. But money isn't everything. Indeed money is very little compared with our determination to put a stop to the terrible cruelty with which so many cattle and pigs and sheep are killed for our daily use. I don't say that we shouldn't eat meat, but I do say the poor cattle should be put to death as painlessly as possible, and not in the barbaric way that is still too common in some of our abattoirs, and especially in small villages where there isn't proper supervision. I know that you all agree with me about this matter, but I've often felt that some of you are not sufficiently *earnest* in your desire and your determination to bring about the necessary reforms, and that may be because you don't really know what goes on in a slaughter-house, or, on the other hand, because you don't realize that it's quite possible to be kind to animals even while you are killing them. A lot of people won't listen to arguments: they only believe what they see. And so this afternoon I'm going to appeal to you not by argument but by example, and you will see two methods of killing a pig, one cruel and one kind. Mr. Bowles, who abhors cruelty just as much as we do, has very kindly consented to be our demonstrator, and he will kill one of these pigs in the old-fashioned way by sticking a knife into its throat, and the other in quite a different way by shooting it with a humane pistol that he himself has invented, a very clever and charitable thing to do, as I'm sure you will all agree when you have seen how efficient a weapon it is. I hope you will all be impressed by the contrast between these methods, and those of you who have never seen a pig being killed will be shocked beyond words to know that it is often done with the disgusting and abominable cruelty that Mr. Bowles, to whom we should all be very grateful, has agreed to demonstrate. It is a truly revolting spectacle, but as you will all see it for yourselves in a few minutes, and as I'm afraid it's going to rain before long — but most of you have umbrellas, I see — I won't keep you longer by describing it in detail, but I shall now call upon Mr. Bowles to begin the demonstration.'

There was no applause when Lady Caroline, having finished speaking, stood aside and pointed to Mr. Bowles. The few hands that came together in mechanical salutation tapped lightly together as dying leaves on a window, and this flickering noise — it might be dead leaves, or the owlet's wings in a twilit lane — was altogether lost in the confused and excited chattering that immediately began. Noise encircled the garden: such a noise as occupies the intermission when the Queen's Hall is filled with the admirers of Wagner, but mingled with the sharper sound of starlings frightened in a shrubbery, and coarsened and hoarsened by protest half-shocked beyond the use of words. There were now three hundred and sixty people present, and not half a dozen had ever seen a butcher working — except upon dead meat — and none would have thought of seeking entertainment in an abattoir. But though they muttered, though they exclaimed, though some were gruffly disapproving and others tittering, and here and there a woman cried she could not bear to see blood, yet a kind of decorum held them where they were; a sort of decency anchored them to the paths; their English habit of preferring to endure an outrage, rather than become conspicuous by rebelling against it, kept them from marching out of the garden. And then again they all disliked the thought of offending Lady Caroline. They decided to stay. It was easier to stay than flamboyantly retreat; and many of them, after the first shock was over, felt curiosity come creeping into their minds; they began to desire the discomforting titillation of horror. A few drops of rain fell, and more threatened. They put up their umbrellas, those who had them, and those who had not resented this curtailment of their view, and thrust their way forward, being now at all costs resolved to outwit the eclipsing umbrellas and to watch for all they were worth that which they had but lately shrunk from seeing.

With the gesture of a conjuror who holds up a magic wand for his audience's approval, Mr. Bowles displayed his highwayman's pistol and loaded it with grave precision.

'I think it will be better to use the knife to begin with,' said Lady Caroline. 'First of all show us the cruel and disgusting way in which many people kill their pigs, and then let us see how *nicely* it can be done by the humane method.'

'Very good, your ladyship,' said Mr. Bowles, and laid his pistol on the lid of his cardboard attaché case. Then from a rolled-up sack he took a long brightly-bladed knife. The spectators stood silent. 'Now you look after that for a minute,' he said, and gave the knife to Patrick. Cecily firmly held the second pig by its tether.

'The first thing to do,' said Mr. Bowles, now addressing his audience, 'is to put the pig on its back. Then you make a little cut in the skin between its neck and its chest, so to speak, and thrust in the knife till it reaches the big veins that go into the heart. Or arteries, they're sometimes called,' he added. A shiver rippled along the dark front of the spectators, and some sidled backwards into the rearward rank.

Mr. Bowles laid expert hands on the nearest pig and cast it on its back. Immediately, in the hellish fashion of a pig, it began to scream. The second pig, sympathetic, squealed in lighter tones. The din was ear-splitting, loud as a factory whistle and infinitely more poignant. Only Mr. Bowles was unperturbed by the diabolical uproar — even the children grimaced — and, kneeling above the thrown pig's head, he put a loop of the rope round its forefeet, pulled them towards him, and took his knife from Patrick. Deftly he made a small incision at the base of the porker's fat throat.

Few of the spectators would have believed that any noise could be louder and more fearful than that which they had heard already — many of them, despite decorum, forgetful of their English phlegm, were now in full retreat — but as soon as the pig felt the knife its voice acquired new strength and a still more hideous tone. To Mr. Bowles, however, that was not unexpected. What he did not anticipate was that the beast would leap so convulsively as to knock him off his balance and break free. But Mr. Bowles was somewhat excited by the proximity of so many spectators, and the rope was wet with the rain, and his hands and the pig were wet, and calamity occurred. The porker kicked its feet out of the rope and galloped headlong for the pergola. It was a fearsome sight. Its black body was convulsive with rage and speed, its huge ears flapped, and as it galloped it diabolically screamed. Panic broke the ranks of those who stood by the pergola. They tumbled over each other to get out of its way, and the pig crashed through the trellis-work, turned right, and ran beneath the crimson and the yellow roses.

Now the second pig, emulous of its brother's liberty, also struggled to get free, and Cecily could hardly hold it. Patrick dramatically came to his sister's rescue. He seized the highwayman's pistol, aimed, and fired. But the pistol kicked abominably and the bullet, scoring a furrow down the pig's back, rose in a ricochet and whined over the rhododendron dell. Yelling with fright and pain the second pig broke loose, turned, and followed the way of

the bullet. The spectators on the path that inter-
sected its line of flight uttered loud cries of alarm, and
bolted at ungainly speed towards the house.

The scene of confusion in the garden was now
almost indescribable. Most of the guests were women,
and many of them were old. But the older they were
the more able they appeared to look after themselves,
and the more determined to save the short residue of
their lives. Brandishing their umbrellas like clubs,
or stabbing with them as though they were assegais,
they drove a resolute way to safety through indeter-
minate clusters of men and betwixt vocal groups of
matrons and excited girls. In a very short time all
the old ladies were inside the house again, with the
doors barricaded behind them, and Miss Montgomery, who was seventy-nine, had rung the bell
and ordered more tea.

Meanwhile the Vicar, with great shouting such as
he used in the hunting field, was summoning to him
all the men whom he could recognize and knew to be
moderately sound in wind and limb. His mind,
released by the prospect of activity from the frustration and worry of the afternoon, was already elabor-
ating plans for the recapture of the pigs. He had
been far from happy since his conversation with
Wilfrid, for his dignified and tactful attempts to
elicit some information about the will from Mr.
Peabody had been quite unsuccessful, and the
sudden revelation of his wife's intention to butcher
pigs in the middle of the garden — she had never
told him the details of her plan to popularize
Mr. Bowles's humane pistol — had startled and

perturbed him. The necessity of repairing her folly, and the chance to forget his disappointment with Mr. Peabody in pig-hunting, cheered him a lot, and he began to give orders for surrounding the dell with great vigour and confidence. His instructions were delayed by old Sir Gervase Flood, a fierce veteran of the Indian Civil Service, who came clamouring for a boar-spear.

'You must have a spear in the house,' he shouted. 'Everybody's got a spear or two somewhere or other. Get your beaters lined up, Purefoy, drive the pig out of the jungle, and leave the rest to me. Only get me a spear first.'

'You couldn't do any good on foot, Flood,' interposed General Ramboise, late of the Rajputana Lancers. 'Now if I had that little grey mare of mine . . .'

'I've stuck pigs on foot a hundred times,' roared Sir Gervase. 'In Orissa, in the 'eighties, with old Abdul Mohamed Chaudhry. You fellows on the other side of India don't know anything about pig.'

'I may say I've ridden, not once, but regularly, in the Kadir Cup meetings,' said the General stiffly.

Sir Gervase interrupted him, and made for the vicarage. 'I'm going to look for a spear,' he shouted. 'Where d'you keep 'em, Purefoy?'

The Vicar called him back. 'There are no boar-spears in my house,' he said, 'so I'm afraid you'll have to put up with my method of capturing the fugitives.' He then marched his party to the dell, and disposed them on its circumference.

The second pig had taken refuge among the

58

rhododendrons, and though it could not be seen its progress might be marked by the shaking of the bushes and the occasional destruction of syringas and the remaining azaleas. It was still yelling at intervals, and was obviously very wild. The Vicar ordered his party to advance into the dell, and this, after some hesitation, they proceeded to do.

In the meantime the first pig, after a spirited pursuit round the garden by Miss Ramboise and several other athletic young women, was busily destroying the rose-garden. In such evident fury as to daunt even Miss Ramboise, it attacked a magnificent Golden Gleam, whose yellow petals fluttered in the air and fell like dapples of sunlight on its black satanic hide. Half a dozen ruined Duchesses of Athol lay behind it, their bloom an orange carpet for the soil, and the dark red blossom of l'Etoile de Holland lay like blood in the wasted snow of Madame Butterfly. The raging pig uprooted a fine Shot Silk; pink petals were mingled with the red, the creamy white, the yellow, and the gold, and the gross black brute, its swart ears flapping, trampled the lovely wreckage underfoot. Rain fell thick and steady now, and the least percipient was sensible of something awful in this sinister spectacle of wrath beneath a hostile sky. Wet petals clung to the swine's dark coat, and a trickle of blood, thinned by the rain, painted its shoulders. Grunting and rooting, its ire increasing, it destroyed the last of the roses, and turned to stare with tiny malignant eyes at the abashed Miss Ramboise.

But now these onlookers received reinforcements.

Lady Caroline had been running to and fro, gravely alarmed lest any of the guests had been hurt, now peering into the dell, now retrieving an umbrella from the snapdragons. Cecily and Patrick had also been running about, but with no apparent purpose except to enjoy the sensations of rapid movement and loud shouting. Mr. Bowles, after sitting for some time in futile contemplation, had risen and slowly walked away, with no special purpose or destination in view, and in this dazed condition the Vicar had hailed him and added him to his party. But now Cecily and Patrick and their mother came quickly to the desolated rose-garden, and Patrick had the highwayman's pistol, reloaded, and three or four of the long cartridges in his trouser-pocket. Without consulting anybody as to the propriety of his action he advanced boldly against the pig, raised the pistol, and fired. But again the pistol kicked hard, and the bullet flew wide and high. The pig raised its head, flapped its ears, grunted, and raced from the ruined roses towards the pond. It tore a wasted furrow through the down-sloping bank of Madonna lilies — for a moment its sooty flanks increased their pallor and made their pale green glow — and plunged into the water. Within a few seconds it was joined there by its brother from the dell.

The Vicar's party had had a strenuous but fruitless time among the rhododendrons. They had invaded the drenched bushes with reluctance; they forced their way through dripping branches with dull determination; and then, exasperated by the slapping of wet leaves and entanglements that took their ankles, they continued the hunt with witless fury. The pig, moving with surprising speed, dodged them easily, for they were constantly confused by shouts intended to direct them, and the Vicar's 'View halloa!' was often contradicted by stentorian exclamations in Hindustani from Sir Gervase or General Ramboise. The hunt was finally at fault when Mr. Bowles, tripping over a root, disappeared into the bushes and cried so shrilly that Sir Gervase mistook the human for the porcine note. *'Bagh gaya!'* he shouted, and hurled himself through the intervening rhododendron and on to the prostrate Mr. Bowles. Others followed suit, and a pretty scramble took place during which Mr. Bowles suffered severely. Taking advantage of this lull in the pursuit, the pig slipped out of the dell and trotted into the pond.

Both pigs were now in the water, flank-high. They showed no sympathy, no realization of their common lot against the rout of pursuers, but after floundering a little on the muddy bottom they stood still, snuffling and blowing, their rage abated by the coolness, and apparently content. Patrick, who had reloaded the wheel-lock pistol, was just in time prevented from firing it again, and before the Vicar's party had extricated themselves from the imbroglio in the dell, Lady Caroline took charge of the proceedings. 'Poor beasts,' she said, 'we must treat them very *kindly* after all they've gone through.' Kilting her skirt to the knee she strode into the pond. The nearer pig stood still. She bent, and plunged her arm into the water, and found the rope that was still tied to its hock. She began to lead it out. The other pig, driven before her, came quickly to the shore, where Patrick took hold of its tether. The adventure was over, and the black swine stood docile as poodles, as though no evil thought had ever entered their upsnout heads. 'Take them back to the shed,' said Lady Caroline, and shivered in her sodden clothes.

Suddenly she began to cry, and the congratulations of those who had surrounded her became murmurs of condolence and little pats of sympathy. The Vicar appeared, and when he saw her plight his story of the hunting in the dell, all ready and impatient to be told, was at once forgotten. His self-importance disappeared. His only emotion was anxiety, and his high-coloured handsome face lost its look of security and grew plain and pitiable with distress. He took off his coat, and wrapped it round his wife's shoulders, and led her, still weeping uncontrollably, towards the house.

Their entrance was hindered by the barricade with which the old ladies had blocked the French windows. The Vicar bellowed like a bull and beat the window-frames. Wilfrid had also retired to the house, not long after the old ladies, and having found glasses and a decanter was now comforting them with sherry. Hurriedly forsaking this charity he pulled away sofas and chairs and let the postulants in. He was horrified by Lady Caroline's drenched and miserable appearance, and while the Vicar took her upstairs to bed Wilfrid ran to the

62

kitchen and bade the maids fill hot-water bottles, and he himself prepared a comforting negus with whisky and ginger wine.

When all the other guests had gone — some excited, some scandalized, some foolishly hilarious, and others merely uncomfortable — Sir Gervase Flood and General Ramboise still walked to and fro in the desolated muddy garden. They had picked up two of the score or so of discarded umbrellas that lay on the flower-beds, and ever and anon they would stop to expound their rival methods of sticking pig: Sir Gervase, grasping his umbrella like a great dagger, would illustrate the downward stab with which the charging boars of Bengal are customarily killed; and the General, disliking the crudeness of this attack, would seriously argue the superior art of riding down a jinking pig, such as he had often pursued at meetings to compete for the Kadir Cup, and leaning from an imaginary saddle he showed the proper technique with a long lance-like reaching of his gamp.

Not for a long time did it occur to them that their umbrellas might be used to better purpose, but when at last they remembered the rain, and put them up, their comfort was so largely increased that a reflective clublike air enveloped them and they turned to the discussion of more serious topics. They found themselves in perfect agreement as soon as Sir Gervase began to deplore the progressive Indianization of the Services.

ARTHUR GANDER had relieved the monotony of
dressing by the invention of several variations on
the theme of the morning toilet, and the order in
which he put on his clothes depended almost entirely upon his mood. There were, of course, limitations to this method of expressing his feelings: he
could not put on his shoes before his socks, nor could
he tie his tie until he had donned his shirt. But
except for these obvious restrictions the sequence of
his toilet was arbitrarily dictated, and its principal
variations were as follows.

Sometimes he woke in a sound Conservative
temper, and then he would demonstrate his belief
in the English constitution and the Church of England, in law and order, in discipline and tradition,
by dressing in a sober and conventional manner:
after scrupulous ablutions he would clothe himself
in vest and drawers, socks, shirt, trousers and shoes,
collar and tie and waistcoat — strictly in this order —
then brush his hair, and put on his coat and choose
a handkerchief, happy in the knowledge that his
progression from nakedness to respectability had
been orthodox and strictly in accordance with the
best of contemporary custom. But when his morning mood was rebellious, when he woke with a
romantic inclination to anarchy — because civilization was effete, and the world was vanity, and a
man must rely on his own strength and offer his

bare breast to the wind and the spears of destiny —
then Arthur would omit to shave, and first putting
on socks and shoes, would take drawers and trousers
next, and having clothed himself upwards as far as
the waist would pause for a few minutes to look
grimly at his reflexion in the glass and think: 'This
is the heroic and the desperate image of man.
Sailors in a gun-turret fight like this. In time of
revolution the pits would spew forth ten thousand
miners clad like this. Naked to the waist and ready
for anything!' Sometimes, in such a mood, he was
betrayed by the sight of his stomach — bisected by
the top of his trousers, its upper quadrant was a
homely sight, a plump domestic shape, like a round
cheese, or a cauliflower, or a pudding in a bag —
but hastily diverting his gaze to the stern line of his
mouth and the resolute set of his shoulders he would
build upon such aspects of determination still more
exalted fantasies. These pleasant exercises in
imagination were usually interrupted by a summons
to breakfast, and when it had been twice repeated
Arthur would put on his shirt as sullenly as if it were
a symbol of defeat, a white flag.

His happiest mornings were those on which he
started from the top. This was the mark of what he
called his Gay Guerrilla mood. It was a whimsical
temper that laughed at the silly world, that mocked
alike the seriousness of the Conservative and the
solemnity of the Rebel. The Gay Guerrilla had no
reverence for tradition, no sympathy with impossible
ideals. He made a long nose at the philosophy of
quieta non movere, and shrugged his shoulders at the

folly of waking sleeping dogs for a high purpose. His creed was laughter, and his plan of campaign a cheerful irresponsibility. In a mad world he alone was sane, because he was an outlaw from the world. He was Yorick, he was Robin Hood, he was elfin as to habits and his perception was sophisticated. Therefore he put on his vest and his shirt, his collar and a bright green tie, he brushed his hair, he added a coat, and for some little while walked about his dressing-room with bare legs. This truncated uniform was a very pretty mockery of conventional attire, and sometimes, when the mirror reflected him in a certain light, his legs appeared so much hairier than they truly were that he saw in them a likeness to the shaggy limbs of a satyr, and was very well pleased by that. Then, when he was called to breakfast, he would pull on his trousers with a chuckle, fasten his belt with a wink, and go down-stairs with the whimsical and private knowledge that his well-creased flannels concealed the hairy shanks of a wild woodland creature.

It was in this fashion that he dressed himself on a Wednesday morning some three weeks after his uncle's funeral. He had defied his wife and refused to get up and go out for the early morning walk that she had lately been urging him to take. He had refused to drink the whisked egg-and-milk that he had drunk, at her persuasion, every morning for the last fortnight. He had simply stayed in bed, which was what he wanted to do, and between the comfort of his pillow and the satisfaction of having defeated his wife's purpose — which impugned his virility — he achieved the singular happiness of the Gay Guerrilla. In the first place he didn't believe that he was to blame for their having had no children since the birth, nine years ago of their daughter Ruth. In the second place he didn't believe that drinking eggs-and-milk and walking to Lammiter and back before breakfast could do anything to remedy such a deficiency. And in the third place he didn't care if it could, for he disliked walking, and hated eggs-and-milk, and in the clarifying light of these aversions he saw plainly that this new regimen of health was avaricious in origin, humiliating in effect, and altogether distasteful. Was he the sort of man to sacrifice his integrity for a beggarly seventy thousand pounds? Not a bit of it. Was he the kind of fool who thought it better to be rich than comfortable? No fear. And in any case it wasn't his fault; it was Daisy's. And it was just like her to put the blame on him. But it wasn't worth arguing about, because an argument with Daisy endured for weeks, and she would bring books from the library to prove her point, and quote the experience of friends — whose real existence Arthur always doubted — to substantiate her views. It was better to ignore her, to be impercipient and bland, to preserve a secret amusement within a shell of polite indifference. Let fools worry, but the Gay Guerrilla had nothing to defend save freedom, and the man whose trousers hid a satyr's hairiness could overleap the tedious concerns of humankind.

Arthur went down to breakfast with a little secret smile on his lips, and in his eyes, so far as he could produce it, the sly glance of a faun. His wife and their daughter Ruth were already at the table, Ruth with a book before her and her mother reading a letter with the look of pride and exclusiveness that was habitual to her when she was reading even a postcard, as though her correspondents wrote to no one but her and as though their news were more interesting than any one else's. Arthur's faun-like gaze went unnoticed. He sat down and looked with no pleasure at the plate of brown husks before him. 'What's this?' he asked.

'Dear Juliet! She does write amusing letters,' said his wife.

'What's this brown stuff?' Arthur repeated.

'It's a new breakfast-food, called Vima-Bran,' said Daisy, without looking up from her letter.

'And what does that mean?'

'Vima-Bran is not only a palatable food, but a powerful tonic,' said Ruth. 'It is manufactured by an entirely new process from vitamins, the best British malt, and fresh wholesome bran. Children love it, and it is confidently recommended to the over-tired business man as a certain cure for lassitude, debility, nervousness, and other modern ailments.'

'Who told you all that nonsense?'

'It says so on the box,' Ruth explained. She was reputed a clever child, and according to the not uncommon assumption that brains are merely a compensation for lack of beauty, there might be some truth in this: for she had lank black hair, a sallow complexion, a youthful propensity to warts, and an astigmatism that obliged her to wear spectacles. Her brain was certainly not inactive, and she also possessed such agreeable qualities as honesty, a reasonably good temper, and the ability to find her own amusements.

Arthur remembered his insouciant character in time to repress the display of irritation to which he was tempted, and removing the Vima-Bran to the sideboard, remarked in a whimsical voice, 'Well, Daisy, if you know any tired business men, you'd better give them what's left of this stuff, because I'm certainly not going to eat it. As I don't suffer from debility, and as my nerves are in excellent form, and as I rather like a feeling of lassitude occasionally, it would be wasted on me, I'm afraid.'

'Oh, Arthur, you are tiresome,' said Daisy, and looked at him through her thick pince-nez with a worried smile. She was a tall thin woman with her hair pulled back to a whorl at the nape of her neck, and a prominent thyroid cartilage. 'Isn't daddy being tiresome?' she asked Ruth, who was too absorbed by her book to pay any attention. 'He knows that we want to make him big and strong, but he won't do anything to help us.'

'I'm as strong as a horse,' said Arthur, and whistled *Over the hills and far away*, as he helped himself to bacon and eggs.

'How do hedgehogs mate?' asked Ruth. Her inquiry was not so irrelevant as it appears, for the book she was reading was entitled *Wild Life in Woods and Fields*. Daisy, though startled by the abrupt appearance of so remote and thorny a topic, amiably abandoned the matter of Vima-Bran to satisfy Ruth's hunger for knowledge. For she felt it her duty to answer questions of this kind, and by diligent attention to duty she had given Ruth an uncommonly confused notion of many natural processes: such as pollination. Daisy herself had always been rather vague about the significance of pollen — the entanglement of flowers, bees, and hay fever was too much for her — and an unfortunate comparison she had once drawn between the moths that frequent fur coats, and the hawk-moth that pollinates the honeysuckle, had for long made Ruth believe that moth-balls were the woodbine's odorous fruit. A pretty fancy, and no more wide of the mark than much of Daisy's teaching. She approached the subject of hedgehogs without a tremor.

'Hedgehogs are just like other creatures,' she said kindly. 'They know that Nature wishes them to become parents, and because wild things *always* obey Nature, they fall in love with each other, and then, at the proper time, they come together.'

'Yes, but how?' demanded Ruth.

'There are some of Nature's secrets into which we mustn't pry too closely,' answered Daisy.

Ruth sniffed, a sceptical sound. 'Do *you* know, Daddy?' she asked.

'You must learn to observe things for yourself,' said her father firmly. 'Whenever you go for a walk, keep your eyes and ears wide open, and what you see and hear will teach you far more than books can.'

'Oh, well, I suppose I'll have to ask the librarian,' said Ruth patiently, and resumed her reading.

After breakfast Arthur filled his largest pipe — Daisy had recently been trying to make him give up smoking — and walked slowly down the road to look at the Houses. The Houses were his largest and most disastrous speculation. They were eight in number, and he had built them soon after the War, in collaboration with a late comrade-in-arms whose profit on the transaction had been considerable. The sight of them generally filled him with gloom: they stood in a row, superior villa residences built of thin red brick, unseasoned wood, and Belgian slates that did not keep out the rain. But to-day he looked at them with amusement, even with satisfaction, for it was in keeping with his mood that he should have carelessly thrown away good money in unprofitable investment. And that damned fellow his comrade-in-arms — his name was never mentioned, he was known simply and definitively as That Damned Fellow — had been a good fellow in his way, amusing to talk to after a roughish manner, and laudably master of his fate. Arthur smiled appreciatively to remember some nocturnal episodes of their service together in St. Omer: That Damned Fellow had known his way about, all right. And he himself — he straightened his shoulders complacently — he himself had called for wine in a soldier's voice, and clapped a girl with a soldier's hand: he had heard the chimes at midnight.

Arthur's service in France had been of a very peaceable kind. He had crossed the Channel with the 4th Brackens in July, 1915, and some nine weeks later, chancing to be within three or four miles of the Battle of Loos and within three or four yards of the battalion transport wagons, he had been seriously hurt by a flying tin of bully-beef. An errant shell, whether British or German no one ever knew, had pitched on one of the wagons, and violently scattered its load of quartermaster's stores. A case of bully-beef had flown out like shrapnel, and one of the tins, a blue-painted contribution from the Argentine, had struck Arthur on the back of the head. Having been admitted to hospital with slight concussion of the brain, he stayed there for six months with shell-shock, and afterwards secured a comfortable billet as Deputy Assistant Accommodation Officer (D.A.A.O.) for Incoming Drafts at St. Omer. There he stayed for nearly eighteen months, till he was appointed A.A.O. (Assistant Accommodation Officer) at Calais. He did valuable service there for another year, and shortly after the Armistice he was awarded the M.B.E. for his efforts — in conjunction with the Military Police — to control the holiday traffic problem in the vicinity of the Garden of Eden.

Very soon after he returned to civilian life, however, Arthur's lively imagination began to embroider his experience, soldierly enough in all conscience, with exuberant details. His description of the battle of Loos, for example, was a masterpiece of heroism too modestly related, and might well have been accepted as the crown of his military career, were it not for his story of swimming the Somme at Péronne, after the last bridge had been blown up, in a storm of machine-gun bullets, shrapnel, bombs, and rifle-grenades. Even this adventure, in some people's opinion, was less striking than the manner in which he had held up the flank of the German advance against Kemmel Hill in April of 1918; and his friends were extremely cynical about the War Office's system of awarding decorations, since they knew that all Arthur received, for so much uncomplaining heroism, was a paltry M.B.E.

He had felt, to begin with, occasional qualms of conscience about these stories, and several times he had resolved to tell no more. But he so enjoyed the sensations of adventure they gave him, and he so truly desired to be a hero — or, more truly still, to have been one — that he could seldom resist the opportunities that his imagination offered, and presently, like an embezzling cashier, he found himself committed to an ever larger borrowing of other people's assets. Like an embezzler, too, he acquired in time the conviction that he had a perfect right to what he had borrowed, and he was genuinely upset if anyone doubted his veracity. Only on the rarest occasions did he squarely face the truth and acknowledge his fraudulent conversion of it: and even then he would soon comfort himself by yielding to humility. At such times he rapidly became a Christian, he confessed his faults — to himself — and he remembered that no one who had not sinned could hope to be pardoned. He luxuriated in self-abasement and took no little pleasure in seeing himself as the chief of sinners. He always slept particularly well after such an orgy of repentance.

To-day, however, he was far from humility. To-day he was a soldier of fortune. A soldier of fortune! He laughed aloud when he thought of the twofold meaning, for indeed he might have been both kinds had not That Damned Fellow persuaded him to squander his fortune and build those wretched houses. He had once had a very comfortable property. His father, dying when Arthur was fifteen, had left rather more than £8,000 in trust for him, which had ripened under the care of the late Major Gander, and though Arthur's connexion with the family firm had never been more than a subordinate one, he was able to retire with £20,000 when American Candy, Inc. bought the business in 1921. Then his ex-comrade-in-arms appeared on the scene, and half that sum had been invested in this prettily named residential estate of Hornbeams: eight houses which already consumed half their rents in repairs, and thirty acres of waste ground too wet to be built on. That Damned Fellow, however, had done well enough out of the venture: he had been the contractor. And because Arthur was not one of those dull people who learn by experience, he had lost money steadily since then in one bogus company after another, till now his whole capital consisted of the house in which he lived, which his father had built; the unprofitable and troublesome estate of Hornbeams; and three thousand five hundred pounds in India Stock. His income was quite insufficient for his needs, and the only way in which he had lately been able to increase it was to sell India Stock or to borrow from his sister Hilary. He disliked the latter method, but it was more economical than the former, and Hilary was both generous and fairly well-off.

Arthur walked as far as the Priory. It was a magnificent old house. Part of it was more than eight hundred years old. It had been in the market for six months, and anybody could buy it who had £12,000 to spare. Arthur greatly desired to be its owner, for its beauty delighted him, the thought of its ancient associations enchanted him, and he perceived very clearly that in such a house, with plenty of money to spend, he would make an excellent squire: he would be genial and benevolent, kind to his tenants and merry with his neighbours, a power for good and a staunch supporter of all that was most worthy of support in the customs and traditions of rural England. The mood of the Gay Guerrilla began to fade, and the larger image of the Jovial Squire crept in to take its place. But neither Priory nor squiredom were possible without money, and the only money in sight was Uncle John's. That handsome fortune, which he had so successfully despised an hour or two before, grew more and more desirable in Arthur's sight, and before he turned to walk homewards he was sincerely sorry for having rebuffed his wife and refused to eat the Vima-Bran.

Daisy was in the garden when he returned. It was a poor and weedy garden, but Daisy was very fond of it. It was true that she could never remember the names of flowers, but she was profoundly convinced of the spiritual importance of growing flowers, and she could sentimentalize very convincingly about a dewdrop or a bud. Arthur, to please her, had been compelled to simulate an equal interest, though try as he would he could not make it real or even realistic. He had never been able to see himself as the Compleat Gardener. The Old Soldier, the True-Blue Tory, the Gay Guerrilla, the Desperate Rebel, the Jovial Squire: all these he could portray, but the Gardener was beyond his power. He had made the best of things, however, and for a very good reason he specialized in rock-plants. There was a small rockery at the foot of the garden, a rough heap of stones scantily covered with sedums and campanulas and alpine pinks and poppies. But its really important feature was not easily discernible, and was indeed known only to Arthur, who had planted it, and to a few of his friends. Daisy had never guessed its existence. Arthur was always a little worried when he saw her in the neighbourhood of the rockery, and now, returning from his walk and observing her busy with a dibble among the pinks, he hurried towards her and said, in a frank and rather boyish way, 'I say, Daisy, do you think you could give me a whisked egg-and-milk? I feel I'd rather like one.'

Daisy, who was perspiring slightly, shook back her straying hair, straightened her pince-nez, and said, 'Of course I will! Oh, Arthur, I'm so glad that you're beginning to realize how *right* I am in what I'm trying to do for you. Just wait a minute and

76

I'll bring it to you out here. It will do you much more good to drink it in the fresh air. Look at those helianthi; aren't they lovely?'

They were two or three double scarlet rock roses that she pointed to, but Arthur did not bother to correct her, and she went very happily towards the house, stopping here and there to pick off a faded flower or sprinkle pansies from the can of guano water that she carried.

Arthur examined the secret part of the rockery, and found it undisturbed. Presently Daisy came back, her lank form ungainly with haste, and exclaimed, 'Hilary's here. Won't you come and speak to her? She can't stay for more than ten minutes, because she's on the way to the vicarage. She came to ask for Ruth, and now she's going on to see Lady Caroline. Hilary says she's worse again, and they've had to get a nurse in to look after her.'

'Oh dear!' said Arthur. News of illness always took him aback, and till he had got used to it — when he saw himself as a chronic invalid, patiently enduring discomfort, and greeting his visitors with a brave smile — it made him feel curiously weak, and wonder if he had run any risk of infection. 'Yes,' he said, 'I'll come and speak to Hilary.'

Hilary, with laudable honesty, had just told Ruth that she had no knowledge of the hedgehog's amatory technique. She turned to Arthur and Daisy, and, with a rather brusque inflection, asked, 'Why don't you see that Ruth gets some friends of her own age to play with? She spends far too much time by herself, and it isn't natural for a child to live alone.'

77

'She's rather a solitary little girl,' said Daisy, 'and surely we ought to encourage her fondness for books?'

'A lot of nonsense about hedgehogs won't do her any good,' said Hilary. 'She's only just recovered from mumps, and what she wants now is good food and plenty of exercise. Why don't you take her to the seaside?'

Daisy, with a deprecatory smile, began to explain: 'It's rather difficult to get away just now.' But Arthur, making no bones about it, said, 'We can't afford to, at present. As a matter of fact, I've just spent a very busy couple of hours trying to contrive some ways of making a little extra money, simply to give Ruth a holiday. She does want a change, but for the moment I'm in difficulties, and unless something happens there's nothing can be done about it.'

'Well, you ought to make an effort,' said Hilary. 'She's as white as paper, and reading about hedge-hogs won't put colour in her cheeks.'

'If Uncle John had only made the kind of will we hoped and expected he would,' said Daisy, 'we'd have been able to do so *much* for her. I can't *think* why he didn't remember our special difficulties, and even our special claims. Arthur's father was the eldest son, and it was only because he died that Uncle John got the chance to come home and make so much money. In a way it was *our* money. At least that's how it appears to me, and I think you must admit that it's a perfectly logical point of view.'

'Oh, I'm tired of talking about that wretched

will,' said Hilary. The Ganders, indeed, had spoken of little else for the last three weeks, and the Major's state of mind, as well as their own state of health, had been canvassed, discussed, and dissected with anger and bitterness, with doubt and despair, and with tireless assiduity. Their first fury had now spent itself, but resentment still smouldered hotly and any little draught of contrary opinion was enough to blow it into flames. There had been no serious quarrel among them, because a feeling of mutual misfortune still united them, and the common asperity of their opinions about the deceased Major was still a sufficient tap for most of their ill-humour. Neither Stephen nor Jane had ever been very fond of Daisy, and their normal dislike of her was now a little aggravated by the thought that she and Arthur, by reason of their daughter Ruth, were apparently the most likely heirs; but they had no greater affection for Katherine, and she had gone off to meet her home-coming husband in Paris, in a mood so blatantly philoprogenitive as to diminish their already small affection for her, and make them doubt the ultimate succession of Arthur and Daisy. Katherine might have twins, and twins again. Her husband Oliver, it seemed, came of a family in which twins were as common as they are in a flock of sheep. Katherine had bought, for her reading in the train, a parcel of books entitled *The Happy Mother*, *Wise Parenthood*, *Radiant Nurseries*, and so forth. Katherine was full of optimism and utterly determined; and Stephen and Jane disliked her so much that their increasing dislike of Daisy was sensibly checked. Daisy herself could hardly bear to speak of Katherine.

'As I've said before, Uncle John's money was his own and he had the right to do just what he liked with it,' Hilary continued. 'And in any case you have nothing to grumble about. You've got one child already and there's no reason why you shouldn't have another, or even two more.'

'I always hoped to have a large family,' said Daisy, and looked reproachfully at Arthur who frowned impatiently, jingled some money in his trouser-pocket, and resolutely changed the subject.

'I hear there's bad news from the vicarage,' he said.

'Poor Caroline's very seriously ill,' said Hilary. 'She got a heavy cold after that dreadful garden-party, and went out long before it was better. Now she's got pleurisy, and they're frightened of pneumonia.'

'How terribly worrying,' said Daisy. 'And though one doesn't like to say so, of course, it was really all her own fault. Those pigs, I mean. It was such a curious idea for a garden-party. And then when she'd caught so bad a cold she ought to have really taken great care of herself, if only for the Vicar's sake.'

'Caroline doesn't know what it means to take care of herself, and that's why she's such a darling,' said Hilary. But Daisy primly responded, 'Any woman who has responsibilities *ought* to take care of herself. I used to be careless enough of my own health before I was married, but when Ruth came I realized that it was my duty to think a good deal about myself, simply for the sake of other people.' Lady Caroline had once reproved Daisy for keeping goldfish in a bowl: 'Oh, those poor fish!' she had exclaimed. 'Don't you know it's simply torture to keep them in a round glass like that where they can't find any shade? You must go at once and buy a proper tank with a dark side, and put stones and things in it. Really, the ignorance and thoughtlessness of people are absolutely incredible!' And Daisy had never forgotten nor quite forgiven this criticism.

Hilary rose to go: 'I've stayed longer than I meant to, and I must hurry. Don't forget what I said about Ruth: the child needs taking care of more than you do, Daisy.'

'Hilary's such a dear,' said Daisy, after her sister-in-law had gone. 'Of course her manner is against her, and people who don't know her very well are often put off by it, but she really is very kind and good-hearted. I understand her perfectly. What a pity she never married. She's just a little bit unsympathetic sometimes, and marriage might have made all the difference. Poor Hilary! It's sweet of her to take such an interest in Ruth, though really she doesn't know anything about children. She can't, of course.'

Arthur was sitting very quiet and still in a large armchair. He had a sad and shrunken look. He was picturing himself ill in bed with pneumonia. He made no reply to Daisy.

She continued thoughtfully: 'I'm awfully glad she's keeping Rumneys. I really didn't think she would be able to afford it, but I suppose she has more than we know of. After all she's never had to *spend* money on anyone except herself, and she isn't extravagant in any way. That costume she was wearing is exactly like her old grey one: I wonder if she had it dyed? Well, I think that's going too far. Economy's all very well, but if you carry it beyond a certain point it simply becomes meanness. Don't you think so, Arthur?'

Arthur shivered slightly. 'I'm feeling cold,' he said.

A cloud, indeed, had blown across the face of the sun. Hilary, walking to the vicarage, strode more briskly, and tried to ignore the discomfort of her mind. She told herself that people habitually recover from pleurisy, that they generally evade the threat of pneumonia, and that even pneumonia is not necessarily fatal. But she could not banish her fears, and though she pretended that her slight feeling of breathlessness was caused by the pace at which she was walking, she knew that it was rather due to her sense of impending calamity. She had for many years been accustomed to think and speak of death in a matter-of-fact way, and to believe that because it was the normal conclusion of life it could be approached, and should be approached, with the calmness proper to other normal events. This happy delusion had been strengthened by the material fact that none of her own friends or relations had died for a long time past: not since the War, when her nephew John was killed at Epéhy, her brother-in-law, Claud Sutton, at Beaumont

Hamel, and Frank Sorley, Stephen's father, at Sanctuary Wood: and War deaths were as difficult to remember as the sensation of one particular bruise after having been knocked down by a motor car. But the Major's sudden passing had torn this useful impercipience from Hilary's mind, and now, still sore from that bereavement, she dreaded another hurt. She could not bear to think of Caroline dying: Caroline who was her closest friend, whose children she loved, whose house welcomed her. She felt fear growing within her, like the sensation of drowning, and she stopped by a gate at the roadside to regain control of herself.

The road, curving and recurving, ran almost on top of the long ridge that rose west and south of Lammiter. The vicarage was in front of her and below her, on the south-western slope of the ridge, separated by the road from the church and the little hill and what had once been the village of Lammiter West, but was now Lammiter's most agreeable suburb. Grassy, and haphazardly wooded, criss-crossed by sweet-smelling untidy hedges, the country fell away into the shallow valley of the Greenrush, the narrow stream that slid so silently through the fields. It was a placid and a lovely view, but, for the moment, it was not comforting. Its loveliness could not be touched, for to grasp a leaf and to brush the grass gave no feeling of the valley as a whole; and its calmness would not comprehend her fear. Hilary, all of a sudden, felt a great desire to be in and of this happy soil, as the hawthorn and the elms were of it: not to be dead in it, but to live in it like a hedge with its flowers at her feet and its birds among her leaves. She was tired of the people who talked so foolishly to her, and complained to her, and of the necessity of death. She was even weary of herself.

This descent into pessimism, however, was short-lived. She was a robust and sensible woman, neither given to absurd fantasies nor to the wickedness of belittling humanity. She was rather shocked by her momentary desire to become a hedge, and the shock was salutary. She mastered her fear and her fore-boding, and walked on to the vicarage with a firm step.

She found the Vicar on the terrace. He was staring at the garden with blank unseeing eyes. His shoulders were bent and his face had lost something of its high colour. Worry had always made him look plainer than he showed in his photographs, for instance, and now, as though the handsome line of his features had been held taut only by confidence or the effort of his will, his chin hung heavy, his cheeks were relaxed, and bewilderment was in his eyes. 'He's curiously like Arthur,' Hilary thought, and bade him good morning.

'You've done wonders with your garden,' she said. 'It looks as well as ever it did.'

'The rose-garden doesn't. Those wretched pigs did a lot of damage there.' The Vicar spoke in a flat uninterested voice.

'How's Caroline?' Hilary asked him.

'She's very ill. Griffiths was here an hour ago, and he's coming back this afternoon.'

'Dr. Griffiths always takes the gloomiest view possible. I shouldn't worry too much over what he says.'

'He sounded her, and said there was still a lot of friction. And the pain in her side is worse. It's very bad when she coughs.'

'Can I go up and see her?'

'I was just going myself; not that I can do any good, but she might want to tell me something.'

They climbed a shallow stair and the Vicar silently opened the bedroom door. The nurse rose with a small crepitation of starched linen, and held up a warning hand. 'She's sleeping,' she whispered.

Lady Caroline lay with a dark flush on her cheeks. Her lips were pale and her breathing was hoarse and quick and shallow. Her body looked slightly contorted, and her left shoulder seemed higher than the right. A flicker of pain crossed her face.

Hilary looked inquiringly at the nurse, who pursed her lips in a non-committal way. The Vicar muttered, 'I think we'd better go down again.'

They returned to the garden. 'You know her brother Quentin has written to say that he'll have to stop her allowance?' said the Vicar.

'Caroline's allowance? Why?'

'He's a director of the Seahouse Investment Trust. They've gone into voluntary liquidation, and Quentin's lost everything!'

'But according to *The Times* they're paying their creditors in full,' said Hilary.

'Yes, and Quentin's bearing the brunt. It was he

who insisted they must go into liquidation. He said his honour was at stake, and his honour's costing him nearly half a million. What will happen to Charles I've no idea.'

Of the late Duke of Starveling's family only one had shown ability to cope with the modern world in as splendid a way as their ancestors had dealt with a simpler age. This was Lord Quentin Whicher, the second son, who, becoming a financier, had on three occasions made a very respectable fortune. His temperament was unstable, however, and as he was subject to devastating attacks of honesty he invariably threw away his millions as soon as he had amassed them. He had recently discovered fraudulent practice in the affairs of the Seahouse Investment Trust, and insisting upon its immediate liquidation with the violence characteristic of his honest periods, he had offered the whole of his current fortune to meet the Company's liabilities. This lordly gesture, though good for his own soul, was disastrous to his two brothers and five sisters, all of whom were dependent on him. Charles, the present Duke, maintained Starveling Castle, in the northern part of the county, only by Quentin's munificence, and for several years Quentin had given Lady Caroline an annual allowance of two thousand pounds.

Hilary heard of the loss of this income with dismay. 'But what are you going to do?' she asked.

The Vicar shook his head. 'I don't know, and I can't think. I can't even worry about it. It was a blow when the news came, but now I can't think of anything but Caroline.'

Hilary said, 'It's a pity you're not eligible to compete for Uncle John's estate. With six of a family you'd be an easy winner.'

The Vicar looked uncomfortable. 'It was a curious will,' he said.

'A very embarrassing will.'

'What was the exact description of the possible legatees? "The legal offspring of the late Jonathan Gander:" was that it?'

' "Whichever of the late Jonathan Gander's progeny shall, five years from now, have become the parent of the largest family born in wedlock," ' Hilary quoted, with reasonable accuracy.

The Vicar looked more melancholy than ever. 'Heaven knows how I'm going to give a decent education to the children now,' he said.

'I expect Quentin will make another fortune in a year or two,' she suggested.

A maid came running from the house. 'Please, sir,' she said, 'her ladyship's just woke up, and she'd like to speak to you, Nurse says.'

The Vicar straightened his shoulders and seemed to grow more confident at once. 'Come back soon,' he said to Hilary. 'I hope you'll be able to have a talk with her the next time.'

THE Ridge road that quarter-circled Lammiter was a social highway for the Ganders and most of their friends. Its northern terminus was the vicarage. Near by, in Lammiter West, lived General Ramboise, and not far away were Miss Montgomery and Mrs. Corcoran. Sir Gervase Flood had a house, stuffed full of tiger-skin rugs and ivory elephants and Benares brass, on the east side of the road, three-quarters of a mile south of Lammiter West. Half a mile farther the road received, as a tributary, Hornbeam Lane, where Arthur lived, and where, at its lower and wetter end, his unprofitable estate was situated. Past Hornbeam Lane the road continued its southern course for ten minutes' walking distance, curved broadly east, and began to skirt the extensive grounds of Rumneys, which stood on the north and higher side. Four hundred yards east of Rumneys a little white-painted gate, demurely set beneath a dark close-clipped arch of hollies, led by a flagged path that presently divided and engirt the house, to the front door of Mulberry Acre.

This was a cottage built after the Tudor style of architecture. It had not, it is true, been built in the days of the Tudor monarchs, but with the help of some old tiles and timbers a contemporary architect had constructed a pleasant little house sufficiently resembling, from the outside, a domestic building of the sixteenth century to warrant the use of the royal name. The interior decoration, however, made no pretence to antiquity, unless the Victorian era may be called antique: for the dining-room, by a pretty piece of affectation, had been furnished with Spanish mahogany and horsehair, with dignified portraits and steel engravings, with a little wax fruit and a chandelier.

The principal bedrooms were boldly of their own age. They were three in number, and they were similarly furnished. The two adjectives, aesthetic and ascetic, so like in sound and sometimes so antagonistic in meaning, had almost equal claims for priority in their description; for though the first bedroom was a symphony of green — the sheets were the pale hue of a duck's egg, and the carpet was like the darker-than-emerald heart of an Atlantic wave — and though the second bedroom was a concordance in blue — the pillows were pale as a thrush's eggs, the brushes on the dressing-table might have been backed with sapphire — and though the third bedroom was a harmony in yellow — the bed-linen was like primroses, and the walls were gold — yet the furniture in all of them was made of steel. The beds were steel, the chairs were steel, and the wardrobes, of steel and enamel, resembled safes. The bathroom escaped luxury only by the sombreness of its colour, which was black, save for the snowy towels and the snow-white mat.

The drawing-room, which was shaped like the letter L, was also the study and the workroom. The furniture, ash-coloured, was pleasantly upholstered

in old rose, and its walls were quaintly decorated
with paintings by Braque, Paul Klee, and their
Surréalist disciples: the happy effect was of that
peace which precedeth understanding and puberty.
The low book-shelves that half-surrounded the room
were mainly inhabited by poets. All the poetry
published in England for the last twenty years was
there, from Abercromby to Auden, from *Hassan* to
A Draft of XXX Cantos. There were also French
poets. There was also a set, in forty volumes and
Spanish, of the selected works of Lope de Vega.

Stephen Sorley had spent a great deal of money,
far more than he could afford, on the furnishing of
Mulberry Acre, and till his uncle's death had
appeared to promise him substantial wealth he had
found unfailing delight in his surroundings. But the
prospect of riches had undermined his pleasure in
imitation Tudor and steel furniture, and he had set
his heart on purchasing the desirable Queen Anne
house, five or six miles away, and decorating it, with
academic precision, in the manner of the period.
His hopes, of course, had been frustrated by the unexpected nature of the Major's will, but the vision of
the house, with its old brick walls and old silver
candlesticks, stayed in his mind so obstinately and so
painfully that he had done no work at all for the last
three weeks. He had been quite unable to attend to
the tedious business of correcting papers, reproving
solecisms, and patting on their backs the occasional
good phrases that appeared in the many exercises
written by pupils of the Mulberry School of Journalism and Short Story Writing. Fortunately for

Stephen, his friend Wilfrid was not only an extremely sympathetic young man, but also a very hard worker, and during Stephen's indisposition Wilfrid had performed the duties of both without a word of complaint. He had, indeed, strongly advised Stephen to take a long holiday. 'You've had a fearful shock,' he had said, 'and it would be horribly unfair to expect you to do a stroke of work till you're *quite* better. I can manage *perfectly* well by myself. The only thing I can't bear is to see you looking miserable, so just go and lie down and have a good rest, and I'll finish these silly papers in *no* time.'

The Mulberry School of Journalism — by correspondence — was a fairly successful business, and though Stephen truly disliked the drudgery of it, and despised it as the last unwanted hare-lipped bastard of literature, he was not unmindful of its profit, and he often gave considerable thought to the elaboration of advertisements by which to increase the number of their disciples. At times he could write preposterous rubrics without a trace of bitterness, without a memory of his own sterile labour to mock him as he scrawled in high capitals:

'HAVE YOU A PEN? THEN YOU CAN MAKE MONEY!
A HOBBY WORTH £500 A YEAR.
If you can write, you can write profitably!
NO HARD WORK!
NO DISAPPOINTMENT!
The easiest way to earn your living
is to write for it!!!'

But there were other days when he invented new captions with acid in his pen and his heart full of gall: 'After six weeks' tuition the majority of our students find no difficulty in writing acceptable articles, and, what is more, in selling them at their own price': there was a pretty thing for him to say, he who had striven for years to give form to feeling that would not be expressed in words, to find in all the tortuous corridors of thought a subject, whole and complete, that he could dress with shining phrases, or, on a poor score of occasions, to sell what he had written for any price at all!

Stephen for years had endeavoured to be a poet, and poetry had run away from him like a child at Blind Man's Buff. Sometimes he had heard her laugh, heard the quick sound of her steps, and sometimes he had felt her frock. But he had never caught her. It was a sad pursuit, for he had a great desire to write poetry, and he had tried to in many styles. He had sought to compose tremendous simplicities in the early manner of Blake: and his simplicities were rarely simple and never tremendous. He had attempted Sitwellism and Prufrockery, but all in vain. He had tried to emulate the fiery hopes and indignation of the young post-post-war poets; but he lacked the faith to move magnetic mountains. He had essayed the composition of obscurely brilliant cloisonné work in the later fashion of Ezra Pound; but the effort to invent a meaning for his lines had defeated him.

Nor could he find a style of his own. And this was strange, because he was more interested in himself than in anything or anyone else. He was egocentric to a far greater degree than Arthur, for instance. Arthur used himself like coloured spectacles through which to see the world, or like litmus paper on which to test the reaction of real or fancied experience. But Stephen looked only at himself, and this, perhaps, was part of the reason for his failure to achieve poetic vision: for he was fat enough to throw a large shadow.

On the day following the day on which Hilary had gone to call at the vicarage, about six in the evening, Wilfrid sat correcting the last of a high bundle of exercises, when Mrs. Barrow, the housekeeper, announced the arrival of Mr. Arthur Gander. Arthur wore a somewhat apologetic air when he came in, for his only purpose in calling was to avoid a lecture on dietetics that was waiting for him at home: one of Daisy's friends had just written to inform her that beans were a very strengthening food.

Wilfrid behaved charmingly. 'How nice of you to come and see us!' he said. 'No, really, I'm not busy, I'd just this moment finished. Stephen went to lie down after tea, he's not *really* fit yet, but I expect he'll be down in a little while. Mrs. Barrow's giving us chicken salad and iced gooseberry fool to-night, and he won't want to miss that. Oh, do sit here, Arthur, this is a *much* more comfortable chair. I was just going to have a glass of sherry: you'll have one too, won't you?'

'I'd rather have a little gin,' said Arthur cautiously. 'A pink gin, perhaps.' Among Daisy's other follies was a shrill hatred of wine and spirits, and Arthur was forced to conform with this injurious prejudice. He had fortunately discovered, however, that gin perfumes the breath so slightly, if at all, that he could drink comparatively large quantities of it without rousing her suspicion. He looked enviously at the decanter of straw-pale sherry, but sherry, like roses, bewrays its presence, and his glance returned with an accompanying sigh to the square and hueless bottle. 'Thank you, thank you, that's plenty,' he said.

Presently Stephen came down. He was wearing a plum-coloured velvet jacket, and he looked pale and tired. He had been trying to write a poem about his own unhappiness: not a mere verse or two of complaint, not an angry squib, but a large and coruscating affair in which the Queen Anne house became the symbol of all artistic desire, and the deceased Major represented the crass and mundane world which for ever frustrated it. He had been working at the poem for a week. It was to be a compound of classical allusion, peacock phrases, assonance carefully substituted for rhyme, and brutally biting colloquialism. But so far it was not going very well. He had a very good dictionary of quotations, and the classical allusions were leading him too many ways at once. Nor could he contrive a proper sheen for the peacock phrases.

Wilfrid poured a glass of sherry for him, and he began to talk about the will. Wilfrid made sympathetic noises, and Arthur nodded his head and helped himself to a little more gin.

After twenty minutes' dissertation on the Major's alleged iniquity, Stephen said, 'And if it hadn't been for Katherine we could probably have upset the will, or at any rate ignored it by mutual consent. She is, without exception, the most vulgar and selfish woman I've ever met. I've come across a lot of selfish people in my time — the egotist is always with us — but I've never seen anyone so utterly and shamelessly self-centred as she is. And simply because she's married to a hulking brute of a soldier she has the chance to rob us all of our inheritance! It absolutely makes my blood boil. Where is she now?'

'She's staying with Oliver's people, I think,' said Arthur.

'At Bognor,' said Wilfrid. 'But they're going up to Scotland in August, to stay with some people called Maitland, who're cousins of Oliver's.'

'Who told you so?'

'Mrs. Barrow. She was in town this afternoon, and she met Mrs. Arbor, the housekeeper at Rumneys, and they had a long talk together. Hilary had a letter from Katherine this morning, and Katherine said she was having a perfectly *lovely* time with Oliver, and she hoped to be able to tell Hilary some very good news when she wrote next.'

Stephen's hand trembled as he refilled his glass. 'It's intolerable!' he said. 'Really, the way that human beings will degrade themselves, simply for money, is almost beyond belief!'

'Money's a great delusion,' said Arthur gravely. 'Of course it's very useful to have some, but to make it one's chief end in life is a terrible mistake. I've lost nearly all I had and I'm still fairly happy. I think I should be happier if I had another few hundreds a year, but I really don't know. I find life very interesting as it is. I spend a good deal of my time thinking, you see, and one can do a lot of thinking on a very small income.'

Wilfrid said, 'There's awfully bad news from the vicarage again. Mrs. Arbor told Mrs. Barrow that poor Lady Caroline had had a very bad night, and they've almost given up hope.'

The shadow of death descended on Arthur and extinguished the mild cheerfulness that company and a little gin had bred in him. Stephen moved restlessly, for he also was frightened of illness and the grave. He took a bottle of bismuth tablets from his waistcoat pocket and shook one into his hand.

'I can't think why she had that absurd garden-party,' he said. 'It was such an unnecessary and humiliating way to catch cold.'

'Life is full of humiliation,' said Arthur. He was on the fringe of his Christian mood. 'It's very salutary to be humbled. I'm often thrown into the very depths of despair, and do you know, I always think that I see things more clearly then, and I feel much better after it's over.'

'Oh, do let's be more cheerful,' cried Wilfrid. 'No one is sorrier for Lady Caroline than I am, but we shan't do her *any* good by getting in the miserables about her. I'm going to put a record on the gramophone, something nice and *noisy*.'

In a moment the room was filled with the alarming clamour of Duke Ellington's band, and Wilfrid, smiling seraphically and snapping his fingers, shouted, 'Isn't that lovely? Oh, I do like a good noisy band, and really there's lots of fun in life, and this is honestly a very nice house, Stephen, however much you want that red-brick thing that was built by Queen Anne or somebody. Stephen! Let's ask Arthur to stay to dinner with us! It was a great big chicken, and the gooseberry fool is simply enormous; I went to the kitchen and looked at it, and Mrs. Barrow gave me a spoonful to try it. And if Arthur stays we'll open a bottle of Liebfraumilch and have a really nice party. Oh, do stay, Arthur! Make him stay, Stephen!'

'Well, Daisy will be expecting me,' said Arthur, but Wilfrid interrupted him. 'We're expecting you, too,' he said.

Stephen, who liked company and was not averse from annoying Daisy, added, 'Yes, you'd better stay, Arthur. There seems to be a good dinner, and if you'd like to hear it I'll read you part of the new poem I'm working on. It's experimental, and very incomplete as yet, but I think you'll find it fairly interesting.'

Arthur, after another little show of hesitation, decided to stay, and Wilfrid, having run into the kitchen to warn Mrs. Barrow, returned and took him upstairs. Arthur was shown into the Blue Room.

'You'll want to brush your hair, and have a wash, and make yourself comfortable,' said Wilfrid. 'Mrs. Barrow's going to bring you a clean towel, and don't hurry, because there's *plenty* of time. I'm going to brush my hair too.'

Mrs. Barrow appeared with the towel. 'Good evening, Mr. Gander,' she said. 'I'm sure it's very kind of you to come and see Mr. Stephen like this. He's been very poorly for the last two or three weeks, and it cheers him up to have somebody come in and talk to him. What he'd do without Mr. Wilfrid heaven only knows. Mr. Wilfrid's a godsend to him. But there, Mr. Wilfrid would be a godsend to any house, he's that nice and cheerful and considering. And Mr. Stephen deserves to have somebody like Mr. Wilfrid, for he's a very kind and well-behaved gentleman himself, and I only wish he could be a bit happier. Indeed two nicer young gentlemen I wouldn't wish to have anything to do with. No bother in the house, and so careful with the furniture, and no trouble over them getting drunk, like so many young gentlemen do, or bringing in undesirable females, which is worse. Why, Mr. Wilfrid often helps me with the dusting, and what could be nicer than that? Now if you've got everything you want, Mr. Gander, I'll go down and take a look at the fish: I got some fillets of whiting and I want the sauce to be just right. There's no need to hurry yourself, for dinner won't be ready for ten minutes yet.'

It was an admirable meal they sat down to, and the hock was so good that Wilfrid brought a second bottle, which tasted even better. Arthur, his fingers holding the stem of a green-tinted glass, felt his soul expand. 'Do you know,' he said, 'the flavour of this wine reminds me of a bottle of champagne that I found — well, that I acquired by the fortune of war

98

in March, 1918. It was during the great retreat, and we were coming back through one of those little Somme towns: Morlancourt, I think, or was it Bray? The strain of that week was so dreadful that one's memory is a little vague. But I think it was Morlancourt. Yes, I'm almost sure it was. The place was deserted, of course, and some of our men forced their way into an estaminet. One could hardly blame them, poor devils, they'd had a fearfully tough time, but one had to clear them out, of course. So I went in and said, "Now, you fellows, this isn't the way to win the war," and got them out. A little jocularity isn't a bad thing on occasions like that, so long as it doesn't interfere with discipline. Now just as I was following them I caught sight of a very old bottle of champagne, quite grey with dust, standing all by itself on one of the shelves, and I thought to myself, "If you don't take it, the Boche will, and that won't help the Allied Cause, will it?" So I reached up and took it off the shelf and put it in my haversack. Well, we had a pretty hard time for the rest of the day. We were doing a rearguard action, with a bit of counter-attacking now and then, and the Boche was coming on fast and working round to the north. But about five o'clock in the afternoon we had a little respite. We had a decent position on the edge of a small wood, and the Boche seemed to be coming to a stop. So I saw that the men were making themselves as comfortable as they could, and I established contact with the people on my right — Rutlands they were, I think. Yes, Rutlands — and then it

seemed time to sample the champagne. So I got
the bottle out of my haversack, and do you know,
it was a bottle of Krug's Private Cuvée, 1892.
1892! It had gone still, naturally, but the flavour,
though somewhat unusual for champagne, was
simply delicious. I drank it all, and no sooner had
I finished it than the Boche started shelling again,
and we were forced to retire. Well, everybody was
absolutely worn out, of course, nerves shot to pieces,
and that sort of thing, but the champagne had made
a new man of me, and I carried one fellow into
safety — a mere youngster, who'd been rather badly
hit — and came back for another — a corporal with
the D.C.M., I remember — and I carried on like that
without feeling a trace of fatigue, or fear, or even
discomfort. It was simply due to the champagne,
of course; I'm not pretending to be a hero, or anything like that; one merely did one's duty, like
everybody else. But I must confess that I got a
nasty shock when I found the Boches had come
round to the north of our position, and a couple of
their machine-guns were playing down a sunk road
that we had to cross. However, there was only one
thing to do, and luckily I had the presence of mind
to do it. I got hold of a Lewis gun and a couple of
drums of ammunition, and jumped down into the
road, and began blazing at 'em like hell. Not
wildly or indiscriminately, of course, but quite
coolly — I remember their bullets kicking up the
white mud all round me, like little fountains, and
thinking it was rather pretty, if one had the time to
watch it — and actually I was shooting rather well,

because in no time I'd laid out the crews of both their guns. Well, all except one fellow, that is, and he left his gun and came belting down the road with a rifle and bayonet, straight for me. Now he *was* a brave fellow. What I'd been doing was nothing at all, really, but that Boche was really a gallant fellow. However, I couldn't let him get away with it, and I had my sights on him in a split second. And then I got another shock. The drum was empty! I'd fired my last shot! Well, I hadn't much time to lose, for the Boche was only eight or ten yards away now, a big fellow he was, too, and suddenly I remembered that in a fit of absent-mindedness I'd put the empty champagne bottle in my haversack. That was a bit of sheer luck. I had it out in no time, got to my feet, and chucked it at the Boche as hard as ever I could. It was a very pretty throw-in, though I say it myself, and took him right on the point of the chin. It bowled him over, of course; a great big fellow, well over six feet, I should say, and he went down hard; and by that time my company, or what was left of them, were all across the road and comparatively safe. Rather a joke, don't you think: bowling an outsize Prussian with an empty bottle? Krug versus Krupp, eh? And this hock of yours, though actually it's quite different, somehow recalled to me the flavour of that champagne, which really was the most delicious wine I've ever drunk.'

Wilfrid had listened to this long recital with flattering interest and little cries of appreciation, and when it was finished he exclaimed a dozen times his wonderment at Arthur's bravery. 'Oh, I'd *never* have been able to do all that,' he said. 'And then to aim so well with the bottle! I think it was simply marvellous. Do have some brandy now, Arthur.'

'A bottle of Krug, 1892,' said Arthur slowly. 'That's what makes the story worth telling.'

Stephen had not enjoyed the tale. He hated all thought of the War. He had been eleven years old when the War Office reported his father as wounded and missing and probably killed; and after the first desolation of grief he had comforted himself by pretending that his father was not really dead, but on secret service behind the enemy lines. The report of his death was a device intended to disarm suspicion, for the work he was engaged on was of the utmost importance. But sooner or later — perhaps not till the War was over — he would come home with medals on his breast and glorious fame. Year by year this hope grew sick, but desperately survived, and died at last with bitter reluctance. Stephen, in violent revulsion and jealousy of those whose fathers and friends had miraculously survived the War, turned his back upon it. But the War, like the sound of footsteps on a lonely road, made him look behind, and when he was twenty-one he had faced it squarely enough for a little while. He had tried, with genuine passion, to write a poem called *War Memorial*. It was to have been a poem in the grand manner, classical in form, restrained in language, but showing beneath restraint such enormities of anger and grief as would make everyone cling like frightened lovers to the sweet shape of peace.

But from the beginning it lacked strength and fluency, and soon its manner became a blurred staccato that hobbled into exhaustion. It limped from mild epigram to milder until it could go no further. There was an early distich that declared:

'We use the earth like a furnished and sunlit room:
They in their bravery took the earth for their tomb.'

That was the best of the completed couplets, and the conceit was old. The War had again defeated Stephen's hopes, and making a more determined effort to shut it out of his mind, he had succeeded fairly well with the kind help of time.

He was irritated, therefore, by the necessity of listening to Arthur, but as Arthur's host he endured the tedious narrative without complaint. Decency kept him prisoner, and the never-ending words fell upon his ear as loudly and tiresomely as rain on a tin roof. He remembered a quotation from Baudelaire — he had come across it that morning in a commonplace-book, side by side with a note on Virginia ham — peanut-fed pork smoked slowly over hickory chips and cooked with brown sugar, black pepper, and molasses — but the lines from Baudelaire were more relevant. He repeated them under his breath:

'*Je suis comme le roi d'un pays pluvieux,
Riche mais impuissant, jeune et pourtant très vieux.*'

It was very satisfying to quote Baudelaire, and Stephen felt a little better.

After a glass or two of brandy Arthur got into full swing with his fictitious reminiscences, and Wilfrid sat spellbound to hear how he used to throw bombs into German dugouts, and lie all night in No Man's Land, and narrowly escape drowning in shell-holes at Passchendaele, and tear off his puttees to tie tourniquets on shattered limbs. Nor could Stephen remain wholly remote from the horrid influence of Arthur's stories. He lay back in his chair, his long pale hands folded over his plum-coloured velvet coat, his eyes half-closed, and listened despite his aversion.

Arthur's adventures became bloodier and more circumstantial and more significant as the night grew older. He let Wilfrid pour, for the fifth time, a little more liqueur brandy into the balloon-shaped glass he held so comfortably in his cupped hands, and staring at the amber transparency as though it were a magic mirror, he said dreamily, 'It's interesting to think that two thousand years ago some Roman soldier was sitting in his villa talking to young men about Caesar's campaign in Gaul, and telling them stories that seemed as strange to them as mine do to you. And a thousand years ago Crusaders came home with stories very like mine, about the Saracens; and English archers . . .'

'Remembered with advantages what feats they did that day,' said Stephen yawning.

'What I mean,' said Arthur, 'is that this is the proper way to learn history. History ought to be a warm and vital tradition, learnt from the lips of survivors of great events. Those cold official narratives are worthless, absolutely worthless. There's not one of them will tell you the things that I've been telling you. You can only hear stories like mine from old soldiers; old sweats, as they used to be called. And such stories are really valuable. There are two episodes in my own experience, for example, that make a real contribution to the history of the War, though they've never been published, and perhaps never will be published. The first is rather too long a story to tell you now, and I'd need a map of Cambrai to make it clear; perhaps it's enough to say that if my advice had been taken the War would have been over by Christmas, 1917. But there was a lot of jealousy between Regular officers and people with Territorial and New Army commissions, and my advice was disregarded, with what results you know. But the second episode can be told in a few minutes, and it's more amusing than the other.'

Arthur sipped his brandy. 'You remember Haig's famous message in April, 1918, when he warned us that we were fighting with our backs to the wall. Well, there aren't many people who know how he came to use that very striking phrase, but I'm one of them, and for a very good reason; it was I who suggested it to him, and the Crown Prince of Germany suggested it to me. Oh, I don't mean that he did it deliberately — we weren't on visiting terms, you know — but by a curious coincidence I happened to overhear a very significant conversation between him and Ludendorff. We weren't far from St. Eloi at the time — between St. Eloi and Zillebeke, as a matter of fact — and we were having rather a rough time. Well, that's an understatement, because it was absolute dog-fighting, here, there, and everywhere. And one night, when it was fairly quiet, I took my sergeant and went over to the Boche line to see if I could pick up any information. We came to a forward sap, and before the sentry in it could utter a sound my sergeant had him by the throat and quietened him for ever. — He was a very fine fellow, Sergeant Allsop: killed at Bapaume, poor devil. — Well, we crept down the sap, and though I get quite excited to think about it now, I remember feeling as cool as a cucumber at the time. Simply as cool as a cucumber! We went down the sap till we came to a bit of a bend, and just beyond that was the trench, and in the trench, not more than two or three yards from us, there were several people talking. Now I don't know much German, but I listened carefully, and I heard someone saying that the evenings were getting longer, and someone else replying it was very cold for the time of year, and that sort of thing. But presently, to my surprise, I heard them talking English. Now that was extraordinarily interesting, and I determined to have a look at them. With infinite caution, moving only an inch at a time, I crept towards the trench and looked round the corner. Fortunately the sap was very dark, and still more fortunately there was enough light in the sky for me to see their faces. There were four or five people standing there, and you can imagine my amazement when I recognized two of them as the Crown Prince and Ludendorff!

I was completely taken aback, and for a little while I couldn't make out what they were talking about. — I suppose they were speaking English so that the other Germans wouldn't understand them. — But then I heard Ludendorff say, "They have no reserves at all," and I realized they were discussing the strength of our position.

' "No reserves whatever," said the Crown Prince.

' "Unless they bring up the Waacs," said Ludendorff.

' "Perhaps they will bring up the Waacs," said the Crown Prince.

' "How would you like that?" asked Ludendorff.

' "That would be very nice," said the Crown Prince. "When we get to Paris I shall invite all the Waacs to a ball."

'Then Ludendorff said it was time for them to return to their headquarters, and I heard no more. But what I had heard was of the utmost importance, and when we got back to our own line I reported to the C.O. and suggested I should make a further report to Sir Douglas Haig in person. He readily agreed, and I went down the line at once. The C.-in-C.'s headquarters were at St. Omer then. There was some delay before I was taken in to see Haig, and I got the impression that everybody there was more than a little worried and apprehensive. Everybody except Haig, that is. He was like iron, like a rock, though he looked very tired and worn. Well, I told him my story as clearly as I could, and he recognized the significance of it immediately: if Ludendorff and the Crown Prince had come up to the front line, it meant there was going to be another big push, and from what they had said about our lack of reserves I had gathered they were feeling very confident. Then Sir Douglas asked me, "Is that all you heard?" Well, I rather disliked the idea of repeating their joke about the Waacs, because Haig wasn't the sort of man to whom you would care to tell that sort of thing. I mean, there was a kind of nobility about him. So for a moment or two I stammered and hesitated a little.

' "What else did they say?" he asked, and frowned a little, and I felt more nervous than ever, and stammered again.

' "Captain Gander," he said, "I order you to tell me what the Crown Prince said next."

'So in absolute desperation I told him. But because I was so nervous I made a spoonerism, or rather two spoonerisms, and instead of saying, "He would like to invite the Waacs to a ball," I said, "He would fight when he liked with our backs to a wall."'

'Haig looked at me very gravely. "The Crown Prince has very little knowledge of the English if he doesn't realize we are dangerous fighters in such a position," he said.

'Then he thanked me for the information I had brought, and I returned to my battalion. A few days later he issued his message to the troops, and no one but Haig and myself knew its full significance. That magnificent sentence, "We are fighting with our backs to the wall," wasn't only encouragement to the soldiers — though of course it did encourage them — but also, and this is more important

I think, it was deliberate and open defiance of Ludendorff and the Crown Prince!'

A little snore, like the far whisper of a foghorn, blew softly out of Stephen's lips. Wilfrid, despite an almost equal weariness, made haste to cover this breach of hospitality and cried, 'Oh, Stephen, you've dropped your cigarette!'

Stephen woke, and felt for his bottle of bismuth tablets.

'You were going to read your poem to us,' said Wilfrid, 'but we forgot all about it. Arthur's stories have been so *perfectly* absorbing.'

'It isn't really ready for publication,' said Stephen. 'I never believe in showing unfinished work.' He yawned without concealment.

Arthur looked at his watch. 'I say,' he said, 'I'd no idea it was so late. I must go home: Daisy'll be wondering what's become of me.' He stood up, tentatively.

'Have a little more brandy,' said Wilfrid with unfailing kindness.

Stephen yawned again.

'No, really,' said Arthur. 'I'm afraid I've stayed too long as it is.'

'Oh, indeed you haven't,' Wilfrid protested.

'Come again,' said Stephen. 'Good night, Arthur, I'm going to bed now.'

Wilfrid led Arthur to the door, and bade him a warm farewell. Arthur trod the high ridge with exhilaration in his steps. He had had a magnificent evening, and he was a little better than sober. He stopped on the starlit road, and stiffened his shoulders, and saluted. 'I have come, sir, to report a most unusual occurrence,' he said. He was talking to his Commander-in-Chief.

He was delighted with the story about the Crown Prince and the Waacs. The idea had come to him between his fourth and fifth brandies, and he had developed it with most laudably swift decision. He had the soldier's instinct, he knew when to attack, and how to consolidate. 'I crept down the sap, sir, and strained every nerve to hear what they were saying,' he announced to the starlight.

Between tall trees the road appeared to grow narrower, and Arthur remembered his first story, of the Lewis gun and the bottle of champagne. There were lime trees in blossom on the one side, and their sweet smell induced a momentary sadness in him. Suddenly he wished — Oh God, how greatly he wished! — that the story of the Lewis gun had been true, and he in very fact a hero. But the stars shone bright, the night was kind, and brandy enlivened his pulse. He put away unmanly repining, and walked on with a soldier's stride.

His lips were moving. 'I considered it my duty to make an immediate report to you, sir,' he was saying, 'and when I suggested this to my Commanding Officer he at once concurred.'

Arthur was very happy. He was still talking to Sir Douglas Haig.

VI

JANE SUTTON went to North Berwick in August, and played golf every day. Her great friend, Bolivia Ramboise, went to Prestwick, and also played regularly. They returned to Lammiter early in September, Bolivia some days later than Jane, and the morning after Bolivia's return they played together on the Lammiter Heath course, and lunched in the Clubhouse. They went out again after lunch, but a heavy shower at the short fifteenth interrupted their accurate and hard-hitting progress. The fairway of the fifteenth ran parallel with the front of the Clubhouse and not very far from it.

'I don't think it's worth getting wet,' said Bolivia. 'We've had a decent amount of golf lately, we can afford to miss a hole or two.'

Jane agreed, and they returned to the Clubhouse and ordered tea. They sat in the bay of a large window and looked with critical affection at the pleasing harmony, now subdued by rain, of green turf and brown heath and yellow sand.

'I want the Committee to dig another trap on the near side of that green,' said Jane, pointing to the fifteenth. 'It's a damned sight too easy at present.'

Bolivia agreed. 'Do you remember Eve Puddifoot in the last Medal Handicap? She sliced her drive, topped her approach, rolled in, and was down in four. Now that sort of thing's not good enough.'

'No, it's got to be stopped,' said Jane. 'I've

several ideas for tightening things up a bit, and if you'll back me I'll make a lot of difference to this course. I want a really big bunker about a hundred and twenty yards in front of the tee at the seventh, for instance. It makes me sick to see the rabbits roll down hill there, and get away with it, and think they're playing golf.'

'Yes, that's a good idea,' said Bolivia. 'And why not shift the eleventh tee about thirty yards west? That would make the brook absolutely deadly, and if you were short . . .'

'You'd be in the trees! Now that's what I call a brilliant suggestion! You know, with a bit of digging, and shifting, we could make this course twice as difficult, and then it would be really worth playing on.'

'You've got the right ideas,' said Jane, and swallowed her tea at a gulp.

They made a magnificent picture of English womanhood as they sat there: Jane thick as an ox, thewed like a wrestler, broad-browed, heavy in the jaw, tawny haired; Bolivia tall as a Guardsman, muscular and swift in movement, black haired, with thick black eyebrows that met in the middle, a Roman nose, a jutting chin, and weather-beaten cheeks. They had for each other a solid friendship, unselfish and undemonstrative, of the kind that is supposed to be more common among men. Bolivia — she had been so christened to commemorate the death of her uncle, the General's brother, who had been killed by Tobas while exploring the Gran Chaco — Bolivia had listened with real interest to

Jane's description of golf at North Berwick, and Jane had paid close attention to all that Bolivia had to say about Prestwick. Without any nonsense or extravagance they admired each other's good qualities — Bolivia was ever the first to admit the superior technique of Jane's approach-shots — and without any tedious parade of their emotions, which were indeed neither complex nor many, they thoroughly understood each other.

Presently Jane said, 'I must go and have a talk with Stephen and Wilfrid one of these days. I've got to get a few clothes before winter, I suppose, and God knows what people are wearing nowadays. It's a damned nuisance having to dress oneself. I'm simply defeated when it comes to buying anything new. But Wilfrid's marvellous at suggesting things, and Stephen's pretty good too.'

Bolivia agreed. 'It is rather a bore. I just go to my dressmaker and let her do what she likes with me.'

'I can't afford to do that, worse luck. North Berwick was filthily expensive, and my new pack of clubs cost a devil of a lot. But I really needed them.'

'It's a pity the Major hadn't made a more sensible will. You'd be all right if you'd got your share of seventy thousand.'

'Yes, I was a bit sore about that to begin with, but I've got over it now.'

'Any news of developments in the family?' asked Bolivia.

'Not so far as I know. Arthur's down with a bilious attack, due to Daisy's attempts to feed him up, and Katherine hasn't written lately. She was very cock-a-hoop to begin with, but we haven't heard from her for the last few weeks, so I suppose she's got nothing to report yet. Some women don't take so easily as others.'

'And you've simply resigned the competition to those two?'

'Well, Stephen's not likely to marry, and Hilary's rising forty. There's no one else, unless George turns up. Nobody's heard of him for years, and so far Peabody hasn't had any replies to the advertisement he put in the papers. I expect George drank himself to death years ago.'

Bolivia said, 'Did you never think of trying for the prize yourself? You'd have a good enough chance. There's only Arthur and his solitary child to set the pace: bogey's only one.'

Jane frowned. 'Well, I did toy with the idea for a week or two. Freddy Hislop began to show signs of interest, and so did young Wheatley — they'd heard the news, of course — and I wondered for a few days whether it would be worth while to whistle them in. But Wheatley's rather a bore, and Freddy's never broken ninety yet, and isn't likely to, so I came to the conclusion that the whole business would try my temper too much, and I dropped it.'

'But Wheatley and Freddy aren't the only men in Lammiter,' Bolivia urged, 'and seventy thousand's a lot of money.'

'Oh, I know, but the truth is I don't like babies, and each one would mean losing at least four months' golf, and probably more. No, it isn't worth it. I've almost decided to put my name in for the Ladies' Open next year, and that means I've got to play steadily and really seriously from now on. I've wasted far too much time in the past, playing with Tom, Dick, and Harry, but all that's got to stop now, and I'm going to concentrate, really concentrate, on my short game. And as that's the case it would be simply ruinous to have a baby.'

'Perhaps you're right,' said Bolivia. 'But if I were in your place, I think I'd say good-bye to golf and marry Wheatley or anybody at all, if only to keep the money away from Daisy and Katherine.'

'Yes, it is rather sickening to think they're going to get it. But I'm not going to stop them, and as I said before, Stephen isn't likely to.'

'You mean . . .?'

'Oh, no, there's nothing wrong with him, but he's so frightened of women that he'll never get married unless somebody bullies him into it. My God, I've got an idea! Why don't *you* whistle him in?'

Bolivia gave a snort of laughter. 'No, thanks,' she said.

'I'm being perfectly serious,' said Jane. 'Stephen's not at all a bad sort when you get to know him. He's very intelligent, and a sensible woman could knock all the nonsense out of him, and make him quite presentable. You see, he started badly. He was terribly cut up by his father's death, and then, when he was about twenty-two, he got a hell of a fright from a girl in Italy. But he only needs somebody to take him in hand and treat him decently and he'd be all right again. It would really be a kindness to Stephen if you married him, and personally I'd be as pleased as a dog with a couple of tails if you got Uncle John's money, and wiped Katherine's eye, and Daisy's too.'

'What was the fright he got?' asked Bolivia.

Jane lit a cigarette. 'Do you remember when I went to Florence, five or six years ago? Well, Stephen was there at the same time, but he'd been staying for months, and a couple of weeks was more than enough for me. There's nothing to do there actually, except go to tea-parties and look at pictures, and though I'm fond enough of pictures in their proper place I got sick to death of them in Florence. There's far too many of them. But Stephen really enjoyed himself, and he seemed to know quite a lot about everything. I remember he took me to the Uffizi one morning, and spent an hour talking about the difference between Botticelli's Annunciation and Leonardo da Vinci's; he said the one had a simple emotional appeal, and the other was full of intellectual excitement; however, they didn't excite me very much, but then I haven't any patience with Roman Catholics.'

'Good Lord, no!' said Bolivia. 'I spent six months in Malta once, with Sylvia Main. You ought to see their priests.'

Jane nodded understandingly. 'I was staying with Elizabeth Chattan,' she said, 'and she had leanings that way. That would have put me off, if nothing else did.'

'Well, I interrupted you,' said Bolivia.

Jane continued: 'I will say this for Florence: there are some very good restaurants there, and Elizabeth and I went quite often to a place called Betti's in the Via Tosinghi, near the Duomo. We were having lunch there one day when Elizabeth suddenly said, 'What a heavenly blaze of colour!' — that's the way she used to speak — and pointed to four people who'd just sat down on the other side of the road. There was another restaurant there, with tables put out on the pavement, and actually these people were sitting in front of a barber's shop, next door to the restaurant. One of the girls was dressed in bright blue, and the other in red, with a big red hat. And one of the men with them was Stephen; he was sitting between the two girls; they were all in a row facing the street.

'Now it's a little difficult to describe what happened, and of course I don't actually know everything that did happen, or what they were talking about, and that sort of thing, because I never liked to ask Stephen about it, and he never knew I'd been there.'

'But he must have seen you,' said Bolivia.

'No, he didn't. Our table was indoors — I don't see any point in having your meals in the street — and it was comparatively dark there, because there was a big awning in front of Betti's. Well, the girl in red was called Giulia Something-or-Other, she was an American, though her father was Italian, and Stephen had known her casually for some time. Who the others were I don't know, but they were all enjoying themselves, and Stephen was playing up astonishingly. He's never really been much of an argument for vice, you know, but he was doing his best that day. I suppose they'd had a couple of drinks somewhere, and they put away a good lot of wine at lunch. Giulia was the kind of girl you'd imagine with a name like that, and I expect she encouraged him, but I was rather surprised when I saw Stephen pinching her behind.'

'Stephen! Pinching her behind!'

'Oh, it's a Florentine custom. When Elizabeth Chattan and I went to a cinema she always came home black and blue. They didn't touch me, but Elizabeth looks like the sort of girl they cast for a nun at Hollywood; that's the kind that always gets pinched. She quite enjoyed it, and so did Giulia apparently. But Stephen was having a proper day out, and the next time I saw him in action he was pinching the other girl. And she liked it, too, and started a tremendous conversation with Stephen, so that her young man was left unoccupied at one end and Giulia was stranded at the other. And that didn't suit Giulia. But why she bit his ear I don't know. It may have been spite, it may be an American or Italian habit, or it may have been just excitement and the heat. I don't know. But she did, and pretty hard too.

'She suddenly leaned across, put her arm round his shoulders, and snapped at his left ear. That was too much for Stephen. He was frightened, and he was hurt too. He jumped up and howled like a dog.

'That made rather a disturbance, but things wouldn't have been so bad if their table, as I told

you, hadn't been just in front of a barber's shop.
There were two Italians in there, getting shaved.
They were sitting right in the window, and they
must have had a far better view of what was going
on than I had, and I suppose the sight of Stephen
pinching both girls in turn, and then making such a
fuss about getting his ear bitten, was too much for
them. It was a very hot day. Anyway, they rushed
out of the barber's shop, all swathed in dust-covers,
and their faces covered with soap, and shouted at
poor Stephen, and shook their fists at him, and
generally made themselves a damned nuisance.
And the two barbers followed them, and they
shouted, and waved their razors about, and the
only person who kept her head was Giulia. She told
everybody to go to hell. But it wasn't any good.
All the waiters in the Via Tosinghi, and half the
people lunching there, joined in the argument, and
a few tables got upset. Then a couple of Carabinieri came along and arrested the barbers, and
that quietened things down a bit.'

'And what happened then?'

'I told Elizabeth she wasn't to say anything about
it, and Stephen took the Rome Express to Paris at
three o'clock that afternoon.'

'And you mean to say that Stephen's avoided
women ever since, just because of that?'

'Well, damn it all, Bolivia! If you were a sensitive
young man, and one day you were tempted to pinch
a girl's behind, and suddenly the whole world went
mad in front of you — Italians covered with shaving
soap, and people brandishing razors, and waiters

flapping their napkins, and Giulia throwing forks at them — well, I mean to say, would you ever pinch anybody again? That's what it amounts to. God knows I'm no psychologist, but that's merely common sense. Stephen got a hell of a fright, and if he's ever going to get married he'll have to be married very gently and quietly.'

'Poor old Stephen,' said Bolivia.

'I like him, you know,' said Jane. 'He may be a bit of a fool in some ways, but potentially he's worth a dozen of Freddy Hislop or young Wheatley. He *is* intelligent. But he's like a salmon when the river's too low; he can't get over the falls, and he's not doing himself any good where he is.'

'Do you remember when I sprained my ankle and couldn't play any golf for a couple of months? Stephen was very decent to me then. He lent me a lot of books, and though they weren't the sort of stuff I'd read normally, I'd nothing else to do at the time, and I dipped into a few of them. And some of them were really quite interesting.'

'I think you'd get on very well with him,' said Jane.

'Well, I think I'd understand him better than most people, after what you've told me.'

'Look here,' said Jane, 'let's go along and see them. I must have a talk to Wilfrid about clothes, and I might as well get it over now; there's not going to be any more golf to-day.'

Bolivia rang the bell and paid for their tea. 'That's all right,' she said when Jane offered her share.

'Thanks very much,' said Jane. 'You've got your car here, haven't you?'

Bolivia had. They drove in silence till they came to Lammiter West, when Bolivia inquired what news there was of the Vicar. After the death of his wife the Vicar had fallen into so pitiable a state of health and mind that his friends had booked a passage for him on a Mediterranean cruise arranged by the Hellenic Club, and trusting to the salutary effect of sea breezes and classical lectures, had overcome his querulous objections, packed his clothes, and taken him aboard the steamship *Alcyone*. The *Alcyone*, her cruise finished, was due to dock in Southampton in a week's time, said Jane, and though the Vicar's letters had been far from gay, they showed a growing interest in his surroundings and a determined effort to face life in a reasonably cheerful manner.

'And how's Hilary getting on with the children?' asked Bolivia.

'She says she's never been so happy in her life before.'

During the Vicar's absence the younger Purefoy children had been living at Rumneys. Lady Caroline's brother, the impoverished Duke of Starveling, had offered to entertain the two elder boys for a month, but he had confessed quite frankly that the cost of feeding six children was more than he could face. — As it was, both Denis and Rupert returned from Starveling Court looking noticeably thin after a prolonged diet of rabbit and stewed gooseberries. — Hilary, therefore, had volunteered to forgo her August holiday and find house-room at Rumneys for Cecily, Patrick, Rosemary, and Peter. The Vicar had thankfully accepted this offer and Hilary, who was devoted to the children, had not only kept them happy, but thoroughly enjoyed herself into the bargain. Her other charities and benevolences had been sadly neglected, and her reputation for common sense impaired by her readiness to share their youthful amusements: on several occasions, for example, she had slept in a tent in the spinney, and she had acquired some knowledge of ratting. Her happiness would have been complete had it not been for an intermittent feeling that she had found consolation, too facile to be decent, for her grief at Caroline's death.

Bolivia drove more slowly than was her custom. She was thinking. They passed Sir Gervase Flood's agreeable residence. Bolivia said, 'It *would* be rather fun to wipe Daisy's eye.'

'And Katherine's,' said Jane.

'If I — if we — actually get the money,' said Bolivia, 'I'll never forget what you've done. I'm taking a lot for granted, of course, but if — well, suppose everything happened as it might happen — I'd insist on Stephen sharing the money with you.'

'Nonsense,' said Jane. 'I'm not a matrimonial agency.'

'No, but you're being extraordinarily generous, and it would only be fair. . . .'

'If you win the prize you can buy Lammiter Heath — it would be a damned good investment — and put me in as permanent secretary. That's all I want.'

'That's a bargain,' said Bolivia.

Wilfrid and Stephen had finished their day's work and were sitting in the garden listening to a gramophone that played Constant Lambert's *Rio Grande*. To the north, over Lammiter West and the Heath beyond, blue rainclouds still cast their shadow, but the garden was full of a golden light, and gold and tawny and crimson dahlias made a proper audience for the gallant music, and in the little orchard ripening fruit shone like rubies in a nest of leaves.

Wilfrid stopped the gramophone and ran to get more chairs. 'Now before we begin to talk,' he said, 'let's play *Rio Grande* just once more. It's too marvellous in this light, and the dahlias make it perfect.'

Jane and Bolivia listened without any manifest enjoyment. 'You do like it, don't you?' asked Wilfrid.

'I'm damned if I do,' said Jane. 'And what difference do the dahlias make, anyhow?'

Wilfrid looked hurt, and Stephen shrugged his shoulders.

'I think it's rather good,' said Bolivia.

'And you see what we mean about the dahlias?' asked Wilfrid.

'Yes, I think I do,' said Bolivia, and avoided Jane's eyes. Stephen looked at her approvingly.

Jane said, 'Look here, Wilfrid, I want you to help me about clothes again. Winter's coming on, and I suppose I'll have to get one or two new things, but the only thing I can think of is a leather jacket. Have you any good ideas?'

Wilfrid turned to Stephen with a little smile of

123

excitement. 'Isn't that funny?' he asked. 'Stephen and I were talking about clothes last night, and he had a perfectly magnificent scheme for making everybody look ten times nicer than they do now, and feeling ten times happier, because they would, wouldn't they?'

'It was a very reasonable suggestion, though I don't suppose you'll agree with me,' said Stephen, a trifle coldly.

'Do tell us about it: it sounds most exciting,' said Bolivia. Jane looked at her with amazement that slowly changed to understanding.

'Quite roughly,' said Stephen, 'the idea was to make fashion a yearly pageant of the seasons. You start in March with pale daffodil hues and very tender greens, and slowly you make your palette richer till in summer everybody is dressed in a whole medley of colours, with either red or blue predominating. Then in September you look for autumnal shades, ripe yellows and orange and russet. And in winter . . .'

'We go into mourning, I suppose?' asked Jane.

'On the contrary. In winter we choose scarlet and holly-green, crimson and white furs, gold buttons and gold braid, and everything that's brightest. The present system of fashions would be discarded altogether, or revolutionized at least, and people would be encouraged to design their own clothes within these very wide limits of colour. The mass-production of modes is an abominable thing: it's designed for a slave mentality and it breeds a slave mentality. Of course the really brilliant *couturière*, the dress designer of genius, would survive, and be stimulated to even richer invention. But apart from the creations of genius, I'd like to see a state of anarchy in dress — significant anarchy if you like — governed only by a seasonal change of colour-scheme.'

'Do you mean for men as well?' said Jane.

'Indeed I do. Don't you agree that corn-coloured hose, a rich brown doublet, and an orange cloak would look better than this dull suit?'

'They wouldn't be much good for people who've got any work to do.'

'You have the vulgar idea,' said Stephen, 'that nobody in the history of the world ever did any work till the invention of dungarees and the office suit. That, let me tell you, is a fallacy.'

'But anarchy and four fashions a year would be far too expensive for most people,' said Bolivia.

'Red cloth costs no more than grey,' said Stephen, 'and people who can only afford drugget would feel better, and look better, in brightly coloured drugget. I myself paid eleven guineas for this suit: one could buy a lot of yellow silk and brown velvet for that. And if we did spend more on our clothes we would revive moribund industries in Yorkshire and Lancashire, and by reducing unemployment we would increase the general prosperity of the country, and so be able to afford a more luxurious style of dressing.'

'Well, you can start your revolution without me,' said Jane. 'All I want is a suit and a frock or two that will do for the autumn and carry me over the winter. What do you suggest, Wilfrid?'

'There's a lovely evening gown in lamé and shot poult in *Vogue* this month,' said Wilfrid. 'I bought it just a day or two ago. It's in the house. I'll go in and look for it.'

'I think there's a lot in what you say, Stephen,' said Bolivia thoughtfully.

'Of course there is! But my God, how difficult it is to persuade people to think for themselves and see for themselves! Now take your own case, Bolivia: you'd benefit enormously if you could choose your clothes without regard for convention or the current fashion. You've got a magnificent figure, and you're not allowed to make the most of it simply because fashion is dictated by dressmakers who deliberately cater for mediocrity. I should like to design clothes for you.'

'I think I'll go in and help Wilfrid to look for *Vogue*,' said Jane, and left them together.

Bolivia took off her hat and patted her hair. 'Tell me what you'd really like me to wear,' she said.

'Stand up,' said Stephen.

Bolivia stood up. Stephen, reclining in a deck-chair, furrowed his brow and stared at her, with purely aesthetic appreciation. He did not observe the kindliness of her smile. 'You could wear an Empire gown with classically simple lines,' he said, 'and you'd look remarkably well in Early Tudor costume with one of those tall conical head-dresses. And I think an Elizabeth collar of starched lace, very high at the back and cut low in front, would suit you. I must consider that. I'll ask Wilfrid too; he's very clever that way.'

'No, don't bother him. I'd much rather know what *you* think I'd look nice in.'

Her tone was a trifle too warm. Stephen's gaze of pure aesthetic apperception was blurred by a slight embarrassment, as the image in a mirror may be blurred by the vapour of a bath. His pale face lightly flushed. 'It wouldn't do any good,' he said. 'You wouldn't wear my design.'

He stood up and folded the deck-chair. 'You've been playing golf?' he asked.

'Yes. Don't you ever go out nowadays? You used to.'

'I haven't played for years.'

'It's lovely on the Heath in the morning.'

'I suppose it is, in this weather. I must get Wilfrid to come and have a round with me some day.'

With an effort Bolivia restrained her annoyance, and they went indoors.

VII

By the exercise of much patience and more tact than one would have been inclined to credit her with, Bolivia succeeded in taking Stephen out to play golf before the weather became cold enough to give him yet another excuse for postponing the occasion. Having once enticed him on to the links, her task became easier, for like many other people he succumbed to the strange fascination of the game, and at the end of their first round it was he who proposed another on the next day but one.

He played better than Bolivia had expected. There was no length in his drive, and he showed a fastidious distaste for the rough compulsion of a niblick; but as he very seldom went off the fairway he had no great need for a niblick. He played pretty little shots straight down the middle, addressing his ball with a certain fussiness, and walking after it in a prim self-satisfied way. His principal fault was talking too much. As soon as he had recovered from the nervousness he felt at being alone with a woman, he displayed such inordinate loquacity as put the greatest strain upon Bolivia's self-control. He discussed everything from the advantage of striking the ball on a flat arc to the suitability of Persian floral designs for crewel-work. He had an annoying habit of holding up the game while he developed some phase of his argument, and when interrupted by a querulous cry of 'Fore!' he would calmly beckon the approaching foursome to come through, and leading Bolivia aside he would continue his dissertation at leisure. Bolivia, who had hitherto taken her golf at a great pace, found it difficult to subdue her inclination to bustle on, but she hid her discomfort with remarkable success.

Her prudent toleration of his talkativeness turned, however, almost to admiration after she had heard him put down her father in argument. It was not without misgiving that she asked Stephen to dine, for General Ramboise, though by no means an ill-tempered man, was inclined to be dogmatic on certain subjects, and sensitive people had been known to resent his forceful enunciation of what were — as he was the first to admit — merely his personal opinions: 'But opinions,' he would add, his long jaw snapping, 'opinions I have formed after a lifetime of practical experience of the problems presented: and I say, sir, that opinions formed in such a way are not lightly to be disregarded!' Stephen, however, introducing a view of his own, succeeded in winning the General's highest commendation.

The dinner was small and informal. Mrs. Ramboise, who preferred to live abroad, was in St. Jean de Luz, and Richard, the General's only son, was in a gunboat on the Yang-tse-kiang: Stephen sat lonely at the long side of the table, with the General at one end and Bolivia at the other. The meal was rather highly seasoned, and the concluding savoury was largely compounded of chillies and mustard sauce. Stephen, bravely endeavouring to cover the embarrassment of weeping and sweating simultaneously, said breathlessly, 'I used to think, General, that fire-eater was only a metaphorical description of you.'

The General chuckled and scattered red pepper over his plate.

'He's behaved very well so far,' said Bolivia. 'He hasn't contradicted either of us yet.'

'I never do contradict people unless they start talking damned nonsense,' said the General. 'There's a lot of people in the world to-day who think that everything they don't like, from cavalry to the Ten Commandments, is out of date and dead and done for. Well, they're fools and I tell 'em so. And people who believe in Communism, and vegetarianism, and teetotalism, and pacifism: they're fools too. I like decency and I hate fads, and when I meet a faddist or a cad I tell him the truth about himself. But apart from that I'm the mildest man in Brackenshire.'

'I'm a pacifist myself,' said Stephen.

'Then you're a fool,' said the General.

'I'm very far from being a fool,' said Stephen.

The General's eyes were light blue as to the iris, and a mottled yellow as to the cornea, which in time of anger received also a suffusion of blood. They now darkened appreciably, but his voice, though louder than is usual for a dining-room, was, by host's politeness, muted several tones below the ringing quality of the parade-ground when he answered: 'Pacifists, so far as I understand 'em, believe that war is neither necessary nor desirable.

But in six thousand years of the world's history there's been a major war in every decade, if not oftener. Why? Because war is necessary, and very often it's desirable! And war isn't going to come to an end now simply because a lot of chicken-livered decadents choose to tell the world they're gun-shy!'

'I don't care if war goes on for ever,' said Stephen. 'All I mean, when I say I'm a pacifist, is that I neither desire nor intend to go to war myself.'

'But if Britain declares war, you'll have to. In a time of crisis the individual will is subjugated to the national will. . . .'

'Just a minute, General. I've heard you say that the last war was, to put it mildly, clumsily handled, and, from the soldiers' point of view, unsatisfactory in many ways. Why?'

'Because of the damned civilians who tried to tell us what to do!' roared the General. 'Because a parcel of half-baked time-serving politicians thought they could run it better than we could! Because a horde of amateurs with no traditions came and tried to teach us our jobs! That's why the War was a damned poor war, and gave soldiering a bad name.'

'Quite so,' said Stephen. 'I agree with you entirely. And because I'm a civilian and not a soldier I intend to have nothing to do with the next war in case I impede the conduct of it. I believe, as you do, that war is a science and that only highly trained scientists can carry it on. The gravest mistake in all military history was the decision, in 1914, to put responsibility for the War in the hands of the people as a whole. War should be waged by the

Army, because the Army knows how to do it, and civilians should keep out of it, because they don't.'

'I must think that over,' said the General.

'If you read St. Paul you'll find that he agrees with me. St. Paul says: "We will not boast of things without our measure," and warns us quite clearly elsewhere to mind our own business. Now I realize that war is no business of mine. And you must realize this: that if war is to retain its good name it will have to be conducted in a proper way. You simply can't afford to let civilians come in and make a mess of it, because if they do they'll give people a totally false impression of war, as they did between 1914 and 1918, and the world will get so sick of it that, sooner or later, the world will prohibit it, and then the science and the art of war will disappear from the face of the earth as the art of hunting mastodons has disappeared. And then, of course, you'll lose your job. No, no, General, for your own sake I insist on leaving the conduct and execution of the next war entirely to the soldiers.'

'I've got to consider this very carefully,' said the General. 'Have a cheroot, my boy.'

He passed a box of black Trichinopolis to Stephen, who dubiously selected one. Bolivia made a move to go. She was filled with admiration for Stephen. She had always been accustomed to see her father win his arguments by a knock-out blow in the first round, and here was Stephen leading on points, confident, fresh, unmarked, while her father, clearly staggered by his attack, was playing for time! Bolivia reverenced her father. Till now she had had no reverence for Stephen, though, in a fashion hard to describe, she had been increasingly aware of a mild affection for him: an affection independent of the fortune that might be its harvest: for she was truly a nice girl, and when a nice girl sets out to marry a man she is always apt to become fond of him, whatever may have been the initial reason for her pursuit. But she now felt such a surge of mingled feelings, all warm with excitement, that something was born, so closely compact of reverence, enthusiasm, surprise, and relief, as to be indistinguishable, in her present state of mind, from love itself; and she looked at Stephen with kindly eyes and resolved beyond a quaver of doubt to hold him captive in her arms before another month was out.

'Now just repeat that last part of your argument,' said the General. 'I want to get it quite clear in my mind.'

Stephen, who preferred talking to any other of life's activities, reopened his case with a cogent allusion to Hannibal. Hannibal, he said, crossed the Alps and waged war in Italy with reasonable success — considering the odds and difficulties against him — for three years: could he have done that if Carthage had been linked by telephone to him, and his strategy had been at the mercy of political intrigue and the necessity of reporting monthly victories in the Carthaginian newspapers? Of course he couldn't. The civilian populace, with all its silly theories and foolish expectations, was merely a nuisance in time of war, and the Army should ignore it. Would Parliament, in time of peace, welcome the intervention of the Army in a General Election? Indeed it wouldn't. Why then should the Army suffer the intervention of Parliament in time of war? 'War,' said Stephen, 'is a specialist's job. I'm no specialist, in that sense, and so I propose to leave it alone. It's a pity for your sake, General, as well as for ours, that all the other civilians in Europe aren't as modest and sensible as I am.'

'You've given me a great deal to think about,' said the General. 'Have some more brandy, my boy. Have another cheroot — no, don't try to light that one again, take a new one.'

The argument found other fruit, and Stephen continued to have the best of it. It was midnight when he reached home, and it was not till the following morning that he realized, with any apprehension of its significance, that Bolivia had kissed him goodnight and that he had responded. The memory of their embrace made him very uncomfortable and not a little ashamed. He was patently ill at ease when Wilfrid, at the breakfast table, asked him how he had enjoyed himself and what had been the nature of his entertainment, and throughout the morning he was subject to a recurrent flush of embarrassment. But Bolivia, calling for him at two o'clock to take him to the golf course, showed nothing of the complementary shame that he had feared, but rather treated him with a new confidence and a curiously protective and even possessive manner.

It was the General, however, who, more than anyone else, gave substance to the gossip which his daughter's sudden friendliness with Stephen had naturally promoted. The General began to talk in the highest terms of Stephen. He made a point of praising him. 'He's an uncommonly sensible fellow', he told Sir Gervase; and Miss Montgomery reported a conversation in which the General had ascribed to Stephen 'a sounder grasp of modern problems than I've observed in any other young man of my acquaintance'.

'The significance of such a remark is obvious,' said Miss Montgomery to her tea-party.

'I don't follow you,' said Mrs. Corcoran.

'He's developed a high opinion of Stephen because Stephen is about to become his son-in-law.'

'That's very clever of you, Harriet,' said Mrs. Corcoran.

'You mean the General is trying to make the best of it?' suggested Miss Foster.

'Oh, not deliberately. But there's a natural tendency to magnify the good points of one's new friends and prospective relations-in-law.'

'I must confess that I'm surprised at Bolivia,' said Mrs. Sabby. 'I did *not* think she was a girl like that.'

'Like what?' asked Mrs. Corcoran.

'Surely it's clear that she's marrying him for money?'

'But he hasn't got any money. Not yet, at any rate.'

'That's what I mean. I think Bolivia's behaviour is absolutely shameless.'

'Perhaps she's in love with him,' said Miss Foster. 'I myself have always found him very agreeable, and I see no reason why Bolivia shouldn't have made the same discovery.'

'I think it's a pity,' said Mrs. Fowler decisively. 'I think it's a great pity. And I'm very sorry indeed for poor Wilfrid: he and Stephen always appeared to be so happy together.'

'Indeed, Wilfrid was looking miserable when I saw him last,' said Miss Foster thoughtfully.

There was a general murmur of commiseration.

'I hope Bolivia gets married quickly, or it will be too late,' said Miss Montgomery.

This observation caused considerable surprise, and Mrs. Corcoran asked sharply, 'What d'you mean, Harriet?'

'Katherine Clements returned to Rumneys yesterday, and I am told that her very first words to Hilary and Jane were that she expected to have twins in May.'

'Twins!' exclaimed Mrs. Sabby. 'How does she know?'

'She doesn't, of course. But I believe her husband's family makes rather a speciality of them, and Katherine is being optimistic.'

The tea-party discussed this new and important development of the drama with relish and a keen appreciation of all its niceties. There woke within them, and became vocal, that interest in the mechanism of creation which had dominated so much of the aggregate three hundred years of their lives, and old Mrs. Fowler, brushing a crumb from her bosom, set down her tea-cup and flatly contradicted Miss Fowler's rash assertion that twins were an accident which no one might prognosticate and none explain. The fire burnt brightly, the yellow curtains were drawn against the October dusk, and the half-emptied plates on the cake-stand showed twice the look of comfort they had worn when full. The vanished frail slices of bread and butter, the diminishment of the cherry-cake, the toasted and now absent scones, had taken their place in three hundred years of life, and the trio of mortal centuries they had strengthened spoke like a college of midwives — but with ladylike regard for decency — about the immortality that flesh can make. They would have listened with sympathy to Juliet's nurse, and all sound women. Had a man come in they would have fallen silent as stone, not so much with embarrassment as with impatient scorn of the episodic as opposed to the progressive partner.

Presently, with the tone of conclusion, Miss Fowler said, 'Well, if Katherine is justified in her expectation — though for my part I don't believe she will be — Arthur and Daisy will have to take a back seat, because I don't for a moment suppose . . .'

'Now don't say anything rash,' said Miss Montgomery with a little smile so gentle that it could not be called a smile of triumph, and yet, to those who knew her, betokened a most pleasurable satisfaction. She was very small and delicate in person. She had weak eyes, and a thin wrinkled face, and a black ribbon round her neck; and she gathered more news, and gathered it more quickly, than anyone else in Lammiter.

Mrs. Sabby, Mrs. Fowler, Miss Foster, and Mrs. Corcoran spoke together. 'You don't mean to say,' they exclaimed, 'you don't mean . . .?'

'Indeed I do,' said Miss Montgomery. 'I was talking to their little girl, Ruth, only this morning. She's a very clever, rather old-fashioned child, and her information was quite definite.'

Again the room was filled with a clamour — so far as old ladies' voices may produce a clamour — of speculation and annotation, comment, and criticism. Again the warm air was fluttered with obstetrical dialectic and the *brouhaha* of three hundred years of gynaecology. Endless were the permutations and combinations of vital statistics, interminable the reminiscences and anecdotes of lying-in. The world was narrowed, in Miss Montgomery's drawing-room, to a likeness of the Great Bed of Ware, and womankind for ever contemned the sterile theories of T. R. Malthus.

It was with a noticeable diminution of interest that the conversation turned at length to the reputed growth of friendship between Hilary Gander and the Reverend Lionel Purefoy. This was a minor matter. Sentimentality had no flavour after the strong substance of procreation. 'She'll be forty in December,' said Miss Montgomery with a deprecating smile.

'And the Vicar's children wouldn't count, would they?' asked Miss Foster.

'Count? Count for what?' asked Mrs. Corcoran.

'Well, if Hilary married the Vicar — of course I don't suppose there's anything in the story, but just for the sake of argument, suppose she did — then she'd have six step-children: that wouldn't mean that she won the Major's legacy, would it?'

138

'No,' said Miss Montgomery decisively. 'That possibility occurred to me some time ago, and I had a little conversation with Mr. Peabody. I was extremely tactful, and naturally I mentioned no names, but I had Hilary's case in mind, and I satisfied myself beyond doubt that step-children, however many, were no qualification in terms of the will.'

'None the less, it would be a very good thing if she did marry him,' said old Mrs. Fowler.

'Why?' asked Mrs. Corcoran.

'Because the Vicar is the sort of man who *must* have a woman to look after him,' said Mrs. Fowler. 'All men are the better of a wife, but he really needs one. There was no conviction in his voice last Sunday, and there won't be till he's married again.'

It was clear, however, that dissection of the putative relations between Hilary and the Vicar would be an anti-climax, and the party showed little inclination to pursue it. Katherine's condition and Daisy's gave them enough to think about, and like wise women they were satisfied with plenty.

Miss Montgomery's party had been a great success, and Miss Montgomery had wit enough to be grateful to Major Gander for his ingenious will.

VIII

THE winter migration began of mist and cloud, of
wind and rain and biting airs. As though with a
huge flock of arctic birds the sky was filled with cold
grey plumage and feathers that in their flight flung
spray they had caught far off in northern seas. On
reluctant wings the morning mist rose wearily, the
hovering clouds obscured the sun, and in the slip-
stream of the flighting winds the last leaves fluttered
wildly on bare branches. The birds of winter came
and struck at the land with cold sharp beaks, and
shook their wet wings over house and field. They
invested the hills and beleaguered the snug valleys.

This was the season when, if Stephen had his way,
the streets would flower with crimson and with
ermine, with cloaks of scarlet and gaiters of holly-
green, and glittering tassels and gold braid would
gleam in the sombre air. But as Stephen had no
disciples, not even Wilfrid or himself, the people
subdued their outward guise to an aspect even
gloomier than the firmament, and secure from envy
walked abroad in dingy hues and the dripping
shade of dark umbrellas. And yet, though these
were indeed the colours of mourning, it would be
foolish to think they were defeated or afraid. These
dismal winter trappings were only the relics of a lost
habit of hibernation — the umbrella their vestigial
cave, the grey waterproof a memory of some hollow

tree-trunk — and in the heart of hibernation there is always the thought of spring. Strip off the hideous clothes of winter and underneath them you will see divine impatience for trees in blossom, buds again, and the brightness of tall blue skies. April is always astir in December's womb, and in the darkness of the year green buds are germinating.

It was this impatience, or the joy of realization after long months of impatience, that so often made the *renouveau* a poet's topic, and helped Chaucer's daisies to grow so white. When the seasons were closer to them than they now are, the poets rose and sang like larks in spring. But even the poet who sang, between March and April, of his love for Alysoun; or he who saw love and Lent come into town together; or they who sang for ever the nightingale, the white moon, and the Provençal dawn; or she who cried to the west wind for rain and to heaven for her lover; or they who hymned a *bel oil vair* in cowslip time — take them all, hot clerk and fevered girl and passionate *trouvère*, and make a sweet sum of their longing, and however much it differed in quality, it would be no greater in quantity than the pother and impatience and flustered expectancy with which plump Arthur and bespectacled Daisy and shallow Katherine, and indeed some three hundred busybodies and kind gossips of Lammiter attended the promised burgeoning of the new year.

Katherine was more honest than Daisy in her maternal expectancy. She simply made herself a nuisance to everybody with whom she came in contact by talking for ever about her anticipated child, or rather children, for the law of averages and the numerical odds in favour of a singleton did not for a moment diminish her assurance of two. Every morning, with impressive regularity, she described, for the benefit of Hilary and Jane, the current state of her health, and such was her simple faith in the perennial interest of this subject that even Hilary's patent boredom and Jane's frequent rudeness did nothing to check the copious details of her matutinal narrative: a narrative not too aggressively matutinal, however, for the delicacy of her condition now made it advisable for her to eat breakfast in bed.

'I'm taking no risks,' she would bluffly say. 'A lot depends on me now, and I'm going to take every possible care of myself and build up my strength, because it will be a bit of a strain to nurse two children. I'll be able to do it, of course — I haven't any doubt about that — but I'm going to be sensible and really study my health for the next few months. It's only fair to *them* that I should. I was wondering, Hilary, if we could have dinner at seven instead of at eight — it won't be for very long: just till the spring — because I think an earlier meal would give me a better night's rest.'

Daisy was also determined to take every care of herself, and in this pious resolve she was encouraged by Arthur, who was relieved to find that his own health was no longer a matter of interest. Daisy still bought patent foods in great quantity and variety: all the newest agglomerations of vitamins, proteins, peptones, diastase, phosphates, hormones, galactogogues, and glandular extracts, as well as other boluses, plasters, carminatives, cathartics and nostrums, were delivered in profusion to Hornbeam House, and applied or swallowed according to the confused aggregate of directions: but now it was Daisy herself who consumed the innumerable pills, potions, and farinaceous messes: not a husk or a capsule was given to Arthur. And Arthur was content.

But though Daisy took such inordinate trouble to maintain her health and prepare for motherhood, she did it all in secret and was very much offended if Arthur made any allusion to her diet or to her state of health. It was not, she thought, a matter to be discussed. She could not refrain from informing people of her condition, but as soon as she had told them she regretted her indiscretion, and desired them to say no more about it. She assumed, for the world's benefit, an aloofly smiling delicacy of temper, and revered as a miracle that which had happened: and indeed it was a miracle.

It was a pleasant sight to see Daisy taking her walks abroad. Her nose might be a little red with the frosty weather, her sloping shoulders might seem unapt for her enormous weight of clothing they supported, the long feet burdened with gaiters and goloshes might seem larger than they were; but her eyes had a whimsical and dreamy look, and a little smile was on her mouth. It was a pity that so few flowers grew in November, for Daisy would have liked to gather blossom as she walked, but she did her best with hips and haws and a few catkins, and the winter melody of thrush and hedgesparrow, nut-hatch and titmouse, pleased her greatly, though she did not know which was which. She made a brave attempt to live in spiritual communion with the prettiest of nature's activities, and though she never forgot the proper hours at which to eat her unnatural compounds of vitamins, phosphates, peptones, and so forth, it was perhaps a mark of grace that she insisted on consuming them in private.

She fortified her sense of living beautifully by reading the poems of W. H. Davies and the works of W. H. Hudson, and whenever she could she reso-lutely banished from her mind all thought of the financial significance of her expectations. This, however, was not always possible, for Katherine made a point of calling on her every week or so, and Katherine's conversation, the mere sight of Kather-ine, would rouse in her such feelings of hostility and discomfort as banished, for the time being, all the complacency and consanguinity with birds and trees that her reading had so happily suggested, and made her feverishly desirous of winning the Major's legacy simply to spite her cousin-in-law.

Katherine would come in looking boisterously maternal. At a very early stage in the proceedings, and long before there was any need for them, she took to wearing loose gowns and corselets designed to support her increasing figure. Enlarged with these wholly redundant garments, she gave forty times more promise of fecundity than Daisy, whose modesty bade her do everything possible to retain a slender fallow look; and Daisy's temper was invariably ruffled by this too procreant spectacle and by the objectionable confidence of Katherine's manner.

Katherine would come in and say, 'Well, Daisy, how are you feeling? Looking a bit down, aren't you?'

Daisy would glance with a slight shudder at the exuberant folds of Katherine's dress, and answer primly, 'Thank you, Katherine, I'm perfectly well. There's no reason why I should be otherwise, is there?'

'I don't know about that,' Katherine would continue. 'It takes different people in different ways. I'm extraordinarily fit myself, but some women I know become chronic invalids as soon as . . .'

If Ruth were in the room, Daisy would rise, at this point, with purposive interruption, and ask her daughter, 'Wouldn't you like to go for a walk, Ruth? It's quite a nice afternoon, and I think a little walk might do you good.'

Ruth's response to these suggestions was always immediate and acquiescent. 'She's getting so good,' Daisy would say. 'A child's intuitive sympathy is really wonderful. It's as though she realized and understood that my life must be calm and peaceful. I can't bear an argument, and even a jarring atmosphere upsets me. It always has. I think that's why I spend so much time in the garden, talking to my flowers, for they always agree with me and sympathize with my little worries.'

Daisy had said nothing to Ruth about her expected baby. Despite her earnest explication of the wonders of nature, as they occurred among bees and flowers and guinea-pigs, she had come to the conclusion that it would be too difficult, and certainly embarrassing, to explain the quickening of her own procreant faculty, and she had excused the evasion of a task that to other mothers she would have called imperative, by pretending to herself that she was withholding the news in order to give Ruth a charming surprise. Ruth, however, as Miss Montgomery had already discovered, was not in a position to be surprised. She was an inquisitive child, and having early suspected the existence of a secret she had set out in a quiet and unobtrusive way to discover it. She had succeeded by skilful eavesdropping. The healthy walks on which she was dispatched when Aunt Katherine came to tea had never taken her farther than the garden, where, oblivious of the cold, she would crouch and listen outside the lee window that was generally left discreetly open. Sometimes she had even succeeded in returning, unobserved, to the drawing-room, and crawling silently behind the couch that stood a little distance from the wall that was adjacent to the door. She had been very interested in what she heard, and her success in learning so much gave her a feeling of virtue: her father had once told her not to rely on books for information — this had been when she was studying hedgehogs — but to use her own eyes and ears; and now she was very profitably obeying him.

One evening, tempted by a frosty moon and a brisk air, Katherine walked down to Hornbeams after dinner and found Daisy alone. Arthur had gone into Lammiter with Wilfrid to see the Lammiter Amateur Dramatic Society play Mr. Milne's comedy of *The Dover Road*, and Daisy, with a petty pensive air, was sitting in the lamplight sewing childish garments.

Katherine also had brought a bag full of wool, flannel, knitting-needles, and so forth, and after inquiring, in a challenging voice, the state of Daisy's health, she produced a half-made vest and vigorously began to knit.

'I've got a lot to do before May,' she said.

Daisy looked at her with distaste. She herself, as soon as her visitor had been announced, had put away her sewing and laid an open copy of *Green Mansions* on her knee. 'I suppose a baby does need a lot of clothes,' she said. 'I ought to remember what Ruth required, but I'm not a very practical person, and I'm afraid I was too intent on the wonder of it all to think a great deal about tiresome details. And when you consider how Nature does without our help in the woods and the fields, it's a little ungrateful, I think, to distrust her in the home.'

'Nature won't supply you with nappies and binders,' said Katherine, knitting vigorously.

Daisy sighed. It was difficult, she felt, to maintain conversation with a person who lived on a different plane, a lower plane, of existence. 'Is that a binder you're making now?' she asked.

'No, it's a vest.'

It was curious, thought Daisy, how much Katherine had changed. There had never been any great sympathy between them, she admitted, because

Katherine had always been unnaturally self-centred, but her manner had been so light, chattering, flimsy, and effervescent, that it had been fairly easy to remain friendly with her, so long as one didn't see her too often. But now her temper had become brusque and overbearing, her voice had hardened, and instead of babbling about a dozen foolish interests — hopping from this to that, lively and avid as a flea on the sand — she had one topic only, that she pursued with unrelenting zest. It was like a monomania. It *was* a monomania, thought Daisy with sudden perspicacity. Katherine was obsessed by the dream of winning seventy thousand pounds: how evil a thing was money! And because of this dreadful dominating greed she had come to believe she was going to have twins. She was at the mercy of a complex, a fixation, the tyranny of imaginative wish-fulfilment. That was the explanation of course, and really it scarcely bore thinking about.

'Have you read *Green Mansions*?' asked Daisy. 'I sometimes think it's the most perfect book in the world.'

'I haven't much time for reading,' said Katherine. 'It's all right for you: you're only making clothes for one baby. . . .'

'I really haven't begun to make anything at all,' Daisy interrupted gently. 'It's so far far away that I hardly dare to think about it yet.'

'What's in the sewing-bag under that cushion?' asked Katherine.

Daisy flushed. 'Oh, nothing really. One or two little things I was sewing in a whimsical way. But nothing of any use — nothing so practical as that binder you're making.'

'It isn't a binder, it's a vest. I told you that before.'

'So you did. How stupid of me to forget! But it doesn't look very like a vest, does it?'

'It will, in time. I've got to make another dozen of these things, and the same number of jackets, pilches, pull-ons, and barrow-coats. I'm buying some, but I want to make as many as possible myself.'

'A dozen of each! Will you really want as many as that?'

'Two children need a lot of clothes,' said Katherine.

In spite of her recent discovery of the pathological nature of Katherine's belief in the imminence of twins, Daisy was irritated by her calm enunciation of it. 'Really, Katherine,' she said, 'for your own sake I wish you wouldn't talk like that, and especially that you wouldn't *think* like that. You're only preparing for a bitter disappointment. I had a long and extraordinarily interesting letter from Juliet last week — Juliet Morrow, you know. You've heard me speak of her? — and she happened to mention this very subject: she's done an enormous amount of welfare work, and among the poor, of course, babies are far more of a common occurrence than they are with us: but Juliet says that even among the *very* poor she's only seen twins half a dozen times, so it's *most* unlikely that you will have them. Please don't set you heart on it, Katherine, for I should hate to think of your being disappointed.'

'I'm going to call them Randolph and Ulrich,' said Katherine. 'Oliver suggested Hengist and Horsa, or Romulus and Remus, but he was joking, of course. I think Randolph has a very manly sound, and Ulrich is rather nice and uncommon, don't you think?'

'Well, I've warned you what to expect,' said Daisy crossly, 'and if you persist in being silly it won't be my fault. Good heavens! I might have twins myself. But I'm not so foolish as to believe that I shall.'

'No, that *would* be foolish,' said Katherine.

'I'm just as likely to have them as you are,' retorted Daisy.

'Oh, no, you're not.'

'But I am!'

'Rubbish,' said Katherine. 'Damn it, I've dropped a stitch.'

Arthur and Wilfrid came home early. The Lammiter Amateurs had scarcely done justice to *The Dover Road*, and Wilfrid was not in the mood for polite comedy however well it had been acted. They left the theatre at the first interval, and after having a drink or two at the bar, they returned to Hornbeams, walking smartly under the frosty moon. 'Daisy will be in bed, I expect,' said Arthur. 'She's been turning in fairly early for the last fortnight or so.'

But he took the precaution of looking through the drawing-room window before going in, and saw not only Daisy but Katherine there. He turned to Wilfrid with a sibilant warning.

'Ssh!' he whispered. 'Daisy's still up, and Katherine's with her. It won't do you any good to go in and talk to them, but if you don't mind sitting outside in the fresh air for a little while, I've got something in the garden that will buck you up in no time.'

'That's just what I want,' said Wilfrid: he had on two or three occasions been permitted to share the secret of the rockery.

Arthur tiptoed over the gravel and led the way to the bottom of the garden. In the milk-white light of the moon the grass was pale and quivering with frost, and the little rockery had a black romantic look. Their shoes made dark smudges on the lawn.

At the side of the rockery farther from the house Arthur, in a jocular voice, said 'Welcome to the smuggler's cave, my boy!' Then he stooped to a large flat stone, and having brushed aside some icy tendrils and dimly sparkling leaves, exerted his strength and lifted it from the frost-bound earth. Beneath it were two tin biscuit-boxes, set side by side among the rocks and the hard soil, to which it served as a lid. In the one were two square quarts of gin and a couple of glasses, and in the other half a dozen bottles of ginger-beer.

It was Daisy's insensate prejudice against spirituous liquors, and her equally intemperate enthusiasm for gardening, that had driven Arthur to establish an alcoholic cache in the rockery. He liked a drink, and he disliked working in the garden. But Daisy forbade him to drink and drove him to dig. Therefore, as was natural, Arthur had sought ways of evading her prohibition and ameliorating his unwelcome toil; and after three or four unsatisfactory devices he had struck upon the happy idea of constructing a little cellar among the stonecrops. Here it served a general purpose and a particular purpose: it was a cellar, and therefore a pleasing and a useful possession at any time; and being situated in the garden it was of special service in lightening such distasteful tasks as weeding, mulching, bedding, raking, and sweeping up leaves.

Arthur opened a quart of gin and poured a generous three-finger peg into each of the glasses. Then he added the ginger-beer, whose bounteous froth, reduced by the gin, quickly subsided and floated on the surface in little moonlit arabesques of foam. The mixture was icy-cold and very agreeable to the palate.

Wilfrid and Arthur sat side by side on convenient rocks and nursed their glasses. 'I often come out here and have a quiet drink,' said Arthur. 'Daisy doesn't like the idea of keeping wine or spirits in the house. She's very broad-minded about most things, but she has rather a prejudice against drink — her father inherited a remarkably fine cellar and then neglected his business, you know — and it's easier to pretend to agree with her than to argue with her. The way to treat a woman is to humour her: give in to her, Wilfred, and if you have a scrap of ingenuity you can do it without sacrificing any of your own amusements, though you may have to re-arrange them a little.'

'I wish I had as much confidence and knowledge of the world as you have, Arthur,' said Wilfrid.

Arthur experienced a feeling of genial satisfaction to be addressed in this way. A man of the world! Of course he was: soldier, adventurer, speculator, man of property, husband and father — how could the title be denied him? But none the less it was pleasant to know that Wilfrid recognized his quality. The sensation of well-being that filled him, as though his arteries had been plumped-out by a transfusion of new blood, was commingled with protective affection for his young friend. He tilted his hat, leaned backwards against the rockery, and contemplated the sky with a wise and tolerant smile.

'Knowledge of the world isn't acquired without pain,' he declared. 'We old fellows who know the ropes, or think we do, have had to pay for our wisdom by bitter experience. We've knocked about a bit, you know. We've been through the mill. I don't think you've any reason to envy us, Wilfrid. I remember going through hell, absolute hell, when I was your age; or younger, perhaps, yes I think I was younger; a woman, of course, it's always a woman. A magnificent creature she was, too, very tall and dark, with a bold and rather insolent manner.'

'Like Bolivia?' Wilfrid asked.

Arthur, who had been enjoying his painful memories, was slightly put out by the question.

'Like Bolivia?' he repeated. 'No, I wouldn't say that. She may have resembled her in a general way, but not really. I don't think — well, perhaps she did, after a fashion, though she was better looking, of course.'

'I do wish you could tell me what to do about Bolivia,' said Wilfrid dolefully.

Arthur coughed judicially. 'Have some more gin,' he said.

'I would never do anything to interfere with Stephen's happiness; you do believe that, don't you? But honestly I can't think he'll be happy with her. They're not suited to each other. Stephen must have somebody with him who's really interested in him, and really sympathetic: but Bolivia doesn't understand him properly, and I'm sure she won't put up with all his little peculiarities. He has moods, you know. But she's obviously determined to marry him, and I'm simply in despair.'

'H'm,' said Arthur. 'H'm, h'm. Have you ever discussed Bolivia with him? Have you ever told him that you think she wouldn't make a suitable or sympathetic wife?'

'No, I've never said a single word about her.'

'Why not?'

'Because Stephen would think I was jealous,' said Wilfrid. 'And I'm not, Arthur, I'm really not. It's just that I know he'll be unhappy with her.'

'Well now,' said Arthur, 'we must consider this very carefully. We mustn't come to a rash conclusion, or to any conclusion, without taking everything into account. So let's begin at the beginning, and tell me, first of all, if you think that Stephen is in love with her?'

'He can't be, with a woman like that.'

'Now that's where you show your lack of experience,' said Arthur wisely and a little reproachfully.

'When you've lived to my age you'll discover that one of the fundamental frailties of the social fabric is that almost anybody, given the proper conditions, can fall in love with almost everybody. It sounds fantastic, I know, but it's true, Wilfrid, it's all too true. Ah, passion's a curious thing. I remember, when I was a young man, becoming infatuated, absolutely infatuated, with a little gipsy-like creature — a chorus girl, Wilfrid — a vulgar little soul, but strangely fascinating, strangely vital, and very warmly attached to me, of course. Nothing could have been more unsuitable, but there it was: a passionate attachment between this gay, vulgar little gipsy, and me!'

Arthur broke off his reminiscences in order to refill their glasses with gin and ginger, and Wilfrid took the opportunity to reintroduce the topic of Stephen and Bolivia.

'Well, anyway, I'm quite sure she isn't in love with him,' he said.

'Who isn't?'

'Bolivia.'

'Ah, yes, Bolivia. Bolivia, of course. So she isn't in love with Stephen, eh?'

'She's marrying him simply to get Major Gander's seventy thousand pounds.'

'Oh, abominable!' said Arthur. 'That's depravity, nothing but depravity, if it's true. To marry for money is a beastly thing. I know, for I had opportunities myself, but I said no. I said, "When I marry I shall marry for love," and so I did. And I've never regretted it, never for a moment. I'm very much disappointed in Bolivia, to hear that she's a girl like that, and the more I think of it the more I believe that you're mistaken, Wilfrid. Bolivia isn't capable of such depravity!'

'Why not?'

'Because Stephen isn't going to get the seventy thousand pounds! We're going to get it, Daisy and I. That proves it, doesn't it? Have some gin and ginger and don't you worry about Bolivia. She's a good girl, Wilfrid, I'm sure she is.'

'But she isn't good enough for Stephen,' said Wilfrid stubbornly, 'and if she marries him she'll make him unhappy. And if they don't get the Major's money they'll be still more unhappy. Stephen couldn't bear to live in a house full of children.'

'Children,' said Arthur portentously. 'They're a great responsibility, Wilfrid, and yet the more I think about it the more I come to believe in what you might call the natural hypothesis. I see myself sitting at the head of a long table that is crowded, simply crowded, with young and happy faces. Now when you consider the sort of life that I've led, roughing it here and there, an infantry officer in the greatest war in history — a soldier for four years, living the fearful, squalid, and reckless life of a soldier — and then coming home and gambling on the Stock Exchange, gambling in real estate, with all the recklessness of a soldier; when you consider that, and remember the women I've known — the little gipsy creature who used to perch on my knee: what a leg she had! A trim warm-hearted vulgar little creature: what a life we led! Dancing, gambling, laughing, and making love. Utterly poor and recklessly happy. And there were others, of course, many many others — and after this vagabond existence I'm content to settle down in Lammiter! It's astonishing, isn't it? The domestic scene, a house full of children, a quiet patriarchal age: that's all I want nowadays. Perfectly amazing, absolutely astounding, and yet there it is! It's a natural law, Wilfrid, and the soldier of fortune comes home to his own fireside just like everybody else. You can laugh at Uncle John if you like, but he was right, he was absolutely right, when he said that a full quiver is a full quiver, and ripeness is all. Ripeness is all: that's the word. Have another drink!'

'That's all very well,' said Wilfrid sullenly, 'but it isn't helpful to me. I thought you were going to give me advice and tell me what to do.'

'And so I shall,' said Arthur. 'You can rely on me absolutely. All my experience is at your service. Tell me what you want to do, and I'll tell you how to do it.'

'I want to keep Stephen from being made unhappy.'

Arthur sadly shook his head. 'Unhappiness is our mortal lot,' he said.

Wilfrid hurriedly added, 'I want to prevent that horrible woman Bolivia from marrying him.'

'Never come between man and wife,' said Arthur.

'But they're not man and wife!'

'That's just it,' said Arthur. 'I was just coming to

that. Now as they're not man and wife your task is much, much easier. Much, much, much easier. There are two instincts in nature, Wilfrid: one is centripetal, and the other is centrifugal. Sometimes you come in like this, and sometimes you go out like that. There's the force of gravity on the one hand, and on the other hand there's the force of levity. The whole thing's like a see-saw. D'you understand? So what you've got to do is to leave it to Nature.'

'You mean I can't do anything at all?'

'On the contrary, you've got to do a great deal. You've got to abstain from action like Fabius Maximus. Quintus Fabius Maximus Cunctator did nothing, and was very successful. So be wise and cunctatious like him, and leave it to Nature. If Nature's going to be centrifugal, they'll fly apart like bows and arrows. And that's what you want them to do, isn't it? Very well, then.'

'You really think they'll break it off before it's too late?'

'After a great deal of experience,' said Arthur solemnly, 'I've come to the conclusion that Nature is more inclined to be centrifugal than centripetal, and the force of levity is greater than the force of gravity. So everything's going to be all right. You see what I mean?'

'Oh, I do hope you're right,' said Wilfrid. 'I'd feel so happy if I thought they were going to break it off.'

'Have a drink,' said Arthur.

'No, really, Arthur, I must go home, because she

was dining with Stephen to-night, and goodness knows how late she'll stay if I leave them alone together. And besides, I'm getting cold. Aren't you?'

'Not a bit,' said Arthur. 'Have another drink.'

He divided between them what was left in the bottle. It gave them no more than a tablespoonful apiece, and they drank it without delay. Arthur, with a sudden access of high spirits, lifted his face to the refulgent sky and began to sing:

'The moon has raised her lamp above,
To light the way to thee, my love,
To li — ight the wa — y
To the — ee my lo — ove!'

'Hush!' cried Wilfrid. 'Hush, Arthur, hush! You'll wake Daisy, if you're not careful.'

'Poof!' said Arthur. 'Pish-posh-poof!' But he put away the bottles and glasses, and carefully replacing the slab of stone, arranged a negligent fringe of climbing plants across it.

'I really must go,' said Wilfrid nervously.

'This way, then,' said Arthur, and started to scramble up the rockery. His hand encountered a cushion of moss and one or two surviving flowers. He pulled one, and held it up to the moon. 'Edelweiss,' he said happily, and began to yodel.

'Oh, *do* be quiet,' cried Wilfrid.

'Tirra-lye-eee-ooh!' shrilled Arthur, and with miraculous dexterity leapt from rock to rock and came down safely on the other side, caught Wilfrid's arm, and ran with him across the lawn. The lower part of the house was in darkness, for Katherine had long since gone home, and Daisy had retired to bed. Wilfrid led his host to the front door and begged him to be careful as he went upstairs.

'That's all right,' said Arthur, 'trust an old campaigner. I'm sleeping in my own room now, so there's not the slightest, smallest possible danger. And don't you worry about Stephen. Remember that Nature's centrifugal: it's just as centrifugal as my hat.' And with a magnificent gesture Arthur threw his bowler hat high into the tall naked branches of a tree, and before Wilfrid could protest he had flung open the door and gone noisily into the house.

Wilfrid hesitated. He would have liked to retrieve Arthur's hat for him. But the beech tree was tall, and its smooth trunk felt so icy cold that he abandoned the thought of climbing it. Reluctantly he closed the gate behind him — among the thin branches the bowler hat was black against the moon — and hurrying now, for he was colder than ever, he trotted up Hornbeam Lane towards the Ridge. He was quite sober, for in addition to owning a harder head than Arthur's, he had drunk less, a lot less, and his preoccupation with the threat to Stephen's happiness had sensibly diminished the exhilarating effect of the gin. He felt rather breathless when he reached the Ridge road, but still he hurried, for he was anxious to get home and drive Bolivia away.

BOLIVIA had shown considerable resource and a most admirable self-discipline in the wooing of Stephen. Nothing had been said or done that was likely to alarm him. She had not repeated the impulsive embrace with which she had bade him good night after the dinner-party *à trois*, but a week or so later she had kissed him, coolly and casually, on the cheek, and having accustomed him to this non-committal salute by a seemingly careless repetition of it, she had ultimately been rewarded by his regular expectation of it, his apparent enjoyment of it, and even by reciprocation. Habit, however, had not yet succeeded in transforming the salute into a caress: Bolivia was too cautious to put any warmth into it, and Stephen had no wish to: and the Cytherean bark was temporarily in irons.

It was sadly ironical that Bolivia's able prosecution of the wooing had brought it to a deadlock, but that, for the moment, was the situation. Her initial aim had been to make Stephen feel at ease in her presence, and by avoiding all mention or even thought of marriage, to persuade him to accept her as a friend; and she was in danger of succeeding too well, for he was on the point of settling down into a permanent state of loquacious and quite unfruitful *camaraderie*. He was delighted to have a new companion — for he was poor in friends — and especially such a one as Bolivia: she was a woman, and therefore in several ways more agreeable to talk to than a man; but taking no advantage of her sex she did nothing to remind him of it, and she found manifest pleasure in his conversation. Stephen was delighted with this enrichment of his life, and well he might be: for Bolivia, having heard that nothing pleased a man so much as permission to talk about himself, had encouraged him in this delightful course, and Stephen had responded with a ceaseless torrent of egotism. But to Bolivia's surprise and disappointment he had discussed his thoughts rather than his feelings, his plans and his visioning rather than his sentiment and emotion. It is true that he had complained of the drudgery of his work and the inconvenience of not having as much money as he wanted; but he had never displayed the loneliness of his heart and asked for comfort, as she had hoped. He had told her at great length what he would do if he were the Prime Minister, or Sir Henry Wood, or Sir John Reith, or the Archbishop of Canterbury, or Mr. Cochran; but he had never told her what he would do if he were to think of looking for a wife. His conversation, indeed, in spite of the I's with which it was studded, had never been intimate. Though Bolivia had given him every opportunity, they had never enjoyed what she could think of as a really cosy chat. His talk, like that of so many men, was simply a profitless discussion; it led, perhaps, to some vague theoretical conclusion, but that was no use to a girl. He merely played Narcissus over a pool of various speculation, while Bolivia was supposed to peep over his shoulder and look at the refraction of his image in these watery postulates. And she was getting very worried by so much waste of time.

With Daisy and Katherine both announcing, in their own way, the ripening of their hopes, there was indeed no time to lose if she and Stephen were also to make a bid for the Major's money. But how to persuade him to leap, without looking, the fence between friendship and love, was a problem that threatened to defeat her. One false move, or overt warmth, and Stephen would bolt like a rabbit; and without a move of some kind, without warmth enkindled by some device, he would sit where he was and talk, simply talk, for ever and ever. The horns of a dilemma can seldom have been so sharp to impale and so fish-hooked to retain.

On this evening, when Arthur and Wilfrid were seeking distraction between *The Dover Road* and the rockery, Bolivia went to dine with Stephen in a mood not far from despair. It was not by any means the first time she had dined at Mulberry Acre, and Mrs. Barrow was almost as perturbed by the frequency of her visits as Bolivia was by their fruitlessness: for Mrs. Barrow knew too well that the perfect comfort of Stephen's bachelor establishment would never survive under the tiresome discipline of a fellow-woman. Only her professional integrity prevented her from deliberately spoiling the dinners she cooked for Bolivia, and not even that could persuade her to prepare her choicer dishes on such occasions. Leg of mutton and an apple charlotte was the best that Bolivia ever got from Mrs. Barrow.

During dinner Stephen had been more tedious than usual, for he had been talking about poetry in general and the later work of Ezra Pound in particular, and try as she would Bolivia could find little interest in the former and no sense in the latter: for it seemed to her like a jig-saw puzzle before the pieces had been arranged. And when she asked Stephen what certain of the Cantos meant, he told her that that was hardly a fair question, poetry being what it is; but she could take it that each of the Cantos was the expression of a significant emotion.

'What emotion?' asked Bolivia.

'The emotion expressed by the poem,' answered Stephen.

'And what does it signify?'

'Pound's response to the emotion, of course.'

Deep melancholy settled upon Bolivia, and for a moment she thought spitefully that if this were a true sample of Stephen's mind, then not even seventy thousand pounds would compensate her for having to live with him; but that thought passed, and was replaced by distrust of her own mental ability, for her intellect had often been derided at school, and she came to the unhappy conclusion that she wasn't good enough for him; and then the stubborn soldierly spirit she had inherited from her father ousted that ignoble doubt, and she determined to marry him yet, by hook or by crook.

Stephen at last observed her sorrowful inattention, and asked if anything was troubling her. Bolivia, with sudden resolution, determined to employ a ruse she had previously elaborated. She had devised a story that would, she thought, raise his amorous temperature by means of jealousy. She was alternately proud of the device, and ashamed of it. But for good or ill she made up her mind to use it.

'Yes,' she answered, 'I'm very worried by a letter I got this morning. Did you ever meet a man called Smith?'

'Frequently,' said Stephen.

'I mean a man who came to Lammiter about two years ago, and tried to make love to me?'

'No, not that one.'

'Well, he's just written to say he's coming back, and he wants to see me again. I'm rather frightened, Stephen.'

'Of what?'

Bolivia flushed. She realized that she wasn't flying her kite very skilfully. The tone of her voice should have told Stephen of what she was frightened, and roused in him the reaction of jealousy and the male's protective instinct. But her voice had remained disappointingly matter-of-fact; there had been no reaction; and now she must make her fear of Mr. Smith embarrassingly explicit. She made a brave attempt.

'I couldn't tell anyone else,' she said, 'but you're clever enough to understand and sympathetic enough to — well, to sympathize. He's extraordinarily good-looking, Stephen, and he's very attractive to women. Not only to me, but to nearly every woman he meets. He's that kind of man. I had just sufficient strength of mind to say no, when he came here two years ago, and I hope I'll have as much sense and determination this time.'

'Does he want to marry you?'

'No. He's married already.'

'I see.'

Stephen concealed his emotion. At all times he had a fastidious distaste for the Casanova *motif* in conversation, and he was not only displeased by Bolivia's introduction of it, but genuinely upset to think she was subject to womanly frailty. He saw no reason to doubt her story: fearing and disliking passion, he was the more ready to believe in its existence: he was credulous of the world's vice, as a Fascist of Communist plots. And he was shocked by the thought of Bolivia's weakness, as selfish and sentimental people may be shocked by the sight of a poor child weeping with cold and starvation; or an old blind beggar in the rain; or an ill-used horse. He grieved also for the hurt to their friendship, that had been so calm and platonic, and now was bruised by man's attack. He leaned back in his chair by the fire, and joined the tips of his fingers, and contemplated them, and tried to be calm.

'You can refuse to see him, I suppose,' he suggested.

'But don't you understand that I *want* to see him? It's foolish, I know, but I can't help it.'

Stephen rose from his chair and walked to the other side of the room. He took a book from the shelves, and put it back again. He was profoundly disturbed. With his back to Bolivia he said, in a voice that was meant to be casual, 'Tell me more about him.'

Bolivia's power of invention was slight, and because she disliked telling lies she already half-regretted her introduction of the fictitious Mr. Smith. She embarked upon the description of his physical, mental, and social attributes with marked reluctance, and stumbled unhappily from an outline of his nose to a platitudinous encomium of his charm of manner. But Stephen's critical faculty had been temporarily destroyed, and her hesitation and lack of conviction seemed to him the natural embarrassment of a girl in her position. He returned to his chair and listened without comment until her halting recital came to an end. And still he said nothing.

Bolivia waited anxiously. Her conscience was troubling her, and she was shame-faced till she saw if her strategy were successful.

'I sympathize with you,' said Stephen at length.

Bolivia's hope revived. If he truly sympathized, if he were moved to a natural jealousy, or even to a human dog-in-the-mangerism, then all would be well. 'Stephen!' she murmured. But Stephen ignored her.

'I sympathize with you,' he said wearily, 'because I have had the same sort of experience myself. It was in Florence. I'd been living there for several months. You know Florence?'

'No, I don't,' said Bolivia angrily.

'At least you know the obvious difference between the Venetian and Florentine schools of painting? One is wordly and magnificent, and the other is spiritual and splendid. On the west side of the Uffizi you can see the overfed Venus of Titian, and on the east the exquisitely reluctant Venus of Botticelli: you remember the rhyme:

"He painted Venus on an oyster,
With little waves that should be moister" '?

'Never heard it before,' said Bolivia.

Stephen continued: 'It seemed to me that Botticelli, by showing Venus obviously reluctant to come to earth, had given her an unusually interesting interpretation, and I began work on a poem that was going to justify and popularize his conception. On the other side of the medal was the Titian Venus, which in my opinion is simply a travesty of Love. Now it's rather curious that by moving a little to one side of the Botticelli Venus you can see, in the next room, Leonardo's Annunciation, and Leonardo's Angel will give you the clue to Venus's reluctance. The Angel has a purely intellectual interest in his message: a passionately intellectual interest: he understands the whole consequence of Christianity in the very moment of annunciation: there's nothing sentimental in his message: it's simply the first caption in a syllabus of the modern world. And now you see why Venus is so unwilling to come ashore.'

'No, I don't,' said Bolivia.

'Because she realizes that she is out of date and a hindrance to civilization. The modern world is an intellectual conception, and Love is hostile and destructive to the intelligence. The tragedy of Love is that she is waved ashore, and beckoned ashore, and pulled ashore, against her will; and that was the thesis of my poem. It was going to be a long poem, with a good many references to other pictures in the Uffizi, and I was working very hard on the first canto when I met a girl called Giulia — well, it doesn't matter what her name was.'

Bolivia showed rather more interest in the narrative. This, she remembered, was the girl of whom Jane had spoken: the girl who had bitten Stephen's ear.

Stephen said slowly, 'I suppose she attracted me almost in the same way as this man Smith attracts you. I fought against the influence, and I was very unhappy about it. It interfered with my work, you see. But I wasn't sufficiently determined — I didn't want to hurt her feelings — and one day I agreed to go out with her.'

'Yes?' said Bolivia.

'I can't tell you what happened,' said Stephen, 'except that she took advantage of her position and behaved abominably. There was a very painful scene, typical, I imagine, of what generally happens when one gives way to a desire for vulgar pleasure. I was thoroughly upset, and my poem, with its vision of an intellectual world and Venus retiring to a nunnery — for that was to be the last canto — simply went to pieces. But I learnt a useful lesson, and I've never been tempted to repeat my folly.'

Stephen's version of the story came to a feeble conclusion compared with Jane's, thought Bolivia, and she was partially consoled for her fabrication of Mr. Smith by Stephen's suppression of some relevant details in the anecdote about Giulia. He had said nothing of his indulgence in the Florentine habit of bottom-pinching. Bolivia was tempted to ask if he had enjoyed it, but she wisely refrained, and took the better course of sympathy. She made some apt remarks on the pain of disillusionment, and implied, as a consequence of Stephen's warning example, her half-framed intention of rebuffing Mr. Smith. Stephen grew more cheerful. His confession, incomplete though it was, had established a certain intimacy between them, as though he had undone his waistcoat buttons, and Bolivia's demi-promise to nonsuit the libertine Smith made him grateful to her. He stood beside her and patted her arm. Bolivia's heart beat quicker and her shoulders made a confiding movement towards him.

'I like the cut of that dress,' he said, 'but I don't think dark blue is really your colour.'

Bolivia came to the end of her tether. 'I give it up!' she exclaimed, and stood up to mark her words. 'I'm sick and tired of the whole business!'

Stephen, who had no clue to the meaning other than his last remark, thought she referred to the difficulty of looking well-dressed. They had discussed the problem on an earlier occasion.

'You really must let me take you in hand,' he said gaily. 'You remember we talked about clothes once before? Well, the very next day I found exactly what I wanted, in a book on theatrical costumes, and I quite forgot to tell you about it. It was a design by Inigo Jones.'

Stephen, busy at once, went to the bookshelves, and maintaining as he searched a series of encouraging remarks, presently found what he wanted. 'Here it is,' he said, and opened a large volume at a fac-simile of Inigo's design for Thomyris in Ben Jonson's *Masque of Queens*.

'Now don't you agree?' he asked. 'You'd look absolutely superb in a dress like that, and as a matter of fact I've got a piece of velvet upstairs that would be the very thing to make it. Wilfrid and I bought it for curtains, but we never used it, and it's still in his wardrobe. I'll go and get it, and let you see it.'

Stephen was now in his happiest domestic mood, but Bolivia retained an appearance of comparative equanimity only because she could not decide which of several violent things she really wanted to do first. She was almost equally ready to weep with disappointment, or to swear tempestuously with rage; to tell Stephen to go to hell, or to plead with him to be sensible and marry her on the spot; to leave the house in high dudgeon, or stubbornly declare her intention of never leaving it. Immobilized by these contrary desires she stayed where she was till Stephen returned.

He came back carrying a roll of yellow chiffon velvet, opulently patterned.

'Isn't it lovely?' he asked. 'And it would simply fall into the shape of that Thomyris costume. It's soft enough to be folded and pulled about, and heavy enough to hang in really handsome lines. Hold it up and see for yourself. Now wouldn't that look splendid? If I had a few pins I could fix it up in no time.'

'Go and find some,' said Bolivia.

'It would be rather fun to see what we could

171

make of it,' said Stephen agreeably, and went on his errand.

Bolivia threw down the velvet. She caught a glimpse of her reflexion in a mirror; her cheeks were flushed and her eyes were shining. 'It's the last chance, it's my only hope,' she muttered, and began to unfasten her frock. She undressed rapidly and pulled a big easy chair in front of the fire. When she sat in it she was hidden from all the rest of the room. Stephen returned.

'I've got lots of them,' he said, closing the door behind him. 'I found a whole packet in Wilfrid's room. Are you feeling cold, Bolivia?'

'No, I'm very comfortable,' she answered from her hiding-place.

Stephen came towards the fire. *'Bolivia!'* he exclaimed, and stood with trembling knees and misty eyes. For one terrible moment he had thought she was naked, and even now, after perceiving that she still wore a garment of some sort, he was so horror-struck that he could not move. Bolivia, despite her tall and muscular frame, suffered from defective circulation and consequently the cold, and in winter she always wore good sensible combinations. Her resolution had fallen short of taking these off, and she was, to be accurate, more fully clothed than young women who go bathing from a public beach. But a costume that calls for no comment on a beach may excite considerable surprise in a drawing-room, and Stephen's constitution, being less robust than some, received a shock more staggering than that administered by the story of the libertine Smith.

'Have you gone mad?' he asked in a strained and husky voice.

Bolivia looked surprised. 'You want to drape that velvet on me, don't you?' she asked. 'You couldn't do it on top of my dress, so I took it off.'

'There was no need to make an indecent exhibition of yourself,' cried Stephen.

'Silly Stephen!' said Bolivia. 'I'm not indecent. I look rather nice, I think.'

She stood up, smiling, and put her hands behind her. She was, indeed, a very handsome young woman.

'Sit down,' begged Stephen. 'Sit down, Bolivia. No, don't come near me. I won't have it. I don't want you to come near me. Go away!'

He retreated towards the window, and Bolivia, picking up the loosened roll of velvet, followed him.

'Come and show me how to wear it,' she said.

'I'll do nothing of the sort till you put more clothes on,' said Stephen, and nervously bit his lips, and clutched his hands together, and still retreated to the window.

'Silly Stephen!' Bolivia repeated. 'Nobody's going to hurt you!' And with a quick swirl of the yellow velvet she threw it over him in a great loop, and began to pull him towards her. Stephen gibbered with fright, and Bolivia made little soothing noises to him.

He was saved from whatever fate awaited him by a sudden catcall, a piercing sound muted only by the thickness of the window-panes. Startled, they turned towards it and saw for a second two jeering faces pressed against the glass. Then the faces disappeared, and Stephen realized that the situation, horrible enough before, had now acquired a new and far-reaching element of horror.

'You've ruined me!' he cried. 'They'll tell everyone in Lammiter what they've seen, and my reputation will be ruined, irretrievably ruined. They may blackmail me, they'll write beastly letters to me, they'll make my life a misery!'

Bolivia wrapt herself in the lovely velvet. 'You'd better go and see if they're still in the garden,' she said.

Stephen hesitated only for a moment, and hurried to the door. He took a heavy walking-stick and searched the moonlit garden, but found no one there. The Peeping Toms had fled.

When he came back Bolivia was dressing herself, and Stephen shuddered again, for the casual intimacy of her movements menaced his security. She stepped into her knickers without embarrassment, with the demeanour indeed of being well used to his presence at her toilet. She put her head into a silk slip, she thrust up her arms, she patted and pulled and wriggled it into place with an air of appalling familiarity. She put on the dress, and pulled it, and smoothed it, and stroked it till it hung properly. She took a comb from her bag, and turning to the mirror she leisurely arranged her hair. There was in her activity a careless acceptance of the situation. She seemed to be at home and at ease. They might have been married for years.

'Did you see anybody?' she asked.

'No,' said Stephen dully. His spirit was bruised and beaten. The inertia of defeat lay upon him. He sank into a chair and felt for his bottle of bismuth tablets.

'I suppose you recognized them,' said Bolivia.

'No,' said Stephen again.

'I did,' said Bolivia. 'One of them was Ling, and the other was Hopkins. Ling works at the garage we use, and father thinks a lot of him because he's in the Territorials. And Hopkins does odd jobs in the garden for Miss Montgomery. If they dare to talk, they can tell their story to a lot of people who'll be interested in it.'

'O my God,' said Stephen with a groan. 'I'll be ruined, utterly ruined.'

'That will be my privilege,' said Bolivia. 'I'll suffer more than you will.'

'But it was your fault! It was all due to your beastly behaviour. Good heavens, you come to dinner with me, and then you insist on undressing, and . . .'

'Nonsense. It was you who asked me to dinner, knowing we should be alone, and then gave me too much to drink. . . .'

'I didn't! I wouldn't dream of doing such a thing!'

'No, but that's the story that'll be told. And God only knows what my father will say to it.'

Stephen bowed his head and groaned again.

'There's only one thing to be done!' said Bolivia.

'What's that?'

'If you want to prevent scandal, if you want to

protect my name as well as your own, if you want to
avoid trouble of a different kind — well, father has a
terribly hasty temper. . . .'

'Oh, I'll do anything I can!'

'Then you must announce our engagement
immediately, and we can get married next month.'

'B-b-b-but, but — but,' stammered Stephen.

'It's the only way,' said Bolivia deliberately, and
came to his chair and sat upon the arm of it. She
smoothed his hair and kissed his forehead and held
him when he tried to escape. 'It won't be so bad as
you think,' she said. 'I'm very fond of you, Stephen,
and I'll do everything I can to make you happy. I'll
tell father as soon as I get home, and I know he'll
be pleased, because he's had a very high opinion of
you ever since you talked to him about the next war.
He'll be on our side, Stephen, so don't worry about
that. And now I must get my coat and go home.
Don't bother, I know where it is.'

Stephen sat inert and stunned. When Bolivia
returned he looked at her with meek beseeching.
She bent and kissed him good night. 'I'll be a good
wife to you,' she promised, and went briskly out to
her car. Stephen sat motionless in his chair.

He was still there when Wilfrid came home.
'Bolivia's gone, has she?' asked Wilfrid happily.

'Yes,' said Stephen.

'Oh, I'm so glad! I was afraid she would still be
here, and I've got the most marvellous story to tell
you, about Arthur. He talked so nicely to me for a
long time, about all sorts of things, and then, my
dear, he started to yodel! We were sitting by the

rockery, and suddenly he pretended to be in the Alps and *yodelled*! — Why, Stephen, what's the matter?'

Wilfrid's light-hearted chattering came to a halt, and he looked with dismay at Stephen's face of silent misery.

'Oh, what's the matter?' he cried again. 'Aren't you feeling well?'

'I'm all right,' said Stephen.

'You're not, you're looking dreadful. Stephen! Is it anything to do with Bolivia?'

There was a short and heavy silence. 'We're going to be married,' said Stephen.

'Oh, *Stephen*!' cried Wilfrid, and fell on his knees before him. 'What a *dreadful* thing to have happened!'

THE news of Bolivia's engagement was warmly welcomed by the busybodies and amiable gossips of Lammiter. Not all approved of her exploit, which was generally understood to have been Amazonian work, or a Sabine rape gone topsy-turvy, but none would have wished her campaign to end otherwise, for its successful conclusion gave their conversation a lot of fine lush pasture. There was a great deal of speculation as to the part that love had played in the making of the match, and more debate about the influence exerted by hopes of gain: the sentimental-ists were staunch but few, the cynics were numerous and dogmatic. It was generally agreed that Stephen and Bolivia were, on the surface at least, ill-suited to each other: but everyone knew of a dozen matri-monial alliances in which apparent antipathies — he the chalk, and she the cheese — had succeeded in living together for a long period of years in seeming contentment: so by the majority their contrariety was discounted. Flippant young women would wonder, with a smirk and a titter, how Stephen had phrased his declaration, while their elders excogi-tated with wise instance the problems of how and in what state and comfort the young couple might expect to live. Many old ladies were preoccupied with Wilfrid's future, and thought a grave injustice had been done to him.

Fortunately for everybody the Peeping Toms,

Hopkins and Ling, had been dissuaded from describing their garden view except to a few vulgar friends in their own walk of life, by whom it was received with improper pleasure but not wholly believed. Bolivia had confronted Ling in the garage where he worked, Hopkins in Miss Montgomery's garden, and said to each in turn, 'I'm half-inclined to give you a damned good horse-whipping, and if I hear of your making yourself a nuisance again, I shall!' So menacing had been her aspect, and her size and strength so obviously sufficient to fulfil such a threat, that Ling and Hopkins had been effectively frightened, and they had not spread their story in circles where it could do any damage. Gossip, therefore, was happily not complicated by scandal.

The effect of the news on Stephen's relations was comparatively simple: Arthur was amazed, Daisy was angry in a lofty and acidulous way, Katherine was contemptuous, Jane was delighted, and Hilary was minded to laugh, and disposed to be worried, and inclined to hope that marriage would do Stephen good. Jane, having heard the news on the morning after Stephen's fall, brought it to Rumneys in time for lunch, and Hilary, far as she was from being spiteful, could not resist the temptation to bait Katherine about this unexpected extension, or presumptive extension, of competitive progeniture.

'This changes the whole situation,' she said. 'And what a joke if it turns out to be Stephen who inherits John's money!'

'I don't see the joke,' said Katherine coldly, 'and in any case he hasn't a chance.'

'One can never tell,' said Hilary. 'There are two years to go.'

Katherine corrected her: 'A year and ten months.'

'Well, a year and ten months. A lot can happen in that time.'

'He can't possibly have more than two, and I'll have two by May.'

'Bolivia comes of very prolific stock,' said Hilary. 'Her father had seven brothers and three sisters.'

'That makes no difference,' said Katherine. 'She can't have more than two children in less than two years.'

'The General was a twin, wasn't he?' asked Jane.

Katherine put down her fork. 'I don't believe you!' she exclaimed.

'It's perfectly true,' said Hilary. 'His brother, the other twin, died of dysentery in South Africa. John met him there.'

'Anyway,' said Katherine defiantly, 'a casual twin means nothing at all. But in Oliver's family they're a regular occurrence. The Clementses expect to have twins: it's the normal thing for them to do.'

'Butter, please,' said Jane, and looked at Katherine with a wicked smile. 'Don't you think there's something suspicious about the suddenness of their engagement?' she asked. 'Nobody expected it. It was announced without any warning, and Bolivia says they're going to get married next month.'

'They don't want to lose time,' said Katherine.

'Perhaps they can't afford to.'

Hilary and Katherine protested together, Hilary

because she disliked the suggestion, Katherine because she was startled by it.

'All right,' said Jane, lavishly cutting cheese, 'I may be wrong, but personally I think there's something fishy about the whole business. And if I'm right, you haven't such a long start as you imagine.'

For ten minutes after the throwing of this mayfly of innuendo, the spreading of this birdlime for suspicion, there was argument that would have been meat and drink to a moralist. For Katherine showed, too clearly, her share of mankind's credulity of evil, that betokens not so much a kindred evil in the listener as a fearful cognizance of the frailty of our barricades of virtue; and Jane, fabricating details, displayed a feature, a nose as it were, of the anti-social nature of art that has troubled all clear thinkers from Plato to Lenin; but Hilary, after reproving Jane for improper invention, and Katherine for believing it, left them at the table and went about her household business so calmly and happily intent upon immediate tasks that the moralist, dubious before of humanity's sufficient ballast, would have recognized in her such a bottom of decency and good sense as would restore, for an hour at least, his failing confidence: for moralists before all others require constant reassurance.

Katherine, however, was worried for several days. Her reason bade her disbelieve Jane's suggestion, but something below reason, something base but more largely basic, repeatedly whispered that you never knew, you never could tell; even a man so latently caprine as Stephen, a respectable golfer like

Bolivia, had the power to surprise and to shock. Obsessed by this anxiety she refrained, for several days, from talking about her prospective children, and spent a lot of time in dividing, upon small pieces of paper, a varying number of calendar months by the normal period of gestation.

The probable effect of Stephen's engagement upon what had come to be known as the Nursery Stakes was, of course, its principal claim to interest. The tea-parties in Lammiter West might, and did, discuss its minor aspects with relish: what did the General say? — Bolivia was a little older than Stephen, wasn't she? — the ring was plain but good — matters of that sort: but all this was preliminary to a concluding movement whose theme, ever the same though infinitely varied, was the Ganders' ability to reproduce their kind with profitable speed. All winter that was the dominating topic. Wherever ladies met in twos or threes, at their morning coffee, in Lammiter High Street, on the golf-course, in tram-cars, at the hairdresser's, at the dressmaker's, at a wedding, at the Brackenshire Ladies' Club, at a bridge-party, at the florist's in Green Street, at the theatre, at the new picture-house, at a popular lecture or a political rally, conversation turned inevitably to the Nursery Stakes, to stable gossip and the question of form: nor was it ladies only who were interested, for the qualities of the several runners were discussed with almost equal knowledge and regularity by gentlemen over their morning sherry, in the golf-club, in the Conservative Club, in the Yeomanry Club, at the hairdresser's, at the

Turkish baths, at the Racquets Club, in tram-cars and in motor-cars, at the tobacconist's, at the Green Dragon and the Red Lion, and in many other places. In the winter of that year was April indeed astir, and beneath skies that bore grey galleons of snow, and trundled athwart the zenith Aquarius' slopping water-carts, all Lammiter was ceaselessly aware of the germination of green buds and counted on curious fingers their possible distribution.

But though the topic was debated in many localities and divers situations, it was at tea-parties that its plenitude was properly honoured. There, with a clear fire to warm the air, and Miss Montgomery's baton to order the statement, the enlargement, the variations, and the conclusion of the theme, the theme was fully orchestrated. The muted violin of a spinster's tone most delicately revolved the proem, and out of consciousness cried a faint trumpet 'Spring! Spring! Spring!' Talk spread rapidly, fiddles and second fiddles argued backwards and forwards, and on the branches of their bows a bird called 'Spring!' Now with a broad chuckle laughed a bassoon, 'Who, who who?' and 'When, oh, when?' Swift counterpoint debated Arthur and Katherine, Daisy and Stephen, and a faint far-off drum, with hollow mockery, asked where was George, who drank and was driven from home. '*Boom!*' said the drums, 'in Africa! *Bang!*' said the drums, 'in India! *Bump!*' said the drums, 'in America! And it's not very like,' said the drums, 'that he'll come back in time for a christening now, from India, Africa, or even from America. Bang-bang!' said the drums.

And the silver chattering of spoons on porcelain, tuned like a xylophone, prattled of twins and tattled of triplets, and an aged instrument, whose name no one could remember, solemnly chanted:

> 'No thyng ys to man so dere
> As wommanys love in gode manere.'

But a flute, wheezing a little, like Juliet's nurse, whispered, 'Susan and she — God rest all Christian souls! — were of an age;' and then took heart, and turned merry as a blackbird, and cried 'I cannot choose but laugh!' So laughter called to the wood-winds and the brass, and they puffed a dozen jests into the air of skirts too short in front, and cuckoos in the nest, and horns for husbands, and the like. But the silver trumpets sang:

> 'Blow, northern wind,
> Send thou me my sweeting,'

and a pizzicato, like the pin-prick pattern of April rain, softened all hearts and all desired that Daisy and Katherine and Bolivia should have twenty pink-bottomed babies apiece, a festoon of them, wreaths of them, troops of them, with no thought of prizes but simply to match May and fulfil the turning of the year. The triumph of all who'd begotten, and the travail of all who'd borne, were as warp and weft in their lot, and flute and fiddle, brass and drum, would join in a great cry, 'Ripeness is all!'

Such, without making any more to-do about it, was the temper and thought and talk of Lammiter tea-parties that winter.

With matter of this kind to fill their minds it was natural, though perhaps unfair, that the Vicar's accident should receive less sympathy and attention than otherwise it would have commanded. It was, however, an accident serious in itself and charged with more serious consequences.

After returning from his Mediterranean voyage the Vicar had made a brave attempt to resume not only his duties but a normal course of existence. He was handicapped by grief that still weighed upon him like the after-effects of concussion, and even, at times, enwrapped him like a fog, in whose gloomy light he appeared half-blind to the outer world; but he did his best to overcome the enervating effect of bereavement, and performed his parochial duties with the somewhat distracted air of a man who, though absent-minded, is eager to oblige. In November, being partly persuaded thereto by Hilary, he resolved that fox-hunting would be good for him, and though his new poverty imperatively declared he must dispose of the stable he had previously maintained, and indeed compelled him to sell three-fourths of it, he kept a hard, ewe-necked, short-legged brown gelding which, though not handsome, was able to get through the mud and do a long day.

Neither the Vicar nor the horse could be blamed for what happened. They enjoyed several days of moderate sport and one superlative four-mile point over the best of the Lammiter country, after which the Vicar, greatly cheered, preached so rousing a sermon from a text in the Book of Kings —

'The dogs shall eat Jezebel by the walls of Jezreel' —
that Sir Gervase excitedly muttered 'Get along
forrad!' in the middle of it, as though he were
hunting the Lord's hounds himself; and everyone
believed the Vicar to have made a complete re-
covery. But on the following Wednesday, in pursuit
of a dog-fox that obligingly and immediately quitted
woodland for cow-pasture, the Vicar, well to the
front, jumped a rough fence, and the good brown
gelding landed disastrously on the stump of a
willow-tree. The Vicar was picked up unconscious,
with a couple of cracked ribs and a fractured femur.

In the nursing home where he lay for seven weeks,
his most regular visitor was Hilary. She was the
first to call on him after the operation for reduction
of the fracture: he lay with a look of bewilderment
and three days' growth of reddish beard on his face.
His injured leg, elaborately tied to a black steel
splint that protruded from the foot of the bed,
endured the drag of a huge lead weight which prevented the distal part of the broken bone from over-
riding the proximal end. A cage, over which the
blankets made a kind of wigwam, covered his lower
limbs. The room was bare and heartlessly clean. A
tumbler and a jug of barley-water stood on a bedside
table.

'My poor Lionel!' said Hilary. 'It must be torture
to lie like that!'

'Torture,' repeated the Vicar, 'simply torture.
And why, Hilary, why!'

'But it might have been worse,' said Hilary.
'Thank heaven you weren't killed.'

'I don't understand it,' said the Vicar. 'I've suffered so much already. Caroline's death was more than I thought I could bear, and now this happens. There was no reason for it, no reason whatever.'

'Anyone's liable to fall off a horse.'

'Yes, but why should I be the one? It's so unfair. Caroline's death was unfair. I relied on her for so many things, and her death crippled me. And now I'm crippled again.'

'You'll get better,' said Hilary comfortingly. 'Do what the doctor tells you to do, try not to worry, and you'll be all right in a few weeks' time.'

'But don't you see the unfairness of it?'

'Of course I do. But grown-up people can't afford to grumble simply because life isn't fair to them. Well, I must go now, because the nurse said I wasn't to stay more than two or three minutes, but I'll come back to-morrow, and I expect you'll be feeling more comfortable then. Good-bye, Lionel, and whatever you do, don't worry about yourself.'

'Do you think I'm under a curse?' asked the Vicar.

'I never heard such nonsense,' Hilary replied, and paused to smooth his sheets before she left him.

On the following afternoon she returned and found him flushed by a high temperature. He had been shaved, and his eyes were bright. Despite his cramped and comfortless position he looked remarkably handsome; but he soon began to talk in a feverish and foolish style. He complained once more about the iniquity of being singled out for injury from among a whole field of fox-hunters, and when

Hilary reproved him for his childishness, kindly but firmly, he hotly exclaimed, 'How should man be just with God?'

Hilary was surprised. It was not his habit to talk of God, except in the pulpit, and she experienced a certain embarrassment, as though at some indelicacy, when she heard him mention his Creator without the appropriate ritual and vestments.

'Your pillow's very crumpled,' she said, 'let me straighten it for you.'

The Vicar thrust out a restraining hand. 'I will not refrain my mouth; I will speak in the anguish of my spirit; I will complain in the bitterness of my soul,' he shouted.

Hilary grew rather frightened. She looked for a thermometer, but the nurse had removed it.

'Am I a sea, or a whale, that thou settest a watch over me?' demanded the Vicar in a voice that was hoarse and wild.

'Really, Lionel, you mustn't excite yourself like that,' said Hilary. 'If you lie quietly and take things easily you'll get better very quickly; but if you worry about trifles . . .'

'Who ever perished, being innocent?' cried the Vicar.

'Now do be sensible, please.'

The compulsive tone of her voice had a brief effect. The Vicar lay motionless and silent for half a minute. Then a frown corrugated his forehead, his head moved recklessly on the pillow, and he muttered: 'I have sinned, I have sinned. If I were pure and upright He would make my habitation prosperous. The hypocrite's hope shall perish, he shall lean upon his house but it shall not stand.'

'What on earth are you talking about?' asked Hilary.

'My transgression is sealed up in a bag,' said the Vicar.

Hilary tiptoed to the door, but before she reached it, it opened and a nurse came in. She was a brisk, capable woman with percipient quick eyes and a hairy mole on her chin. She whispered to Hilary, 'It's all right, Miss Gander. I was listening outside, and I heard him getting restless. He's been upset all day. I think you'd better go now. I'll tidy him up and make him comfortable, and I expect he'll drop off and have a sleep then.'

Hilary waited in the corridor. Presently the nurse came out and closed the door firmly behind her and without apparent regard for the patient. She had a Bible in one hand.

'I took this away from him,' she said. 'He asked for it this morning, and Matron said he could have it, though I knew it wouldn't be good for him, in his state. He's been reading about Job all day. The very idea!'

'He's delirious, isn't he?' asked Hilary.

'No, not really. Job's gone to his head a bit, that's all. I remember the same sort of thing happened to me when I was training: I had to go into hospital with a floating kidney, and while I was there I borrowed a book on surgery from a medical student. Well, you'd never believe all the complications I had: cysts, and embolism, and congestion, and

double ureters, and Bright's disease, and I don't
know what all. And that's what's happened to Mr.
Purefoy: he thinks he's got everything that Job had.
Well, I'll never let a parson read the Bible again,
not in this nursing home.'

Hilary was partly reassured by the nurse's
confidence and her good sense, but while she was
walking home she could not help speculating about
the nature of the transgressions that apparently
burdened the Vicar's conscience. As it was impossible to believe he had committed any of the
major sins, she supposed he was thinking, with
morbid exaggeration, of some youthful peccadillo
of the kind that everyone is guilty of and has long
forgotten. Or perhaps he was beginning to reproach
himself for having lived so long on his wife's money.
Hilary herself had never thought the worse of him
for this, though some of her less amiable acquaintances did, but she realized that in his present condition, hotly fevered and recently bereaved, he
might well have discovered sentimental grounds for
remorse in a memory of past luxury.

His financial status was now deplorable. His
stipend was £450 a year, the Vicarage was large
and expensive to live in, and to educate six children
in a manner suitable to their ancestry — on the
distaff side — and to his position as a Churchman
and a fox-hunter, cost as much as might keep in
comfort a score of working-class families. The two
elder boys, Denis and Rupert, were at a highly
esteemed public school; Cecily had gone to a school
in Surrey that boasted a swimming-pool, a Greek

theatre, and six mistresses from Roedean; Patrick was at a small but expensive preparatory school a few miles from Lammiter; and Rosemary and Peter attended a suitable day-school for infants in Lammiter West. The aggregate of their annual fees for tuition and board was £1140, and though Denis and Rupert were both clever at travelling without a ticket, a considerable sum had to be added to that for train-fares, clothes, and holiday entertainment.

The Vicar had made no attempt to solve the problem of paying annual bills of £1140 out of a yearly stipend of £450. In the grief-stricken days that followed his wife's death he had said to all his friends, 'I am a beaten man', and left it at that. Such was the simplicity of his confession that it achieved the likeness of dignity. His grief, indubitable and obvious, had disarmed criticism. He had retired, for months, into a trance of sorrow; passivity had made him handsomer than ever. And in this seemingly helpless state he had seen re-enacted the miracle of the loaves and fishes: his brother-in-law, Lord Quentin Whicher, the quixotic financier, having rescued more than he expected from the wreckage of his lost company, had promised to pay for Denis and Rupert for at least a year; Hilary had offered to pay Cecily's fees; and the Duke of Starveling, on the strength of dreaming that he would win a prize in the Dublin Sweepstake, had sent a cheque for £100. The Vicar had accepted this manifestation of the expansive power of five loaves and a few small fishes with gratitude but no great surprise: it is likely that the majority of those present on the shores of the Sea of Galilee also failed to notice the miracle that had occurred.

The Duke damned and confounded his generosity as soon as the result of the Cambridgeshire was known. Lord Quentin also regretted his benevolence, for no sooner had he contracted to pay the boys' fees than a chance came to get in on the ground-floor of a new process for the mass production of gas-masks (civilian pattern) for daily use in the next war,·and he naturally wanted every penny he could lay hands on to invest in an enterprise so useful and, with good luck, so enormously profitable. Hilary alone remained well pleased with her one-sided bargain; she delighted to think that Cicely's education was proceeding out of her purse, and she began to budget for a blissful future in which Rosemary and Peter should also be dependent on her. She told herself that this care for Caroline's children was no more than she owed to the memory of her dead friend, but she had the grace to admit that she thoroughly enjoyed her piety. They were charming children, for they had inherited their father's looks and the enthusiastic vitality of their mother.

XI

WHILE the Vicar uncomfortably waited for his broken leg to mend, Stephen expected a union at least as painful. Pride compelled him to hide the apprehension that grew greater as marriage came nearer, but under a mask of equanimity there lay often terror and dismay. Fortunately for them both, Bolivia was so busily engaged in preparations for the wedding that she had little time for the show and practice of affection. Naturally she had said no word to Stephen of her basic motive in desiring to marry him, and no suspicion of such a motive had occurred to him: he knew that all young women most ardently desire to be married, and he knew that he was by no means unattractive: the terrible Giulia, indeed, had shown conclusively, by biting his ear in the Via Tosinghi, that he was almost indecently desirable. He had no need to search Bolivia for any motive deeper than that. Sometimes he tried to comfort himself by thinking he might now inherit the Major's fortune; but he could not persuade himself that this was really probable. He had never reconciled himself to the unfairness of his uncle's will, but he had long abandoned, in bitterness of soul, all hope of sharing in the estate; and even now, though marriage confronted his morning thoughts as closely and insistently as the nine o'clock postman, his imagination refused to conceive an ululation of infants in the decent quietness of Mulberry Acre. He would have been startled to the depths of his being had he known that Bolivia, having already decided to turn Wilfrid's room into a nursery, was consulting an architect about the possibility of cutting off part of the drawing-room to make a playroom.

Bolivia had already acquired a busy domestic look. She had almost given up golf, and her manner towards Stephen was a curious mixture of maternal solicitude, a little girl's pride in a new frock, healthy amativeness when she had time for it, and an elder sister's impatience with a schoolboy brother. They had a long argument about the rehabilitation of the principal bedroom which was typical of all their intercourse.

Bolivia disliked the steel and enamel furniture that suited Wilfrid and Stephen; and Stephen was repelled by the pale and massive suite that Bolivia desired. But Bolivia sensibly told him, 'A single bed isn't going to be much use to us now, is it?'

Stephen bit his lip, and fidgeted with his ring, and said querulously, 'We could have two single beds, I suppose.'

'You are a darling,' exclaimed Bolivia irrationally, and gave him a sudden hug and a loud cheerful kiss.

Stephen made a petulant gesture, as one who slaps at a mosquito.

'Now don't be silly,' said Bolivia.

'But we *could* have two,' Stephen repeated.

'We could have three, for that matter,' said Bolivia, 'but the fact remains that we don't need more than one. Now don't argue, dear, because I know more about this sort of thing than you do. I admit that you and Wilfrid have made the house very attractive to anyone who likes modern furniture, but it's not suitable for a married couple. You must allow me to know best in matters of this kind. I'm going to make you very comfortable, and we're both going to be tremendously happy. Now we'll just go down to the furniture shop to say that we'll take the suite, and then I want you to come to the Club and meet some old friends of mine. They've heard all about you and they're just dying to see you.'

'I can't go out this morning,' said Stephen irritably. 'I've got a great deal to do, and I can't neglect my work simply because I'm going to be married. It wouldn't be fair to Wilfrid, for one thing.'

'And it wouldn't be fair to me if you didn't come,' said Bolivia, kissing him again. 'Wilfrid won't mind doing a little extra work at a time like this, when he knows you're so busy. I'll go and speak to him, and tell him you won't be back till after lunch.'

Wilfrid was now a pathetic figure. He made brave attempts to conceal his unhappiness, and even to simulate a festive air, a jovial interest in the approaching nuptials: he bought Stephen a dove-grey wedding waistcoat of unusual design, and cuff-links for himself: but his heart was desolate, and the old ladies and the elderly ladies who had found him such a merry companion shook their heads over him, and some of them prophesied that he would go into a decline. Now, when Bolivia came into the room where he was working, he appeared very pale and small beside her. She wore a winter coat of tweed, whose rough material seemed to accentuate the hostile abundance of her figure; and Wilfrid, in a slim smooth suit of clouded blue, was looking his daintiest. He winced at the sight of her.

He listened silently while she explained that Stephen had important business to attend to, and acidly agreed that he could conduct, by himself, the affairs of the Mulberry School of Journalism and Story Writing until after lunch. He watched them pass the window, Stephen reluctant, Bolivia possessive and assured. 'Pig, beast, cow, bitch!' he cried. 'You fat cannibal, you horror, you creature!'

A few minutes later, while he was sniffing unhappily, and staring blindly at a story written by a young man in Birkenhead — who had been told to put more punch in his work — Mrs. Barrow came in with a cup of tea and a biscuit for him. 'Drink this, Mr. Wilfrid,' she said, 'and you'll feel all the better for it. I thought you might be a bit upset, with them going out together like that and leaving you all alone, and a cup of tea works wonders sometimes. I feel upset myself when I think what this house is going to be like with Miss Bolivia ruling it, and I for one will never be happy when I think of you having to go in lodgings to make room for her.'

Wilfrid drank his tea gratefully. 'This is just what I wanted,' he said. 'You're one of the cleverest and nicest people I've ever met, Mrs. Barrow, and goodness knows how I'll ever get on without you.'

'It was too good to last,' said Mrs. Barrow mournfully. 'We were that happy, just you and I and Mr. Stephen, it was like Paradise till she came and spoilt it all.'

Mrs. Barrow began to sniff, to grow red and watery, and it was Wilfrid's turn to play the comforter. 'There, there, Mrs. Barrow,' he said, 'we mustn't make ourselves *too* unhappy, because that would make Stephen unhappy, and he's miserable enough already, poor dear. This marriage isn't his fault, you know, and he's going to find things so terribly difficult that if we don't do all we can to help him he simply won't survive it.'

'She's a perfect cannibal,' said Mrs. Barrow.

'I know she is,' Wilfrid agreed, 'and that's why we've got to be very kind and good to poor Stephen, and never do anything to worry him.'

Mrs. Barrow regarded him with reverent affection. 'You're an angel, Mr. Wilfrid, that's what you are,' she said.

'Oh, what nonsense you talk!' cried Wilfrid. 'I'm not in the least bit like an angel!'

Mrs. Barrow seemed disposed to argue the point, but Wilfrid, happier now, took her by the shoulders and playfully pushed her out of the room, crying, 'Run along to your kitchen, Mrs. Barrow, because I've lots and lots of work to do, and if you don't make something extra specially lovely for lunch I'm going to be very *very* angry with you.'

Greatly cheered by sympathy and Mrs. Barrow's high opinion of him, he returned to his desk and quickly dealt with the young man from Birkenhead.

Then he wrote an encouraging letter to a typist in Wolverhampton who had composed, for Lesson III, a bright little article entitled 'Why I Am Romantic'; and, with less approval, criticized a pessimistic essay from an unemployed riveter on Tyneside, who had chosen the alternative exercise, 'Are We Really Civilized?' 'You will never be able to sell work of this description,' he wrote. 'To be successful you must be cheerful. No editor will buy a gloomy, morbid article when he has the chance of printing something bright, joyous, optimistic, and, of course, well-written. Your vocabulary is good, and so is your power of description, but you will have to avoid a tendency to pessimism if you want to make literature profitable.'

Meanwhile Stephen and Bolivia, having bought the sinister double bed and various other articles of furniture, went to the Brackenshire Ladies' Club and ate lunch in the company of three of Bolivia's friends with whom she had obviously no more in common than they had with her. One was short, bottle-shouldered, bespectacled, and apparently inclined to literature and Communism; another was shrill, blonde, flirtatious, and at twenty-seven more than a little faded and jaded; and the third was amiable, negative, and inconspicuous beneath the protective coloration of domesticity: but they had all been at school with Bolivia, and she, being anxious to show them her new fiancé, had found them correspondingly curious to see him. They made themselves very agreeable to Stephen, flattered him occasionally, frequently deferred to him, and Stephen, though he liked none of them and the cooking was poor, began to enjoy himself. There had been several of these exhibition parties, and he had discovered that his engagement at least bestowed upon him a certain unexpected importance. It might be fleeting, it was probably unsubstantial, but none the less he liked it. An audience, no matter how obtained, was not to be despised, and Stephen could find pleasure in the company of almost anyone who had the grace to listen to him. He felt a certain affection even for Bolivia so long as she let him talk, but though in the early days of their friendship she had been a willing listener, she had become less patient of late, and Stephen's monologues were restricted to occasions such as the present: he was allowed to be eloquent when his eloquence served the useful purpose of impressing Bolivia's friends: but not otherwise.

With Bolivia's father he continued to be on surprisingly good terms. The General had been greatly taken by Stephen's unusual, and, as he thought, ironic defence of pacifism; and though he later heard him utter some heterodox opinions about painting, poetry, politics, architecture, and social obligations, his conviction was never shaken that his prospective son-in-law had sound ideas about everything that really mattered. He would introduce Stephen to his elderly cronies — excellent gentlemen with cast-iron convictions and meagre imagination – and tell them that here was a young man whose views on the conduct of war were a credit to him. Whereupon Stephen would repeat his inspired discovery that war was a matter for soldiers only, and that civilians had no claim, call, or title to interfere with it. The implications of this doctrine were never apparent to the General's friends, who came to share his high opinion of Stephen; with the result that Stephen was offered a commission in the Brackenshire Territorials, and invited to address a meeting of Junior Imperialists. But these triumphs of mockery, and the brief interest of Bolivia's friends, were the only compensation his engagement offered; and their inadequacy can hardly be denied.

The wedding was to be celebrated two days before Christmas. Despite her anxiety to be married as soon as possible, Bolivia had found it impossible to complete her arrangements for an earlier date. The alterations at Mulberry Acre, opposed as they were at every step by Stephen, or Wilfrid, or Mrs. Barrow, took longer than she had thought; and the purchase of a trousseau was also unexpectedly slow, for confronted with a luxurious range of wedding garments Bolivia revealed a sudden passion for clothes that delayed her choice and multiplied her desires; and, as a final obstacle, Mrs. Ramboise refused to come home before the twenty-first of December. Though loathing the English winter, a motive obscurely pious always drove her to abandon Bordighera, Cannes, Mentone, or wherever she might be at the time, in order to spend Christmas at home. But she never stayed for more than a few days, and she wrote to Bolivia, quite sensibly and pleasantly, 'I very much hope to see your wedding, but I have no intention of making a second journey, in the depths of winter, for that purpose, nor of staying in Lammiter for more than a week. If, then, you want me to be there — and I expect you do — you will have to be married between the 21st and the 28th of December, or put it off till May'. All these circumstances combined to fix the twenty-third as the wedding-day; and to Stephen the thought of Christmas grew horrible beyond words.

Two days before the wedding Hilary gave a dinner-party at Rumneys. It was a family affair. Hilary sat at the head of the long table, on her right was Stephen, next to him Bolivia, then Arthur, Mrs. Ramboise — who had reached home the night before — and Mr. Peabody. On Hilary's left were General Ramboise, Daisy, Wilfrid, Katherine and Sir Gervase Flood, who had been invited as a complement to the General. At the foot of the table, between Sir Gervase and Mr. Peabody, sat Jane, looking enormous in a white taffeta frock so voluminously frilled, fluted, flounced, and scalloped that she might have been tarred and feathered: but thickly feathered, closely feathered: the tar was invisible, yet the feathers, the white flocculence, the hispid fringes, must have had something to stick to.

Hilary was relieved when she got them all seated, for the previous conversation had been embarrassingly dominated by Mrs. Ramboise's narrative of an uneventful afternoon at the bridge-table. Stephen and Bolivia were the guests of the evening, and in Hilary's opinion they should have been the centre of attraction, and their affairs the principal topic of discussion. Sir Gervase and the General had done their best, making a number of appropriate observations in a bluff and humorous vein; Arthur had confided to Bolivia his belief that domesticity was the true crown and purpose of a woman's life; and Daisy and Katherine, in the intervals of jealously regarding each other's figure, had made some pleasant remarks about wedding-presents and the like. But Mrs. Ramboise — she had had ten minutes' conversation with Stephen in the early afternoon, before going to the bridge-party, when, greeting him without emotion, she had said, 'So you're going to marry my girl, are you? Well, marriage is a gamble at the best, but it's no use trying to prevent people gambling. It's in their blood. And Bolivia's old enough to know her own mind by now. It's a pity you're not in the Navy: that would have given you a better chance. A husband and wife generally get on better if they're separated for eight or ten months in the year. But there's no use wishing for that now, and I'm not going to say anything to discourage you. I expect you'll be as happy as most people are, so long as you don't let Bolivia bully you. Keep her under your thumb, that's my advice.' — Mrs. Ramboise, breaking in upon the epithalamic chatter, had loudly demanded, 'Are we going to have any bridge after dinner? I had the filthiest time this afternoon I've ever had in my life: not a partner with a grain of sense, not an opponent with an ounce of grit. In the very first hand the dealer opened with One

Diamond, and I'd a strong two-suiter — five spades to the Ace, King, Knave, and five hearts to the Ace, Queen — so naturally I made a skip bid and called Two Spades. Well, what d'you think happened?'

Attention was partly deflected by the entrance of Mr. Peabody, and Mrs. Ramboise continued her narrative to a diminished audience. Hilary ventured to interrupt, in order to introduce the newcomer. 'How d'you do?' said Mrs. Ramboise with obvious resentment, and concluded her story in a voice of unrestrained savagery: 'So I said to her, "Don't you know that a Jump Overcall's a strength-showing bid? Don't you know the difference between a strength-showing bid and a pre-emptive overbid? Have you read your Culbertson or haven't you?" '

'And had she?' asked Wilfrid.

'Pah!' said Mrs. Ramboise.

Daisy whispered to Wilfrid: 'What *is* a Culbertson?'

'Oh, Daisy!' cried Wilfrid. 'What a lovely thing to ask! You are being sweet.'

Mr. Peabody finished his glass of sherry, and Hilary led the way to the dining-room. She was sorry for Mr. Peabody, who was sitting next to Mrs. Ramboise; but it was too late to do anything about that now, and the general spectacle reassured her. Tall glasses reflected the light, the flowers were good, the silver shone. A dinner-table, hedged by guests, was a lovely sight, she thought; and hospitality, once a virtue, had now become a chief grace of life. And the dinner was going to be a good one: clear soup that was clear as sherry, and rich as stock and steak and sherry could make it; lobster vol-auvent, for which the cook had fingers deft as a card-sharper's, and the knack of imprisoning the sea's flavour as cleverly as a shell; cutlets that were to the sheep from which they came as dainty lyrics inset in solid drama; a turkey, white and massive, with a host of little sausages about it like *putti* round a Rubens goddess; exuberant meringues; and for a savoury soft roes in bacon. An excellent dinner, thought Hilary complacently: a little heavy, per-haps, but it was Christmas time as well as wedding-time, and most of her guests had hearty appetites at any time. It was a pity that Lionel could not be there to share it, for he appreciated a good table and a clever kitchen as well as any man.

As though influenced by her thought — but this was unlikely, for he took pride in thinking for himself — General Ramboise asked what news there was of the Vicar.

'I'm worried about him,' said Hilary. 'He's getting on very well in a way, and he's certainly much better, but he's behaving rather strangely. I went to see him the other day and he asked me if I'd ever read Karl Marx.'

'Good God!' said the General.

'He was very worried because Marx apparently says that the proletariat are *bound* to turn on their masters and overthrow them — a sort of natural law, like steam and that sort of thing — though that seems silly to me, because there's no reason to suppose every working-man's going to think what Marx thought, or do what he says they ought to do.'

'It's all a pack of nonsense,' said the General. 'I

don't know what's gone wrong with Purefoy, if he's worrying about stuff like that.'

'He'd never actually read any Marx before,' said Hilary, 'so it came as a shock to him.'

'It didn't come as a shock to me,' said the General. 'I read the fellow twenty years ago, and I saw at once what it was: a pack of seditious nonsense. So I chucked the book away, and I've never thought about it since. How did Purefoy get hold of it?'

'Rupert sent it to him.'

'That boy of his?'

'Yes. He's a Communist, or pretends to be, and I think he must be trying to convert his father.'

'But, good God,' said the General, 'he's at Tugborough, isn't he? There can't be any Communists there.'

'There's quite a lot, according to Rupert. And Denis, who's a Fascist, says there are just as many of them.'

'Well, I'm damned,' said the General. 'I don't know what the school's coming to.'

Any reflections upon the declining respectability of his old school were cut short by an outburst from the other end of the table where Mrs. Ramboise had unfortunately discovered a sympathetic listener in Mr. Peabody. Her voice, hard and resonant, demanded with sudden indignation, 'And do you know what she'd the impudence to say? She said she thought an overcall in your opponent's suit meant a Slam try to show no losers!'

'Too bad,' murmured Mr. Peabody, 'too bad indeed.'

'So far as a woman like that's concerned, Culbertson might never have existed!'

'I know, I know,' said Mr. Peabody. 'It's really dreadful.'

'Well, I told her the facts. I said my overcall, coming as it did, was equivalent to a strong Take-out Double with a freak, and Culbertson himself says that's one of the most beautiful inferential bids in Contract. Beautiful, that's his word. And who's going to contradict Culbertson?'

Hilary turned to ask Stephen if the reconditioning of Mulberry Acre was now complete. But Stephen, already patently nervous and ill at ease, had been seriously shaken by the ringing brutality of Mrs. Ramboise's observations, and at the sound of Hilary's voice, so close beside him, he started convulsively and knocked over a tall hock glass.

'Oh!' cried Daisy. 'I hope that doesn't mean bad luck.'

'Why should it?' asked Katherine.

'Well,' said Daisy, 'I remember being at a dinner-party once, and a glass broke on the table without anyone having touched it, and the following day we read in the paper that Foch was dead. Or was it Arnold Bennett? No, I think it was Foch. At any rate it was somebody very well known.'

A puzzled silence followed.

'And that isn't all,' Daisy continued, 'because a long time ago, before we were married, I happened to pick up a butter-dish one day, and it simply flew into a thousand pieces. A thousand pieces!'

'And who was dead that time?' asked Jane in a sepulchral tone.

'My eldest brother,' said Daisy simply. 'A cable came from Australia the very next day to say he'd died suddenly by falling out of a window.'

Again there was a brief silence.

With a prim little gesture of renunciation Daisy refused the cutlet. Katherine took two, and said boisterously, 'I'm as hungry as a hunter. My appetite gets better every day.'

Daisy, pleased both by her superior delicacy and her psychic anecdotes, sat with a small cold smile on her face. Hilary said to Bolivia, 'Do you think Stephen will learn to ski at Lauterbrunnen?'

They had arranged to go to Switzerland for their honeymoon.

'I expect he'll tumble about a bit,' said Bolivia, 'but I'll look after him all right.'

'Oh, you musn't get hurt, Stephen!' cried Wilfrid.

'I don't suppose Stephen will mind taking a knock or two,' said the General.

Sir Gervase, who had been talking to Jane about *shikar*, grunted complacently. 'I broke every bone in my body when I was a young man,' he said.

'Whatever for?' asked Daisy.

Wilfrid giggled, and Katherine said proudly, 'Oliver got a greenstick fracture of his collar-bone playing polo last year.'

Stephen shifted uneasily in his chair. The mere prospect of honeymooning with Bolivia made him miserably unhappy, while the thought of being compelled to slide down precipitous slopes on vast unmanageable skis — that would assuredly trip him up, and dislocate his joints, and hit him on the back of his head — filled him with terror. And now, hearing these people talk so glibly, so heartlessly, about serious accidents, he trembled in impotent fury. The succulent turkey became sawdust in his mouth, and champagne turned to vinegar.

The General leaned forward and shouted down the table to Sir Gervase, 'Did I ever tell you Stephen's ideas about the next war? That the Army must control everything, and the politicians and civilians will have to do what we tell 'em?'

'Yes, I think you did,' said Sir Gervase. 'Very interesting indeed.'

'I said nothing of the kind,' snapped Stephen.

'What's that?' asked the General.

Stephen muttered, 'What I meant was that war is so stupid a thing that only people as stupid as soldiers should have anything to do with it.'

Fortunately the General did not properly hear this outrageous remark, but he caught the word 'stupid', and indignation, occluding his veins, empurpled his face and lit the yellow striae in his eyes.

Bolivia, with opportune good sense, laughed heartily and proclaimed, 'There's no use expecting Stephen to say anything sensible to-night. He's got stage-fright — haven't you, darling? — and I only hope he gets over it before Saturday. I don't want him to panic at the church door.'

Her laughter was loud and jovial, but the glance she flashed at Stephen was hard and threatening. 'Sit up and don't look like a fool,' she whispered fiercely.

The situation was saved by a great chattering of female voices, a chorus of inconsequent and protective comment upon anything at all and nothing in particular. Hilary and Daisy, Katherine and Jane, aware of discord in the air, sensitive to the General's displeasure, to Bolivia's anxiety, and to Stephen's danger, all began to talk with great zest on a variety of harmless topics, and their voices raised a screen behind which the crisis peacefully expired. Then, with obvious relief, the barrage slackened and ceased; and Mrs. Ramboise, who had remained aloof from the pother, was heard to say, 'A bluff One No-Trump overcall without a stopper in the bid suit; simple and absolutely effective!'

'Culbertson agrees, I think,' said Mr. Peabody.

'Culbertson states the case,' said Mrs. Ramboise decisively.

XII

As soon as the ladies had withdrawn Wilfrid came round and sat beside Stephen. 'Christmas is going to be perfectly hateful this year,' he said with a sigh.

'It's going to be worse for me than for you,' said Stephen.

Arthur helped himself to brandy. The glass was of the generous balloon shape, and held a lot. Arthur took handsome advantage of its capacity. Before Daisy's watchful eyes he had been compelled, throughout dinner, to let the wine pass him by, and now he was naturally eager to make up for lost time. He gulped the brandy as though Bisquit Dubouché, nearly sixty years old, were meant to quench a man's thirst. It quenched, more happily and almost immediately, his sense of reality. He set his elbows on the table and leaned forward to listen to the General and Sir Gervase. This was the kind of company he preferred above all other. A soldier and a proconsul! Arthur felt the twin flames of war and imperialism warm his heart. He also had been a soldier. He had helped, if not to build, at least to defend an empire. He waited impatiently for an opportunity to say so.

Sir Gervase was talking about a study he had read of the Mahratta campaigns. 'Rapid movement, decisive action, and independent judgment were the reasons for our success,' he declared.

'There was damned little opportunity for any of those in the last war,' said the General.

Arthur finished his brandy. 'It's interesting to hear you say that,' he said to Sir Gervase: and turned with a bland smile to the General, 'because I once had a most unusual chance to exercise independent judgment, and also to show the effect of rapid movement.'

'Where was that?' asked the General.

'At the battle of Cambrai,' said Arthur.

The General grunted. His own war service had been confined to garrison duty in India.

A dreaming beatitude made Arthur's eyes more soft and velvety, a deeper brown. He replenished his glass. 'We'd gone forward behind the tanks, you know,' he said, 'and really the first day was quite easy. We had to do some mopping-up, of course' — Arthur passed over this unpleasant detail with a deprecatory smile — 'and the Fifty-First, poor devils, were held up for a while in front of Flesquières. But except for that it was really quite good going. We pushed on very fast, and cut round behind Flesquières — we and the Fifty-First — and to keep the story short we got to Fontaine-Notre-Dame, on one of the main roads to Cambrai, and found ourselves practically in open country. We'd gone right through the Boches, and there was really nothing to stop us from simply walking ahead.'

'What about Bourlon Wood?' asked the General.

'Yes, they still held part of Bourlon Wood,' said Arthur quickly, 'but what I mean is that in front of us, actually in front of us, there was no opposition and the road to Cambrai was open. But of course we couldn't do anything about it, because the men were exhausted, and we'd no reserves.'

'You'd have had plenty of reserves if they hadn't all been wasted at Passchendaele,' said Sir Gervase fiercely. 'Four hundred thousand casualties, and what did we get in return? Nothing, absolutely nothing!'

'I think that's arguable,' said the General. 'Very arguable indeed. Haig's strategy wasn't a narrow one. It was conceived in terms of the whole front.'

Arthur coughed impatiently. If Sir Gervase and the General began to debate the ethics and military value of Third Ypres, there would be no stopping them and his story would never be heard. 'As I was saying,' he continued, 'we found ourselves, on the night of November 21st, in possession of Fontaine-Notre-Dame, and the road to Cambrai was open before us. But we were utterly exhausted, and we couldn't exploit the situation. It was maddening, simply maddening. And then, while I was looking round, you know, I found a bicycle, a German bicycle they'd left behind them, and I got an idea. It was a fantastic and a rather rash idea, but curiously enough I very nearly put it into practice, and if I'd been successful — well, I don't believe in boasting, and it was a forlorn hope from the beginning — but it almost came off, and if it had come off the battle of Cambrai would have been one of the decisive victories of the War.'

'Oh, Arthur, how wonderful!' cried Wilfrid; but the General and Sir Gervase looked very sceptical.

Arthur drank a little more brandy. 'The bicycle had a good strong carrier,' he said, 'and that's really what put the idea into my head, because it was big enough to carry a box of Mills bombs. So without saying a word to anyone I got a box, and strapped it on, and set out for Cambrai. I don't think I've ever had a more thrilling ride in my life, but I kept very cool: being on a bicycle helped me, because a bicycle is such a reasonable thing to ride, not a bit like a horse. It was very cold, and the road was rough and wet. I skidded and nearly fell two or three times. But except for that there was no danger. There were a few stragglers and walking-wounded on the road, and a gun or two in the ditch, and some French peasants who evidently thought the Germans were in full retreat. I remember ringing my bell to make them get out of the way, and some-how or other that seemed a very funny thing to do. Well, I came to the outskirts of Cambrai, and there was a good deal of confusion there. The streets were unlighted, of course, and there were a lot of people running about, and they all seemed very alarmed. But they didn't pay any attention to me: did I tell you I was wearing a German tunic and steel helmet that I'd taken off a dead officer in Fontaine-Notre-Dame? They were quite a good fit, as it happened. Now my plans were naturally very vague, and a good lot depended on luck, but what I hoped to do was to create a panic in Cambrai and disorganize the nerve-centre of that part of the German army. As it happened I very nearly suc-ceeded. There's a big square in the middle of the

town, it's called the Place d'Armes, I think, and
when I reached it I saw exactly what I wanted to see.
On one side there was a battalion of infantry drawn
up — all in the dark, you know, and I vividly
remember the noise their boots made on the cobbles
— curious how a thing like that sticks in one's mind!
— and on the other side, in front of a big building,
the *hôtel de ville*, I expect, there was a group of
officers: two or three generals, and a lot of staff
officers, and any number of colonels. They were all
very excited, and there was a great argument going
on. This was the situation I'd been praying for!
No other officer in the whole war had such a
magnificent opportunity to exploit the element of
surprise, and I was determined to do everything I
could without thought of my own life or safety.
Well, I dismounted about thirty yards away from
them, and concealed myself and my bicycle behind
a convenient corner. I unfastened the box of bombs
and took one out. I pulled out the safety pin and
flung back my arm in readiness to throw it.'

Arthur demonstrated the movement with his now
empty glass.

'Look here,' demanded the General, 'is this a
true story?'

Very politely Arthur said, 'I don't think you
served on the Western Front, sir, did you?'

'No, I didn't,' said the General, 'but I've talked
to a hundred people who did, and I've read a score
of books . . .'

'Books are almost useless,' said Arthur. 'The only
people who really know what happened during the

war are humble regimental officers like myself. I could tell you any number of remarkable occurrences that no historian has ever so much as mentioned, that no historian ever will mention, and, perhaps, that no historian would believe. There was, for example, a really vital mishap at Monchy . . .'

'Oh, tell us about the bomb,' cried Wilfrid. 'I'm dying to know what happened. Did you really throw it?'

'Ah yes, the bomb,' said Arthur. 'Yes, I threw it, and two more in quick succession.'

'And blew them all up?'

Arthur shrugged his shoulders. With an expression that signified a humorous resignation to misfortune he reached for the brandy: 'If I had, as you say, blown them all up, the rest of the war might have taken a very different course. But the bombs didn't burst. One of them hit a staff officer in the face, but that was all the damage they did. By some mischance the detonators hadn't been put in, and a Mills bomb,' he explained to Wilfrid, 'will not explode unless there's a detonator in it. It was my own fault, I admit. I should have examined them. But I was, not unnaturally, I think, somewhat excited by my venture, and I forgot to do so.'

'And how did you manage to get back?' asked Wilfrid.

'There was a great uproar, but the confusion helped me. I rode right across the square, shouting as loudly as I could, in German, of course, and then unfortunately I got lost. I turned into a very narrow street, almost a cul-de-sac, for the only way out of it was by a little passage between two houses. I got off my bicycle, and suddenly a door opened and a woman spoke to me. Now what she said was one of the most astounding things I've ever heard.'

Sir Gervase interrupted him. 'Talking of women, he said, 'I think it's time we joined the ladies.'

The General, who for some time had barely concealed his impatience, agreed with him. Mr. Peabody was already on his feet.

'What a marvellous adventure,' said Wilfrid, following them to the drawing-room.

'I wish they had let me finish it,' said Arthur. 'The next part was still more interesting. It was a green bicycle, you see, and green is my lucky colour.'

Mrs. Ramboise summoned Katherine, Sir Gervase, and Mr. Peabody to play bridge. Bolivia, who had had a long and friendly talk with Jane, took charge of Stephen.

'Poor old man,' she said, 'have you had a very boring evening? I know you didn't enjoy yourself at dinner, and I don't suppose things were any more amusing after we left.'

'They talked about the War,' said Stephen.

'Well, daddy's interested in that sort of thing, of course.'

'It was Arthur who did most of the talking.'

'He had a lot of adventures in France, hadn't he? Let's go into the little parlour and talk quietly for a while, and you can have a rest. I don't want you to get tired out before Saturday.'

The little parlour opened off the drawing-room. It contained a sofa, a couple of chairs, a writing-table, a bookcase, and two pictures of roses painted in oil. The window was heavily curtained and so was the door. It was a comfortable little room.

Bolivia sat on the sofa and invitingly patted the place beside her. Stephen dully accepted the invitation.

'Darling,' she said, 'I know you're not feeling very happy, but everything will be quite different after Saturday. We're going to have a lovely time as soon as we get away from all these people. Won't it be heavenly, just you and me, all by ourselves, in Lauterbrunnen?'

'Lauterbrunnen isn't a desert island, is it?'

'Silly Stephen! You know perfectly well what I mean. Oh, we're going to be terribly happy! And being married to me is going to do you a lot of good too. I'm not going to let you wear rings, for one thing, and I'm going to see that you get plenty of exercise, and then you won't need that bismuth stuff that you're always taking. You've no idea how much I'm going to enjoy looking after you. Kiss me, Stephen.'

'No, I don't feel like it to-night.'

'Just a little one.'

'No, really, I hate being pawed and messed about.'

'Silly Stephen!' repeated Bolivia, but now in a somewhat harder tone. Stephen turned petulantly away from her, but Bolivia, with a strong arm, pulled him backwards and clutched his head to her bosom. Stooping, she kissed him several times with the gusto of victory.

'Oh, stop it!' cried Stephen. 'Let me go, Bolivia!'

He struggled to free himself, his large plump body writhing, half on and half off the sofa, his pale face flushed, his shirt front crackling. Excited by the contest, Bolivia bent to kiss him again. Stephen twisted his head away, and Bolivia, with a sudden disastrous madness, fastened her teeth in the lobe of his left ear.

It was a painful bite. Her teeth drew blood. And on the instant the hideous memory returned to Stephen of that afternoon in Florence when Giulia Whats-her-name had assaulted him. He saw again the dreadful turmoil in the Via Tosinghi: waiters gesticulating, the soap-smeared shouting men from the barber's, the shining razors, the crowd gathering in the sunshine between the striped awnings, the coming of the Carabinieri. He heard Giulia's shrill voice, he felt himself pulled again into that vortex of fear and embarrassment. His nerves, ragged already, fretted by weeks of emotion, snapped like the check-chains at the launching of a liner: and panic slid free. He sprang to the door. The curtain got in his way, and Bolivia nearly caught him. But just in time he pulled it aside, tugged open the door, and hurled himself into the startled drawing-room.

He traversed it like a bolting horse. He knocked down chairs and a table. He frightened Hilary and all her guests. He cried shrilly to Wilfrid to come and help him, and reaching the farther door disappeared from view.

Bolivia, noticeably slower but with an expression of fierce determination, ran after him. But Wilfrid, gallantly sticking out his foot, tripped her and brought her to the floor.

There was an outcry of confused expostulation, inquiry, and fear: 'He's gone *must*!' shouted Sir Gervase. 'Give me a gun! We've got to stop him. Where can I find a gun? He's dangerous, I tell you. He's gone *must*! Surely there's a gun of some kind in the house?'

'Don't be a silly old man!' exclaimed Hilary. 'Oh, Bolivia, whatever have you done to him?'

While Bolivia was annotating the catastrophe, as best she could, Wilfrid hurried after Stephen and found him, bareheaded and dishevelled, walking swiftly down the drive. Wilfrid hailed and pursued him.

'I've come to take you home,' he said. 'Now don't start explaining, because there's no need to. I've been expecting something of this kind to happen all the time, and you mustn't worry about it, or be afraid of anything. *I'm* going to look after you now. We're going straight home . . .'

'But you're taking me back to the house,' said Stephen.

'Only to get a car,' said Wilfrid. 'That will be quicker than walking. I think we'll take Bolivia's, shall we?'

There were three cars in front of the house, and Bolivia's was the leading one. Stephen, whose panic had left him dazed and acquiescent, got in, and Wilfrid made a flying start as Bolivia and the General appeared at the front door.

'They'll follow us!' cried Stephen, once more alarmed.

'But they won't catch us,' said Wilfrid, and swung out of the drive with reckless speed.

Neither spoke again till they reached Mulberry Acre. Stephen, more sensitive to cold as his excitement waned, was shivering slightly. But Wilfrid was filled with triumph and drove with exultant speed. Like silver scissors ripping an old black coat, his headlights tore the darkness. The rushing tyres shrieked their defiance of the road. The cylinders purred their swift delight and the divided air, meeting behind, clapped its hands. Every lamp-post rose to the salute as they approached, and doubled-down with friendly laughter as they passed. Their invading gleams made Wilfrid's fair hair shine, and lit the heroic gladness of his face. He had, like so many heroes, rescued his friend from dire peril. He was, perhaps, like Britomart when she saved Amoret from the enchanter Busyrane and the foul mansion where cruel Cupid, riding on a ravenous lion, for ever led Reproach, Repentance, Shame, Strife, Anger, and Unthriftihood, Disloyalty, Infirmity, Poverty and Death, in the Masque of Love. And like Britomart, Wilfrid found ample reward for his exertion in the thought of Stephen's escape from such company; like Amoret, Stephen had already begun to feed on hope.

Wilfrid swerved across the road and stopped abruptly by the little gate that led to Mulberry Acre. They hurried into the house. Wilfrid turned on the light and saw for the first time the damage done to Stephen's ear. Had Stephen submitted to the caress he might have suffered no hurt; but as it happened Bolivia's teeth had slightly torn the skin.

'She bit me,' Stephen explained.

'But that's dreadful,' said Wilfrid indignantly. 'Why, it's nothing short of vandalism! I shan't have a scrap of sympathy for her now, whatever she says. A woman who can do a thing like that is a perfect fiend. For goodness' sake go upstairs and wash it, Stephen, and dab some iodine on it, or you'll get blood-poisoning.'

'They may come after us,' said Stephen.

'Go upstairs and bathe your ear,' Wilfrid repeated. 'I'll lock the doors and put the house in a state of defence. Mrs. Barrow will help us, won't you, Mrs. Barrow?'

Mrs. Barrow was indeed willing to help, as soon as she had been told what had happened. 'We'll give her a warm welcome if she has the impudence to come here again!' she declared; and with much puffing and panting pushed a table against the front door and piled a couple of chairs on top of it.

'Are all the windows fastened?' asked Wilfrid.

'They are, Mr. Wilfrid, but she might break them.'

'We'll go upstairs and keep guard from the guest-room, and if she tries to do that we'll bombard her.'

The guest-room overlooked the front door. In preparation for the new regime it had lately been used as a dump for wedding-presents, surplus furniture, pictures, and books that Bolivia had removed from the downstairs shelves to make room for her own collection of schoolgirl, romantic, and golfing literature. There was, then, plenty of ammunition available, should Bolivia try to force an entrance.

Among the books were the forty volumes of the selected works of Lope de Vega, that Stephen had once bought with the hope of discovering, in the works of the prolific Spaniard, plots, characters, and situations that he could use in a modern context. But as he had never fulfilled his intention of learning Spanish, Lope had been of no profit to him.

Wilfrid opened the casement window and waited anxiously. Presently he heard a car approach and stop. The sound of voices broke through the darkness: angry voices, the one rising clear and coppery as when a well-bred Englishwoman berates a porter or commands a foreigner, the other brusque and decisive as when 94 Piccadilly interprets Pacifism. 'She's brought her father,' whispered Wilfrid.

Bolivia leading, the invaders arrived and knocked loudly at the door.

'What do you want?' asked Wilfrid from the window.

Bolivia looked up, and shouted, 'I want to see Stephen, of course.'

'Well, you can't see him,' said Wilfrid.

'Look here,' roared the General, 'my daughter's been insulted . . .'

'And my friend's been bitten,' said Wilfrid.

'Open the door!' bellowed the General.

'This is a private house,' said Wilfrid, 'and you've no claim to admission when the occupants obviously don't desire your company.'

'Where's Stephen?' cried Bolivia. 'I've a right to see him, and I'm going to see him.'

'If you don't come down and let us in, you'll suffer for it, young man!'

Bolivia hammered on the door, and Mrs. Barrow handed Wilfrid two volumes of Lope de Vega. They were *Jerusalen Conquistada* and *El Galan Castrucho.* 'Here you are,' she said. 'Knock their blooming heads off!'

'If you don't go away I shall have to resort to violence,' said Wilfrid sternly.

'I demand to see Stephen!' shouted Bolivia. 'I'm not going to leave here till I settle with him. Stephen! Stephen!'

'Will you go away, or will you take the consequences?' asked Wilfrid.

'Open the door, you puppy!' roared the General.

Jerusalen Conquistada flew down the cold night air and knocked his hat off. *El Galan Castrucho* followed. It opened its leaves in the outflowing light, it flapped in the darkness, and fell like a shot woodpigeon at Bolivia's feet. She jumped backwards into the winter soil of an herbaceous border.

'Here's plenty more,' said Mrs. Barrow, and gave Wilfrid *Las Fortunas de Diana*, *El Maestro de Danzar*, *Las Flores de Don Juan*, and several other plays, novels and pastorals. In rapid succession Wilfrid hurled them at the enemy. The air was noisy with the fluttering of Spanish drama, the General's oaths, and Bolivia's indignant outcry. *Las Fortunas de Diana* scored a hit, and so did the *Arte Nuevo de Comedias.*

Some thirty volumes had descended — and effectively restrained the invaders from further attack upon the door — when the third car arrived, bringing Hilary, Arthur, and Mr. Peabody.

'My God, there's more of them!' cried Mrs.

Barrow, and feverishly began to load the table at Wilfrid's side with fresh ammunition: wedding-presents now, travelling clocks, toast-racks, etchings of Lammiter Bridge and the Fifteenth Century house in Green Street, decanters, hock glasses, walking sticks, a cushion, a patent putter, napkin-rings, a fruit dish, finger-bowls, book-ends, and so forth.

'Wait a minute,' said Wilfrid, 'let's see what they're going to do.'

It was soon apparent that the newcomers were not reinforcements for the attack. They were, indeed, a relieving force. Hilary took Bolivia by the arm and talked to her severely about her folly. Mr. Peabody lectured the General on the rights of house-holders and the sanctity of private property.

'But he's insulted my daughter,' shouted the General.

'To force an entry into a private house,' said Mr. Peabody, 'is a very serious offence, and however grave the provocation I fear no magistrate would excuse your taking the law into your own hands in so violent and unwarrantable a manner. I myself am not only a lawyer, but a Justice of the Peace . . .'

'So am I!' said the General.

While this discussion was proceeding, Mrs. Barrow observed that Stephen had entered the room. 'Why, here's Mr. Stephen,' she said. 'Oh, what a dreadful injury you've got!'

Stephen had put on a dressing-gown. He had also bedaubed his ear and the adjacent part of his cheek so lavishly with iodine as to resemble a skewbald pony. Mrs. Barrow closely examined the punctured lobe. 'There now,' she said, 'it's not so bad as I thought it was. That'll be all right in a day or two.'

'It's very painful,' said Stephen.

'Well, we don't have to worry any more,' said Mrs. Barrow. 'Not with Mr. Wilfrid here to protect us. He's been a perfect hero, Mr. Stephen. You ought to have heard him telling off the General!'

'I did,' said Stephen.

'Didn't I do it beautifully!' asked Wilfrid, his face flushed and his eyes shining with delight. 'Oh, I've been having a lovely time. I've never felt so brave in my life before.'

'What are they doing now?' asked Stephen, and went to the window. He carried two pillows with him.

The disputing groups had coalesced. The General and Bolivia were still protesting. Hilary and Arthur and Mr. Peabody were yet persuading. But the latter were now dominant, and all five were gradually moving away. Stephen leaned out of the window and viciously hurled his pillows after them — white, soft, and heavy, they sailed through the air and mistook their targets; for one took Mr. Peabody on the nape of his neck, and the other struck Arthur somewhat lower down.

'Why didn't you throw a clock or a picture at them?' asked Mrs. Barrow. 'There wasn't any need to dirty two nice clean pillows.'

'They were the pillows off Miss Ramboise's double bed,' said Stephen, and slammed the window.

XIII

THREE days after Christmas Mrs. Ramboise returned
to the Riviera, and Bolivia went with her. There
had been no communication between her and
Stephen. *The Times* and the *Lammiter Morning Post*
had announced that the marriage previously
arranged would not take place, but details of the
rupture were kept comparatively secret — Mrs.
Barrow had discretion, while none of the others
would ever mention the horrid scene again — and
even the most assiduous gossip-hunters had little but
the bare bone of fact to supplement their Christmas
dinners. Wilfrid, having packed up the wedding-
presents, sent them to Bolivia to dispose of, and
persuaded the furniture dealer who had supplied the
bedroom suite to repurchase it at a somewhat
reduced price. He and Stephen spent a very happy
Christmas together, and settled down to work
again in great content.

After five weeks in hospital the Vicar had gone
home, where he propelled himself about the ground
floor of his house in a wheeled chair fitted with a
horizontal support for his broken leg. He was
unduly sensitive about the grotesque appearance of
the immobilized limb, and did not encourage
visitors. Even Hilary found him reserved and sometimes unamiable, but despite her lack of welcome she
went regularly to the Vicarage during the Christmas

holidays, when all the young Purefoys were at home.

She found Rupert, the eldest of them, very busy with plans for a new school-magazine of which he was to be the editor. 'But don't think it's going to be like the ordinary school-magazine,' he said. 'You know what dismal stuff they are. This is going to be serious and very good. The general idea is to put across the necessity for Communism in the Public Schools. You see we *must* do something about the present state of society, and if we don't tackle it nobody will, because older people — well, my father's generation — have never been taught to really understand how life is conditioned. We've got a marvellous design for the cover, a Red Hand holding a Hammer, and we'll probably call it *Red*. Just the one word, you know. It's going to create a terrific sensation, and I shan't be a bit surprised if I get expelled.'

Rupert sat on the arm of a chair and smiled at Hilary. He was a very good-looking boy with long eyelashes and a finely shaped jaw that was a more delicate edition of his father's. His hair, a wavy dark brown, was rather long, and his voice had a light-hearted clarity. He was carefully and attractively dressed.

'But surely you're not serious when you say you're a Communist,' Hilary objected. 'Think what they did in Russia: murdering hundreds of thousands of people, and stopping others from going to Church, and plotting against everybody, and putting people in timber-camps, and I don't know what else. You can't wish to see that sort of thing going on in England?'

Rupert laughed. 'You've got all the facts, haven't you? But they don't make any difference, because Communism is inevitable. It's an historical necessity.'

'But why?' asked Hilary.

'Well, of course, you've got to read Karl Marx and Lenin to find out really why. But they prove it quite definitely. You see, what has always counted most in history is the Class Struggle. Oh, I know you hear a lot about Hannibal, and Agincourt, and the Treaty of Utrecht, but that's all eye-wash, because till now history books have always been written by Capitalists, or at any rate by the Bourgeoisie, and they didn't know about the Class Struggle. But it's the most significant fact in history because it has never stopped. There have been Tyrants, and the Feudal System, and Aristocracies, and the Bourgeoisie, and now it's the turn of the People. In the new order of things there's bound to be a Dictatorship of the Proletariat.'

'So you've become a Communist simply in order to be on the winning side?'

'Oh, hang it, Hilary, that's not fair! I'm a Communist because it's the reasonable thing to be, and because I, and most of my friends, are simply sick to death about the stuff that all our politicians talk. They're such ghastly frauds that one simply must be different from them. All the most intellectual men at Tugborough are Communists, and quite a lot of decent fellows too. It's really one's duty to try and clear up all the mess in the world, and naturally one wants a bit of excitement as well. And Communism seems the proper ticket, don't you think?'

'And what happens to the Class Struggle after you've established the Dictatorship of the Proletariat?' asked Hilary. 'Does it still go on?'

'No, because there won't be any different classes then, there'll simply be the Proletariat. Of course I don't pretend we're going to skip right into a kind of Utopia. In fact, everything will be fearfully difficult and hideously uncomfortable for years to come, before the Dictatorship of the Proletariat is really established. But that's part of the fun, and it's bound to be worth it in the long run.'

'And when you've established the Proletariat, and there's nobody else left, don't you think the Proletariat will begin to develop into Aristocrats, and Capitalists, and Bourgeois, and start the Class Struggle all over again?'

'Oh, no, that's not at all likely.'

'Why not?'

'Well, Marx says nothing about it, and I don't think Lenin does either, and they'd thought about that sort of thing for years. I really don't think you need worry about that.'

'Human nature . . .' said Hilary.

'Human nature depends entirely upon environment and the economic conditions of life,' said Rupert firmly.

'But Denis has the same environment as you, and he hasn't become a Communist,' Hilary objected.

'No,' said Rupert judicially, 'and that's a good debating point. But Denis is very young yet. He's eighteen months younger than I am, and he's been led astray by Mosley. He says he's a Fascist, you know, and actually I suppose he is, because he's just the age to like walking about in a black shirt, and saluting people. He was in the Scouts till a year ago, and the Fascist uniform's a lot smarter than theirs, and Fascists haven't got to do good deeds or anything boring like that. We don't deny — well, all the people who think as I do, I mean — we don't deny that Mosley's a very clever fellow, because he's really invented something that does appeal to boys who've got a bit fed-up with Boy Scouting. But there's no need to worry about Denis. He's only sixteen, and he'll get over this Fascist nonsense all right. I say, do you mind if I leave you now? It's horribly rude of me, but I'm composing a Manifesto for the first number of *Red*, and it's rather a job, you know, because I've got to get all my facts absolutely right, and I want to re-read *The Coming Struggle for Power*.'

'I'm waiting to have tea with your father,' said Hilary, 'so perhaps I'll see you again.'

'I do hope so,' said Rupert, 'but not this afternoon, I'm afraid. You really don't mind my cutting away like this?'

He was indeed his mother's son, thought Hilary. He had all her charming gift of enthusiasm. It was a wild and wayfaring enthusiasm, but none the less a delectable heritage. Caroline had once endeavoured to provide the poor with window-boxes, and Rupert meant to give them the whole earth. It was a delight to be with him and to listen to him. Hilary felt a vast affection, a loving and laughing affection for him, and while she was savouring these happy thoughts she was loudly reminded of the existence of several other young Purefoys.

She heard the sound of marching feet on the terrace outside the window. She heard a stern but youthful voice.

'Halt!' it cried. 'Stand still, don't wobble about like that .... Right dress! Tuck in that beastly stomach of yours, Cecily, and try to stand still. Look to your right, Peter ... Eyes Front! Now when I give you the order to dismiss, remember to raise your right arms in the proper salute, and then double smartly away ... Squad, dis-miss!'

A minute later Denis came in and greeted Hilary with a rather abstracted manner. He was a sturdy boy, with untidy reddish-brown hair and his father's square-cut handsome features. He wore a black shirt tucked into a pair of dirty grey flannel trousers, and a belt that supported an empty holster.

'Well, Denis, have they been drilling well?' asked Hilary.

'No,' said Denis. 'You haven't any idea how difficult it is to get these little beasts to march in step or do anything really smartly. Cecily giggles, and Peter's absolutely hopeless.'

'He's only six,' said Hilary apologetically.

'He's quite old enough to realize that drill is important,' said Denis. 'If a boy can't drill he can't fight, and if he can't fight he's no good to the Empire.'

'But whom do you want to fight?'

'Oh, I don't know. Russia, I expect, or perhaps Germany, or Japan. It doesn't matter, does it? We're bound to be at war with someone pretty soon, and the sooner the better, because if we don't go to war I expect I'll be expelled. Old Picker, my housemaster, has had a down on me for years, because I'm a Fascist and he's a Liberal or something beastly like that.'

'Are there many Fascists at Tugborough?'

'Hundreds of them,' said Denis. 'All the decent fellows are, and quite a lot of clever ones too.'

'But Rupert isn't. I've just been talking to him, and he's a Communist.'

'Oh, but that's different. He's getting pretty old. He's seventeen, and when people get to that age they're usually a bit soured and hopeless about things, and they think there's nothing left but Communism. And he's a bit of a snob too, and thinks it's superior to be one of the Proletariat. But don't worry about Rupert, Aunt Hilary. We won't stand any nonsense from him.'

'I hope you won't be too rough with him,' said Hilary gravely.

'He'll have to take his chance,' said Denis. 'In these days the State is everything and the Individual doesn't matter. I say, Aunt Hilary, you won't mind if I leave now? No, I don't want any tea, I'm in training. I've got to go and have a look at my stamp collection, to see if it's worth selling. I must raise some money before going back to school.'

'What for?'

'Well,' said Denis, a trifle shyly, 'I want to get a revolver if possible, and if I can't manage that I might buy a pair of knuckle-dusters.'

It was curious, thought Hilary, how completely their interest had been diverted, within the last year or two, from machinery to politics. A little while ago their thoughts had been filled by the mysteries of wireless telephony and aeroplane engines, but now they had forsaken short waves and cylinders for social problems. And that, despite the paradox of Rupert's Communism and the adolescent bloodiness of Denis's ideas, was a step in the right direction, Hilary believed. For she had always felt that aeroplanes and other mechanical devices, being simply things to use, a handsome enlargement of the bathroom tap, so to speak, were not worthy of the devotion they inspired in so many people. The proper study of mankind was man, and politicians, though often with unhappy results, did occasionally seem to realize that.

Hilary picked up a book that Rupert had been reading and had left on his chair. It was an anthology called *New Country*. She turned over the pages and read, in some surprise and not without bewilderment, occasional stanzas. Here was more vigour than she had grown to expect in poetry. It was true that she had no sympathy with the pervading motif of rebellion, and it was also true that many lines read as though the writer's pen had not been thrown properly into gear — there was, she thought, an unnecessary amount of noise — but her senses were forced to acknowledge a real exhilaration in most of

233

the poems. Rupert had underlined a number of
passages. There was a stanza he had framed with
thick black pencilling:

> 'And we whom winter days oppress
> May find some work to hand;
> Perfect our plans, renew parts,
> Break hedges down, plough land.'

Caroline would have approved of that, thought
Hilary; and turning a page or two found another
marked line:

> 'Turning ᵣeᴅellion to a fanning breath and
> tradition to a jet of flame.'

It was more exciting poetry than the contents of the
Georgian Anthologies that had been her last, but
now almost forgotten, enthusiasm; and obviously
Rupert had read it all and quite properly been
excited by it. His manner, while he spoke of his
plans for a Communist magazine, had been light
and easy, but that proved nothing. He could not be
expected to talk in the fervent voice of his favourite
poets. However hot his belief, he would not throw
red cinders on the carpet for conversation. But his
secret thoughts might be glowing as red as these
young poets'.

Hilary read the last poem in the book. It had a
brief chorus:

> 'Come then, companions. This is the spring
>   of blood,
> heart's hey-day, movement of masses, begin-
>   ning of good.'

— And of course, thought Hilary, Denis feels that too, in his small-boy fashion. And though his idea of the movement of masses and the beginning of good is much much sillier than Rupert's, that's because he's so much younger. I wonder if, for the first time since the War, the Spring of blood is really being felt by young people all over England? Oh, I wish I were young again, so that I could *know*!

The door opened and the Vicar, preceded by his leg, rolled in upon his invalid chair. He was looking tired and rather querulous. His leg resembled a shelf for guillemots to perch on.

Hilary said, 'Do you know, Lionel, those boys of yours are better stuff than we ever were?'

The Vicar cocked an inquiring eyebrow.

'When we were their age,' Hilary continued, 'we weren't interested in the welfare of nations. We were only interested in ourselves.'

'I don't agree with you,' said the Vicar. 'When I was sixteen I intended to reform the whole world. People always do, when they're sixteen.'

'And then give up hope?'

'Inevitably.'

'Well, Rupert hasn't given up hope — he's dominated by hope — and so he's better than we are now.'

'Perhaps,' said the Vicar. 'But I'm tired of trying to think young men's thoughts.'

'Is your leg still hurting you?'

'It's not very comfortable.'

Mrs. Finger brought in tea. Mrs. Finger had been the Vicar's housekeeper for the last six months. She had formerly been in the employment of the Duke of Starveling, and was accordingly inured to hard work and well-trained in the art of making a pound do the work of thirty-five shillings. She was a shrewd, smooth-haired, tightly clad, buxom, solid woman with short legs and very bright inquisitive brown eyes. She allowed herself the liberty of a half-smile to Hilary.

Hilary said, 'Those boys have a curious breadth of understanding. They're possibly narrow and mistaken in their own enthusiasms, but they make allowances for each other. They're instinctive psychologists, though I don't think that Denis is a very reliable psychologist. But when we were their age . . .'

'You're being sentimental about youth,' said the Vicar.

'I don't think so. I believe the young people of to-day have sharper eyes, and a better understanding, and a more urgent desire for honesty and justice than we ever had: or than I ever had.'

'And your evidence for this belief is what Rupert and Denis have been telling you?'

'Not altogether. Have you read this book?' She showed him *New Country*.

'I've done nothing but read books for the last six weeks, and I'm tired to death of them. The world is in a state of anarchy, and each book I read depresses me more than the last one.'

'But everyone knows . . .'

'I didn't know!' The Vicar's voice rose to a thin parody of his old healthy tone of pompous indignation. 'How was I to know that the foundations of life, as I thought of them, were being attacked, and weakened, and burrowed into? There was no one in Lammiter who talked of such things. The newspapers I read paid no attention to them. I was allowed to live in ignorance of four-fifths of contemporary thought.'

Hilary refrained from making the obvious reply.

'It's a dreadful thing to find there is no justice or honesty in the world,' said the Vicar.

'I suppose all revolutions start from that discovery.'

'There are spiritual as well as political effects.'

Hilary took another sandwich; and there was silence for a full minute.

The Vicar's head sank forward at a dejected angle. His features, as they often did in the relaxation of defeat, showed a curious resemblance to Arthur's weak lines. His brief puff of indignation had left him deflated. He mumbled, as though speaking to his lower waistcoat buttons, 'I think I have lost faith.'

Hilary said sharply, 'Don't be a fool, Lionel.'

The Vicar muttered to his waistcoat buttons, 'I believed in a Just God. Then Caroline died, then I fell and broke my leg, and then I found I had been left in ignorance of all that was going on in the world.'

'Really, Lionel, I've no patience with you sometimes!' said Hilary. 'Simply because of a trumpery — well, because of a perfectly natural series of accidents, you have the folly and the audacity to say you have lost faith! I never heard of such silly, childish egotism in all my life.'

'A bruised reed shall He not break,' muttered the Vicar.

'What on earth have reeds got to do with it? You say you've just discovered — what everyone else has always known — that the world is full of injustice, and Communism, and war, and poverty, and dissatisfaction, and Heaven knows what else: and hasn't it occurred to you that all these things are due, not to Christianity, but to lack of Christianity? Didn't it strike you, in your marvellous studies, that if the world put into practice, whether they believed it or not, simply one fraction of Christian Teaching, the bulk of their troubles would disappear? Don't you see that such things as loving your neighbour, and refraining from covetousness, and not laying up excessive treasure on earth, are *practical* advice? Whether Christianity is divine teaching or not — and personally I haven't any doubt — it's obviously sensible teaching: but you have the silly audacity to deny both its origin and its use simply because you fell off your horse and hurt your leg.'

'You don't understand,' said the Vicar.

'I understand too well,' said Hilary.

'I have a guilty conscience.'

'So has everybody else. You can't claim distinction because of that.'

Hilary, roused to anger by the Vicar's parade of self-pity, became still more angry because of her display of anger. Anger fed anger, and embarrassment blew the flames. The Vicar had shocked her by exhibiting his weakness, and she had shocked herself by unclothing her faith. She intensely disliked such spiritual nudism. She preferred to keep her piety secret as her ablutions, and she hotly resented the provocation, the successful provocation, to publish it. She rose, noisily and abruptly, and prepared to go.

The Vicar still seemed more interested in his waistcoat buttons than in his visitor. He said, as though confiding in them, 'I see no possibility of sending Rupert and Denis to Oxford. I haven't the money, and I don't know what's going to become of them.'

'They're provided for at present, and you've no reason to worry about them till next autumn. Good-bye, Lionel, and for heaven's sake stop grovelling.'

Hilary marched out of the Vicarage with the stamping impatience of a right flank guardsman advancing to fix bayonets. She walked home through the late afternoon dusk with indignation sounding in every footfall. Never in her life had she been so angry with anyone. She went so far as to say to herself that she wouldn't go back to the Vicarage. But a moment later she was rehearsing a little speech that might, on her next visit, help in restoring him to his senses. After all, she thought, it's common enough for people to lose faith in adversity, and even commoner to forget it in prosperity. Most people are fools; or half-fools; or, at the best, quarter-fools. Lionel's certainly a fool. But he's the father of Rupert and Denis, Cecily, Patrick, and Rosemary and Peter: so there's a lot to be said for him, after all. And when he's happy, and not

239

showing-off, he can be very pleasant. But five days out of seven he's a fool. He needs someone to look after him. He lost his backbone when Caroline died. . . .

Mr. Peabody was waiting to see her at Rumneys. His smooth grey cheeks showed, with more difficulty than most people would have found in repressing it, a certain animation. The pleasurable anticipation of giving a surprise endeavoured, but almost in vain, to twist his facial muscles into a smile. He was a man with news to tell.

'I have received a letter of unusual interest,' he said, and thrust his hand into an inner pocket. 'A letter that we had almost ceased to expect. It came with the afternoon post, and under the circumstances I thought it best that I should deliver it to you personally.'

'What is it?' asked Hilary. 'News of George?' Her interest in human affairs was temporarily exhausted by the demands already made on her sympathy, and she showed nothing of that eager astonishment which Mr. Peabody had been looking forward to.

He was disappointed by her ready guess and lack of excitement, but he saved what he could from the ruin of his surprise, and answered, 'Not of him, but from him.'

'Where is he?'

Mr. Peabody removed the letter from its envelope: 'He gives an address in Parel, near Bombay.'

'Let me see,' said Hilary.

George's notepaper was thin, cheap, and not very

clean. It retained a slight domestic smell, not of English cooking, but of more pungent ingredients. The letter was as follows:

'Dear Peabody,

'The malice of circumstance — and circumstance can be damned malicious when it likes — obliged me to leave Bombay a few months ago, though at the time I had a very good job there, and take up a secluded residence in Goa. But Time is the Great Healer — it wasn't the police I was afraid of, not on this occasion — and I returned a week ago to my former abode in this select garden-city suburb of Bombay the Beautiful. I was then told, by a certain friend, that during my absence an advertisement, of that frequently fallacious "will hear something to his advantage" type, had appeared in three separate issues of *The Times of India*.

'I promptly repaired to Bori Bunder and searched the files — a dusty job it was, too — and found the cheerful news of my favourite uncle's demise.

'I suppose it is too much to expect that the old boy has made me his sole heir and successor, but apparently he's left me something, and I shall be much obliged if you will transmit my cut without unnecessary delay. I would come home to claim it if I thought it was big enough, but my nature is too sensitive to run the risk of being presented, after so much travelling, with a gold watch and chain and a signed photograph of the deceased in regimental uniform.

'How are all my revered cousins? I suppose

they've done pretty well out of Uncle John. Well, I'm not jealous — and that's a lie if you ever heard one.

'Be a good sort, Peabody, and send my estate by return, if you can.'

Hilary read and re-read this shabbily cheerful effusion. 'He's not abashed by misfortune,' she said.

'Reading between the lines,' said Mr. Peabody cautiously, 'I gather that he is in reduced circumstances. Perhaps very reduced circumstances.'

'Very very reduced, I should think. Have you replied to him yet?'

'I've had a copy of the will made, which I propose to send him to-morrow.'

'I wonder if he's in a position to benefit by it?'

'Mrs. Clements and Mrs. Arthur Gander will be sadly disappointed if he is.'

'Simply to know that George has turned up will make them very frightened and furiously angry,' said Hilary.

'Perhaps you will inform them of his letter?' Mr. Peabody suggested. 'I think they had better be told about it.'

'I've always felt that George would turn up in time to make a nuisance of himself,' said Hilary.

'A rolling stone,' sighed Mr. Peabody.

'And we don't know where he has been rolling,' said Hilary.

XIV

JANUARY, the longest and darkest month in the year, fell tardily from the calendar with the painful deliberation of water-drops on the victim of a Chinese torturer. Like an endless chain of buckets, draining a cold quarry, reluctant February followed. And March came limping in on frost-bitten feet.

Neither Daisy nor Katherine could find hobby or employment to whip on the tedious slowcoach days. Long before the old year was finished they had made infant clothes enough to stock a crèche; and that occupation came to an end. They were afraid to take much exercise, and nervous lest they took too little. They grew somewhat ill-humoured. Hilary found it difficult to keep the peace between Katherine and Jane, who had been inclined to surliness since the unhappy conclusion of Bolivia's engagement; and Arthur, driven with increasing frequency to seek comfort in the rockery, caught a severe cold through drinking gin in the rain.

Everybody had been very upset by George's letter. Daisy and Katherine had made little or no attempt to hide their anger: they said that such a man as George had no business to be alive, he should have perished from one or other of his excesses long, long ago, and the Law should prevent him from coming home to compete for their inheritance. Even those whose interest in the Nursery

Stakes was merely academical — Miss Montgomery, Mrs. Corcoran, Miss Foster, and some two or three hundred other friendly observers — were genuinely perturbed by the possibility of George Gander's return to Lammiter. He was not only a nuisance, but a dangerous nuisance. He borrowed money, he encouraged young men to drink more than was good for them, his own drunkenness was open and shameless, and he had an old-fashioned habit of seduction. On his last visit to Lammiter both Miss Montgomery and Mrs. Sabby had lost parlour-maids through his attentions, and there were many who still believed that it was on his account the charming but light-headed teacher of gymnastics at the Girls' High School had been compelled to resign. Nobody in Lammiter had any desire to meet George again, and even those who would hate to see good money going to Daisy or Katherine, were horrified to think that George might inherit it instead of them.

After the first shock, however, a certain degree of equanimity returned, and everybody concerned was increasingly eager to discount the likelihood of George's interference. Katherine said, 'He can't possibly have a family, because if he ever did get married, which isn't likely, no woman would live with him long enough to have more than one baby, and he'd have left her months before that anyway. I'm not afraid of George, and I don't suppose we'll ever hear from him again.'

Daisy was less emphatic, but after a few anxious days she became equally sure of the impossibility of

George's intervention. 'Poor George,' she said, with a kind smile and a tremulous movement of her thyroid cartilage. 'I don't believe that he's really wicked, you know, he's only weak. And how he must be suffering now! Because this will bring home to him how terribly he has wasted his life. If he had been sensible, and married and settled down, he might be as happy as we are, and be in a position to benefit by poor Uncle John's will. The wild nomadic life he leads isn't natural, and in the long run I'm sure that beachcombing — well, he isn't a beachcomber, of course, but he's that kind of a person — I'm sure they become very embittered. I myself had something of the gipsy in me when I was a girl, and I've always been grateful for being able to suppress my romantic craving to have done with civilization, and wander for ever in the woods and fields. But poor George hadn't my strength of mind.'

In February there was another alarm. George wrote again, from the same address, to acknowledge Mr. Peabody's communication and to make further inquiries. 'I never thought the old boy had it in him to spring such a surprise on his collection of Willy-wet-legs and Dora Don'ts — I mean my charming cousins,' he wrote. 'I'd like to have seen their faces when you read the will to them. Personally I think it's a good joke, and I hope you'll do something to satisfy my curiosity about the present state of the field. I can figure out who the nominations were, but who were the actual starters? And how are they running? Who's in the lead, and by how much, and who's coming up on the rails? In plain language with no frills, who's got how many babies, who's expecting more, and when?'

Mr. Peabody sought Hilary's advice before he undertook to answer these questions. 'George is, I think, entitled to know the actual statistics,' he explained, 'but I very much doubt whether I would be justified in telling him of the potential statistics, though in the circumstances the latter are of greater importance — of greater news-value, if I may be allowed the phrase — than the former. And yet it is common knowledge that Mrs. Clements and Mrs. Arthur hope shortly to increase their families, and were I merely to tell George that the former has no children, the latter one, I should come dangerously near to being guilty of *suppressio veri*. You see my dilemma? On the one side *suppressio veri*, on the other indelicacy, breach of confidence — though, as neither of them has personally confided in me, we may perhaps disregard that — or at the worst mis-representation — for even medical men, I under-stand, have sometimes been deceived in such cases.'

'Give me George's address, and I'll tell him every-thing,' said Hilary. 'I'll write a nice gossiping family letter, without saying a word about his letters to you, and you can reply to him as officially and formally and discreetly as you like.'

'An excellent suggestion,' said Mr. Peabody gratefully, and on his way home he thought, with as near an approach to idle sentiment as his nature permitted, that it was a great pity Hilary could not inherit the money. She was in no real need of it, of

course, though on account of her recent extrava-
gances — school fees for the Vicar's children, and
another loan to Arthur — she had lately been living
beyond her income. But she was the kind of person
whom good fortune would suit. It would seem
natural to her, and she would wear it as becomingly
as a pretty child a daisy-chain. Mr. Peabody, walking under his umbrella on which the rain beat
noisily, felt a pang as sharp as the rheumatic twinges
that sometimes darted through his right shoulder.
He felt lonely. For nearly thirty years he had been
such a stranger to all kinds of feeling, except
occasional rheumatism and a desire to play Contract Bridge, that he gave to this sensation a greater
importance than it deserved. For a few unhappy
minutes he saw himself, beneath his umbrella, and
Hilary, by the fireside where he had left her, in the
magnification of a sentimental close-up. His feeling
of loneliness became desolation, and through this
emotional telescope he perceived, as never before,
Hilary's honest charm, and kindliness, and good
sense, and physical attraction. Her forty years were
a lighter burden than Daisy's thirty-two, and his
vivid unexpected realization that her lips were firm,
her teeth white and even, her hair a pleasant brown,
her complexion good, induced in Mr. Peabody yet
another novel and bewildering sensation.

Fortunately his nature was unable to sustain or
nurture such feelings. Long abstinence from emotion had destroyed his capacity for it, and his early
instincts to avoid it had been reinforced by an
acquired instinct to get rid of it whenever, with

increasing rarity, it came his way. But he was still
so shaken when he reached home — where his
sister, who resembled him in looks and temper, kept
house for him with impersonal efficiency — that he
tried to open the door with the wrong key. Habit,
however, and a column of foreign news restored his
calm. In the morning it was his custom to read only
the financial pages of *The Times*. The rest of the
paper was reserved for the peaceful hour before
dinner, and under the spell of alien intelligence
Mr. Peabody forgot the emotional squall which
had struck him. Reading of bloodshed and tyranny
in Germany, of France's martial hysteria and helical
finances, of devilment in Manchuria and simplicity in Downing Street, of preparations for war
and demonstrations for peace, of modern inven-
tions and medieval mentality, of Mussolini's
imperialism and de Valera's rural isolation, of
poverty in America and prosperity in the Faroes,
of discontented minorities in Croatia and Catalonia
and dissatisfied majorities everywhere else, of new
designs for death and ancient miseries for life —
reading such matters as these, and forty other signs
of our age and manifestations of civilization, Mr.
Peabody thought, as he had often thought, how
sensible a paper was *The Times*. It did not despise
the events it chronicled, but it did not overrate
their importance. It saw them already with the
calm eye of posterity. *Tempus fugit, Tempora stat*
might be its motto. Men may come and go, but
history is there for ever: looking at the silly world
with the impartial gaze of history Mr. Peabody,

though contemning its folly, was not oppressed by its unhappiness. And he forgot all about Hilary and the other Ganders till the next morning, when he dictated a brief business-like letter to George in Bombay.

Arthur and Daisy and Katherine found this second reminder of George's existence less easy to dismiss than the first had been. They began to remember stories not only of the profligacy of the Orient but of the prolificity of the tropics. Arthur told Daisy that the last Indian census had shown an increase in the population of forty million souls. Daisy suspected, and Katherine declared, that a score or so of George's begetting might well be included in this monstrous growth. They were having tea at Rumneys when she made this uncomfortable suggestion. The enormous fertility of Hindustan darkened their thoughts. Dim visions of obscene temples and procreant jungles and swarming bazaars filled their minds.

Half-spiteful and half-frightened, Katherine said, 'Out of forty million babies some are sure to be George's.'

'But he can't possibly bring them home,' said Daisy.

'Why not?' asked Katherine.

'Well, think what people would say if he came to Lammiter with a huge coffee-coloured family. Even George wouldn't outrage decency to that extent.'

'There's no need for him to come home,' said Jane. 'Twenty children in Bombay are worth as much as twenty children in Lammiter. All he has to do is to send Peabody copies of their birth-certificates, and the money's his.'

Hilary intervened. 'John didn't leave his money to the parent of the largest family, but to the parent of the largest family born in wedlock. And if George has twenty, or even twelve children, they can't all be legitimate.'

'How long has he been in Bombay?' asked Daisy.

'I don't know. We thought he was going to America when he left here the last time.'

'That was seven years ago,' said Katherine thoughtfully. 'But he had been in India before that.'

'He may have become a Mohammedan,' said Jane.

'What difference would that make?' asked Katherine.

'He could have four wives, all perfectly legal, and the children of those wives would be no more illegitimate than Ruth.'

'You couldn't possibly compare them with Ruth,' said Daisy stiffly. 'Arthur and I were married in church . . .'

'And George was married in a mosque. Or probably in four mosques,' said Jane.

'But this is a Christian country . . .'

'There are far more Mohammedans than Christians in the British Empire.'

'That makes no difference at all. Nobody whose parents weren't married in church or a proper registry office can be really legitimate, in our sense of the word, and to compare Ruth with a lot of Mohammedan children is simply disgusting.'

'They'll be her cousins,' said Jane.

'I shan't acknowledge any relationship with them whatsoever.'

'But you won't be able to deny it, and I'm perfectly sure that George will expect Ruth to play with them even if they are a bit black.'

'This will ruin Oliver!' exclaimed Katherine with sudden bitterness. 'He'll have to resign his commission. He can't possibly stay in the Army if it becomes known that he has Indian relations.'

'It's curious to think of your having twenty Mohammedan nephews and nieces,' said Jane.

Further unpleasantness was prevented by Hilary's opportune reminder that they had no real grounds for supposing George had become a Moslem, and in reaction to the sepia pictures they had been painting of a quartet of wives and a multitudinous progeny, they gradually came to assume, and to persuade themselves, that George was still a bachelor and a barren branch.

Meanwhile Hilary's housekeeper, Mrs. Arbor, was also entertaining friends: Mrs. Barrow had come to tea, and Mrs. Finger, the new housekeeper at the Vicarage. Mrs. Finger had a lot of good stories about ducal eccentricities at Starveling Court and the manners and the quiddities of people far remote from the knowledge of Mrs. Barrow and Mrs. Arbor, who valued her friendship accordingly. She had a dry unemotional way of speaking. She would suck in her lips and stare at her interlocutor with black beady eyes that were sometimes more startling than her conversation.

She finished her description of a house-party at Starveling Court during one of Lord Quentin's recurrent periods of affluence, and Mrs. Arbor remarked, 'It must be quite a change for you at the vicarage, Mrs. Finger.'

'He's got water on the brain,' said Mrs. Finger.

'You mean the Vicar?'

Mrs. Finger nodded. 'I've seen it before,' she said. 'Lord Eustace got it: he was the old Duke's brother. It's a puddle under the skull, and it soaks down. Lord Eustace was a bit of a rip in his young days — it was him that had tied a bell under Mrs. Lovely's bed before Lord Everipe went into the wrong room, which he always did, and woke up everyone thinking it was a fire — but after Lord Eustace got water on the brain he began to think he was saved, and sat in the w.c. all day singing hymns. Only it's had a different effect on the Vicar, because he's an atheist now.'

Mrs. Arbor gasped. 'An atheist!' she exclaimed.

'He told me so himself. He said he'd lost his faith.'

'Then he's very, very ill,' said Mrs. Barrow solemnly.

'What did you say to him?' asked Mrs. Arbor.

'I told him he ought to cheer up and get married again. He's the sort of man who needs a wife.'

'But that wouldn't restore his faith,' said Mrs. Arbor.

'Of course it would, if she looked after him properly. Some people can't be Christians unless they're comfortable, and others can't unless they're miserable. There was the Honourable Harry Gallop, for one: he always used to go to church after he'd made a good bet, just to show how happy he was. And there was old Lord Liable who used to give cheques for thousands of pounds to Foreign Missions whenever he went bankrupt: they weren't worth anything, of course, but they showed his piety. Religion takes people different ways, and the Vicar's one of the first kind. If he got another wife, and twenty thousand pounds in the bank, he'd be a roaring Christian in half an hour.'

Mrs. Arbor and Mrs. Barrow were obviously worried by this explanation. They recognized heresy, and suspected blasphemy. Mrs. Barrow made a vague remark or two, and Mrs. Arbor smoothed her dress with a decisive gesture. 'And how is Mr. Stephen getting along?' she asked, signalling a change in the conversation as ostentatiously as a traffic policeman who stops and starts opposing motor streams.

'He's a different man from what he was before Christmas,' said Mrs. Barrow enthusiastically. 'It's a treat to see him now, him and Mr. Wilfrid, they're as happy as sandboys, and working hard, and the letters they write to the students are just a joy to read. I often go in and take a look at them, there's always some lying about, and the sheer human kindness of them is simply a revelation.'

'They're paid for it,' remarked Mrs. Finger.

'Of course they are!' said Mrs. Barrow. 'And so were the teachers who taught you and me and Mrs. Arbor, and all the encouragement I ever got was being hit across the knuckles with a ruler. But Mr.

Stephen and Mr. Wilfrid are like a father and mother to their students. I was reading one of their letters only this morning, and really if you knew the circumstances, it was a marvel they could do it. Because I read the composition it was about — the students all write compositions, and Mr. Wilfrid and Mr. Stephen correct them and say what's wrong with them — and this one was from a young man in Scotland, and he was writing about the Modern Girl, and for all he knew about them he might have been bedridden from birth. Why, he couldn't even spell knickers! But Mr. Wilfrid wasn't angry a bit. He wrote: "Dear Mr. Campbell. We were delighted to receive your Second Exercise and to note the real advance you have made in your studies." Then he went on about his style having improved, and how he'd learned to come to grips with his subject, though of course he hadn't and probably never will, from the sound of him. But Mr. Wilfrid said, "We have taken special interest in your work from the beginning, and we feel quite sure that if you persist in your literary endeavours you will soon find a market for anything you care to write." Then he explained what was wrong with the composition, but all so nicely that it was more like praise than blame. Now if that isn't real Christian kindliness, I never hope to see it.'

'Good business, I call it,' said Mrs. Finger.

'That may be,' said Mrs. Barrow, 'but kindness never did any harm, even in business, and Mr. Wilfrid's kindness itself, and so is Mr. Stephen. I've said from the start, and I still say it, that if the

Major wanted his money to be used with charity and understanding, he should have left it to them.'

'Mr. Arthur needs it more than they do, poor soul,' said Mrs. Arbor with a sigh.

'She can't be more than two or three months off her time now,' said Mrs. Finger.

'The first week in May, I understand,' said Mrs. Arbor.

'It'll be a boy,' said Mrs. Finger.

'I'm sure we all hope so,' said Mrs. Arbor, 'and I won't be surprised if you're right. I was talking to that cook of hers not long ago — a poor thing she is too — and she said that Mrs. Arthur had been eating half a dozen tangerine oranges every day for weeks past, and according to my experience they're much more inclined to fruit when it's a boy, and to solid things like suet puddings and macaroni-and-cheese when it's a girl.'

'I've heard that, too,' said Mrs. Finger, 'and I don't put much trust in it. But you can always tell by their shape. Now Mrs. Arthur's carrying well forward, high, and on the right side. And that's always a boy. You watch her closely and you'll see that her right eye's brighter than the left, though her glasses hide it a little, and there's another sign. And unless I'm much mistaken she steps off with her right foot, which makes it proof positive.'

'That's true,' said Mrs. Barrow, 'I've heard it often and never known it come wrong.'

'Now, Miss Katherine, or Mrs. Oliver, as I should say, is quite different,' said Mrs. Arbor.

'She's certainly spread out,' said Mrs. Barrow.

'Those thin ones often do,' said Mrs. Finger. You wouldn't think they could, and then about the fifth month they begin to open out like an umbrella. I never showed much myself, righ⁺ till the end, I was always stout and thick-set, but my girl Jenny was as slim as a reed, and when she got into trouble we all saw it in no time. She couldn't hide it, being built that way.'

Mrs. Arbor nodded sympathetically.

'Does Miss Katherine still think it's twins?' asked Mrs. Barrow.

'She's sure of it,' said Mrs. Arbor.

'She's preparing for a disappointment,' said Mrs. Barrow. 'They don't often come, and she's got nothing to go by. What do you say, Mrs. Finger?'

Mrs. Finger pursed her lips. 'I wouldn't like to commit myself,' she said, 'but it *might* be twins. She's showing both fore and aft, as you might say, and unless she's farther on than she thinks, and I've seen a lot of mistakes that way, well, she may be right. But you never can tell with a shape like hers.'

'I wouldn't wish for twins myself,' said Mrs. Barrow, 'no matter how much I was going to be paid for them. One at a time's trouble enough, heaven knows.'

'She'll be fit for them,' said Mrs. Finger. 'Her kind always make the best nurses. There was a sister of my own, married well in Rugby, they had The Light Horseman, she was as fat as a cow and never had any milk worth speaking of. But my girl Jenny, who looked like a stick of celery beforehand, could have nursed a dozen.'

The scope of the conversation grew wider. The ripples spread outwards and touched cousins, aunts, grandmothers, friends, and sisters-in-law. Mrs. Arbor put away the tea-cups and brought out a bottle of sherry. The rain beat steadily on the dark window-panes.

A mile away, in Mr. Peabody's office, *The Times*, neatly folded, lay on his leather-topped table ready to be taken home, to be largely opened, to proclaim its sober and dignified tidings of civilization in disgrace, and the renaissance of tyranny. But unmoved by politics, disdainful of alarm, more remote from panic than *The Times* itself, Mrs. Arbor and Mrs. Finger and Mrs. Barrow discreetly sipped their sherry and gave, in their wisdom, their minds to the primary issue of life and the essence of humankind, before which tyrants are impotent and civilization is but a printed page in a gale of wind.

On the first of May, a cold and windy morning, Arthur woke in a resentful mood and clothed himself in the order and manner that betokened, in his code of dressing, a mutinous hatred of the petty surroundings in which he lived. He omitted to shave; he put on pants and trousers, socks and shoes; he considered his bare-chested image in the mirror; and with a grim and bitter smile declaimed:

'Give me a spirit that on this life's rough sea,
Loves to have his sails filled with a lusty wind,
Even till his sail-yards tremble, his masts crack,
And his rapt ship run on her side so low
That she drinks water and, and, and . . .'

He frowned, and clicked his tongue impatiently, but could not remember the next phrase. The passage, a short one, was in an anthology called *Texts and Pretexts* that he had borrowed from Stephen, and in which he had found much to interest him. He had, as he thought, got by heart this brief and stirring extract. It had seemed to fill a want in his utterance. It was a mood with which he had long been acquainted, but which he had never been able to crystallize into speech. The thought was native to him, and the sharp glittering words in which it was caught and essentialized made him hotly and angrily in love with it. Not to re-member the conclusion was exasperating. But the book was downstairs, he would get it and refresh his memory. He opened the door of his dressing-room and marched out as he was, naked to the waist, frowning, unshaved, a rebel who loved to have his sails filled with a lusty wind.

Miss Chiblet, the monthly nurse who had lately taken up residence in the house in preparation for Daisy's lying-in, met him in the passage. She was a refined and severe young woman, a protégée of one of Daisy's friends. 'Oh, Mr. Gander!' she said. 'What a fright you gave me!'

'Tchah!' said Arthur, and went downstairs.

Ruth was in the sitting-room, reading an old Sunday newspaper that she had borrowed from the kitchen. She looked at her father in some surprise, but without sufficient curiosity to ask him what had become of his shirt. She was more interested in the story she was reading. 'It says here,' she exclaimed, 'that a boy in America swallowed a newt, and it wouldn't come out again. So he ate a lot of salt, pounds and pounds of it, and went to a river where there was a very loud waterfall, and lay down on the grass . . .'

Arthur took no notice of his daughter, but searched the bookshelves. He found what he wanted and walked sternly out of the room. Ruth followed him to the foot of the stairs, and shouted, 'But would the newt really come out again when it heard the waterfall? Oh, would it, Daddy? Tell me, please, I want to know!'

Arthur, paying no attention, re-entered his dressing-room and firmly closed the door The anthology opened at the wanted poem. He faced the mirror, the book in his left hand, his right thumb hooked into the top of his trousers, a lowering and belligerent expression on his face. He completed his quotation:

'That she drinks water and her keel ploughs air.
There is no danger to a man that knows
What life and death is; there's not any law
Exceeds his knowledge; neither is it lawful
That he should stoop to any other law.'

'It's absurd,' he muttered to his image, 'it's fantastically absurd that a man like me should be cribbed and cabined by mean and meagre domestic bonds. A soldier, by God! And I spend my time telephoning for the doctor and reading *The Wind in the Willows* to Daisy! I've had enough of it. This isn't the life for me. I want to live where there's no law but the law of life and death. A battlefield, a frontier, a pioneer's cabin: they're the places for me. And it isn't too late to change! I could go to Kenya, to the Peace River country, to, to, to — well, there's a dozen other places. Or gun-running. In Manchuria, to Paraguay, to the Communists in South China: a man's life, beyond the law, desperate and unafraid till the masts crack and the sea comes in, and there's an end!'

The door opened and Ruth's solemn bespectacled face came round the edge of it. 'Daddy,' she asked, 'would the newt really come out when it heard the waterfall? Because the boy had taken lots and lots of salt?'

'I don't know and I don't care,' said Arthur.

'Why were you making faces at yourself in the glass?'

'Get out of here! Go and have your breakfast!' shouted Arthur.

'It isn't ready yet,' said Ruth.

Arthur pushed her out and closed the door again.

'Children hanging on to my coat-tails,' he growled; 'children filling the house, babies and nurses and cradles in every damned room: by God, it's too much! I'm a soldier, not a wet nurse. . . . There are rifles in that crate and machine-gun parts in the other. Fifty short magazine Lee-Enfields, and twenty thousand rounds of ammunition. Get 'em unpacked, quick, and spread your men along that ridge. We'll hold the pass as long as there's a round left, or I'll shoot the first man who turns tail. I'm not frightened of those damned Japs!'

Arthur confronted a particularly sinister reflexion; his eyebrows were gathered in a fearful frown, his lips were twisted to a sneer of cold command. He was not only gun-running in Manchuria but taking command of a rearguard action against the invaders.

There was a knock at the door. 'Go away!' cried Arthur.

'Oh, Mr. Gander,' said Miss Chiblet, invisible but insistent, 'Mrs. Gander wants to speak to you. She won't believe me when I tell her there's no hurry, and she'd like you to telephone to the doctor again.'

Arthur stared at his stern parti-clad image. 'Three hundred yards; half-left, two stunted trees, enemy machine-gun post; three rounds rapid; *fire!*' he commanded.

Miss Chiblet knocked again. 'Mr. Gander,' she repeated.

'Yes, yes!' shouted Arthur. 'I'm coming. Good heavens, do you think I'm deaf?'

He put on his dressing-gown and knotted its girdle with a savage tug. He had telephoned to the doctor at tea-time on the previous day, and again at eleven o'clock. The doctor had said, a little testily, that he was a busy man and they were wasting his time. Miss Chiblet would know when he was needed, and he didn't propose to return till she sent for him. But Daisy, with a woman's mistrust of women, again refused to rely on Miss Chiblet's judgment and thought her symptoms grave enough to warrant the doctor's personal attention.

Arthur went sulkily to the telephone. The doctor had a loud barking voice that made his ear-drum quiver like a stricken gong. He wouldn't accept Arthur's report of the situation and insisted on speaking to Miss Chiblet. Arthur returned to Daisy and tried to reason with her. Escaping at last, he finished dressing and took Ruth to Rumneys, where, it had been arranged, she should stay till the crisis was over.

At five o'clock the doctor threatened to give up the case if Arthur telephoned to him again, and at three o'clock in the morning Arthur was driven out into the darkness to summon him from sleep, and talk to him as man to man, and explain to him that Daisy's constitution was entirely different from that of other women — she said so herself — and that he must come at once, no matter what Miss Chiblet said, or the consequences might be appalling.

After another day of recurrent alarms and a night still more disturbed, the baby was born at the respectable hour of eleven o'clock in the morning. As Mrs. Finger had predicted, it was a boy. The doctor, somewhat resentfully, said it was a healthy child and that Daisy was very comfortable. Arthur collected his gardening tools, and retiring to the rockery drank half a bottle of gin and fell sound asleep.

This notable advance in Daisy's bid for fortune was enthusiastically acclaimed, and in three days more than a hundred people came to inquire about her health, to offer congratulations, and to leave flowers. Her room, and indeed the whole house, looked like a Chicago gunman's funeral in the palmy days of Prohibition; and her cook was incapacitated by a serious attack of hay-fever.

Arthur suffered rather badly from the joint effect of sleepless nights and the half-bottle of gin, and succumbing to the general atmosphere of *malaise*, took to spending most of the day in a dressing-gown. His rebellious mood, his nostalgia for lusty winds and a cracking mast and military operations in Manchuria, vanished entirely, and he luxuriated in a gentle self-pity. Upstairs there was a constant coming and going, the running to and fro of Miss Chiblet as she sought in vain to keep pace with Daisy's ever-changing needs — windows to be opened and windows to be shut, barley-water and malted milk, pillows to be added or subtracted, visitors to be admitted and others to be ushered away, the cradle to be moved out of a draught or out of the sun — but downstairs Arthur sat alone among the surplus flowers, and was pleasantly sorry for himself, for his loneliness and neglectedness, and the increase of his responsibilities.

But self-pity could not dominate his temper for long, and presently, observing the restless commotion of which his son was centre — the bustle of preparing bottles and changing diapers and filling baths — it occurred to him that women were un-businesslike and inefficient creatures, and if the child were to have a proper chance to thrive and grow he had better assume command of the situation himself. So he began assiduously to read several books on the feeding and management of infants, which Daisy had previously bought, and made a great nuisance of himself by testing with a large and dimly-figured thermometer the temperature of the child's bath water, and by insisting that all bottles should be sterilized in his presence. Nor was he content with the orthodox routine of a nursery, but discovering the functional instability of a baby he began to cast about for some method of reducing the incessant labours of its attendants. After several days of anxious thought he hit upon a brilliant idea, and having carried a packing-case, a sheet of glass, and some carpenter's tools into the sitting-room, he set to work.

While he was busy with a saw, Stephen and Wilfrid were shown in. Wilfrid had brought a magnificent bundle of pale yellow tulips. They exchanged greetings, and Arthur assured them that Daisy and her child were progressing favourably.

'How terribly excited you must be!' said Wilfrid.

'It's been a wearing time,' said Arthur, 'very wearing indeed. I wouldn't willingly go through it again. The responsibility's great, and one suffers a lot of natural anxiety, and — well, my feelings were something like those of a Divisional H.Q. during the War, when the troops were going forward, and of course one didn't know what was happening to them. I've seen Headquarters absolutely white with anxiety at such times.'

'What are you making?' asked Stephen. 'A cage?'

'Something of the kind,' said Arthur. 'As a matter of fact it's a new nursery appliance that I've invented. The ordinary methods of looking after a baby are quite hopelessly antiquated — women are conservative creatures, you know, and absolutely without imagination — and as soon as I began to watch Miss Chiblet at work I saw there was room for new ideas. No one has ever thought of babies in a scientific way. No one has tried to classify them. How, for example, would you define a baby?'

'A young mammal, I suppose,' said Stephen; and Wilfrid cried, 'Oh, that's far too easy! I'm sure Arthur's thinking of something terribly difficult and unexpected.'

'Your answer isn't scientific, it isn't accurate,' said Arthur. 'The proper definition is this: a baby is a biological system of uncontrolled apertures. Now consider what that means.'

'Indeed, I shan't,' said Stephen.

'It means,' said Arthur firmly, 'that the nurse or the mother, as the case may be, is always busy changing its clothes. And that's a waste of time, of labour, and of money. Now this invention of mine is not only labour-saving, but by doing away with all laundry-work it will save money as well. I shall probably patent it, and make a steady income out of it.'

'But how does it work?' asked Wilfrid.

Arthur, with obvious pleasure, turned the open side of the packing-case towards them. 'It's simply a cage with a glass front and a sliding floor,' he said. 'On each side, behind an interior wall of wire-netting, I'm going to put a small oil-lamp, and cut holes in the roof for ventilation. That will keep it warm, and the child can lie there quite comfortably, naked, on a carpet of cotton-wool. No bother about dressing or undressing, you see; you simply bath it in the morning and put it straight in.'

Stephen and Wilfrid looked with dubious appraisement at the half-made cage.

'The glass front moves up and down,' said Arthur, 'and the sliding floor can be removed when necessary.'

'It sounds marvellous,' said Wilfrid.

'Do you think Daisy will approve of it?' asked Stephen.

'Daisy will see its advantages and, naturally, defer to my judgment,' said Arthur. Frowning a little, he sat down with a roll of wire-netting in his hands, and plucked idly at it as though it were a banjo.

'You're looking tired, Arthur,' said Wilfrid.

Arthur sighed. 'One can't have a baby without suffering,' he said.

'It's a primitive and disgusting business,' Stephen observed.

'We've been talking *such* a lot about you, and wondering how you were getting on,' said Wilfrid.

'And even you, who are sympathetic, can't properly realize the nerve-racking strain of it all,' said Arthur. 'I myself have often pooh-pooh'd the sufferings of other men in similar circumstances: but I never shall again. For nearly a week I had no sleep, or hardly any sleep. I was worn to a shadow. But I couldn't lie down and admit defeat, I had to keep going, of course, and somehow or other I managed it. I really ought to go away somewhere and have a proper rest, and forget about it, but I don't see how it can be done: I can hardly leave the child alone at ten days old.'

'Dr. Banner's very good at these cases, isn't he?' asked Wilfrid. 'At least I've always heard so.'

'Yes, in a way,' said Arthur, 'but I shouldn't have him again. I think I'd go to Dr. Umble another time. Banner knows his job, of course, but one wants more than mere technical knowledge at such a time. One needs sympathy and understanding, and Banner's rather brusque and off-handed. On Tuesday night, for instance — or rather early on Wednesday morning — I went to see him and explain the situation. I felt it was no use to telephone, I had to see him personally, because I really thought the baby might arrive at any moment, and though Miss Chiblet is fully trained, and said to be very clever, I didn't altogether rely on her judgment. So I dressed, and went out, and rang Banner's night-bell, and really, from the way he spoke to me you might have thought there was nothing more seriously wrong with me than toothache. I was feeling wretchedly ill and worried, and I got no sympathy from him, not even common politeness. Now that isn't good enough. To be treated in that way, considering the state I was in, might have had very serious consequences.'

'I should hate to be a doctor,' said Stephen.

'Their great fault is lack of imagination,' said Arthur. 'To be told to go away, to be driven from his door in the condition I was in that night, was absolute barbarity. Banner didn't realize it, of course, but that's what it was: barbarity. How I ever managed to get home I don't know.'

Wilfrid said, 'Do you think you could get someone to put these tulips in water, Arthur? They're rather lovely, and they won't last if they're not looked after properly.'

'I'll go and find a vase myself,' said Arthur.

'Oh no! You're too tired.'

Arthur rose and picked up the faggot of lovely flowers. 'It was very kind of you to bring them,' he said.

'I thought you'd like to have them,' said Wilfrid.

'I don't think we ought to stay much longer,' Stephen suggested, when Arthur had gone out.

'No,' answered Wilfrid. 'Poor Arthur's looking

dreadfully pulled down. We mustn't talk too much, or we'll tire him.'

But Arthur was unwilling for them to go so soon. 'No, no,' he said, 'this is doing me good, it really is. I haven't had a proper chance to talk things over with anyone yet, and it's a tremendous relief, after having gone through so much, to get it off one's mind.'

'Still, I think it's time for us to go now,' said Stephen.

Arthur sat down and impressively continued his story: 'Wednesday was the longest day of my life,' he said. 'I don't know how I got through it. But it seems, when we're put to the test, as though we have reserves of strength that otherwise we never suspect. I was in constant discomfort, and about eleven o'clock at night, when the pains were definitely getting stronger and more regular . . .'

'But you didn't actually *feel* them, did you?' asked Wilfrid with a horrified expression.

'I think I can safely say that I suffered more than Daisy did,' said Arthur. 'The mind has a greater capacity for pain than the body. The body is a limited thing, but imagination is infinite. You see, women are biologically intended for motherhood, but man, I feel sure, being more finely constructed, is intended only to play the part of the lover. We should love and go free. We were never meant to stand the strain of fatherhood.'

'It sounds a dreadful experience, as you tell it,' said Wilfrid. 'I'd no idea it was so bad as that. I do think you've been brave, Arthur. I couldn't bear it myself, I know I couldn't.'

'But you'll be well paid for your trouble,' said Stephen. 'You have two children now, and none of the rest of us has any. It looks as though you're going to be Uncle John's heir.'

'Oh, money!' said Arthur. 'I'm not obsessed by the idea of money, and I never have been. I shan't be mean when Uncle John's — how much was it? Sixty or seventy thousand? I forget — when Uncle John's estate is handed over to me. If either of you ever want a couple of thousand to play with, all you'll have to do is to let me know.'

'Oh, won't that be lovely!' cried Wilfrid. 'I do think that's generous of you, Arthur. But what about Katherine? Mrs. Barrow told me she went to the nursing-home yesterday morning.'

'We all knew she was going sooner or later,' said Arthur. 'But that won't make any difference. She'll have one child, but I have two.'

'Mrs. Barrow said she wouldn't be surprised if Katherine had twins.'

'Katherine started that story herself,' said Arthur testily, 'and a lot of old women have been foolish enough to believe it. But it's simply nonsense: the wish was father to the thought, but a wish can't produce babies: and I'd willingly wager five hundred pounds to a penny that even though she has a dozen she'll never have twins. Do either of you want to bet?'

'Lend me a penny, quick!' cried Wilfrid; and Stephen gave him one.

'There!' said Wilfrid, throwing it on the table. 'I'll take the bet, and if Katherine has twins . . .'

'She won't,' said Arthur. 'There's absolutely no reason why she should.'

Muted by an intervening wall, the ringing of the telephone bell interrupted him. Arthur went into the hall and took down the receiver. 'Hullo,' he said. 'Oh, yes, yes, we're all well. I meant to have a sleep this afternoon, but Stephen and Wilfrid came in, and I had to talk to them. Yes, we're all getting on as well as can be expected.'

It was Hilary who had rung up. 'I'm speaking from the nursing home,' she said.

'And how's Katherine?'

'Very pleased with herself, I imagine.'

'Good,' said Arthur. 'Is it all over?'

'Well, I hope so. The second one arrived ten minutes ago.'

'Wh — what do you mean?' stammered Arthur.

'She's got twins,' said Hilary.

Arthur put back the receiver with a shaking hand. Instead of a credit balance of seventy thousand pounds, he was faced with five hundred on the debit side.

XVI

KATHERINE'S dramatic feat aroused intense excitement. The human side of her achievement, however, was somewhat overshadowed by its competitive significance. To have vindicated so successfully
her promise of twins — they were fine healthy children, a boy and a girl — was in itself an example of
progenitive virtuosity that deserved the warmest
commendation; but the popular mind was more
taken by the fact of her having so brilliantly
demolished Daisy's lead in the Nursery Stakes.
Starting as an outsider, she had, in a remarkably
short time, overtaken the favourite and was now
running neck and neck with her. She was rewarded
by almost as many letters as Daisy had received, and
by even more flowers. But many of the callers came
out of curiosity, and most of the flowers were sent as
an indication of sporting interest rather than a
pledge of friendship. For Katherine was hardly beloved, even by her acquaintances, and certainly not
by her friends; and though no one could honestly
regret her production of twins — for it made the
most enthralling topic of conversation that Lammiter had known since the marriage of the Duke of
York — there were many who thought it hard lines
on Daisy, and hoped she would not yet give up the
race. There were still sixteen months to go, and a
great deal could happen in that time. Daisy, they
hoped, would not lose heart.

In the Red Lion and the Green Dragon, at the Yeomanry Club, at the tobacconist's in Green Street, and other places where betting was indulged in — books had also been made in the Lammiter Ladies' Club and the Golf Club — Daisy was quoted at three to one against, and at eleven to two when it became known that Katherine's husband was definitely coming home from India on short leave in September: but so much money was available at the latter price that the odds shortened again to fours. In the previous summer Daisy had started odds on, but Katherine's cocksure prophecy of twins had given rise to a great run in her favour, and not till about Christmas time had the betting settled down to a reasonable basis. Between then and March little new money had been forthcoming, but now there was enormous activity in hedging, implementing, and the placing of psychic or inspirational bets.

All the books, however, were hopelessly upset — from the backers' point of view — by a sudden telegram from Marseilles. It was addressed to Mr. Peabody, and the sender was George. It stated: 'Children and I arrive at Plymouth twenty-sixth will wire time of arrival Lammiter later.'

Like a winter squall, opening dark and fanwise on the sea, the tidings ran through Lammiter, and like December sea-wind it chilled the hearts of all who heard it: or nearly all, for it is true that a little minority, naturally coarse or toughened by a slapstick fate, laughed long and loudly at the news: but the large majority were truly shocked, truly apprehensive, and in many cases coldly dismayed.

Katherine was the most violently affected. Daisy, indeed, wept almost continuously for forty-eight hours, but as the weather was fine and she lay all day in a long chair in her garden, she was able to take the flowers into her confidence, and though the loquacious beauty of white lilac excited more tears, the brave sympathy of some purple irises mitigated their bitterness. It would be unfair to say that she enjoyed her grief, but she certainly found relief in facile abandonment to it. Arthur minimized the shock by discreet recourse to gin, and Stephen, though profoundly disturbed by the thought of George's return, could not restrain a small spiteful satisfaction at the prospective defeat of Katherine and Daisy. Hilary concealed her feelings and bade Mrs. Arbor make ready several bedrooms for George and his family; and Jane, hearing this, flew into a temper and swore that if Rumneys were turned into an asylum for half-castes she would leave it and live for ever at the Club. But Katherine neither hid her emotion nor found escape from it. Katherine promptly went into hysterics, and the twins, tuning-in to the wave-length of her distemper, amplified her ululation in a way that would have startled pandemonium. They were robust infants, and howling seemed to do them good. Because Katherine was so distraught a wet-nurse was found for them: they drained her dry and bellowed afresh. They were given bottles, scientifically prepared: they sucked them empty and howled like a double Hecuba. Katherine, tearing the sheets, vociferously demanded

274

their return: she nursed them, whickering the while, and they screamed like an American police car. All the other patients, except an aviator whose parachute had failed to open, got up and dressed themselves and left the nursing-home; and Katherine and her twins continued their symphony of wrath to an angry audience of nurses, doctors, and housemaids.

It was, however, only to be expected that the Ganders should be upset by the prospect of George's return with a family of unknown origin and colour. What no one could have foreseen was the effect of the news on so many other people in Lammiter, and on almost everybody in Lammiter West. The apprehension, the cold dislike, the drawing-room dismay with which it was first received, grew imperceptibly to a kind of panic. Miss Montgomery remembered, with advantage, that George had once seduced her parlourmaid. Mrs. Sabby recalled the rumour that he had ruined hers. The Chairman of the Education Committee, thinking of the similar fate that had befallen a young teacher of gymnastics, gravely warned the assembled headmasters of Lammiter that danger, like a lion in the way, would shortly attend the coming to and fro of all their female assistants. Mothers whose eldest sons had drunk their first glass of beer under the shadow of George's elbow grew alarmed for the safety of their Benjamins. Shopkeepers determined to give no credit to George or to his family, and bank managers told their cashiers to scrutinize with added care all cheques that were presented. The Empire

League of Youth passed a resolution condemning, in the strongest terms, miscegenation; and the Women Citizens contemplated a petition to the Home Secretary to prevent George from landing at any English port. The British Women's Temperance Association was urged to special prayer — but the motion emanated from a somewhat fanatical member — and the Special Constables, in the privacy of their bedrooms, assiduously practised the rapid drawing of their truncheons.

Such, after infinite repetition of gossip and the inordinate exchange of rumours, was the effect of George's telegram. In the course of three or four days he came to be regarded as a monster, a kind of dragon, or evil spectre. The most sober and responsible people yielded to the infection of this superstitious fear, while domestic servants, errand-boys, and children were roused to almost intolerable excitement. It was generally assumed that George's offspring were black: there was no authority for this belief, for no one had seen the complexion of their mother, but it was perhaps a natural supposition: so attendant upon George — at least in the imagination of children, errand-boys, and domestic servants — there would be a troop of swart young heathens, brightly clad. It was, then, with feverish anticipation that Lammiter awaited the day of their arrival.

In the early afternoon of May 25th Mr. Peabody received a radiogram from the s.s. *City of Prague*, then at sea, which read: 'Docking at Plymouth early tomorrow reach Lammiter two oclock Gander.' By tea-time the news was common property, and on the following day a crowd of more than fifteen hundred people assembled at the station to see George's arrival.

Hilary and Mr. Peabody were there, with Arthur and Wilfrid, but Stephen had refused to come, and Jane, thanks to the timely synchronization of unrelated events, was playing in the Ladies' Open Golf Championship at Porthcawl. The crowd was quiet and orderly, but Hilary was sorely embarrassed to see that George's advent had already provoked such interest, and had it not been for Wilfrid she would have fled from so many spectators. Wilfrid, however, was delighted by the crowd's attention, and his high spirits fortified her against the beam of three thousand curious eyes.

The train was signalled. Wilfrid, arm-in-arm between Hilary and Arthur, capered excitedly on the platform. The crowd on the road outside pressed against the railings and closed densely round the station entrance.

Coming smoothly and slowly round a bend in the line, coming almost silently — steel kissing steel and steam with a sigh escaping — the train slid to a standstill. Doors opened, porters hurried, and seven passengers got out. But none of them was George, none was a child, and all were obvious though unassuming Nordics.

Mr. Peabody fumbled in his pocket and found George's telegram.

' "Reach Lammiter two oclock," ' he repeated. 'It's quite clear and definite. I can't think why he

277

isn't here, unless the ship was delayed by fog or some accident, and then surely he would have let us know.'

'Perhaps he's changed his mind and isn't coming at all,' suggested Arthur hopefully. Ten minutes earlier Wilfrid had assured him that the five hundred pounds bet he had lost had not been seriously intended; and Arthur, who had avoided Wilfrid for the last ten days, was so greatly relieved — though he had never meant to pay so monstrous a debt — that his normal tendency to optimism was greatly exaggerated.

'George has missed his train,' said Hilary decisively. 'That's the explanation, and it's what we might have expected from him.'

Mr. Peabody looked incredulous, for punctuality was a condition of his life, and he thought the missing of trains was part of a humorist's stock-in-trade rather than a piece of actual existence; but Wilfrid, calling to the stationmaster, asked when the next train from Plymouth was due.

'Five-thirty,' said the stationmaster, 'but it's a local, and Mr. Gander won't be in that, if he's sensible. The next fast one's nine-thirty-seven.'

'We'd better meet the five-thirty as well,' said Hilary, turning to go. 'George would no more avoid a bad train than a bad habit.'

The crowd was disappointed and somewhat resentful to find they had wasted their time. It was Wilfrid who appeased their curiosity and loudly announced that George had missed the train. The word was repeated, and grumbling comment accompanied it. The pressure of the crowd changed its direction outwards, and, to the sound of hoarse complaint and the cackle of disillusion, dispersion began. The crowd thawed, obstructed its own movement, melted, and vanished. But at half-past five nearly six hundred of them returned to the station, again to be disappointed, and at twenty-seven minutes past nine they were back in full strength, inclined to be noisy now, and many of them smelling healthily of beer.

For the third time their mission was in vain: George had not yet arrived; and the crowd grew angry. Someone, they thought, had tricked them. And they began to show their displeasure. A police inspector escorted Arthur, Wilfrid, and Mr. Peabody from the station, while six constables benignly opposed their strength against the unruliest sections of the mob.

Hilary, after two useless journeys, had stayed at home. She heard the latest news with a slightly irritated composure. 'We might have known what would happen,' she said. 'If George is to be relied on for anything at all, it's for being unreliable. Well, I'm going to no more trouble for him. If he comes here, he can stay here; and if he doesn't, so much the better.'

Wilfrid said, 'I suppose it isn't possible . . .'

'What?' asked Arthur.

'Well, people sometimes play practical jokes.'

Mr. Peabody pursed his lips and raised his eyebrows — because his skin was so tight these were both difficult processes — and looked the very picture of legal scepticism. Hilary seemed thoughtful for a moment, then slowly shook her head. But optimism and credulity, those rosy twins, led Arthur up the garden-path immediately, and ante-dating his instant conversion he declared, 'That's it! Of course it is. George has been pulling our legs! I suspected it from the very beginning. Those letters of his didn't read like serious inquiries — we should never have been deceived by them, and, in fact, I wasn't — and those two telegrams could have been written by anyone. I was never convinced of their authenticity. And now, of course, it's quite clear that he persuaded some friend of his to send them: someone who happened to be coming home, who wasn't too scrupulous, and had the same idea of a joke as George. Well, well! He's had us absolutely on a string, hasn't he? Or most of us, at any rate. Even Wilfrid was caught to begin with: weren't you, Wilfrid? George is a clever fellow, a very clever fellow indeed, but he'll have to get up earlier in the morning if he wants to surprise me. I'm too old a bird to be caught napping. It was a good try, though. I give George full marks for it. A very good joke indeed. And Hilary got their rooms all ready for them, eh? Well, George would laugh if he knew that!'

Arthur stood before the fire, his right hand in his trouser-pocket, his left elbow on the mantelpiece — the fingers amiably waving — and looked down at the others with a plump and happy smile. No one answered him. But he chuckled loudly. 'An extremely good joke,' he repeated. 'I'll remember this, and give George credit for it, as long as I live.'

At the far end of the room a maid came in with a
tray of glasses and a decanter. Hilary looked inquiringly at Mr. Peabody, and suggested bridge. Mr.
Peabody was eager for a game, Wilfrid and Arthur
were agreeable to it. They played for an hour,
intent upon their cards but aware of an underlying
euphrasy that had nothing to do with good hands or
successful bidding: for George and his family had
not arrived, and though Arthur's optimism might
be unwarranted, there was none of them could
wholly withstand the infection of hope. At the least
they had been given another evening's grace.

At a quarter to eleven Mr. Peabody remarked,
with obvious intention to continue, that he hoped
they would have time for another rubber. Arthur
helped himself to whisky and soda, and sat down
again. Hilary, in the act of dealing, paused and
listened. Her ears, attuned to the life of the house,
had caught, or so she imagined, a distant noise,
unusual at that hour and surprising. But she might
have been mistaken: she continued to deal. 'One
heart,' she said carefully.

The door at the far end of the room opened again,
and a maid, in a voice that was high-pitched with
excitement, announced, 'Mr. George Gander,
ma'am.'

XVII

BLINKING at the light, George came into the room, and after a moment's hesitation, stepped cheerfully forward. 'Well, Hilary!' he exclaimed, and before he could say more tripped over a rug, and stumbling violently, broke into a little run to maintain his balance and brought up with a heavy hand on Mr. Peabody's shoulder: for the card-players sat still, their heads turned towards him, but too surprised for any larger movement.

'That bloody rug!' he said amiably. 'If I've tripped on it once I've tripped on it a hundred times. Why don't you give it away, or hide it when you know I'm coming home?'

'How did you get here?' asked Hilary.

George bent and kissed her affectionately. 'You look younger every time I see you,' he said. 'If we hadn't been brought up together like brother and sister. . . .'

'We weren't,' said Hilary brusquely. George's kiss had been too alcoholically scented for her liking.

'. . . if we weren't right in the middle of the prohibited degrees I couldn't stay in the same room for two minutes without making love to you, in spite of old Peabody there. How are you, Peabody? Grave-robbing still profitable? Still plundering widows and orphans at six-and-eight a kick? And Arthur, by God! Arthur, you old hypocrite, I'm damned glad to see you.'

'This is Mr. Follison: my cousin George,' said Hilary.

'How d'you do, old man?' said George. 'Any friend of Hilary's is a friend of mine.' He shook Wilfrid warmly by the hand, who stared at him in simple amazement.

George pulled a chair nearer to the table, and sat down. 'The wanderer's return,' he said, beaming on all impartially. ' "The Good Wife's sons come home again, for her blessings on their head." '

He was a little man, very shabbily dressed in a thin blue suit. His collar was soiled, and his pale brown shoes were cracked. He had a broad, innocent forehead, and dark hair that was growing thin on top. Under briefly smudged brows his eyes, though somewhat bleary, somewhat yellowish at the circumference, were an undefeated and ever-twinkling blue, and his lips, though they parted to show blackened teeth, were well and whimsically cut. His complexion was a pallid yellowish-brown, and his fingers, none too clean, were broadly tobacco-stained. He was by no means the monster, the ogre, of popular imagination, but in Hilary's drawing-room he looked startlingly disreputable, and his voice did nothing to discount his appearance. For his voice was rich and deep and a little too loud; his intonation was vulgarly assured; and his accent was a strange amalgam, such as sailors acquire, with sometimes a hint of American, and sometimes a touch of cockney in it.

Mr. Peabody cleared his throat. 'We expected you to arrive early this afternoon,' he said.

283

'And that's what I expected,' said George. 'But you'd got nothing else to do but expect: you could sit still and expect in comfort: I'd got to catch a train as well.'

'And you missed it?' asked Hilary.

'By an hour and a half,' said George, 'and so did three of my fellow-voyagers and a bottle of brandy that one of them was taking home to cure his father-in-law's rheumatism. And the next one I missed by all eternity, because I knew nothing about it till it had gone. But I caught the third. I caught it very comfortably indeed. I was nestling in the arms of Morpheus, in a corner-seat with my back to the engine, half an hour before it started.'

'But that must have been the nine twenty-seven,' said Mr. Peabody, 'and you certainly didn't arrive by it. I was on the platform myself in order to meet you.'

'If Gabriel and God's own string-band had been there I'd have disappointed them. I'm no sleep-walker, and I didn't lift an eyelid till we got to Wishington. Then the girls began to tickle me, so I woke up, and they said they thought we must be getting near Lammiter.

'The girls!' said Hilary.

'By God!' said George. 'I'd forgotten all about 'em. They're downstairs somewhere: they were too shy to come up, I suppose. And that *badmash* of a taxi-driver's there too. He wants thirty bob for driving us back from Wishington, the *suar*, and I've lost my pocket-book somewhere. Lend me a couple of pounds, Peabody, will you? You can charge it to the estate.'

Hilary led the way downstairs, closely pursued by Wilfrid and Arthur. George and Mr. Peabody followed as soon as George had received his two pounds.

Four steps from the bottom Hilary halted to look, with dismay, at the picture of George's family. It was worse than she had expected. It was as bad as she had ever feared . . . Sitting on the oak settle were two small boys in dirty sailor-suits: they were thin, coffee-coloured, black-haired, with bulging foreheads and very bony knees: one was sniffing and sobbing, the other, open-mouthed, was silently weeping. Beside them sat a dumpy girl of about fifteen, rather lighter in colour, with a khaki topee on the back of her head. On the opposite side of the hall, in a tall brocaded chair, sat another girl intently scrutinizing an illustrated magazine: on closer inspection she was seen to be extremely pretty, and the magazine turned out to be the *Illustrated Nudist Gazette*. The eldest of the family stood near the door talking to the taxi-driver. She was a slim and lovely young woman, and from her animated demeanour she was clearly enjoying herself: the taxi-driver was not ill-looking. Lying untidily about the hall were eight or ten pieces of luggage: two battered fibre trunks, a bruised tin trunk, a string-bag, and several brown-paper parcels.

With a last bewitching smile the oldest girl left the taxi-driver and came to meet Hilary. Her manner was self-possessed, her voice was thin and rather metallic, and she spoke with a quick sing-song intonation.

'I am Miss Doris Gander,' she said. 'You are my Aunt Hilary, no doubt. Our father has told us all about you, and I am very pleased to meet you.'

'How do you do,' said Hilary faintly. 'I'm sorry you were left downstairs, but George — your father, that is. . . .'

'Oh, that is quite all right. We have been admiring your bungalow. I think it is ripping.'

'You must take your little brothers to bed,' said Hilary. 'They look tired-out.'

'There is nothing the matter with them,' said Doris. 'They are just cry-babies, that is all.'

George, with Mr. Peabody's two pounds in his pocket, came briskly downstairs. 'Well, Hilary,' he exclaimed, 'what d'you think of them? Isn't this a girl to be proud of? Aren't they a healthy-looking crowd? "And they learned from their wistful mother to call Old England home".'

'Where is their mother?' whispered Hilary.

George pointed to the floor with his tobacco-brown index finger. 'Under the sod in a foreign soil,' he answered cheerfully. 'The tragedy of my life, Hilary. Don't let's talk about it. Have all the children been introduced to you?'

'Only Doris,' said Hilary.

'Well, that's Tessie, with the magazine. A very studious girl, quiet and bookish in her tastes, like me. Come and say how-d'you-do to your Aunt Hilary, Tessie. What have you been reading, eh? Good God, where did you get this?'

'You bought it at the station,' said Tessie.

'Our father is always taking pains that we shall be

286

well educated,' said Doris. 'We are all great readers. Our father. . . .'

'Don't call me "our father",' said George irritably. 'You make me sound like a bit of the Lord's Prayer, and for a modest man that's most embarrassing. Now, the other girl, the fat one with the hat on, is Clarice, and the boys are Edward and Timothy. What are you crying for, Timmy?'

'*Bahut bhukha hun,*' wailed Timothy, and Edward, between sobs, cried shrilly after him, '*Bahut bhukha hun!*'

'Can't they speak English?' asked Hilary.

'Sometimes you'd be surprised by their command of our rich and flexible language,' said George. 'But in moments of stress, in the hours of emotion or fatigue, they're liable to fall back on Hindustani.'

'They have learnt it from their *ayah*, no doubt,' Doris explained, 'and they have also heard it from the *mali* and the other servants when they are playing in the compound.'

'*Bahut bhukha hun,*' whimpered Timothy.

'But what does he want?' asked Hilary.

'He says he's hungry,' said Doris, 'but he is only a cry-baby. He has been eating cakes and such-like delicacies all day, and he ought to be highly thankful for so many good things instead of making tantrums in other person's bungalow.'

'Mrs. Arbor,' said Hilary.—Mrs. Arbor had silently joined the company.—'Take these children to the nursery, and the little girl with the hat on too, and get them to bed, and give them some hot milk.'

Mrs. Arbor led the little boys upstairs, and Clarice, a phlegmatic child, obediently followed.

Hilary turned to Doris: 'I expect you and your sister are almost as tired as the children?'

'Oh, no, indeed!' said Doris. 'We are well used to late nights. In Bombay we are constantly at balls and parties, in the Yacht Club and the Byculla Club and elsewhere as well, and there the merriment never finishes before the wee small hours.'

'I'm afraid you'll find Lammiter rather dull in comparison,' said Hilary.

They all returned to the drawing-room except George, who was arguing with the taxi-driver. 'I repeat, for your benefit,' he said, 'that I've just come home from India, and I haven't had time to change my several lakhs of rupees into pounds, shillings, and pence. So tell your employer to send the bill to this address, and meanwhile here's half a crown for yourself. You won't do any good by being rude, because this is all the English money I've got. So take it or leave it.'

Having got rid of the taxi-driver without wasting Mr. Peabody's two pounds, George, well pleased with himself, joined the others in the drawing-room.

He found Arthur, Wilfrid, and Mr. Peabody sitting side by side on a couch. None of them had spoken a word since their first glimpse of these new exotic Ganders, and they were still silently entranced by the spectacle of Doris in lively conversation with Hilary, and of Tessie on a *pouf* beside her. The latter view, indeed, was intermittently disconcerting to Arthur and Wilfrid, for the *pouf* was low, and she sat in such a way that beyond her stocking-tops a segment of unclad thigh was visible, on which, ever and again, by horrid accident, their gaze embarrassingly fell. But even without this disturbing peep-show they would have been far from comfortable and just as attentive. Every glance from Tessie's lustrous eyes put them out of countenance, and Doris, with a sidelong look, brought blushes to their cheeks. Even Mr. Peabody betrayed something like emotion, though in a negative way: for his attitude was that of a small boy confronting for the first time a mandril or giraffe — notionless, blankly staring, transfixed by wonder, lost in uncharted seas beyond experience. Nothing like Tessie or Doris had ever been seen before in Lammiter, unless in the talking-picture theatres.

They were disturbingly lovely, and their complexion made the pink and white of English cheeks appear, in comparison, crude colours carelessly applied, mere afterthoughts, by a daubing amateur: for the pallor of their faces, a moonlike pallor, seemed inseparable from the smooth texture of their skin, like the faint hue of ivory, or the pale glow of a primrose in woody shade. Moonlight was Arthur's comparison. 'Like moonlight on a cloud,' he thought, and blushed, and smirked with exquisite discomfort when Doris, from under thin black brows, shot a warm glance at him. Their eyes — but metaphors grow mixed, for their eyes were dark and liquid, their eyes were deadly marksmen, their eyes were eloquent and all their honeyed phrases spoke of love. They were, thought Wilfred — recalling with

T   289

distaste a vulgar expression he once had heard —
they were bedroom eyes: but not of that draughty
chamber, that aseptic dormitory, that cold prelude
to a colder bath, the English bedroom: rather of a
cushioned and fountain-loud seraglio, or perfumed
cabinet whose walls were delicately lewd from
Aretino's inspiration. Wilfrid quite frankly disliked
their eyes, but could not keep his own from meeting
them.

Their figures were slim, their movements volup-
tuous. Their thin bare arms and their legs, almost
as thin beneath airy stockings, suggested the rippling
agility of an Oriental dance. And their *chi-chi* voices
— or rather Doris's voice, for Tessie appeared to
speak only with her eyes — had the exotic charm of
novelty, for neither Wilfrid nor Arthur nor Mr.
Peabody had ever heard before that bright scalloped
rhythm, or encountered their slightly dislocated
idiom.

George's voice woke Mr. Peabody from his trance.
George had helped himself to a drink, and George
said heartily: 'Well, Hilary, are you going to admit
that I've done you a good turn? Don't you think
they'll do credit to the ancient and honourable name
of Gander?'

Mr. Peabody thought: 'I must make an early
opportunity to have a long and serious talk with
George. He will have to produce a marriage certificate and five — or is it six? No, five — birth
certificates; and I must satisfy myself as to their
authenticity. Because this extraordinary family, if
indeed they are his and were born in wedlock, will

certainly make him the heir to seventy thousand pounds. Dear, dear! I was prepared for a surprise, but not for a *dénouement* so astonishing as this.'

Hilary, in a strained, unhappy voice, answered George's questions. 'I'm sure we shall get on together as well as can be expected,' she said, 'and perhaps even better than that. But I hope Doris won't be disappointed in Lammiter. She seems to have led a very gay life in Bombay. Going to dances, I mean, and parties, and so forth.'

'Oh yes,' said Doris, 'we are most enthusiastic dancers, are we not, Tessie?'

Tessie looked meltingly at Wilfrid. 'Can you dance the Valita, Mr. Follison,' she asked, 'or the De Albert? On the steamer not one of the gentlemen knew them, but they are quite my favourite dances, and we always had them at the Institute in Parel.'

'And at the Yacht Club also, and in many bungalows on Malabar Hill,' said Doris hurriedly.

George, laughing suddenly, blew into his whisky and soda like a seal coming to the surface. 'Excuse my boisterous behaviour,' he said, 'but I was just thinking that these girls of mine are going to be a welcome spot of colour in the wide open spaces of Lammiter's experience. And we'll have to keep an eye on 'em, Hilary. They'll make a bee-line for anything in trousers, from a postman to a Privy Councillor. Even the Boy Scouts won't be safe from them.'

Hilary said, 'I don't care for jokes of that sort. That isn't the way to speak before your daughters, and it certainly isn't the way to speak of them.'

'Our father is a highly jocular man,' said Doris. 'Our father . . .'

'I wish you wouldn't refer to me in that damned liturgical style,' complained George.

'It's getting very late,' said Hilary, and rose from her chair.

'Now don't spoil the party,' said George. 'Here am I, home from the gorgeous East, the land of glittering despair, all set for a cosy heart-to-heart talk on the immortal theme that Home is Best, and you tell me it's getting late. Sit down and have a drink, Hilary, and take another look at these girls of mine. Don't you think they're like you? They're Ganders to the backbone. My greatest pride in them has always been that they're the spitting image of you. Not exactly as you are now perhaps — you're handsomer than you used to be — but what you were at their age. Don't you think so, Peabody? Don't you agree with me, Arthur?'

'You're talking arrant nonsense,' said Hilary, and having made her excuses to Mr. Peabody, Arthur, and Wilfrid — who bade good night to Doris and Tessie with bewilderment, a fearful joy, and plain timidity respectively — she shepherded her nieces from the room. She paused for a moment at the door, and said bitterly, 'I hope you sleep better than I shall, George. You'll find your old room ready for you.'

Mr. Peabody also prepared to go. 'You must come and have a talk with me as soon as you can,' he said. 'On Monday morning, perhaps, at my office?'

'With all my affidavits, writs, depositions and certificates in a sealed envelope,' said George agreeably. 'You'll find everything in order, Peabody. My quiver's entirely filled by legitimate offspring — though their colour's a bit off-white, as you may have noticed — and they've all been christened, vaccinated, and prepared for congratulation. The booty's mine, Peabody, and I'd like to touch you for a couple of hundred almost at once. I'm sorry, Arthur, old man, but we've got to face facts, haven't we? I'll lend you a fiver now and then if you're ever hard up.'

'My income is perfectly sufficient for the quiet way in which I live,' said Arthur stiffly.

'You're damned lucky,' said George.

'Well, I must be going,' exclaimed Mr. Peabody. 'No, I want nothing to drink, thank you, and I can find my own way out. We meet again on Monday morning, about eleven-thirty: you will remember? Good night, good night.'

Arthur and Wilfrid likewise refused George's offer of continued entertainment: Wilfrid, shaken by his encounter with Doris and Tessie, was also a little nervous of George; and Arthur, suddenly realizing that these houris who had so embarrassed and enchanted him were finally dispossessing him of fortune, was not unnaturally depressed.

He and Wilfrid left together. Before separating — Wilfrid turning left for Mulberry Acre, Arthur going downhill to Hornbeam Lane — they stood for half a minute in silence, vainly seeking words to ease their minds of an impacted and complicated burden.

At last Wilfrid, indignantly, said, 'I think they're terrible! All of them, simply *terrible!*'

'And they're going to inherit seventy thousand pounds,' said Arthur.

'Girls like that oughtn't to be allowed into the country!' said Wilfrid.

Arthur sighed deeply.

'They're *horrible* girls! I felt as though — well, as if I weren't properly buttoned-up — whenever they looked at me.'

'And yet they had a curious fascination,' murmured Arthur.

'They're too disgusting for anything.'

'They remind me of a woman I met in Constantinople,' said Arthur. 'She had the same complexion, a strange moonlit pallor. I remember crossing the Galata Bridge one night . . .'

'I didn't know you'd ever been to Constantinople,' said Wilfrid crossly.

'Oh, yes,' said Arthur very blandly. 'I went out with Harington in 1920. An interesting show, that. I must tell you about it some day. And then I met this extraordinary woman, very like Doris . . .'

'No, Arthur, please don't tell me! I couldn't *bear* to hear another word about women. Not to-night, not after seeing Doris and Tessie. They were *so* horrible!'

Arthur shrugged his shoulders and walked slowly towards Hornbeam Lane. He amused, and even excited himself, by the story of his Constantinople adventure. It was the first time he had heard it, and he thought it uncommonly good.

XVIII

On the following day, which was Sunday, Lammiter, with rare exceptions, found satisfactory release for all its energy in talking. By twelve twenty-five, ten minutes after the conclusion of morning service, nearly everybody had heard of George's arrival, and various descriptions of his family, some more inaccurate than others, were in rapid circulation. Among the few who experienced a desire for more positive activity were Tessie and Katherine. At five o'clock in the afternoon Tessie went out for a walk, and half an hour later, in a dampish copse at the foot of Hornbeam Lane, she was being very satisfactorily hugged under a tree by Sergeant Pilcher: that same Sergeant Pilcher whose men inadvertently fired a *feu de joie* at Major Gander's funeral. And about the same time Katherine was making arrangements to remove herself and her twins to the home of her parents-in-law at Bognor.

A whole procession of emotions, however, preceded these diverse yet cousinly events — Tessie leaning warmly against Sergeant Pilcher's blue patrol jacket was nearly related to the shrillness of Katherine's voice as she telephoned to her mother-in-law — and Hilary, more than all others, deserved sympathy for the part she was compelled to play. She had slept poorly, and the elastic hours of night, so brief in slumber, so interminable to the wakeful, had been stretched intolerably by alternating thoughts of George and Doris, of Clarice and the dark tearful little boys. She had a strong sense of family obligations, and before seeing them she had never doubted that it was her duty, nor denied that it was her inclination, to entertain them. But in the dreary solitude of sleeplessness she condemned her inclination and regretted her sense of duty, for the game femineity of Doris and Tessie, fortified as it was by such unnecessary loveliness, filled her with foreboding; and scandal, as she knew, was native to George as fleas to a dog.

But in the morning twilight she fell asleep, and was wakened two or three hours later with early tea and the news that Clarice, Edward, and Timothy had disappeared. No one had seen them go out, but they had certainly been gone for more than an hour. Hilary was not greatly surprised. She felt sure they would turn up again. 'We mustn't worry over small mishaps,' she told Mrs. Arbor, who had come in to amplify the maid's story. 'We're going to have a very trying time for the next few weeks, I'm afraid, and we must learn to take things philosophically. We must discipline ourselves to be calm.'

The children were brought home by a policeman a little before ten o'clock. They had been found on the other side of Lammiter, two or three miles away. The little boys were again crying, but Clarice was quite unperturbed. She still wore the khaki topee. They had gone out 'for *hawa khana*', she said, and they had got lost. That was all.

Hilary abandoned her tentative idea of taking them to church. George came down at half-past ten, very well pleased with himself and the world, though he had finished the whisky before going to sleep. Doris and Tessie were still in bed. Hilary went to church alone.

The Vicar was still lame, but he could walk a little with the help of a crutch. The handrail creaked as he hoisted himself into the pulpit; and he preached an excessively dreary sermon on the twenty-seventh verse of the first chapter of the General Epistle of James. Hilary nodded and fell into a light doze. For many years she had visited the fatherless and widows in their affliction, and she felt that nothing Lionel could tell her about it would enable her to do it with greater willingness or acceptability. Miss Montgomery, with whom she walked part of the way home, was of the same opinion.

'I suppose that's what they call an ethical sermon,' she said disdainfully. 'Well, I don't like them, and I never shall. Keep ourselves unspotted from the world, indeed! What hope have I of getting spotted? And then to be told to live a life of service to the community! Good heavens, we might as well go to a Rotary Club. What I want to hear, when I go to church, is *faith*! I know all about works, and so do you. Ethical sermons indeed!'

'Lionel's terribly dull nowadays,' Hilary agreed.

'He needs a woman in the house,' said Miss Montgomery. 'Why don't you marry him yourself, and help to look after those children of his?'

'I've got plenty to look after at present. George came home last night.'

'So I heard.'

'It's going to be very difficult.'

'Are they all black?'

'I wish they were. There are two lovely grown-up girls, no darker than Spaniards, and I don't like the look of them at all.'

'How long has George been married?'

'I don't know. None of us knew that he was married till now. The first time he left home was in 1912, and we've only seen him at long intervals since then.'

'Do you think they're legitimate?'

'I suppose so. He wouldn't have brought them here if they weren't.'

'Then he's going to get the Major's money?'

'It looks like it.'

'I hear that Daisy is very upset.'

'Very. And so is Katherine.'

'Yes, but I can't be really sorry for Katherine. She's been a little bit too obviously mercenary. And in any case children will do her good: they'll make her less egotistical.'

'I must go and see her this afternoon,' said Hilary.

'She's still in the nursing-home?'

'Yes. But she's quite strong again now.'

'Well, don't worry yourself, Hilary. Whatever George or the girls do — and I don't trust George for a minute — nobody's going to blame you But my advice is, get rid of them as soon as you can. If George gets seventy thousand pounds he's going to be much more dangerous, and much more of a nuisance, than he is now. So if I were you I'd look for a little house for them, and get them moved into it as soon as possible.'

Miss Montgomery spoke with unusual decision, now cocking her head on one side to peer sharply at Hilary now vigorously nodding it, so that, with her little red hat, she looked something like a woodpecker at work.

'I hate to see these people imposing on you,' she said.

When Hilary got back to Rumneys she found Doris and Tessie huddled over the drawing-room fire. The morning had been bright, though not particularly warm, but sudden clouds had brought a heavy fall of rain.

'Our father has told us this would be the hot weather in England,' said Doris disconsolately, 'but now it looks more like monsoon.'

'It's only a shower,' said Hilary.

The dining-room was fireless, and, despite the imminence of June, definitely cold. Neither Doris nor Tessie enjoyed her lunch, but George maintained a brisk conversation with questions about Arthur and Daisy, Wilfrid and Katherine. He was immoderately pleased to be told about Katherine's twins and Daisy's belated son.

'That's the best joke I've heard for years,' he said. 'Isn't nature wonderful, as they say in the garden cities? But you can't plant a tree one year, and expect to live in the shade the next. They should have started early, like me. I didn't dash into paternity as a speculation: I was just a simple cockeyed philoprogenitive. And by God, it's paid! Leap before you look, Hilary. That's the wise way! Leap before you look, and you'll land in clover.'

'Have you often found the four-leafed clover, Aunt Hilary?' asked Tessie.

'Well, I used to when I was younger. I haven't looked for any lately.'

Tessie sighed: 'I am hoping to find some. It is jolly lucky. It means you will have a sweetheart.'

They returned eagerly to the drawing-room fire. Doris said, 'It would be nice to go somewhere and dance this afternoon.'

'I'm afraid you can't dance to-day,' said Hilary. 'It's Sunday.'

'But in Bombay,' said Doris, 'we have often danced on Sunday. There is a place called Green's that we make a decided point of going to, on every Sunday afternoon when someone will take us. It is highly agreeable there, and quite a centre of attraction.'

'You'll find,' said George. 'that the amenities of the Orient often scandalize old England. I, who am like God because I despise respectability . . .'

'Rubbish!' said Hilary.

'God made man, but who made his loin-cloth?' asked George amiably. 'As I was about to say, England is lousy with restrictions, but there are many compensations. And the wise man learns to eat peas without cutting his mouth. I grow aphoristic, Hilary. After Sunday tiffin, and especially after port wine — to which I am not accustomed in the unkindly tropics — I become wordy, sententious, and, to tell the truth, rather a bloody nuisance, if

you'll admit such a word. Let us discuss Hinduism:
the Hindu Trinity consists of Brahma the Creator,
Vishnu the Preserver, and Siva the Destroyer, behind whom is Brahma the Universal Reality.
Brahma the Creator, having created, retires hurt;
Vishnu is sometimes said to be another form of
Siva; and Siva is sometimes said to be another form
of Vishnu. Furthermore, Vishnu the Destroyer is
worshipped for his reproductive power, and his
emblem is the phallus. His wife, Kali, is the Mother
of the World, and dances on his chest with a string
of skulls round her neck. The favourite love story
of the Hindus is that of Krishna and Radha:
Krishna was an incarnation of Vishnu, and his fame
as a romantic hero rests on the fact that while his
sweetheart Radha was looking for him in the woods,
he was playing kiss-in-the-ring with a hundred milk-
maids in Brindaban. But this, of course, is the
ultimate simplification of Hinduism. Shall I say
anything about its actual complications? Shall I
mention some of its ten thousand lesser deities, and
the intricate philosophy of their several million
devotees? Perhaps not. Shall I say anything about
the four thousand caste distinctions? No. Yet there
are Brahmans who inherit not only social superior-
ity but sanctity, in the same way as I shall inherit
seventy thousand pounds, who live by eating other
people's sins, and are properly despised for this
practice; and in Madras there are beggars who do
the work of Dr. Barnardo by adopting deformed
children; and that, to a simple man like me, is very
interesting. But far, far more interesting is the

curious circumstance that these Hindus — about 280,000,000 of them — have for several generations been ruled and governed by Members of Parliament whose only comparable subtlety has been their ability to distinguish between Free Trade and Tariff Reform. This proves beyond doubt that the first verse of *Rule Britannia* records an actual fact, and when ignorant foreigners say that Heaven did it for a joke, they're underestimating the place of humour in God's Providence. Now let me tell you something about the Indian princes. . . .'

Meanwhile, from about eleven o'clock till half-past two, Daisy had been hardly less voluble than George. Arthur had briefly described to her the composition of George's family, and their mere enumeration had incarnadined her cheeks with helpless anger. That George the wastrel should come home with five, while she, virtuous she, had painfully borne but two! It was intolerable. Then Arthur had foolishly let fall the fact that Doris and Tessie were lovely beyond the expectation or experience of a quiet domestic man; and Daisy's anger knew no bounds but the genteel circumference of her vocabulary. Had she had words enough she would have made them rattle like hail on a tin roof; but a polite schooling has its disadvantages, and all she could do, after monotonous reiteration of her discontent, was to weep over the Sabbath roast and, half an hour later, take the unexpended portion of her disappointment to the garden, where, in words of one or two syllables, befitting her audience, she told it to the flowers. And Daisy's flowers were never unresponsive. They knew her, she said; though it must be admitted that she did not always know them.

Arthur, having seen that the nurse — whose wages he would have some difficulty in paying — had properly scalded the bottle from which his infant son had fed, wondered how he should spend the afternoon. The baby was thriving, though Daisy and the nurse had flatly refused to have anything to do with the ingenious labour-saving cage he had constructed for it. He thought of devising some simple apparatus for educating its reflexes, but came to the conclusion that it would be waste of time, as female obscurantism would be sure to boycott it. He thought of seeking refreshment on the far side of the rockery; and then found that Daisy was in the garden, so that was no good. Then it occurred to him that he might call at Rumneys. It would be gracious to go and have a talk with George; it would show that he bore him no ill will, and was prepared to accept defeat in a sporting spirit; and it would be interesting, merely on sociological grounds, to see Doris again.

The latter inducement, he found, was more cogent than the former. The thought of Doris inspired in him such sensations as he had not known for several years. His hand was trembling as he put on his hat, and impatience hurried his steps. But when he came near to Rumneys he was assailed by sudden diffidence: he felt, as he had often felt when he was a small boy, that he would not know what to say to her: and telling himself that he had really only come out for a walk, he passed the house with his head averted. A mile farther on, confidence was re-born; he stopped, and returned the way he had come. He felt perfectly confident, and master of the social arts, till through the trees he saw, cynically shining in the sun like a monocle, a dormer window in the steep roof of Rumneys; and it seemed to him that George and Hilary would guess at once the true purpose of his visit, and he would appear ridiculous. Again he passed the tempting drive, and walked on to Lammiter West, beyond the Vicarage, and sat for a little time in earnest thought upon a stile.

When for the third time he came to Rumneys his mind was resolute, and he rang the bell without a tremor. He found Doris alone; for George had gone for a walk, Hilary was sitting by Katherine's bed in the nursing home, and Tessie — Arthur had passed her, without seeing her, on the opposite side of the road — had just caught sight of Sergeant Pilcher, at the top of Hornbeam Lane, looking very smart in his blue patrol jacket and gold chevrons. Arthur, with a fine assumption of ease, asked Doris if she thought she was going to enjoy living in England. . . .

Katherine, like Daisy, was particularly incensed by the news that George had two beautiful daughters. 'And their mother was a native, was she?' she demanded bitterly.

'Well,' said Hilary, 'I'm afraid they're not pure white, though I must admit that the complexion of the elder girls is very attractive. The little boys are darker. though.'

'Just an ordinary *chi-chi* family,' said Katherine. 'Heaven only knows the sort of life that George has been leading. My own brother, with children like that! And I suppose you realize what effect this is going to have on Oliver? His career will be ruined. He can't possibly stay in his regiment if it becomes known that he has a mob of *chi-chi* relations.'

'They're your relatives, not his.'

'And that makes it worse, if anything, because people will say he's deliberately married one of them. They may even think that I'm black too. Don't you see how *fatal* it all is?'

'I think you're exaggerating the consequences.'

'I'm not! A girl like this Doris, or — what's her name? *Tessie!* — can ruin anybody's reputation.'

'That seems possible.'

'Well, that's what I'm saying! And I'm not going to meet George, I'm not going to see any of his family. I'm going to Bognor as soon as they can manage to fetch me, and I shan't come back so long as George is here. He's my brother, I know, but I don't admit the relationship. He can't expect me to, after behaving like this. I've got Oliver's future to think of now. He'll have to be transferred somewhere or other, because obviously he can't remain in India. We'll have to start pulling strings immediately. His father has a lot of influence, thank heaven, because otherwise, I suppose, there'd be nowhere for us to go but Kenya.'

Katherine talked for a long time in this vein. Then she took up the telephone at her bedside and ill-temperedly asked for a trunk-call to Bognor.

Her voice, however, became soft and plaintive when she spoke to her mother-in-law and told her the tentative plan she had made. Hilary endured her comments and self-pity for another half-hour. She did not enjoy them, but she was insufficiently selfish to abbreviate her visit merely because she found it unpleasant. Then she saw the twins being bathed. They also were noisy. Hilary felt rather tired when at last she said good-bye to Katherine.

She walked home beneath a pleasant sky, and at the entrance to Rumneys she abruptly met Arthur, who was coming out. He wore his hat carelessly, somewhat on the back of his head, and his expression was amiable with that faraway and foolish look which is characteristic of a mild and pleasant state of intoxication. Nor was he looking, with sufficient care, to see where he was going: he and Hilary almost collided. But he was quite sober.

He replied vaguely to her startled greeting.

'When did you get here?' asked Hilary.

'About five o'clock. Or perhaps a little earlier, yes, a little earlier, I should think.'

'I didn't go out till half-past four. You must just have missed me.'

'No,' said Arthur. 'Oh, no, not at all, not at all.' He was in the grip of some experience as powerful as the hairdresser's engine that gives enduring undulations to a lady's hair. His consciousness, by the application of heat and pressure, had acquired a permanent wave; and its smooth satisfied ripples were reflected in his shining face.

XIX

With unusual respect for an appointment, George arrived at Mr. Peabody's office punctually at half-past eleven on Monday morning. He carried a bulky blue envelope that he laid on Mr. Peabody's table with easy triumph.

'There you are,' he said. 'Seventy thousand pounds' worth of legal documents, Peabody. Take 'em up tenderly, handle with care: sealed, signed, and indisputable, every one of them: and my passport to a lazy old age. "Why should we toil alone, we only toil, who are the first of things?" '

'This,' said Mr. Peabody, 'is a copy of your marriage certificate to Teresa Rose Mahoney D'Souza?'

George agreed. ' "Dear is the memory of our wedded lives, and dear the last embraces of our wives," ' he added. 'I'm in a poetical mood this morning.'

'And here is her death certificate, and here — one, two, three, four, five — certificates, or copies of them, of the birth of your children?'

'We spared no expense,' said George. 'Everything possible has been done for them, and they all possess documentary evidence of the facts of life.'

Mr. Peabody minutely scrutinized the papers. 'You have been resident in India since 1912?' he asked.

'Legally, yes; actually, no,' said George. 'I'm not a vegetable. I've moved about a bit.'

'You came home, for varying periods, on several occasions.'

'Three times,' said George. 'And I was in Mesopotamia during the War, I've been twice to America, once to Mombassa, and once in Hong-Kong.'

'Perhaps you could give me the dates of your absences from India?'

'They're all there, on that piece of paper, and you can check-up on a lot of them from my passport. It was issued in 1924 and renewed in 1929, so the different visas show where I've been during the last ten years.'

'Ah, yes,' said Mr. Peabody. 'That will be very useful. Now I think you had better leave these documents with me for a few days.'

'While you compare the dates and make sure that none of my children were conceived during their father's absence abroad, eh? All right, Peabody. Go ahead. You're going to be disappointed. They were all born at the appropriate times. Neither Nature nor their poor mother ever made a mistake.'

'Why did you never reveal the fact that you were married?'

'It was nobody's business but mine. Why should I?'

'It's customary to notify one's relatives of such an event.'

'Only when the relatives are going to be gratified by the news.'

Mr. Peabody painfully raised his eyebrows into an expression of inquiry.

'I'm the only one of the family who isn't a snob,' said George. 'I married to suit myself, but I realized that Tessie — my wife — wouldn't suit the taste of my charming cousins, my affectionate sister, my revered uncle, or my beloved Hilary. Because her parentage happened to be a little mixed: her mother was Irish on the one side, but definitely tropical on the other; and her father was said to be Portuguese, but as he was born in Goa his complexion was rather dark. So was my wife's. And as I hate to embarrass people, I said nothing about it.'

Mr. Peabody pursed his lips and tapped upon his desk with a yellow pencil.

'It looks as though I'm the heir, doesn't it?' said George.

'The residue of your uncle's estate is not payable till — let me see: I have forgotten the date — about fifteen months from now. If these documents are authentic — and I see no reason to doubt their authenticity — and if, during the next fifteen months, children in sufficient numbers are borne neither to Mrs. Arthur Gander nor to Mrs. Clements . . .'

'Try to be human, Peabody! They can't possibly beat me in the time, and even to make a dead-heat of it they'd have to have triplets. And you're not going to pretend that that's likely.'

'From the legal point of view . . .'

'From the common-sense point of view! I'm the heir apparent, and you've got to admit it.'

'If I can say so without indiscretion,' said Mr. Peabody carefully, 'it does indeed seem probable, failing any unforeseen occurrence or the emergence of as yet undiscovered but pertinent facts, that you will eventually succeed in establishing your claim to the Major's estate.'

'Eventually succeed!' exclaimed George. 'Good God, I have succeeded. I've got five children and a ream of certificates! What more do you want?'

'I may find it desirable to take counsel's opinion,' said Mr. Peabody.

'Well, the sooner you get things settled, the better I'll be pleased. Because I'm on the rocks,' said George. 'And as we know the money's mine, I think I can touch you for a small advance, can't I? I had to borrow money from a friend for our fares home, and I want to repay it as soon as possible. So be a good fellow and let me have — oh, say five hundred, will you?'

Mr. Peabody shook his head: 'That would be most irregular.'

'I'm on the rocks,' George repeated. 'The girls need new clothes, and so do I. And I'm in debt to my old friend Fewsher.'

'I can do nothing without consulting my fellow trustee,' said Mr. Peabody.

'Hilary?'

'Yes.'

'She'll be all right. Don't worry about her. Give me a hundred, anyway, and the rest can wait.'

Five minutes later Mr. Peabody yielded so far as to give George a cheque for ten pounds. George

310

accepted it without prejudice, and in the course of the next couple of hours renewed his friendship with several time-worn habitués of the Green Dragon.

But though his manner was hearty it soon became evident that George had determined to behave with reasonable propriety. Neither on that day nor any following day did he drink beyond the use of judgment, or show the effect of drink except in such venial respects as a louder laugh, a certain verbosity, and a brightness of the eye. He subjected his more unruly instincts to constant discipline; and to the great relief of the Education Committee, the young female teachers of Lammiter found they could walk abroad, even after dark, without being molested. George made no secret of the reason for his changed behaviour. 'As a man of property,' he said, 'or as a man of prospective property, I intend to conduct myself with a certain dignity. I propose to be affable, but not vulgar. Gone are the happy days when I used to please myself, and myself alone, and take no thought for the morrow. *Carpe diem* is a poor man's motto: a rich man must take care of his health and think of the future: there's no use dying of a plethora when you can live in plenty. So now I'm practising like hell for the honourable exercise of genuflecting in the House of Rimmon. Which is a bloody sensible thing to do.'

Doris also behaved with considerable decorum, though it is doubtful whether she deserved the whole credit for this. It was her misfortune that she preferred men of middle age, or even advancing years, to youth; and the gathering years, especially in a place like Lammiter, bring caution, poverty of spirit, and a more than arterial sclerosis. Her first encounter with Arthur was also her last. Intoxicating though he found it at the time, it proved frightening in retrospect, and he afterwards avoided her, justifying his timidity on the grounds of decency and policy. Thereafter she scraped acquaintance with a retired chemist, a handsome old man who spent his mornings in the Memorial Park, and found to her disappointment that his only interest was British Colonial postage-stamps; she wasted some time pursuing a portly bank-manager who, every evening, took his walk accompanied by a dachshund; and she flirted unsuccessfully with Mr. Glade, the florist in Green Street, who once gave her a carnation. But in justice to her it must be admitted that these expressions of interest were unostentatious — in comparison, at least, with Tessie's activities — and apparently of no great significance to her. They suggested the behaviour of a lady who, by mere habit of amiability, makes herself agreeable to other guests while her husband is engaged with their hostess. For Doris's favourite companion was her father. With him she was always happy, and the gossips of Lammiter began to entertain a more favourable opinion of her, and of George also, when they saw how devoted to each other they were, and how their constant pleasure was in taking long walks together. It was only when her father was busy elsewhere that she opened the dark languor of her eyes to the bank-manager or to Mr. Glade.

Tessie, however, speedily became notorious for the

enthusiasm and catholicity of her affections. In practice she was no snob — though in conversation she and Doris still made great ado about the smartness of their life in Bombay — and every morning she spent an hour or two on the narrow laurel-hedged path to the side door at Rumneys which the tradesmen used. There she dallied in delightful conversation with the milkman, the butcher's boy, the baker's man, and other callers. In the afternoon she often went for a walk with Sergeant Pilcher, who was generally off-duty between office-hours in the morning and evening instruction in the drill-hall. And after dinner she was frequently entertained by commercial travellers at the cinema or the Lammiter palais-de-danse. Tessie enjoyed herself very well indeed.

Hilary was distressed by the frequency of her unexplained absences from home, and talked to her in a firm but kindly way about the desirability and advantages of polite behaviour. But Tessie was stubborn, and George was not helpful. He laughed when he was told that Tessie had been seen kissing the milkman at half-past eight of a fine summer morning, and he complained that Hilary was unreasonable when she objected to Tessie's return from the palais-de-danse at midnight. 'You say it's disgusting to be embraced so early in the morning,' he said, 'but when the poor girl stays up till twelve o'clock, for no other purpose, you're angry again. Try to be logical, Hilary.'

'I'm trying to look after your daughter,' said Hilary.

313

At last, after many similar discussions, George was persuaded to talk seriously to Tessie. He spoke to her in private, and neither his arguments nor her replies were made known to Hilary. But the debate was stormy, and Tessie won. Thereafter George shrugged his shoulders and said she could be trusted to look after herself.

There was no open quarrel till Jane came home. Jane had played brilliantly in the Ladies' Open Championship, finishing only seven strokes behind Mrs. Holm, the winner. After leaving Porthcawl she had paid a series of visits to various friends who lived near good courses, and returned to Lammiter in time for the annual competition for the Captain's Medal. This was three weeks after George's homecoming.

She made no attempt to conceal dislike for her unexpected cousins. She was rude to George, harshly contemptuous of Doris and Tessie, and she ignored the children. Rumneys grew daily more uncomfortable, the air more brittle with strain. A governess who had been engaged to look after the children left within a fortnight, and the servants were discontented. Hilary, under the burden of peacemaking, began to look tired and haggard.

But Jane, as if thriving in a stormy atmosphere, played herself into the final of the Medal competition with relentless vigour and consistent accuracy on the greens. She was always at her best in match-play, and her ultimate victory seemed assured.

Her opponent in the final was a Miss Penny-feather, a tall agreeable-looking girl who had but lately left school. She was a brilliant player, but her nerves had not yet been proved against a gallery, and she was generally expected to crack up.

At the end of the first round, however, Jane was only two up. Miss Pennyfeather had begun very badly indeed, but disaster had produced a fighting spirit, and after holding Jane for a long time she had, by perfect golf, taken three of the last five holes and made a game of it.

They set out for the second round after lunch. It was a lovely day, warm, sunny, almost windless, and they were followed by three or four hundred spectators. At the fifth Jane had not increased her lead. She took the sixth with a swashbuckling drive, a belligerent second, and an audacious and lucky putt. With truculence unassuaged she took the seventh and the eighth. At the ninth her drive lay smugly in the middle of the fairway, two hundred yards from the tee.

This was a pretty hole. The fairway was undulating, and to the right of it stood five tall trees in all their leafy splendour. They grew on the near side of a small quarry. The quarry had not been used for many years. Time had mollified its harsh declivities, grass had grown a carpet in it, and the trees swung their green canopy above. But pleasant though it was to see, it was none the less a danger, and many a hopeful drive, curling maliciously, had been trapped in it.

Miss Pennyfeather's nerve was again forsaking her. She addressed her ball. She bit her lip. She swung a little desperately, somewhat abruptly. She struck a little loosely. Her ball rose, curved to the right like a reed bending in the wind, struck a tree, and rebounding obtusely fell behind the quarry and still farther to the right.

A groan broke from Miss Pennyfeather's supporters. 'Rotten luck!' said Jane gruffly, and walked slowly forward. The crowd followed. Miss Pennyfeather marched into the rough with a niblick. She looked at her ball and looked at the trees. They made a tall rampart before her, but there was a dip in the green crest. With a bitter blow she lofted the ball. It rose like a lark, crossed the trees, and, as a plummet, fell into the quarry. Out of the quarry came a terrified scream.

Miss Pennyfeather advanced through the trees. Jane, from the fairway, approached the quarry. The crowd followed her. And in the quarry they found Tessie and Sergeant Pilcher.

This untimely discovery might have been ignored, with no more unfortunate consequence than Jane's embarrassment and the spectators' annoyance — for golf was a serious matter, and a golf-course should not be profaned by amatory exercises — had not Tessie, far more angry than the spectators and startled by the descending ball, picked it up and thrown it at them.

A hoarse and multifarious protest was the immediate response to this rash action. Even Sergeant Pilcher said 'Coo! You shouldn't have done that!' And Jane, redder than she had been, cried from the lip of the quarry, 'Good God, what the hell d'you think you're doing?'

'Why do you throw your balls at me?' screamed Tessie. 'Take your beastly balls away! I was nearly killed, I was nearly dead! What do you mean by throwing things at me?'

Ponderous, furious, Jane descended the grassy slope to the floor of the quarry and confronted Tessie. 'Look here,' she said, 'do you realize what you've done? Do you realize you've interfered with a most important match?'

'And you have interfered with me!' cried Tessie. 'Go away, and take your little balls and throw them to other places.'

'You little fool!' said Jane. 'Get out of this and go home immediately, or I'll put you across my knee and smack your confounded bottom!'

'I say!' said Sergeant Pilcher, 'that isn't the way to talk to a lady.'

'I'll speak to your Colonel about you,' said Jane.

'We haven't been doing anything wrong, Miss!'

'Wrong!' shouted Jane. 'You come and perform your childish antics on the golf-course, you pick up my opponent's ball, you ruin the match, and you say you haven't done anything wrong!'

The Sergeant was abashed. He said that Tessie didn't understand the importance of golf.

'Take her away at once,' said Jane. 'Get out of my sight, both of you, before I lose my temper!'

Tessie was led away, shrilly protesting. The spectators, who had been excitedly telling each other who she was, now muttered, with righteous satisfaction, 'A most disgraceful episode! Well, let's get on with the game.'

There was some argument about the correct position of Miss Pennyfeather's ball, but Miss Pennyfeather sportingly insisted on its being returned to the quarry. She lofted it out, was pin-high with her fourth, and down in five. Jane topped her second, pitched her third into a bunker on the edge of the green, and took three more. Miss Pennyfeather also won the next two.

Jane pulled herself together, controlled her temper, and halved the twelfth and thirteenth. At the short fourteenth Miss Pennyfeather got a two. At the fifteenth Jane drove out of bounds and they were all square.

Jane won the sixteenth. On the next tee she unhappily caught sight of Tessie and the Sergeant: they had joined the crowd and were following the match with great interest. Jane, purple with rage, hooked her drive into the stream. Miss Pennyfeather won the match and the Medal on the last green.

Jane went home and with vehement anger told Hilary the story of Tessie's outrageous behaviour: 'And as though it wasn't enough to make an exhibition of herself like that, she had the confounded impudence to follow me round! I tell you, Hilary, she's absolutely shameless. When I saw her standing there, at the Long Stream, I could hardly control myself. Well, I couldn't control myself, because I pulled my drive and lost the match. It was her fault entirely. I've tried to make allowances for her, but what she did this afternoon is impossible to forget and impossible to forgive. To behave like that, on a golf-course, was absolutely unpardonable. And though I hate to say it, you can't expect me to live in the same house with a creature like that. Either she or I must leave at once.'

Hilary sighed, and talked reasonably, and tried to soothe Jane's temper. But Jane's mind was made up. She had been insulted, not in her private capacity, but as a golfer, and the insult was unforgivable. It was, however, impossible to turn Tessie out of doors, and Jane was compelled to sacrifice her comfort to her dignity. She slept that night in one of the cheerless little bedrooms at the Ladies' Club.

Hilary was so tired that she went to bed at a quarter to ten. But she could not sleep, and after half an hour's vain importunacy of sleep she turned on the light and looked for something to read. There were several books on the table beside her, and, still in its wrapper, the latest number of *Red*, the school magazine that Rupert was editing. She chose *Red* because it was lighter to hold than a novel.

The editorial was entitled 'Sexual Barbarians'. It was headed by the rubric, apparently meaningless: *A slice of cuttle-fish and a red mullet to Priapus*. Boldly it began: 'These are the Dark Ages of Sex. So far as sexual matters are concerned we live in ignorance and superstitious fear. The authorities of all the Public Schools of England have entered into a conspiracy of silence. They teach us many things — most of them badly — but they teach us nothing about Sex.'

'I should hope not,' thought Hilary, and with growing apprehension continued to read. The first three numbers of the magazine had dealt with political and literary subjects, and they had all been sensational, though somewhat conventionally sensational: that is to say, they had attacked the Officers' Training Corps, the Victorian Tradition in Literature, and the Financial Dictatorship of the City of London. Hilary should have been able to guess what would come next. The next topic was inevitably Sex. But she was innocent in many ways, and her only conjecture had been a foreboding that some day Rupert would go too far. And now, she felt, the day had probably arrived.

Sexual starvation was the crying scandal of the Public Schools, said Rupert. Elsewhere he described their life as an emotional famine. He referred to their pitiful attempts to find a proxy for true emotion; to the lurid novels that battened on their plight; and to well-meaning but useless experiments in co-education. He quoted Lawrence: 'A man who is emotionally educated is as rare as a phoenix. The more scholastically educated a man is generally, the more he is an emotional boor.'

'The remedy for this kind of boorishness is not co-education,' said Rupert. 'We can learn nothing from girls of our own class, because they know no more than we do. So far as we can see, the only remedy is this: that every housemaster should engage a suitable number of young but accomplished doxies. Call them hetairae, if you like. And these young women should be at the disposal of the Upper School in the same way as, for example, tuition in Extra Maths.

'This idea, sufficiently advantageous as it stands,

could be made still more profitable. We suggest that the *prettiest* girls should be reserved as weekly prizes for proficiency in Greek Verse Composition or an English Essay. Because it is obvious that something must be done to reduce the absurd prestige of the First Eleven, the Fifteen, and other athletic louts, and restore learning to its proper place. This is a School, not a Ham and Beef Shop. And if the Scholars get the pretty girls, while the Hearties are left with Plain Jane, then scholarship will be given a much needed fillip, and the Hearties will learn their proper place in society.

'We who enjoy the many advantages of a Public School education are supposed to be the future leaders of our country. But how can we be good leaders when, during the most impressionable years of our life, we suffer from this grievous lack of emotional vitamins? A remedy for this deficiency must be found, and we believe that the remedy here suggested is eminently reasonable.

'We seriously commend it to the attention of the authorities.'

The last sentence, thought Hilary, is the silliest of all. Such opinions ought to be concealed from the authorities, not commended to them. She wondered if Rupert would be expelled, and foresaw, too clearly, another crisis at the Vicarage. Then with a click of the tongue, a little noise of irritation, she put these thoughts from her. And presently she began to laugh. She put out the light and lay for a long time laughing quietly, her cheek moving against the pillow. She fell asleep and saw, in a dream, Rupert's dignified headmaster in the act of presenting prizes at end of term. Instead of the table with its customary pile of calf-bound poets there stood behind him a long row of lightly-clad chorus-girls, arms locked and knees high, stepping rhythmically, cheerfully singing. 'Rupert Purefoy!' said the Headmaster. Rupert stepped on to the platform. The Headmaster detached from the dancing row a flaxen-haired, plump and bright-eyed beauty. '*Hoc ingenii feliciter exculti praemium donant academiae Tugburiensis gubernatores*', he said; and with a smile handed her to Rupert.

Two days later, in the afternoon, the Vicar telephoned to Hilary and asked her to come and see
him. His voice was dull and hopeless, and Hilary
went to the Vicarage in fear of the worst.

'Rupert and Denis have both been expelled,' he
said.

'Both of them!' Hilary exclaimed.

The Vicar picked up the fourth and fatal number
of *Red*.

'Yes, I've seen that,' said Hilary, 'and though I'm
terribly sorry to hear about Rupert, I can't honestly
say I'm surprised. For my own part I thought the
article rather amusing, though I might take a
different view if I were a headmaster. But what has
Denis done? He's got nothing to do with the
magazine.'

'You know as much about them as I do,' said the
Vicar. 'You know that Rupert pretends to be a
Communist, and Denis calls himself a Fascist.
This wretched magazine is supposed to be a
Communist organ. Denis and his friends have
always disliked it. And the editorial in this last
number infuriated them. The Head, I gather,
didn't take it very seriously, but the Fascists did.
What especially annoyed them — you remember the
article? — was the suggestion that Hearties would
have to be content with the plainer girls, because
most of the Fascists, apparently, are Hearties. So

there was a riot. A very serious riot, in which Rupert and Denis were prominent. They were, in fact, the ringleaders. Dobbin has written very sympathetically to me, but he makes it quite clear that, for the sake of the school, expulsion was necessary. He tells me they have caused him a great deal of anxiety for the last six months or more.'

For some little time Hilary said nothing, and the Vicar lay sunk in his chair, his chin on his breast, his hands lying idly on his thighs. He had aged, grown thin, his knees were sharply pointed, and his hair was grey.

Hilary said, doubtfully, 'Well, I'm glad to see that you're taking it philosophically.'

'There is no philosophy in defeat,' said the Vicar. 'I admit I am beaten. That's all.'

'You've been admitting that for months,' said Hilary sharply.

'But this is the end. I can't go on any longer. I've suffered blow after blow, and I've no strength left to out-face a scandal of this kind. I've written to the Bishop.'

'And what have you said to him?'

'I have offered him my resignation.'

'Have you posted the letter?'

'Not yet.'

'Good. Now listen to me, Lionel. I've come to a certain decision, and the only problem that now remains is how to put it into words. I needn't tell you, I suppose, that you've been a source of constant worry ever since poor Caroline's death. I needn't remind you that we — you and I, that is — have been friends for more years than I care to remember. And in many ways I'm very fond of you, though you often make me intensely angry by your selfishness, your display of wounded vanity, your childish egoism, your ridiculous self-pity, and absolute lack of common sense. I thought, for some time, you were feeling better, and getting rid of your pessimism. I hoped that you were. But it seems I was wrong. It seems as though there's only one cure for you. However, I didn't mean to upbraid you. What I did intend, and what I still intend, is to suggest that we get married. I've given a great deal of thought to this matter, and I feel it's the sensible thing to do. I'm devoted to the children, and . . .'

'You fool!' shouted the Vicar.

He had risen from his chair. Stooping slightly, leaning on his stick, he glared at Hilary with an expression she had never seen before. Not anger, but violent dislike of her was its arresting quality. And Hilary, who had been talking rapidly, quick-firing her sentences — she had no desire to linger sentimentally over her declaration, she had made it sound like a scolding rather than a proposal — Hilary was abruptly silenced. She had been ready for an argument, but she was not prepared for this display of physical aversion. She was dreadfully taken aback. She turned rather pale, and spoke with difficulty.

'I was thinking only of your good,' she said. 'Or rather, of your and the children's good. You needn't suppose I have any other reason for wanting to marry you.'

The Vicar said, 'If you only knew the abhorrence I feel . . .'

'If you think you have any physical attraction for me, you're mistaken,' said Hilary.

'I pray God I haven't.'

'Don't bother to bring God into it. You haven't.'

'Then don't say another word about so revolting an idea.'

Hilary began to feel angry. 'Will you try to realize,' she said, 'that in some ways the thought of marrying you is probably just as distasteful to me as it is to you. But I was prepared to sacrifice my comfort, and the very real pleasures of my present manner of life, in order to look after you and give your children the benefit of a secure and sympathetic home. I was Caroline's friend — her true friend, I hope — and it was my deep regard for her that finally persuaded me to make this suggestion. But if you find it revolting . . .'

'I do.'

'Then I've been wasting my time. But *I* won't suffer from your refusal to be sensible. It's you who will suffer, you and your children, and if you weren't ill, both in body and mind . . .'

'My mind is absolutely healthy, and my mind rejects this abhorrent plan with every scrap of strength it possesses. Our marriage is impossible. The mere thought of it is shameful and humiliating and disgusting. I refuse to say another word to you. I must ask you to go, to go now, and do not come back till you have given me time to forget — if I can forget — this horrible suggestion.'

Limping and leaning on his stick the Vicar turned his back on her, and walking to a table, with trembling fingers picked up a book. Hilary stood for a moment or two in silence. Words, half-sentences, explanatory phrases and indignant phrases struggled within her against a feeling of breathlessness, a kind of nervous asphyxia. They struggled and were defeated. She could say nothing. She turned and fled. With difficulty she restrained herself from running down the drive.

Above all thoughts of her own, above all other memory of the Vicar's words, she could hear the hatred in his voice, when, breaking into the clatter of her explanation, he had shouted, 'You fool!' All thought dissolving, she began to cry. An endeavour to understand gave place to more urgent endeavour as she tried to withhold her tears. She walked at a great pace, and the tears came faster than she could sniff them back. She saw Mrs. Sabby approaching her, and crossed to the other side of the road. She passed Sir Gervase without seeing him, and Sir Gervase stood and stared after her in great astonishment. She came to Rumneys with no desire in her mind except the desire to hide herself: and a maid, looking curiously at her, told her that Mr. Peabody was waiting in the library.

'Say I'm sorry,' she said, 'but I can't see him now.'

She went upstairs, and took off her hat, and bathed her face before she looked in the mirror. 'He'd no right to say that,' she whimpered. 'I'm *not* revolting! I'm *not* disgusting!' And tears flowed afresh.

She heard a tap at the door. The maid came in and said, 'Mr. Peabody asked me to tell you that his business is most important, and he would be obliged if you could see him for only a few minutes.

Ten minutes later Hilary was ascribing her unhappy appearance and malaise to the heat, and to walking too fast in the late afternoon sun. Mr. Peabody was sympathetic in a perfunctory way, but his news, he said, was so urgent that he had felt it necessary to impart it without delay. He opened his brief-case and made a busy little rustling noise among its papers.

'I have been in communication with a firm of solicitors and various other agents and authorities in Bombay,' he said, 'and the result of my several inquiries is somewhat startling. George, as you know, gave into my keeping the certificates referring to his marriage, the death of his wife, and the birth of his children. Now all these certificates appeared to be copies, such as may be obtained on payment of a small fee, and after some thought I decided to cable to the Registrar in Bombay and ask him to confirm them. He presently replied that he was unable to find the entries I referred to. Thereupon I established communication with Messrs. Lighterwood, Lighter & Webb — solicitors with whom my late partner had some connection — and asked them, among other things, to search the files of the local newspapers for the usual contemporary notices of these vital events. Their information is that the columns devoted to the notification of births, marriages, and deaths, in *The Times of India*, and several journals of smaller importance which they also examined, make no mention either of George's marriage or the birth of any one of his children. They further state that he had recently been employed, in a humble capacity, by the Bombay and Rajputana Railway, and for some time had been living, with such a family as I described, in a small house, the property of the railway company, in Parel. But according to local evidence there had also been living, in the same house, a middle-aged or elderly woman whose present whereabouts cannot be discovered.'

'A servant, I suppose,' said Hilary.

'Possibly,' said Mr. Peabody. 'Messrs. Lighterwood, Lighter & Webb were also thoughtful enough to give me some information about George's previous movements. That is, activities prior to his employment, or rather re-employment, by the Bombay and Rajputana Railway. He apparently incurred the displeasure — though why, or to what extent, is not known — of one of the Indian Princes, and he seems to have been . . .'

'Does that matter now?' Hilary asked. 'I think you've told me enough to show what you suspect, and frankly I don't believe you. I'm not feeling very well, and perhaps I'm not being very intelligent: but if these aren't George's children — and that's what you're implying, isn't it? — then whose are they and how did he get them? And where did he get these copies of their birth-certificates? There are too many difficulties that you can't explain. Perhaps the children were registered somewhere else, and perhaps he couldn't afford to send a notice to the papers.'

'The forgery of documents such as these,' said Mr. Peabody carefully, 'is happily a rare occurrence, at least in this country. But it is not entirely unknown, even in Great Britain. And in India, or so I have heard, it is possible to procure evidence of a much more unusual and seemingly impossible character. I have been told, though I cannot say with what truth, that one may there procure a dead body in order to charge a man with murder.'

'But George has procured five living bodies, and surely that's very difficult, even in India?'

'But if these birth-certificates cannot be confirmed . . .'

'You must talk to George himself about it. I really can't give my mind to it now, and I don't much care what happens, anyhow.'

Mr. Peabody was disappointed. 'You are my fellow trustee,' he said, 'and it was my duty to give you this information. But, with your approval, I am willing to postpone any further action till I have had a talk with George.'

Hilàry took some aspirin and went to bed. She went to bed calmly and with a reasonable purpose: she wanted to avoid George, to escape the necessity of talking to Doris and Tessie. But she took the aspirin with an almost theatrical gesture: she was a stranger to drugs, even to those mild domestic tablets, and she swallowed them — four of them — with the recklessness of one who seeks oblivion by reckless means.

George, on the other hand, sought stimulants when he heard that Mr. Peabody wanted to see him on business so urgent that it could not wait till the morning. He dined well and drank a good deal of brandy before going to the small square house that Miss Peabody kept in such cold and perfect order for her bachelor brother; and so fortified he listened with great confidence to Mr. Peabody's clear but cautious narrative, and vigorously denied the imputation.

'It's a damned good thing for you, Peabody,' he said, 'that I'm not a touchy sort of fellow. You're suggesting that I've committed a very serious crime, and unless I'm much mistaken that's actionable.'

'No, no, no! I'm merely asking you to provide an explanation for the very curious fact that no original entries can be found to authenticate these certificates.'

'You're suggesting they're forgeries? Well, they're not! And your implication is that I'm claiming seventy thousand pounds on false pretences. Let me tell you this: you're sailing on a damned dangerous tack, and you ought to put about before it's too late.'

'Various sums have already been advanced to you, amounting in all, I think, to two hundred and sixty pounds . . .'

'To which I'm perfectly entitled.'

'I shall be delighted if you can prove that. This inquiry, this necessary inquiry, is very painful to me, and nothing could make me happier than to hear your explanation of what is, at present, a very perplexing situation.'

'So far as I'm concerned, there's no explanation needed. I made certain claims, and I provided you with legal proof in support of them. If you want to question the children, you can. And if you want to apologize to me, you can. But you'll have to do it pretty smartly, because I tell you quite plainly that if I don't get an apology within the next twenty-four hours, I'll get another man of business when I succeed to my inheritance. So put that in your pipe and smoke it!'

George went home and drank some whisky and soda. He repeated, for no one's benefit but his own, his parting words to Mr. Peabody, and felt very well satisfied with them. He thought of several other questions that Peabody might have asked, and invented replies that carried conviction in every word. He continued the debate until Peabody, beaten in every attack, grew vulnerable at every point, and with another peroration, more valiant than the first, he reduced him to silence, to a shape of abject defeat, and so left him with the valedictory echo of a triumphant apodosis ringing in his ears.

'Or it'll be the worse for you, my man!' he repeated: and went to bed, not quite steadily, carrying in one hand the decanter and in the other a siphon of soda-water.

He whistled cheerfully while he undressed. He poured himself another drink and set it conveniently on his bedside table. He took from the bookcase — his boyhood's bookcase — a shabby little red leather volume called *Plain Tales from the Hills*, and got into bed. But presently the print grew blurred, and his memory repeated the story of McIntosh Jellaludin quicker than he could read it. He laid down the book and whistled half a dozen bars of the song to which he had undressed. But suddenly recognizing the tune, he stopped, and exclaimed, 'Damn the road to Mandalay! I'm going to live in blasted England henceforth and for ever, and a bloody dull life it's going to be, with a halo of respectability, like a bowler-hat too big for me, falling on to my ears, and nothing to listen to but the bleat and *gup* of my Willy-wet-leg neighbours, like sheep in a field, like a penny rubber ball bouncing in an empty skull. Me with a stake in the country, and tied to it, by God, henceforth and for ever! And four meals a day, all on plates, and clean shirts so I don't stink of over-eating. If a man's got any richness in him he ought to stink. God, what a fug there must have been round St. Francis! And ploughmen's sweat, and a stoker's sweat, go up to God like an acceptable sacrifice. But cow-dung, and smoke, and ghi, and pan-supari: that's the stink I like. Oh damn respectability to everlasting hell!'

George swallowed his whisky and soda at a gulp, and taking a cigarette, angrily struck a match.

He lay muttering to himself, his cigarette moving between his lips. He was not wholly sober, and not thoroughly awake. He moved restlessly, and pushed the clothes away from him. He felt hot, and kicked impatiently at the sheets. Pale beneath the electric light, a little flame thrust its black edge over the crumpled whiteness.

George, in a fright, leapt out of bed and grabbed

333

the siphon. The stream of soda-water hit hard against the burning clothes, and soon extinguished the small fire. But George was taking no chances. He watered the whole bed, and emptied the siphon before he felt satisfied that danger was averted. And then it seemed that he had nowhere to sleep, for the bed was as wet as a marsh. But George, after a little display of annoyance, was not noticeably worried by this. He shrugged his shoulders and put on his dressing-gown.

He turned out the light and stepped quietly into the corridor. A few yards away, round a corner, he opened another door, and went in. Doris turned over and looked at him with sleepy eyes. She did not appear surprised to see him. He got into bed beside her, and still she showed no surprise. She seemed, indeed, to welcome his visit.

XXI

IT was the result of taking drugs, thought Hilary. It was well known that drugs impaired the moral fibres, and as compensation for this damage they apparently induced a delicious feeling of lassitude. Hilary had slept soundly all night, and in the morning she calmly announced her intention of eating breakfast in bed. It was nine years since she had done such a thing — and then only during the aftermath of influenza — and she admitted that she would not have had the strength of mind to do it now had it not been for the immoral effects of aspirin. It was with a little holiday feeling, a sense of triumphant escape, that she sat up and surveyed the bed-table like a well-laden bridge across her knees.

But the major benevolence of aspirin — or perhaps of Hilary's subjective submission to drugs — was the comparative calmness with which she read, and realized the significance of, a letter from the Vicar. There was, indeed, nothing to perturb her in what he himself had written: but his enclosure was, to use a meiotic figure, to employ a very mild sort of metaphor, a bombshell. Aspirin, fortunately, blanketed the force of its explosion.

His letter read as follows:

'I feel that I owe you both an apology and an explanation for the violence of the mood in which I received your quite unexpected suggestion. I find no difficulty in apologizing. But it is very

335

difficult to explain. It means that I must reveal a secret, and expose a pretence, that I have kept and maintained for nearly twenty-five years. You are charitable enough, I know, to forgive me — if forgiveness is needed — for my long deception. And I think I can trust you to keep my secret. You will understand why it *must* be kept. And you will also understand that I make you a partner in it, after long consideration and with considerable distress, because I was unjust to you, and perhaps caused you unhappiness: and this knowledge — I cannot bring myself to write it, but the enclosed letter should make all clear — will inform you why. I beg you, and I trust you, to tell *no one else.*'

The missive enclosed was of an elder date. The ink was faded and the writing showed a thin outmoded angularity. The note-paper was heavily black-edged.

'Dear Mary,' it began, 'I'm not convinced by the arguments you state for wanting another £50. But sooner than squabble I enclose a cheque. Don't take this for a precedent, though. I'm glad to hear that Lionel is doing well. He must take after you, religion and all. My liver is bad again, and Margaret's death has upset me. I may have another pupil for Charlie before long, and I've told one or two of my friends about him. Do your best for Lionel, he's the handsomest of all my gets, whether official or unofficial. And don't waste the £50.

'Yours affectionately,
'Jonathan Gander.'

Lifting the bed-table from its bridge-like position across her legs, and carefully placing it lengthwise on the quilt, Hilary got out of bed, carried it towards the fireplace and set it down before the fender. Then returning to bed, and making herself comfortable, she re-read Jonathan Gander's letter. Blanketed by aspirin, its force reduced by lassitude, the bombshell burst in her mind. But it was shrapnel, not high explosive. The detonation was not single and destructive, but scattered the news in a hundred directions. She perceived in the tidings a score of explanations, a round dozen of implications, and forty existing or potential consequences. If Lionel was the illegitimate son of her father — but the derivatives ran too fast, the results came pell-mell upon her, and chasing now one, now the other, she missed the effect of the whole. Her heart beat quicker, she pursued a consequence with some excitement, but she escaped that homologue of shell-shock which major news, of a totally unexpected nature, may sometimes bring.

Within a short time, indeed, she found herself thinking, with barely shamefaced satisfaction, that Lionel's children were in some sort her nephews and nieces, and so she enjoyed a quasi claim to look after them. She felt suddenly fonder of Lionel than she had ever been before, and her relief at discovering the reason for his aversion from her — it had not been physical aversion, but merely canonical aversion — was so great as almost to blow back the very shock of discovery. And to find that her father, the munificent patriarchal Jonathan, had been guilty of an immorality, scarcely troubled her at all: but this insensitivity was almost certainly due to aspirin. In less than half an hour the summation of her emotions became something no more troublesome than a curiously sentimental exhilaration: and it was in this condition that she was found by Ruth — projecting her pale spectacled face round the door, after a shallow 'May I come in, Aunt Hilary?' — who proceeded to give her yet more news: such is the irrational bounty of Nature and the untimely profusion of Fortune.

Ruth, by virtue of one of those obscure predilections of childhood, had taken a great fancy to George's little girl, Clarice. Clarice's khaki topee, that she obstinately wore under Lammiter's temperate sun, had possibly something to do with it; or her seeming obtuseness and taciturnity may have appealed to Ruth's lively curiosity. At any rate, she became very fond of Clarice, and having overborne by sheer pertinacity her mother's prejudice against George and his family, she had come, on her own invitation, to spend the last two week-ends at Rumneys.

Ruth stood by Hilary's bed and looked at her with a supercilious gaze. 'Are you ill, Aunt Hilary?' she asked.

'No,' said Hilary. 'I'm feeling very well indeed. But I thought I'd like a treat to-day, so I had my breakfast brought to me.'

'Doris and Tessie are still in bed, too,' said Ruth.

'They never get up very early,' said Hilary.

'Do all grown-up people get lazy?'

'I'm afraid a good many do.'

'I shall never be lazy,' said Ruth virtuously.

'I hope not,' said Hilary.

'Aunt Hilary, is Doris frightened to sleep alone?'

'I don't think so. Why?'

'Because when I went in to see her this morning, quite early, Uncle George was there with her.'

'Well, I suppose he'd just gone in to speak to her. He's her father, you know.'

'But he was in bed with her.'

'Oh, nonsense, Ruth.'

'But he was, Aunt Hilary. I saw him, and he said, "Get to hell out of here".'

'Uncle George often says things that he doesn't mean. I suppose he frightened you, and you got a little bit confused, and so you think you saw . . .'

'I wasn't a bit frightened. And he *was* in bed with Doris.'

'That's quite impossible, Ruth. You're talking rubbish, I'm afraid.'

'But he was! And I asked Clarice, and she said yes, he often sleeps with her. So I thought perhaps she was frightened of the dark or something.'

'Well, run along now, Ruth, and I'll ask Doris herself what she's frightened of. Oh, Ruth!'

'Yes, Aunt Hilary?'

'Don't talk about this to anybody else, to your mother, or the maids, or to other little girls, because Doris mightn't like it.'

'No, Aunt Hilary, I wasn't going to,' said Ruth, and closed the door behind her with ostentatious care.

'So that's that,' murmured Hilary, and was grateful to Mr. Peabody for his timely investigations. She tightened her lips a little to think of illicit pleasure finding house-room at Rumneys, and then she remembered Lionel's letter, and her father's, that he had enclosed: this might not be the first time that Rumneys had given shelter to unlicensed lovers . . . She had been eleven when her father died: her dutiful grief had largely consisted of shame for not having loved him: he had been a noisy domineering old man, sometimes querulous and sometimes facetious. It was curious to think he had once enjoyed emotions so human and so improper as George's apparently cordial regard for Doris.

And what was to be done about George? If Ruth's story were true — and there seemed no reason to doubt it, for she was a truthful child, and according to her Clarice had said that George and Doris regularly cohabited — if this were so, then Mr. Peabody was right, and George was an impostor. Doris and Tessie and the children were not his: they were certainly not his by virtue of having begotten them. And so . . . but in any case Lionel had six children, and George's immigrants were only five. And John had bequeathed his money to 'whichever of the progeny of the late Jonathan Gander shall become the parent of the greatest number of children born in holy wedlock.' Those were the words. As far as she could remember there was no qualification for progeny — legitimacy was not essential — though holy wedlock was insisted upon as the prelude to a second generation. So Lionel . . .

Hilary bathed and dressed in a hurry. She had better see Mr. Peabody as soon as possible and then she must have a long talk with Lionel. But first of all she had to listen to Mrs. Arbor, who wanted to tell her about the damage to George's room. Hilary went with her to examine it.

'We might all have been burnt in our beds if he hadn't taken the siphon upstairs with him,' said Mrs. Arbor.

'That was very prudent of him,' said Hilary.

'But what puzzles me,' said Mrs. Arbor, 'is where he slept. Because if you feel the clothes you'll find they're almost dry now, so it wasn't this morning that he set himself on fire, or they'd still be sopping. It must have been last night, just after he went to bed.'

'You're quite a detective, Mrs. Arbor.'

'Well, I take an interest in things.'

'I suppose he slept in a chair. But I'll ask him when I see him.'

Without looking for George, Hilary went straight to Mr. Peabody's. If Mrs. Arbor was suspicious of George's nocturnal habits, the other servants might also be gossiping, and a scandal of appalling magnitude was probably imminent. George's relationship with Doris could not be left longer in doubt, and whatever the result of further inquiry — though there could be only one — he must quickly be got rid of. And that, thought Hilary, was Mr. Peabody's duty.

He listened to her story with obvious pleasure. In his satisfaction at receiving confirmatory evidence for his case against George, the impropriety of the evidence escaped him entirely.

'No happier discovery could have been made,' he said. 'I'm delighted to hear this, quite delighted. It will save us an enormous amount of trouble and expense, though it brings us face to face, of course, with the fact that George has behaved with — I say so most reluctantly — with criminal folly, and rendered himself liable to a criminal charge: he has been guilty of fraud in a very aggravated degree. I imagine, however, that the idea of bringing such a charge against him is as repugnant to you as it is to me.'

'All I want to do is to get him and the children out of Lammiter as quickly as possible. If he decides to go back to India I'll pay their fares myself, and do it gladly.'

'I must have another talk with George,' said Mr. Peabody. 'When I saw him yesterday he was inclined to be contumacious. He endeavoured to take the upper hand. So far from being apologetic, he was defiant. He actually shouted at me. My sister, in the adjoining room, heard him quite distinctly. But I do not think he will shout this time.'

'I leave it to you, then,' said Hilary, and rose to go. She hesitated, and asked, 'What was the exact wording of John's will? The money was to go to 'whichever of Jonathan Gander's progeny . . .'

' "shall have become the parent, whether father or mother, of the greatest number of children born in wedlock ".'

'That seems to make a distinction between the first and second generations, doesn't it?'

'The word *progeny* is not the one I would have used myself had I drawn the will,' said Mr. Peabody. 'Its connotation is too general for a legal document. And, as you say, the fact that holy wedlock is definitely mentioned in regard to the second generation, while there is no such proviso attached specifically to the earlier generation, might well be interpreted as an intention to enlarge the application of the word *progeny* beyond the happily delimited eligibility prescribed for the grand-children.'

'In other words,' said Hilary, 'if my father had left any illegitimate children, and they married, their children would be acceptable in terms of the will?'

'It's a hypothetical case, of course, but my opinion is that the will might be susceptible of such an interpretation, and had the occasion for such interpretation arisen, it might even have been argued that Major Gander had intentionally phrased the will so as to make it permissible. And there you see how dangerous it is for a man to make his own will. A solicitor, whose training has taught him to foresee dubiety and so to evade miscon-struction - - and who has, if I may say so, a far more precise apprehension of the significance of words than any literary man – a solicitor would never have made such a mistake. I invariably advise my clients to consult a solicitor in any difficulty, no matter how small. It saves time and trouble, and often enough, when a client's instructions have been somewhat vague, I have been able to essentialize or reconstruct them with the most fortunate results.'

'Yes, it's a great profession,' said Hilary. 'But I must go now. And I can leave you to look after George?'

'I shall look after George,' said Mr. Peabody with a steely smile.

Hilary walked briskly along the Ridge road, and having left her principal difficulty behind her, arrived at the Vicarage with a feeling of confidence so lively that it almost amounted to gaiety. The Vicar, leaning on his stick, was pacing the sun-bright terrace. He turned with a look of shame and confusion. But Hilary, ignoring his expression, advanced upon him and soundly kissed him.

'Dear Lionel!' she said. 'I'm so sorry I asked you to marry me. But why did you never tell me that you were my brother?'

'Hush!' said the Vicar nervously. 'Mrs. Finger may be listening. She's a very inquisitive woman.'

'But what does it matter now? Everybody will have to be told before long.'

'Never!' said the Vicar. 'Nobody will ever know, at least in my lifetime.'

With a purposeful though irregular stride he walked down the steps, and along the path to a seat that overlooked the little pond where once two Large Black pigs had taken refuge, and Lady Caroline had bravely followed. Hilary sat down beside him.

'Do you realize that you're the heir to seventy

thousand pounds?' she asked; and explained to him the peculiar phrasing of the Major's will, and Mr. Peabody's interpretation of it.

'That makes no difference,' said the Vicar. 'I've known, or supposed, for a long time that I had a good claim to the money. But no amount of money could persuade me to reveal the circumstances of my birth. From boyhood I've been made miserable by the shame of it, and ever since I grew up I've done my utmost to conceal it. Till now I've been successful. I never even told Caroline. She always believed that my father was Charles Purefoy — as everybody else believes. And after a lifetime of pretending to have been respectably born, I'm not going to be bribed into confessing my illegitimacy now. Think what my friends would say, what Caroline's relations would say!'

'And think what you could do for Rupert and Denis and the children with seventy thousand pounds,' said Hilary.

Slowly the Vicar shook his head. 'It's no use,' he said. 'I *can't* do it.'

'Then I'm going to,' said Hilary. 'I'm certainly not going to let you lose all that money simply in order to flatter your silly pride.'

'But your own name, your father's reputation . . .'

'The family name is ruined already, or will be as soon as my maids have had a chance to talk,' said Hilary; and told him about George.

'Some men will do anything for money,' said the Vicar. 'But I'm not one of them. You're trying to persuade me to be as shameless as George.'

345

'There's all the difference in the world between you and George. He's an impostor . . .'

'So am I, and I don't intend to confess it.'

After a little while Hilary said, 'I thought of a very good plan while I was coming here. It's a plan that really makes things much easier for both of us. You see, we can't get married now — and perhaps that's just as well — but as I'm your sister, or your half-sister, I can come and keep house for you, and help you to look after the children. It's going to be very expensive to educate Rupert and Denis — I know exactly what we should do with them — and probably the others will be just as difficult when they get a little older: but we shall be quite well off with your seventy thousand and my . . .'

The Vicar said, 'My seventy thousand will do us no good, for I shall never claim it.'

'But suppose I claim it for you? I still have your father's letter.'

'I forbid you to make any use of it whatever.'

'But Lionel . . .'

'You don't know the whole story of your father's misconduct.'

'Then tell me.'

The Vicar hesitated: 'I'm not the only one who would suffer if it were made public. He was guilty of immoral association on more than one occasion. And there are men living to-day . . .'

'In Lammiter?'

'Not only in Lammiter. One is a well-known peer, a leader of political opinion, and a millionaire. I believe Lord Fosgene . . .'

'Not Hubble-Bubble?'

'His name was Hubble. The poor man who was supposed to be his father made lemonade. But it was your father — and his — who gave him his real start in life, and so helped him to become prominent during the War: our most effective gas-shells were produced in his factory, if you remember. Your father — my father — was very generous to all his children.'

Hilary was silent for some time. Then she said, 'I'm not particularly interested in Lord Fosgene. I don't admire him, and I don't see why we should worry about his peace of mind or his reputation. I'm going to take the letter you sent me, the one my father wrote, to Mr. Peabody . . .'

'No, no,' said the Vicar, 'not to Peabody!'

'Why not?'

'Because . . .'

'Well?'

'Because he's another.'

'*Mr. Peabody!*'

'Yes. Both he and his sister.'

Hilary sat aghast.

'You see,' said the Vicar, 'my father — your father . . .'

'Their father,' said Hilary.

'Was a most remarkable man,' said the Vicar.

XXII

GEORGE's attempt to defend himself against the
new weapon with which Fortune had armed Mr.
Peabody was not even half-hearted. It was less than
quarter-hearted. It was the duodecimo edition of an
attempt. Compared with the large flamboyance of
his previous defiance, it was a Persian miniature set
beside the Antwerp *Baptism* of Peter Paul Rubens.
Mr. Peabody swept it aside, ignored it, refused to
look at it, and told George that unless he proffered
a full confession, and withdrew all claims to the
Major's estate, he would be liable to immediate
arrest. 'But,' he added, 'if you do confess, and if
you do withdraw your claim, then I am authorized
to say that there will be no prosecution, and the cost
of your return to India will be defrayed by my
fellow-trustee.'

'Good old Hilary,' said George.

'So you are going to be sensible?' said Mr.
Peabody.

George leaned back in his chair and thoughtfully
whistled a little tune.

'I'm tired of this bloody place, anyway,' he said
at last. 'You've never been East, have you? Well,
about the middle of the Red Sea you generally run
into a following wind, and you begin to get hot.
Then your pores open, and you sit on deck in a sweet
and lovely muck-sweat, and you begin to feel things,
and smell things. You begin to live! You've got

nothing but a remnant of weather out of God's bargain basement in this country, and I'm tired of it. All your lousy virtues come from ignorance and fog and frustration; and virtue, to be honest, isn't suited to my constitution. So if you warble Hallelujah! when I sail away, you'll have the doubtful satisfaction of knowing I'm singing seconds to you in the Bay of Biscay. I don't envy you, Peabody. You're a dry stick. But Hilary's a damned good sort, and I'm going right away to say thank-you to her with all the stops out.'

Human traffic to India falls to a minimum in July, and when Mr. Peabody discovered that the *Mahadeo* was sailing from Liverpool to Bombay in five days' time, he had no difficulty in booking second-class passages for George and his pseudo-family. This brief but necessary interval between *dénouement* and departure was not so embarrassing as it might have been: except for a tendency to jeer at Mr. Peabody, George showed no ill-will, and took disgrace, the failure of his plans, and the loss of a fortune with commendable resignation. Pride in his defeated scheme outweighed the shame of discovery.

'It was a great idea, wasn't it?' he said to Hilary. 'And if I'd never been found out, you'd never have known how good it was. I'll tell you all about it, shall I? Well, to begin with, Doris and I are practically Darby and Joan: our lives have been romantically entwined for at least a year: no, we can't get married, because I did that once before, under the influence of boot-leg mint-juleps, and so far as I know the lady's still alive. But Doris and I get on quite well together, and we're lying to a sea-anchor as snugly as to permanent moorings.'

'But whom do the children belong to?'

'I'm just coming to that. You see, about seven or eight months ago I got into a bit of a bother with one of the Native States — though actually it was a friend of mine who started the trouble — and I went down to Goa and lay low for a while till the horizon cleared. And when I came back I found that Doris had brought in her mother and the rest of the family to live with her. Well, it was a bit of a nuisance, but I didn't say much. They'd nowhere else to go, and I'd got my old job back: a clerical appointment in the Traffic Manager's office of the B.&R.R., grossly underpaid at two hundred and fifty rupees per mensem, but better, as you'll agree, than a stalled ox and hatred therewith. So we all lived together in our salubrious *chawl* at Parel, and presently it looked as though my lavish hospitality was going to pay handsome dividends. Because when I heard from Peabody that children were the essential ante in Uncle John's poker game, I took steps to adopt the whole litter. Their mother was agreeable — I promised her a good rake-off — but we had some trouble with the younger ones: Clarice and the *bachche* had a rather dingier father than the others, and they weren't very clever at learning their parts. But we gave them some intensive drill, and presently sailed for England, Home, and Booty. Now honestly, Hilary, don't you think it was a damned good *bandobast*?'

'How did you get the birth-certificates?'

'You can get anything you want on this earth, if you know where to go for it,' said George.

As though to demonstrate the truth of this daring aphorism, George, on the day of his departure, entertained Arthur to lunch at the Green Dragon. Neither had heard anything of the latest pretender to the Gander fortune — for Hilary, not yet having persuaded the Vicar to publish his claim, had said nothing about it — so both believed that Arthur was once again a probable winner. Arthur, indeed, was now convinced of his title to at least thirty-five thousand, and in such a faith it was easy to be generous and to forgive George for the impudence of his would-be fraud; while George was not insensible of the fact that a man who has money may, on occasion, be induced to part with some of it.

He ordered a bottle of burgundy. It was a roughish and hearty Richebourg, that rubbed the palate like horse-hair on a G string. He said, 'Yes, I thought I could depend on you to take a broadminded view of my little escapade. It was a damned good idea, wasn't it? It's just the sort of thing that you might have thought of: though if you'd set out to do what I did, you'd have managed things better and probably been successful. Well, here's luck, Arthur.'

'Good luck,' said Arthur. 'It's rather funny you should say that: I mean that I might have thought of the same idea. Because actually I did. It was several months ago that I began to toy with a scheme identical with yours, though I never put it into practice, of course. But I suppose that's why you never really deceived me.'

'I didn't, eh?'

'No, not really. I was doubtful for a while — you acted the part very well, George — but I can't honestly say that you ever wholly took me in.'

'You're a shrewd fellow, Arthur.'

'Well, I've had a certain amount of experience, of course. I've knocked about rather more than most of the people here.'

'Yes, you're a man of the world.'

'Oh, in a very modest way. I learnt a good deal during the War, and since then, in business and affairs generally, I've always kept my eyes open and tried to think a little bit ahead of the other fellow, you know.'

'And I expect you generally succeeded.' George refilled the glasses. 'I wish I'd seen more of you during the last few weeks. We've got a good deal in common, you know: we've both seen life in the raw, and survived a peck of uncommon experiences, and neither of us has any great respect for conventionality. If it ever came to a trial between us, I fancy you'd turn out to be a whole lot more of the husky adventurer than I am.'

Arthur laughed a little laugh of pure delight, and closed a wicked eye. 'I haven't always lived as quietly as this,' he said.

'I bet you haven't,' said George.

'Nowadays, of course, I'm rather tied down. Daisy and the children, you know. They're a responsibility, and I can't shirk it. I'm not grumbling, far from it, but sometimes I wish I was free to live my own life, as you do.'

'It's a pity you can't come out to India with me,' said George. 'I've got a little bit of business on hand that would suit you down to the ground. There's a mint of money in it, and a lot of fun as well. You'd see the humour of it.'

'There's nothing I'd like more, but I'm afraid it's impossible. You mustn't tempt me, George. It wouldn't take much to persuade me to go, and my conscience would never forgive me. I've a wife and family to think of, and they must come first. But it's a bitter disappointment to have to say no.'

'You could take a share in the business, and a share in the joke and the profits too, without ever going outside Lammiter if you think it would amuse you, and if you'd like to make some easy money.'

'My capital is rather tied up at present . . .'

'Let's have another bottle of burgundy, and I'll tell you all about it.'

With an easy mastery of his subject, George spoke for several minutes about the romance of India, and alluded in some detail to the enormous wealth of the Indian princes. The second bottle was brought, and fresh glasses, and the robust wine enabled Arthur to see, with ever increasing clarity, the gorgeously crowded scenes that George described. He drank his burgundy in generous gulps.

'Now, there's a friend of mine in Bombay,' George continued, 'who's negotiating, at this very moment, with the Maharajah of Cooch-Parwanee, with a view to installing up-to-date bathrooms and modern sanitation in the royal palace. This friend of mine — fill up your glass, Arthur — was once a contractor and plumber in a very big way of business. But he had a lot of bad luck, and now he's hard put to it to find enough capital to go ahead with. So I've gone into partnership with him, and I'm trying to raise a little money so that we can start right away, as soon as I get back. As an investment it's an absolute gold-reef.'

'But I don't see anything humorous about it.'

'You haven't had a chance to yet. Plumbing's only the start of it, Arthur. — Have some more burgundy — You see, this friend of mine is also an expert photographer. Now by virtue of his plumbing he has the *entrée* to the innermost recesses of the royal palace, and being a Kodak enthusiast he brings away lasting souvenirs of his happy visit. In other words, he goes in with a green marble bathroom and chromium taps, and comes ðut with a complete pictorial representation of Saturday Night in the Harem. And, as you know, in the present state of journalism such records are valuable, especially in America. But our Indian princes are great believers in the privacy of the home, so it's likely the Maharajah would also be interested in the copyright of our pretty pictures, and might even be induced to bid handsomely for it.'

'It's a dangerous job,' said Arthur, 'a very dangerous job indeed.'

George laughed loudly. 'That sounds funny, coming from you,' he said. 'When did the thought of danger ever prevent you from doing anything?'

'Never,' said Arthur. 'And that'sh why I say it's a dangerous job, a cateristically dangerous job. And from the legal point of view . . .'

'Now don't say that I'm suggesting anything illegal! Damn it, Arthur, I thought you knew me better than that! This is a very sound business proposition, built on the two axioms that supply creates demand, and competition is the life of trade.'

'It's a racket,' said Arthur.

George, with an indignant fist, thumped the table. 'It's nothing of the sort,' he said. 'It's a commercial venture, pure and simple.'

'Then I don't want to have anything to do with it. But if it's a racket, I'll invest two hundred pounds in it.'

George stared at him in amazement.

'I'm a natural racketeer,' said Arthur proudly. 'Cribbed, cabin'd, and confined in sordid domistecity, I don't get much scape for my inclinotions. But you're different. You're free. You go where you like and do as you please. All over the world!' — With a magnificent gesture Arthur swept a wine-glass and a toast-rack from the table.— 'And if you're going to be a racketeer, I'll help you. Because that's what I am too. A spiritual racketeer.'

Arthur thrust his hand across the table, and George, concealing his astonishment, shook it warmly.

'You're a grand fellow, he said, and suddenly shouted with laughter.

355

'True words often spoken in jest,' said Arthur solemnly.

'I'll send you a complete set of all the photos we take.'

Arthur began to sing: ' "Pale hands I loved, beside the Shalima-ar".'

'Shut up,' said George. 'We've got a lot of business to talk yet. When can you give me the money?'

'Going to the bank right away,' said Arthur. 'Cash a cheque for two hundred pounds, hand it over, and instantatiously become a racketeer.'

'I'll see that you get more than your fair share of the profits,' said George.

They shook hands again. 'I trust you implicibly,' said Arthur.

The bank was round the corner, and Arthur, after a short consultation with the manager, cashed his cheque and handed George a crackling sheaf of twenty-pound notes. George thanked him heartily; and looked at the clock. 'My God!' he said, 'it's ten to three!'

'Time for another drink,' said Arthur.

'Like hell there is. My train goes at three!'

Fortunately they found a taxi not very far away, and drove hurriedly to the station. Arthur, with his arm round George's neck, sang loudly,

' "Farewell and adieu to you, gay Spanish ladies,
Farewell and adieu to you, ladies of Spain!" '

Hilary, in the meantime, waited anxiously on the platform with Doris and Tessie and Mr. Peabody. Clarice and the little boys, with a good deal of luggage, were already in the carriage: Clarice contentedly read a gaily bound book, while the little boys beat large toy drums that Hilary had given them.

Doris, with admirable regard for the conventions, maintained polite conversation of the proper valedictory kind: 'It has been ripping of you, Aunt Hilary, to put us up for so long, and give us such a jolly good time. We have enjoyed ourselves no end, haven't we, Tessie?'

Tessie nodded glumly. She had been hoping to see Sergeant Pilcher at the station. She had already said good-bye to her other admirers, and she wore, with some pride, two engagement rings, a silver bracelet, and a brooch with red and green stones in it. But at five minutes to three there was no sign of the Sergeant, and her feelings were hurt.

Hilary said nervously, 'If we only knew where to look for George!'

'Do not fear,' said Doris, 'he will be here in a jiffy. Our father is always in plenty of time.'

'He isn't your father,' said Hilary with a flicker of irritation.

'Here he comes!' cried Tessie, and waving her hand excitedly, ran to meet, not George, but the Sergeant.

Doris said politely, 'We shall have such lots of news to tell to all our friends in Bombay when we get back to India. They will be highly interested to hear about our visit home to England, and it is nice that we can say how much we have enjoyed it.'

One of the little boys put down his drum and began to cry: '*Bahut bhukha hun, bahut bhukha hun!*'

357

'He is a cross-patch,' said Doris. 'He cannot be hungry now, when he has had such a good dinner only a short time ago.'

Mr. Peabody looked at his watch and compared it with the station clock. Both showed two minutes to three.

'Here's George now,' exclaimed Hilary with great relief. 'And Arthur too,' she added.

Arm-in-arm, George and Arthur advanced to the train. Arthur was still singing.

'Hurry up!' cried Hilary.

'Plenty of time,' said Arthur, and boldly putting his arm round Doris's shoulder, kissed her warmly.

'Oh, Uncle Arthur, what a flirt you are!' she said.

'Tessie! Get into the train at once.'

Reluctantly Tessie parted from Sergeant Pilcher. She now wore a string of pearls whose large refulgence put all the oysters in the world to shame.

The guard, the stationmaster, and a porter converged on the diminishing group, and Doris was persuaded to go aboard. Arthur, for the third time, was singing 'Farewell and adieu to you, gay Spanish ladies,' and George was still shaking Hilary's hand in warm farewell. 'You must come out and see us some day,' he said. 'We'll give you a fine time in Bombay. And you too, Peabody. Forgive and forget: that's my motto. We'll paint the old town red: moonlight picnics at Juhu, drinks at Mongini's, trips to Elephanta, dinner at Green's: it's a grand place, Bombay!'

'Good old George!' said Arthur. 'All racketeers together! Don't forget the pretty pictures, George.'

George was thrust into the carriage, and the stationmaster slammed the door. Shrilly a whistle blew, and the engine answered with a huge belch of steam. Clarice pressed her nose whitely against the glass, and the little boys, like catfish in an aquarium tank, stared from the dim interior. From the open window emerged a pyramid of faces as George and Tessie and Doris looked their last at Lammiter. With a loud dactylic rhythm the train gathered speed, and spilled from innumerable passing windows the momentary dark images of those who waved good-bye.

'Good old George!' shouted Arthur, and flourished his hat, and danced a little dance on the platform.

XXIII

HILARY's task in converting the Vicar to reason was long and arduous, and on several occasions she found it difficult to maintain her own common sense. She began by persuading him to tell her all he knew about their father, the late Jonathan Gander. It was a remarkable story, and it affected Hilary in much the same way as the Vicar had been affected by his discovery of Karl Marx and religious doubt. She had the sensation of being uprooted, of suddenly waking to find herself in a foreign country. She was afflicted by a feeling of perilous insecurity, and by a recurrent dread that all her friends were strangers under their skins. For Jonathan Gander, whom the years had dignified but devitalized, whom time had enthroned as that exemplar of scarcely human probity, the Victorian parent, was now revealed as a cunning and persistent libertine. More than once she was tempted to concur in her brother's desire for secrecy, and only by the exercise of considerable resolution was she able to turn her back on this easy escape. Though it was beyond question that the comfort of a living Vicar, and of his children, was more important than the reputation of a dead manufacturer, yet Hilary's baser and more timid self could not refrain from questioning, and her good sense had to tell her the proper answer several times a day, to keep her aware of it.

Jonathan Gander had had at least seven illegitimate children; but unlike his son the Major, who had desired above all things a multiplication of Ganders and the increase of their name, he had exercised great ingenuity and no little expense in concealing his fertility and planting his offspring in other nests. Lionel's mother, when Lionel was eighteen months old, had married an amiable young man called Purefoy. Her liberal *dot* had purchased a small preparatory school in the northern part of Brackenshire, and Purefoy, who had taken a good degree at Cambridge, and was industrious as well as sensible, had done very well there. Jonathan had sent him two pupils, and several of his friends, it appeared, had also found the institution useful: Purefoy was discreet, and turned out to be an excellent teacher, while Mrs. Purefoy was devoted to small boys and happily extravagant in her house-keeping.

She maintained her friendship with Jonathan till his second marriage, in 1892. She had been his confidante, and apparently his accessory in certain negotiations, and so long as she lived — she had died in 1910, two years after her husband — she had spoken of him to Lionel with admiring fondness. At the age of fourteen Lionel had learnt by accident who his father was, and for five years he had con-cealed his knowledge in the miserable silence of youth. Then, in the heat of some petty quarrel, he had told his mother what he knew, and she, without shame, had replied that he had a father to be proud of. 'And so,' she added, 'have several other young people of my acquaintance, if they only realized it.'

361

But Lionel had not learnt the full extent of his father's activities till 1904, when Jonathan died. Mrs. Purefoy, greatly moved by his death, had then told him the whole story, together with the names and whereabouts of the other children. She was still proud of her friendship with Jonathan. She admired him not only for his manliness and generosity, but for the cleverness with which he had conducted his affairs and camouflaged their consequences; she entrusted his secrets to Lionel in the spirit of one who could not bear to see the fame of a great man forgotten or neglected, and at her death she bequeathed to him a sealed bundle of letters and other papers that fully confirmed all she had previously told him.

These papers he still possessed. He had preserved them, he had worn the knowledge of their existence, like a hair-shirt. He had kept them to punish himself, by constant awareness of them, for letting the world believe that Purefoy was his father. He had tormented himself by watching the fate and fortune of his fellow by-blows: Jonathan's illegitimate family had acquired a European amplitude, an international significance, for one of them, the son of a French maid, had been killed while fighting in defence of Verdun, and another, the offspring of a German governess, had died, no doubt with equal bravery but on the wrong side, in the Battle of the Marne; a third, an Australian six feet high, had fallen, all the long length of him, on the beach at Anzac.

'So that's what his love-making came to,' said Hilary.

'They were brave, but they didn't live long.'

'Except the Peabodies, and Lord Fosgene.'

'I've always felt very uncomfortable with Peabody,' said the Vicar.

'So have I, for the last few days.'

'It would ruin his life, as it has ruined mine, if he knew the truth.'

'But there's no need to tell him the truth. Not the whole truth! There's no need to say anything about six out of the seven. You're the only one we're thinking of, and your claim can be proved without a single word about the others. Peabody is a bachelor, his sister is older than I am, and Fosgene, so far as I know, has one daughter. So we're doing them no injustice by ignoring them, and I'm going to look through all these papers and burn every one that refers to them. But the others, the ones that concern you, I'm going to take to Peabody, and Peabody will do whatever's necessary to get you the money.'

Lammiter was nearly empty, in the social sense of the word, when the last and most astonishing news about the Gander estate began, by devious paths, to circulate, and was eventually admitted to be true. Miss Montgomery and Mrs. Sabby, Sir Gervase, Mrs. Corcoran and Miss Foster, and all who could afford a summer holiday were at the seaside, or in Scotland, or cruising in the Norwegian fjords. Distance somewhat reduced the impact of the tidings, and the comparative isolation of those who heard them — at Teignmouth, or Crieff, or Molde — diminished their effect. But even in these adverse circumstances they caused such astonishment that all who received them grew aware of a lessened interest in their foreign surroundings and an impatient desire to return to Lammiter and see for themselves how, in the Vicar's familiar countenance, the light of their new knowledge might be reflected, and to observe the effect of this amazing discovery on Arthur and Daisy, on Hilary and Stephen and Jane.

But when, about the end of August, most of them did return, their curiosity, or the greater part of it, found no satisfaction; for Hilary and the Vicar and all his family had gone. He had written to the Bishop asking leave to resign his charge immediately, on the plea of ill health; a *locum tenens*, a malaria-thin chaplain from Bankipore, was living at the Vicarage; and Rumneys, with blinds drawn and gates locked, was deserted. Hilary had fled, and the Vicar had fled. It was only when she suggested flight as a lenitive for the gaping wound of revelation that he had capitulated, and allowed her to inform Mr. Peabody of his birth and claim to the estate. Hilary had taken for three months a large house near Applecross, in the remote parts of Scotland, where, with the aid of solitude, and the sea and the Atlantic breeze, the Vicar might mend his strength and his mind, and where plans might be made for the future, and in particular, for the education of his difficult family.

Hilary had conceived the excellent idea of sending Rupert to Russia, to work on a collective farm, and Denis to Italy, to continue his education in a Roman school.

'If Rupert is a Communist he ought to see something of Communism in action,' she said, 'and as Denis is a Fascist, he'll feel more at home in Italy than in England. If their political views are well-founded, the experience will be valuable, and if they change their minds they can just come home again.'

Denis and Rupert warmly approved the idea, but did not let it interfere with their present enthusiasm for sailing and fishing and mountain-climbing. The younger children were also showing signs of becoming politically minded, and as Cecily avowed a romantic admiration for Mr. de Valera, while Patrick protested his fervent sympathy with the Catalonian Separatists, and Rosemary and Peter had become Scottish Nationalists, it seemed as though the new generation of Ganders — the Vicar had bravely determined to adopt the name — might achieve a wide geographical distribution.

It was evident, however, that the Vicar would become Hilary's permanent care. He was growing rapidly older. By the publication of what he still imagined to be his shame, he had achieved peace; but it was the peace of premature age. He was happy, but happy to be inactive. Hilary, who had so recently discovered him to be her brother, soon began to think of him with the protective feeling due to an older generation. She had already taken full charge of the children, and assumed responsibility for the future of the household. The children manifestly enjoyed her light authority, and the future — if indeed time will admit of control — was in good hands.

Mr. Peabody had no holiday that summer. He was too busy. He investigated and confirmed the Vicar's claim, he took counsel's opinion, he interviewed the other members of the family. He advised Katherine that litigation would be expensive and unprofitable. He informed them that the Vicar desired to offer each of them a solatium of five thousand pounds — the Major's residual seventy thousand pounds had become nearly eighty thousand in the little cheerful prosperity of 1934 — and he finally persuaded them that it was time to wind up the estate.

As he said to his sister, 'A will like that is simply an invitation to trouble. I've had trouble enough with it already, and I want no more. A man who is fool enough to draw his own will should claim an early resurrection and come back to execute it. During his lifetime I had a great respect for the Major, but since his death I have had none. His will condoned, perhaps deliberately, what I for one think of as immorality, and it was a powerful incentive to fraudulent practice. Nor can I reconcile my memory of Jonathan Gander . . .'

'I remember him quite well,' Miss Peabody interrupted. 'He was a handsome man, and he often made humorous remarks. I always admired him. When I was a little girl he used to give me sweets called Grandmama's Bon-bons. You can't get them nowadays.'

XXIV

STEPHEN and Wilfrid came back to Lammiter in September. They had spent a delightful holiday in Brittany and were most engagingly sunburnt. The Mulberry School of Journalism and Short Story Writing had had a profitable year, and Stephen, with his unexpected windfall of five thousand pounds, was busily making plans to enlarge his establishment. But what excited them even more than their bright vision of a college busy with five assistants, ten stenographers, and the constant arrival of cheques, was to see waiting for them a proof copy of Stephen's new book of poems. Wilfrid carried it into the garden, and beneath a tempered sun they sat down to read it.

Stephen had turned again to literature after his disastrous engagement to Bolivia, and found in that strenuous exercise, as many men have found, both comfort and forgetfulness. He had, moreover, invented what he believed to be a new technique in poetry, or at the best a new linear design, and the novelty had been sufficient to win approval from a publisher. The book was already advertised, and described in the most flattering way, in his autumn list.

It was called *A Hundred Patterns*, and consisted of a hundred short poems printed in geometrical forms. By this device, or so Stephen believed, their literal content became diagrammatic: a transformation cleverly designed to appeal to an age whose culture was largely dictated by machinery. Their meaning, in other words, was made manifest, for those who found difficulty in reading, by linear design, or isomorphism, or other spatial harmonies. The first of the poems was a very simple example called *The Paradox*. It read, and looked, as follows:

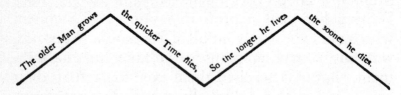

'You see,' said Stephen, 'the rise and fall in the verse is made marvellously clear by the pattern, and that double rise and fall is typical of human life. The first upstroke is youth. Then, after about the age of thirty, there's a descent to forty-five, during which the contemplative or spiritual part of Man is dominated by economic circumstance and the necessity of productive work. Then we go up again, not on a spiritual ascent, but on a gradual emergence of philosophy, which may be either good or bad, but is generally serviceable. The second peak is about sixty years old. Even though it only represents material success, it is still a peak; sometimes, however, it represents a considerable worldly knowledge, or even wisdom. The second downstroke is physical decline, and the end is death.'

Wilfrid said, 'I think it's perfectly wonderful. . . .'

'But there's more in it than that,' said Stephen, 'because in shape it is a diagrammatic representation of waves. It represents waves as a child would draw them, and nowadays, of course, only children really know how to draw. And as waves are a symbol of eternity, so this poem is symbolic of the everlastingness of life, or it would be if it were repeated over and over again. It seems to me, in fact, that it really represents, or even draws, the essential quality of life more simply and more compellingly than has ever been done before.'

'It really is a marvellous poem,' said Wilfrid. 'But I think I like this one almost as much.' He pointed to a stellate arrangement:

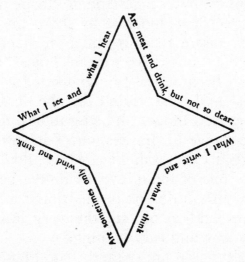

'I'm not quite sure about that one,' said Stephen judicially. 'It's just a little bit cynical. The Star of Hope, you see, combined with rather bitter denigration. No, it's just a shade too clever to be really good. But here's one that's very nearly perfect.'

Wilfrid turned the proof, turned it upside down

and round again, to read a poem like a picture-frame or double square:

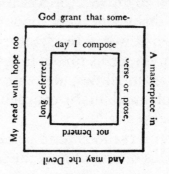

'It ought really,' said Stephen, 'to be a series of infinitely receding squares, to show the levels of thought or desire receding into the depths of the sub-conscious. But there were technical difficulties in the way, because the printer's smallest type was Nonpareil, and that didn't in the least suggest invisibility. So I thought it better to be quite simple, and merely give an impression of inwardness and *reculade*. And I do think it's effective, don't you?'

'It's like one of those lovely Chinese boxes,' said Wilfrid, 'with a little box inside it, and a littler one inside that, and so on, till the very last of all is absolutely tiny and *most* exciting.'

'I thought you'd understand,' said Stephen gratefully. 'If all critics were as clever and helpful as you are, there'd be more hope for the future of English literature.'

Wilfrid blushed with pleasure and cried, 'Oh, Stephen! how *awfully* nice of you to say that!'

In this mood of kindness and mutual esteem they

370

continued to read the poems with unfailing appreciation. A thin haze diffused the sun and shed upon
the garden a warm powdery light. Leaf and fruit
were tinted with September's mellow hues, and
Wilfrid and Stephen, themselves coloured by hot
weather, had an appearance of well-being that was
agreeable to the season and their surroundings.
But their happiness, unlike that of the anchored
trees and the pendant fruit, made them restless and
eager for movement. They wanted to show-off the
poems and excite a wider admiration.

'Let's go and show them to Arthur,' Wilfrid
suggested. 'He really has very good taste in some
ways, and I'm *sure* he'll like them. He can't help
liking them!'

Stephen found the proposal agreeable, and in a
few minutes they were walking briskly, talking
amicably, along the Ridge road. A little while
before they reached Hornbeam Lane, however,
their conversation was interrupted by the imperative
blast of a motor-horn. A car, approaching, had
abruptly reduced speed, and stopped a few yards
beyond them. They looked round and saw a
beckoning hand, a young woman's hand, imperative as the horn.

Stephen turned a little pale. Wilfrid's muscles
grew taut and defensive. They hesitated. The hand
grew more insistent. Reluctantly they obeyed, and
with uneasy minds approached the car.

Bolivia had been abroad for the better part of a
year. They had not seen her since that dreadful
night when she and her father were beaten from the

door of Mulberry Acre by a bombardment of books. They were, not unnaturally, ill-at-ease. But Bolivia showed no sign of embarrassment. She greeted them calmly, with friendly condescension. She was looking well, and was smartly dressed. Sitting beside her was a young man, very handsome, rather sallow, dark-haired, *soigné*, admirably tailored. He seemed hardly so broad or so tall as Bolivia, but his figure was lithe and active, his expression was full of energy.

'This is my fiancé, the Marchese Cellini di Boccadimagra,' said Bolivia.

The Marchese made himself agreeable, and Stephen and Wilfrid, standing in the road, felt the disadvantage of their position.

'Is Jane here?' Bolivia asked. 'I'd like to play some golf if she is.'

'She's gone to America,' said Stephen.

'She'll be away for a whole year,' added Wilfrid. 'She's going to play golf all over the country, and go in for lots of tournaments, and have a perfectly lovely time. I helped her to buy clothes before she went, and honestly, Bolivia, if you saw her frocks you'd *die* with envy!'

'She must have come into some money,' said Bolivia.

'She has,' said Stephen.

'Good,' said Bolivia. 'Well, we must be getting on. I may see you later. I'm getting married next month, and I'll be here till then. Good-bye, Stephen. You're not as fat as you used to be. Good-bye, Wilfrid.'

'Well!' said Wilfrid, 'she *is* a horrid girl! I hate

her as much as ever. And I'm terribly sorry for the Marchese, because I liked him very much indeed, and she's bound to make him miserable.'

Stephen said nothing.

'Did it worry you, seeing her again? Don't think any more about her.'

'She means nothing to me,' said Stephen.

'She just hated me when I told her about Jane's frocks,' said Wilfrid happily. 'She went simply *livid* with rage. I was going to tell her a lot more about them, that's why she went away so quickly, because she knew just what I was thinking, of course, and she couldn't *bear* to listen. She wants to tell everybody that she's going to marry a Marchese, but she doesn't want to hear anything about anybody else's good luck. I'm so glad I made her angry. But I do hope she'll ask us to the wedding. I love weddings: they're so *emotional*. I think I'll give her some rather nice brandy glasses, because they'll be more use to the Marchese than to her.'

Wilfrid chattered all the way to Hornbeam House. They met Arthur just inside the gate. He carried a walking-stick, and he was solemnly beheading a fine growth of tall blue Michaelmas Daisies.

'Arthur!' cried Wilfrid. 'Whatever are you doing?'

Arthur turned a grim face to them. 'These flowers,' he said, 'though you may not believe me, told my wife that beauty was truth, and if a man lived as sweetly and healthily as they did he would never grow fat or bald. That was this morning. Yesterday they told her she was bound to be misunderstood by human beings, because her nature

373

was too fine and delicate for their gross perception; but her flowers would always understand her, and sympathize with her, and though they hated to see her cry, yet her tears were as grateful to them as the morning dew.'

Arthur struck down another bloom. 'Come and have a drink,' he said. On the way to the rock garden he swung viciously at a rose-pink Kaffir Lily. 'That damned hybrid told her that God meant our hearts to be full of joy,' he explained. 'And those pansies have been babbling and blethering to her all summer. But they won't babble any more.'

The long border of pansies, indeed, had suffered total execution. A scythe lay at one end of it, and all the way down was a little, scattered, multi-coloured rivulet of decapitated flowers. 'Garrulous things, pansies,' said Arthur.

'But what will Daisy say?' asked Stephen.

'There'll be a row,' said Arthur briefly.

This ruthless destruction, and the grimness of Arthur's manner, filled Stephen and Wilfrid with awe.

'I never did like gardening,' said Arthur, 'but for Daisy's sake I pretended to, and if she were reasonable I'd go on pretending. But she isn't. She won't be satisfied with flowers that do nothing but grow; she wants them to tell her things. And they do: or so she says. They tell her the sickliest, dampest, out-of-tune, futile, false simplicities, I've ever heard. And I've heard enough of them.'

He strode purposefully to a Red-Hot Poker and uprooted it. 'That thing told her something about the soul of a little child,' he said, 'that I'd be ashamed to repeat. Have another drink.'

Stephen began to discuss the historical aspect of the Pathetic Fallacy, but Arthur begged him to say no more about it.

Wilfrid said, 'We really came to show you Stephen's new poems. They're rather wonderful, and I'm sure they're going to be a tremendous success.'

Arthur showed a very flattering interest in the triangles, pentagons, spirals, ladders and other shapes — the crenellated, zoomorphous, right-angled or whirligig shapes — of Stephen's invention. He turned the book this way and that, and read some six or seven poems aloud, to which Stephen listened with a critical ear and an approving smile.

'Here's another very good one,' said Arthur. 'Now I call this really clever, and it's sound stuff too.'

He pointed to a word-embroidered swastika:

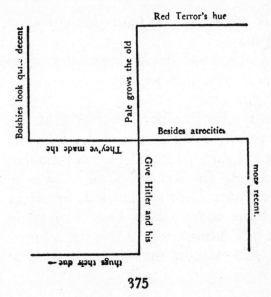

'Perhaps that's just a little crude,' said Stephen. 'I think, on the whole, it's a mistake to bring current events into poetry. Poetry should be timeless and universal, applicable to the present moment only because the moment is part of all time.'

'Well, you know more about it than I do,' said Arthur. 'I only know what I like; and I like that one. I like 'em all, Stephen. You're a damned clever fellow, and here's my very best wishes for the success of your book!'

In this admirable harmony they discussed the poems for a little longer, and then Arthur said, 'I had a letter from George the other day. We're in business together now, you know, and he told me to expect a handsome dividend in a few months' time.'

'What sort of business is it?' asked Wilfrid.

'Very private business,' said Arthur with a knowing wink.

'I think we all behaved very leniently to George,' said Stephen.

'He's a very good fellow,' said Arthur, 'and those were two lovely girls he brought home with him. Especially Doris.'

'I didn't *really* like her,' said Wilfrid.

'She reminded me of a woman I knew in Constantinople,' said Arthur. 'I don't remember if I ever told you about her? Well, it was a curious little adventure. Not so unusual, or on so large a scale as some other affairs I've been mixed up in, but still quite interesting. It was useful, too, because I succeeded — almost entirely by luck, I don't take much credit for it — in averting another war with Turkey. Have some more gin, and I'll tell you about it.'

Stephen and Wilfrid settled themselves comfortably, leaning against convenient stones in the rockery, and Arthur sipped his gin and ginger with a reflective air.

'I went out to Constantinople with Harington,' he said, 'and Harington's not only a brilliant soldier — I once told him that he and Plumer were the finest soldiers on the Western Front — but a brilliant administrator. He's a statesman if ever there was one. And I'm proud of having saved his life, though actually it was more by luck than by anything else. Now I suppose you remember the state of affairs in Constantinople in the latter part of 1920 and '21?'

'I don't,' said Wilfrid.

'Well, everything was in a great muddle,' said Arthur. 'The Allied Forces were in occupation, the Angora government was quarrelling with the Sultan's government, the Greeks were making a thorough nuisance of themselves, the Turks were still fighting the Armenians, the Soviet was intriguing with Angora, and our job was very dangerous and very delicate. Constantinople was a hot-bed, an absolute hot-bed, of spies and plots and attempted assassinations. We'd a very nerve-racking time there, very nerve-racking indeed.

'However, there were compensations, and I happened to meet a woman called — well, I used to call her Cecilia, because her own name was rather difficult to pronounce. She was an Armenian, a lovely creature, quite like Doris, but better-looking. I met her in a very casual way: a busy narrow street in Stamboul, the usual Oriental crowd, a porter fellow with a pole over his shoulder carrying a dozen sheepskins, still warm and dripping with blood, and Cecilia coming in the opposite direction: the porter fellow swung round, nearly slapped her with his horrid cargo, and I knocked him out of the road just in time: there was a bit of a rumpus, but I soon put a stop to that, Cecilia thanked me, and we walked away together.

'Now in a place like Constantinople affairs of that kind develop quicker than they do here, and in a very short time she became my mistress. — I'm not boasting about it, I detest a man who brags about his love affairs, but there's the fact, and there's no use blinking it. — Now, as you know, a woman in love is a very confiding creature, and I soon discovered that Cecilia was a member of a small terrorist group, who believed that we, the British, that is, hadn't given the Armenians a fair deal, and they were plotting some kind of revenge against us. However, Constantinople was full of plots, and most of them came to nothing at all, so I didn't pay much attention to this one. In fact, I forgot all about it till I heard one day that Harington himself was going to have a secret interview with a couple of Armenians who pretended to have information of some tremendous kind that would break up the alliance between the Soviet and the Angora government. Information of that sort would have been invaluable, of course, and Harington, who was quite fearless, was probably justified in running the risk of interviewing these people himself.

'But I took the first opportunity to ask Cecilia if she knew anything about them. She turned pale immediately. I questioned her closely. She couldn't meet my eyes. I repeated my questions, I was absolutely pitiless, and at last I forced her to confess.

'It was a plot to kill Harington. One of the men was her brother, and she herself, at a given signal, was to enter the room and fire the fatal shot. Neither of the men with Harington had weapons of any kind, knowing, of course, they would be searched before going in. Well, I was faced with a very unpleasant duty, but I didn't shirk it, not for a moment. I said to her, "You must consider yourself under arrest," and I stood up and prepared to escort her from the hotel. — We were lunching at the Tokatlian: I forgot to tell you that.

'But Cecilia put her hand on my arm and said, "You cannot leave this hotel alive. Sit down at once, or that waiter . . ." I turned to see a waiter standing immediately behind me. One hand was hidden in his coat. He also was an Armenian.

'I sat down again, and asked Cecilia for an explanation. She said there were two of her accomplices outside the hotel with orders to kill anyone who tried to follow her. And if I attempted to send a message, or otherwise draw attention to my predicament, the Armenian waiter would instantly stab me in the back. She herself, she said, would leave the hotel at a quarter-past two, and proceed to fulfil

379

her mission. She told me I was the only man in the world she had ever loved, but she loved her country more. Her strength of character was as remarkable as her beauty.

'This, then, was the situation. I couldn't leave the hotel alive, and I was no use to anyone as a corpse; nor could I send a message to warn Harington of his danger. Obviously, therefore, there was only one thing to be done: *I had to prevent Cecilia from keeping her fatal appointment!* But how? That was the problem. I couldn't use force to restrain her, or the Armenian waiter would have come into action. I couldn't persuade her to drink too much, because she wouldn't drink anything at all. What was I to do?

'I looked at my watch and saw it was still only ten minutes to two. I had twenty-five minutes' grace. With a great effort I concealed all signs of dismay, and began to talk to her. At first she could not understand me. She saw me looking cheerful, she heard me talking light-heartedly. It was incomprehensible. She suspected a trap. She was sullen, she would not respond. But by-and-by, half against her will, she listened to a certain story. She was captured, she was enthralled by it. At a quarter-past two, oblivious of time, she was hanging on my words, intent on every phrase, lost in the excitement of my narrative. I doubled and redoubled my efforts. I used every art to maintain her attention. I hypnotized her with sentences. I wove a noose of words round her. She couldn't escape! I deliberately set out to enchant her, and I succeeded. Talking without a break for another forty-five minutes I held her there, forgetful of everything but my ceaseless flow of stories, each leading to another, every one more exciting than the last. She was powerless, she was my slave, she was my audience for evermore, had I had the strength to continue. But at three o'clock my voice broke. I made a desperate effort to control it, and fell to the floor in a dead faint.

'But Harington was safe! He had granted an audience of fifteen minutes only, and the conspirators, after waiting in vain for their accomplice, and concocting some wretched story that wouldn't deceive a child, had gone away bitterly disappointed. The plot was foiled, war was averted, and Harington was safe! That was all I cared about when I returned to consciousness. I forgot my long-drawn anxiety, my great effort, my consequent exhaustion. I scarcely even regretted the loss — the temporary loss — of my voice. I had succeeded in these great objects, and that was reward enough.'

For some time after the conclusion of the story, Stephen and Wilfrid sat without saying a word. The spell of the narrative still lay upon them.

Then Stephen asked, 'Why didn't the Armenian waiter interrupt you and remind Cecilia that it was getting late?'

'He didn't know it was getting late,' said Arthur. 'He also was listening to me.'

'What were the stories you told her?' asked Wilfrid.

'I told her several,' said Arthur, 'and I threw in quite a lot of general conversation as well. One of the stories, I remember, was rather unusual, because, quite incidentally, it revealed the identity of the Unknown Soldier. I think it might interest you . . .'

'No,' said Stephen, 'not now, Arthur. Tell us some other day. But not now. It's time we were going home.'

Wilfrid said earnestly, 'You ought to write your autobiography, Arthur. It would make a *wonderful* book.'

Arthur shook his head. 'Im not a literary man, like you fellows. I'm just a simple soldier. And we soldiers aren't much good with a pen, you know.'

'I'm sure you could do it if you tried,' said Wilfrid.

'It's getting late,' said Stephen. 'Come along, Wilfrid. Good-bye, Arthur. Thanks very much for the gin.'

'And for the *lovely* story,' said Wilfrid.

For some time, rapt in thought, Arthur remained by the rockery. He was thinking, and thinking ever more kindly, of Wilfrid's suggestion. 'Why not?' he said at last. 'I could write it under a *nom de guerre*, to save awkward questions. I might even pretend it was a work of fiction. And as Wilfrid said, it would make a wonderful story.'

With sudden decision he took a tumbler and a new bottle of gin from the rockery cellar, and returned to the house. He had turned rebel against gardening, he would rebel against prohibition too. He set the bottle on a desk, took a sheaf of Daisy's best notepaper, and began to write. The words flowed from him. His creation rivalled the spawning salmon. He saw a new world unfold its countries and its seas before him. As Drake, in the branches of the great tree on the Isthmus, beheld green savannas and virgin ocean, and cloud-capped mountains, so Arthur descried new growths of imagination, a sea for all his fictive argosies, and the high snow-peaks of fantasy. He had found his vocation.